RAVE REVIEWS FOR
STEVEN A. ROMAN

LORELEI: BUILDING THE PERFECT BEAST

"Steve Roman's *Lorelei* is sexy, wild, and entertaining! A page-turner with a real punch."
—**Elizabeth Massie**, two-time Bram Stoker Award–winning author of *Sineater*

"What struck me was that Steven Roman was approaching his [graphic novel] storyline in the manner of a novelist, that he was giving his characters room to grow. It works."
—**Charles de Lint**, World Fantasy Award–winning author of *The Blue Girl* and *The Painted Boy*

FINAL DESTINATION: DEAD MAN'S HAND

"Author Steven Roman does an excellent job here, delineating the five characters, showing how their lives intertwine in the run-up to their own, personal brush with death and revealing what happens thereafter, as the terrible truth dawns that they haven't escaped, only delayed the inevitable."
—**The Third Alternative**

"Great American pulp fiction!"
—**Jay Slater**, Editor, *Eaten Alive! Italian Cannibal and Zombie Movies*

BEST NEW ZOMBIE TALES 2: "Laundry Day"

"Laced with a brutal humor and some seriously gory violence, this one is a slaughter-fest crowd pleaser for sure. Action from the get-go, with a surprising twist ending that I really didn't see coming."
—**Paperback Horror**

X-MEN: THE CHAOS ENGINE TRILOGY

"A powerful roller coaster of a novel. This trilogy is not just for Marvel lovers and has something for every reader to enjoy, including romance, action and demise, with a cosmic twist. Roman pulls you right into the action as it unfolds, leaving you gasping from the first book to the last."
—**Celebrity Café**

THE FIEND CLUB GATHERS

BLOOD FEUD

THE SAGA OF PANDORA ZWIEBACK

BOOK 1

STEVEN A. ROMAN

StarWarp Concepts
www.starwarpconcepts.com
NEW YORK, NY

Starwarp Concepts
P.O. Box 4667
Sunnyside, NY 11104

Visit our Web site: **www.StarwarpConcepts.com**

Visit Pan on the Web at:
www.PandoraZwieback.com
www.facebook.com/pages/Pandora-Zwieback/122630931125833

Library of Congress Control Number: 2010900846

ISBN-13: 978-0-9841741-0-2
ISBN-10: 0-9841741-0-9

First Edition: June 2011
10 9 8 7 6 5 4 3 2 1

Cover painting by Bob Larkin
Frontispiece by Eliseu Gouveia

Edited by Howard Zimmerman
Cover and interior design by Mat Postawa

Printed in the USA

This one's for
Uriel Caton,
Pan and Annie's co-creator
and "artistic dad,"

and Michael Z. Hobson,
who knew a winner when he saw one

ACKNOWLEDGMENTS

As much as writers often enjoy being shut-ins who keep their own counsel, no book is ever really written in a vacuum. It's always good to have your work looked over by a fresh pair of eyes—actual live ones, I mean, not just the ones you collect in a jar on the bottom shelf of the refrigerator.

...

I've said too much, haven't I...?

Anyway, here's a hearty shout-out to Vaughne Hansen, Bob Larkin, Clarice Levin, Mat Postawa, Mike Rivilis, Dan Weiss, Sui Mon Wu, Scott Zwiren, and especially my editor, Howard Zimmerman—the folks who offered much-appreciated advice along the way as Pan sets off on her journey. *Blood Feud*'s a much better book for it, so thanks!

Now I can finally go back to my hermitlike existence—it's scary out there in the real world!

Whoever fights monsters should see to it that in the process *he* does not become a monster.

—Friedrich Wilhelm Nietzsche
Beyond Good and Evil

Prologue

"Oh, for the love of God, would you just die already?"

A man. A woman. A star-filled, moonlit night. Under normal circumstances they would be the classic ingredients for a romantic evening . . . except there was little that was either normal *or* romantic about the combination of these ingredients on this particular night. Not when the full moon that hovered over the rocky, volcanic landscape glowed with the color of freshly spilled blood, the woman was an immortal monster hunter standing on a plain littered with the corpses of human and otherworldly combatants, and the man she had run through with a sword wasn't just an ex-lover but a former heavenly messenger recently added to her to-do list. And certainly not when said messenger had designs on unleashing hell on earth in a mad attempt to take revenge on God Himself.

As breakups went, this one probably ranked just short of the long-prophesied battle of Armageddon—but not by much.

Ebon wings spread wide behind him, the handsome, dark-skinned angel took a moment to glance down at the sword protruding from his bare, sculpted chest before turning his attention to the woman who was attempting to shove the remaining two feet of steel through his rib cage.

"I hope you won't take this the wrong way, dear Sebastienne," the angel commented glibly, "but if this is how you normally show affection to your lovers, I'm beginning to understand why you live alone."

"Go to hell, Zaqiel. Or go back to heaven, if He will have you—I don't care which it is. But your madness ends here. Tonight." Gripping the ivory hilt with both hands, she threw her weight against the sword, grunting loudly from the exertion as she tried to force the blade deeper. The night air echoed with the nerve-jangling rasp of metal scraping bone.

"Do you want me to say it tickles more than the whisper of your sweet breath caressing the nape of my neck?" he asked with an infuriatingly playful grin, which quickly evaporated into a sneer. "Because it doesn't, actually. It's rather quite painful."

"Good," Sebastienne snapped through clenched teeth. "I'm just getting started."

"No, I rather think you've had enough fun for one evening," Zaqiel said. "You can stop now."

Sebastienne dug her boot heels into the earth and pushed harder on the weapon. Sweat beaded on her temples as she strained, but the blade wouldn't penetrate any farther.

"No, really," he insisted. "Stop."

"Shut up and die," she growled.

The fallen angel sighed melodramatically—and then smashed her across the face with a backhanded slap. Sebastienne lost her grip on the sword and staggered back a few feet before crashing to the ash-covered dirt on her rear end. Too dazed to move, she could only sit and watch numbly as the former prince of heaven wrenched the blade from his chest. The wound healed instantly.

Zaqiel hefted the blade in his fighting hand and nodded appreciatively. "Good balance . . . well crafted," he commented, "but not a very effective weapon against the Almighty's favorite children—"

"The Almighty's *rejects*, you mean! Admit it, Zaqiel, that's what you really are— you and Lucifer and all the other traitors He cast out! You're an embarrassment to your creator. That's why he banished you Watchers to that stinking pit for the rest of eternity—so He wouldn't have to look at you anymore . . . so He wouldn't have to remember you ever *existed*." She flashed a wicked smile. "Forgotten by all . . . mourned by none."

Zaqiel's lips pulled back in a snarl; a flash of lightning in the ever-rising pyroclastic cloud above them gleamed off razor-sharp fangs. She'd hit a nerve with that remark, doing far more damage than her useless sword ever could. She hoped they left a ragged scar on his heart, as his betrayal had left on hers.

"Perhaps you are right," he growled. "But I escaped the crucible, did I not? While God looked the other way and busied Himself with offering salvation to his monkey-children I regained my long-denied freedom—unlike my brothers who still beg Him for release!" He pointed up toward the rim of the volcano. "And now I have returned to free them!"

Zaqiel strode toward her, tightly gripping the sword hilt. "And yet who should arrive at my hour of triumph, to disrupt my plans? The lowly *beast* I had the poor judgment to choose as my lover—who now has turned on its master. A mongrel that doesn't know whether it should be human or animal!" He sneered. "And you have the temerity to speak to *me* of God's rejects."

Sebastienne blinked back tears. Her words might have hurt his pride, but his tore at her soul. "Damn you, Zaqiel . . ." she whispered hoarsely.

"I am already damned!" the angel roared, and raised the sword above his head. *"But I will not suffer alone!"*

The blade swept down, and she screamed.

1

If Dalibor Frantisek hadn't already been dead for a quarter century, the fifty-caliber bullets that punched a hole through his brain and tore into his chest might have really hurt. As it was, he just found the unexpected barrage annoying as hell—and that was only because the snipers had utterly decimated the latest addition to his wardrobe.

A two-thousand-dollar, hand-fitted, gray Gucci suit fresh from the tailor, ruined in a shower of blood and cranial fluids just seconds after he'd stepped from the Humvee; not even the most skilled dry cleaners back in Prague would be able to get out those stains. *Well,* he thought dourly, *that's what happens when you decide to wear fancy dress to a recovery mission. Everyone else will be wearing body armor, but you just had to go and show them up, didn't you? You've no one to blame but yourself.*

But, honestly, who would ever expect a bunch of Roman Catholic *priests* to be so well-armed? With high-powered army-issue sniper rifles, no less?

Dalibor sighed and patted down his brown hair to cover the ragged but already healing exit wound in the back of his skull. Then he turned his attention toward the source of his annoyance.

Sitting atop a hill on the outskirts of the remote Czech Republic village of Mariz, the Church of Saint Adalbert of Prague wasn't a spectacular-looking house of worship by any means—not after five hundred years of neglect. Its plain stone walls were pitted, its single bell tower was crumbling around the edges, and the weed-choked grounds of the church were littered with masonry that had fallen off and never been carted away. But Dalibor and his soon-to-arrive companions weren't interested in lighting votive candles or admiring baroque architecture. It was the Prize rumored to lie somewhere within its underground passages they were here to claim—if one of the other houses hadn't already gotten to it.

And if they could make it past the damned sharpshooting priest...

The screech of tires behind him caught Dalibor's attention but didn't concern him. It was only his backup finally making their appearance—fashionably late, of course. As always. After he'd drawn the first round of enemy fire. Again. He gazed at the half dozen strike-team members from House Karnstein as they swarmed out of two black Humvees to take up defensive positions. A mix of the living and the undead, they formed the Special Ops branch of the Prague chapter: warriors outfitted with FN P90 submachine guns and the latest in magick-enhanced body armor designed to protect its wearer from most kinds of explosives and weapons fire.

Dalibor gazed down at his raggedy clothing, then sighed. *It certainly would have come in handy tonight . . .*

Jenessa Branislav, of course, had to comment on his bullet-assisted wardrobe malfunction. Shapely and tall, the black leather jumpsuit that she wore under the armor covering her like a second skin, she was easy to spot since she was the only soldier not wearing a protective Kevlar helmet; despite the risk of getting her head blown off, she just didn't like the way the oversized metal bowl flattened her shoulder-length, bright-red hair. Not exactly the best example to set as strike-team leader, especially with those flame-colored tresses presenting such an inviting target for a sniper's bullet, but Dalibor had long ago given up trying to convince her otherwise. Her boots' two-inch-thick rubber soles crunching loudly on the asphalt, she jogged over to join him, paying no attention to the bullets that whipped past her to gouge baseball-sized holes in the grassy field, the cracked pavement, and her company's vehicles.

"Hey, Dalek," she called, addressing him by his childhood nickname, "is that a new look for you?" She gave his tattered suit a quick glance and smiled, revealing gleaming fangs. "Very cutting edge. Where can I get one?"

He nodded toward the church. "Take another five steps in that direction. I'm sure they'll be happy to custom-tailor it for you."

She took a closer look at the suit and raised an eyebrow. "With what? A howitzer?"

He gingerly stuck a finger into the dwindling hole in his head and poked around. "Felt like something smaller. Can't really remember, though." He frowned. "I think it took out my short-term memory."

She shrugged—"Whatever."—then turned to her group. "All right, children, our first order of business is that snipers' nest on the roof. I want Milkors all around, loaded with HE warheads. Zuzana! Krystof!" A woman and man—with the body armor and helmets it was hard to tell who was the vampire, and who the human—tilted their heads toward Jenessa. "Take the east! Dusana! Sionek!" The other female/male team turned to face her. "The west! Vincenc—you're with me!" The remaining male soldier nodded in response, then began making his way over to join her as the others hurried to their positions.

"And what would you like *me* to do?" Dalibor asked.

Jenessa nodded toward the church and smiled. "Take another five steps in that direction."

Dalibor laughed mirthlessly at her joke. "I'll pass."

"Then just stand back and watch the fireworks. This won't take long."

She reached over her left shoulder to unhook the weapon that was clipped to a harness on the rear panel of her armor: a South African–made Milkor MGL-140 multishot grenade launcher. Dalibor caught sight of Vincenc doing the same as he sauntered over. The one-forty was a formidable weapon, capable of firing all six of its shots in less than three seconds. Looking somewhat like a single-barrel, sawed-off shotgun with a pistol grip and a large rotating cylinder in the middle, it fired a variety of shells, from 40mm ammunition to tear-gas canisters and rubber slugs. But it was the HE—high explosive—warheads that Jenessa had ordered her team to use. HEs were shaped like miniature missiles, constructed mostly of plastic, and their tips were tinted in red and yellow hues—the colors of flame. There was good reason for that.

Vincenc followed Jenessa's lead as she unfolded her one-forty's shoulder stock, then slipped on a pair of ballistic goggles to protect her eyes and inserted foam plugs into her ears. She flipped off the safety on her weapon.

"Hey, Dalek," she warned as she lined up her shot. "Cover your ears."

Dalibor, who'd been examining his already-healed chest wound in his Humvee's passenger-side mirror, turned around. "What?"

The roar of the grenade launchers almost permanently deafened him. Dalibor staggered back, his hands clasped over his ringing ears, and cried out a string of curses in Slavic. At least he thought he did—he knew his lips were moving, but the only thing he could hear was the booming echo reverberating in his head. Or was that the sound of the grenades blowing apart the church? It was hard to tell the difference.

Jenessa fixed him with a withering look and shook her head. If he hadn't forgone the earplugs that went with the same body armor he'd neglected to wear, he might have been able to make out what she was saying to him. It certainly wasn't anything complimentary, if the lopsided grin Vincenc flashed at him was any indication.

His hearing finally returned in time for him to catch the last echoes of the barrage, mingled with the pitiful groans of dying clergymen. When the smoke from the multiple explosions cleared, Jenessa walked forward, loudly counting out five paces. Then she stopped and waited. After a few seconds—during which Dalibor was certain he'd be witness to her head exploding from one last sniper round—she turned and looked over her shoulder at him.

"Drama queen," she said lightly. "Seems perfectly safe to me."

The damage to the church, and to its defenders, was far worse than anything done to Dalibor's expensive suit—which, in his opinion, was only right. The thermobaric HE warheads used a fuel-air mixture to create their devastating effect: on impact, the warheads released a flammable liquid in aerosol form, thoroughly dousing their target just before the payload detonated, creating a high-pressure blast wave that burned anything—and anyone—at ground zero, and shredded everything else within a fifteen-yard radius. So with six warheads for each strike-team member, fired from six MGL-140s, there was little remaining of the snipers' nest on the church's roof . . . or the roof . . . or the snipers themselves. Scorched body parts, shattered masonry and brick, and a number of ornamental crosses had rained down on the grass in front of St. Adalbert's, giving the appearance of macabre lawn ornaments. Dalibor gazed at all the blood soaking into the ground and his stomach rumbled.

Jenessa stared at the source of his hunger pangs, then up to his face. "Skipping meals again to maintain that girlish figure?" she commented wryly.

Dalibor snorted. "Hardly. It's just that some of us are too busy tracking down leads on the Prize to think about eating." His stomach roiled again, louder this time.

"Riiiight." The redheaded strike-team leader jerked a thumb in the direction of the Humvees. "Need something to tide you over? We picked up a farmer along the way for snacks—he's a little gamy-tasting, but you get used to it after the first couple of gulps."

Dalibor shook his head. "No thanks. I can always grab something on the way back after we're done here."

Jenessa shrugged. "Suit yourself." She flashed a mischievous grin. "He's a pretty one, though . . ."

He grunted and stuck out his tongue. "Country boys always taste like dirt. And manure." He grimaced and waved a hand in front of his face, as though trying to dispel a nasty odor. "I'm never going back to that."

Her grin broadened. "Elitist. City life has changed you, Dalek."

"And I'm very proud of that fact." He waved a hand toward the church. "Now if you would be so kind as to focus on the mission instead of my feeding habits, *Commander* Branislav . . ."

Jenessa sighed melodramatically. "Very well, Dalek, I can take a hint. To business, then." She folded the stock on her one-forty and slipped it back over her shoulder, swapping the grenade launcher for her submachine gun. The other team members—with the exception of Vincenc, who was busy reloading his weapon—did likewise as they joined her. "The entrance to the catacombs is just past the altar, correct?"

Dalibor nodded. "And I'm sure it will be even more heavily defended than the roof."

She shrugged. "That's to be expected." The sly grin returned as she gazed at his threadbare clothing. "Want to go first and see if you're right?"

"Oh, I think I'm done playing the clay pigeon for this evening, thank you very much. And, as you've obviously noticed, I'm not wearing magically-enhanced body armor to ward off"—he pointed toward the night sky—"*his* influence. So, one step past the threshold and *poof!* Instant bonfire."

Her full lips contracted into a playful pout. "Spoilsport." She turned to her team. "Very well, children, Dalek doesn't want to play anymore. But that's all right—more fun for us." Quickly, she began laying out her attack plan. "Vincenc and Sionek will accompany me on point; Zuzana will follow, with Krystof and Dusana bringing up the rear.

"Ready, children?" she asked, her voice rising in excitement. Her team nodded, and she looked to her right-hand man. "Vincenc, would you be so kind as to open the door?"

The burly soldier hefted the MLG-140 back to his shoulder. This time, Dalibor was alert enough to cover his ears just before Vincenc pulled the trigger, unleashing a hellish barrage that not only removed the church's main door, but a good portion of the front wall as well.

"Move out!" Jenessa barked.

The Special Ops team charged across the lawn before the smoke cleared and dove through the gaping hole. Gunfire immediately erupted from both sides; occasionally the swirling darkness was shattered by the strobing light effect of muzzle flashes. But the conflict didn't last very long. By the time the smoke finally dissipated, the only sound that echoed inside the church was that of Jenessa's sharp voice as she ordered her troops to prepare for whatever obstacle should come next.

Standing on the moonlit lawn, Dalibor sighed. Until the team completed its mission, there was nothing for him to do but wait for their return. And who knew how long *that* might take? According to the maps he'd studied, the catacombs ran throughout the hillside, with numerous twists and turns to scout and countless nooks and crannies to poke around in; Jenessa and her people could be searching for the Prize for hours.

His stomach rumbled again, and he found his gaze wandering over to her Hummer. There, the farmer was tucked away behind all that armor plating—"for snacks," Jenessa had said. Dalibor unconsciously chewed on the lining of his bottom lip as he stared at the vehicle. A snack would certainly help pass the time . . .

He grimaced. Country boys. He'd sworn off those thirty years ago, after he'd walked out of his village and set off for Prague to start a new unlife. It was the earthy smell of them that bothered him the most . . . well, that and the unpleasant memories the odor always brought back. He'd probably start gagging the moment he got a good whiff of snack-boy.

Still . . .

"Maybe just a few sips," he concluded. "To settle my stomach."

His decision made, Dalibor ran a hand through his hair to smooth it out, buttoned the last remnants of his Gucci suit jacket, adjusted his tie, and set off down the hill to silence his gnawing hunger.

"What do you mean it's not here?" Jenessa roared hours later. The playful team leader was gone; in her place now stood a snarling, dagger-toothed monster whose bloodred eyes blazed with anger. And that anger was directed at an elderly priest— the lone survivor of the siege.

"Do I really need to repeat myself?" Vincenc asked over the walkie-talkie. His voice was tight with frustration. "We've made a complete sweep of the place. There's nothing here but rats and old bones."

The old clergyman chuckled. He was well into his seventies, with short, snow-colored hair parted on the left side of his head and a neatly trimmed beard. The brilliance of all that white stood out in great contrast to his weathered, deeply tanned skin—this was a man of God who enjoyed being out in the sun, basking in the glory of his savior. For some reason, that angered Jenessa almost as much as the realization she'd come to that House Karnstein had fallen for a ruse. And a very old one, at that.

"The thing you're looking for is not here, spawn of Satan," he said. "It never was."

"You're lying," she growled. "Every shred of information we compiled over five decades, every rumor and legend we investigated, indicates it's hidden away in the catacombs beneath this church."

He shrugged. "Then search again all you like. There's nothing I can do to stop you."

Jenesa snarled. "Tell me the truth, *knëz*, and you may see the sun rise this morning. Where is the Prize?"

The priest smiled. "Is that what you lot are calling it these days? 'The Prize'? Back in the days of my youth, when I first came to St. Adalbert's, it was known as the Devil's Heart. A far better name, wouldn't you agree? Much more dramatic." The smile widened. "It wasn't here, then, either."

"Then where is it?" she hissed. "You know, don't you? Or at least where we should start looking—true?"

The priest said nothing.

"Fine." She grabbed the old man's throat in a clawlike hand.

He gasped. "H-how can you . . . ?"

"Touch you without bursting into flames?" Jenessa smiled. "Do you know what a dhampyr is, Father? It is the progeny of a vampire and a human—a child that possesses all the strengths of the undead, but none of their weaknesses. Holy water does not burn their flesh, crosses and prayers do not ward them off, sunlight cannot harm them. They are immune to your God's weapons. *I* am immune to your God's weapons."

It took a few moments for that information to sink in—she could practically see the cogs turning in the old man's brain—but at last his gaze tilted down toward his throat, and the bare, unprotected hand of the monster that held him aloft. Slowly, his eyes widened and his jaw began to drop as he stared into her blood-hued orbs. "You . . ."

Jenessa nodded. "That's right, Father, I am such an offspring." She flashed a shark-tooth grin. "Do you know what else I can do? You're about to find out." The grin widened. "Just scream out when you're ready to talk . . ."

The right-side rear door of the Hummer flew open, and Dalibor jumped in surprise. Hurriedly, he wiped his bloodstained mouth with a tattered sleeve and tried not to look guilty at having completely drained Jenessa's snack. His hunger had gotten the best of him—even with his nostrils filling with the disgustingly earthy scent of his prey—and before he knew it a few sips had turned into an out-and-out feeding frenzy.

Not that Jenessa appeared in need of sustenance. Her own lips were caked with dried blood, and twin streaks of crimson ran down from the corners of her mouth to her chin. No doubt she'd feasted on a holy man or two during the search.

"Did you find it?" he asked eagerly.

"No, I didn't find it," she replied bitterly. She stripped off her weapons and tossed them to Vincenc as he and the rest of the team arrived at the vehicle. "It was never here."

Dalibor's eyes widened. "But the information—"

"Was wrong," she snapped, then held up a hand to cut off the question he was about to ask. "But I have a new lead. When we get back to Prague, I want you to contact the council. Get us clearance to move on to the next stage of the operation, and then make the necessary travel arrangements."

His eyebrows rose. "And where exactly are we going?"

"New York." She motioned with her head toward the church. "That's part of what I learned from an old priest in there."

Dalibor nodded. "So the prize is in New York?"

Jenessa shook her head. "Not the Prize, but the person who guards its true location."

"And do you know who that person is?"

The dhampyr smiled wickedly and licked her lips. "Oh, yes. That's the other thing I learned. I know *exactly* who she is, Dalek. And just before I tear out her throat, she'll be *begging* to tell us where we can find the Devil's Heart. . . ."

2

If there was a spot on the face of the Earth more craptacularly boring than the town of Schriksdorp, New York, Pandora Zwieback had never heard about it. Oh, sure, there were probably reference books she could browse through at the library, Web sites she could check out by running a Google search, maybe there was even an article she might find in an old *National Geographic* magazine that profiled it as "The Dullest Place in America," but she'd never been able to work up enough interest to go look. Besides, she already knew any information she'd gather would only confirm her own findings: that the town she liked to call Schriks*dork* was the Suck Capital of the Universe.

And she, unfortunately, had been condemned to live there—*for the rest of her life.*

All right, maybe that was being a little too dramatic. It wasn't like she was locked up in prison, after all. She had her learner's permit, which meant she'd soon be able to try her hand at navigating her mom's Toyota 4Runner, she could leave the house when she needed to, and her mother gave her a fair amount of freedom to live her life. Sure, there were rules she had to follow—helping around the house, letting Mom know where she was going when she went out, stuff like that—but there were no guards at the doors, no bars on the windows, no attack dogs patrolling the grounds. And as long as her grades were good and she didn't get mixed up with things like smoking (a really disgusting habit, in Pan's opinion) or drugs (absolutely not) or drinking alcohol (well, not anymore), she didn't have to worry about Mom getting on her case . . . too much. Besides, in two years she'd turn eighteen, and then she'd be able to make her own decisions about where she wanted to live. And no offense to Mom, but Schriksdorp wouldn't even it make it onto the list of eligible places, even if the English translation of the name for this former Dutch settlement was the admittedly intriguing "Terror Village."

So, no, she wasn't really "condemned" to a life sentence in Stinkville, USA, but there were times when it sure felt like it.

Maybe it was the environment that bothered her. She was a Queens, New York girl, born and bred, used to the grit and the grime and the frantic pace of urban living, and the idea of being surrounded by so much Nature was just a bit ... unsettling. There were too many trees, too much fresh air and wide-open spaces, too much overall peace and quiet. She missed the noise of the city, the feel of unyielding concrete under her boots, the smell of air laden with the grease of Chinese takeout, the smoke of street corner shish kebab, and the steam of overboiled hot dogs.

Maybe it was just because she was an outsider: a teenager with a penchant for occult-themed jewelry, black clothing, and even blacker hair dye—although she kept a streak of the natural blond coloring she'd inherited from her mother as a highlight—who was also a whopping big fangirl when it came to all things horror-related, whether it was movies or literature, comics or television, toys or games. A green-eyed Goth girl trapped in a land of preppy, blond-haired and blue-eyed suburban kids who dressed in the latest oh-so-hip and trendy styles, courtesy of the Gap and H&M and Abercrombie & Fitch. It sometimes made her feel like she was caught in a reality show version of *Disturbing Behavior*, that movie where disobedient kids got their brains rewired by the adults in their town to make them "perfect" sons and daughters. And if she was a stand-in for Katie Holmes's character in that movie . . . well, then Mom must be sort of like Nicole Kidman in that remake of *The Stepford Wives*, where women were forced to become "perfect" wives for their husbands. The difference was, no one had gotten around to rewiring Pan's and Karen's brains. Unless, of course, Mom had already been rewired when she was a kid . . .

Not such a crazy idea, when Pan thought about it. It would certainly explain why Mom had pressed so hard for her to move to Schriksdorp with her: she was hoping to get her daughter "fixed." Get her to wash out the dye and have her shoulder-length locks styled into something a tad more ladylike. Suggest tossing out her battered black leather jacket, the cuffs and back panel of which Pan had painted with images of demons and damned souls burning in the fires of hell. Convince her to trade in the combat boots, black T-shirts, and distressed jeans she tended to wear for tasteful pumps and a bright, frilly sundress.

Like that was ever gonna happen. At least not without a fight to the death first, and then Mom could dress up her corpse however she wanted for the funeral. Pan wouldn't care by that point, anyway, just as long as she'd gotten in the last word before she croaked. A clever declaration like *You can take away my VampireFreaks T-shirts and my T.U.K. boots, but you'll never take . . . my freedom!* Only not, y'know, such a direct swipe from *Braveheart.* Something a little more original.

On the other hand, maybe some mental fine-tuning was just the thing she needed to finally put an end to the psychotic episodes she'd started experiencing . . . again.

The most recent psychosodes—her latest therapist, Dr. Nicole Farrar, preferred calling them "visions" (probably so it didn't make Pan seem quite so crazy)—weren't as bad as others she'd suffered through over the past decade, and were nowhere near as bad as the ones she'd had during that tumultuous period when her life was being torn apart by her parents' disintegrating marriage and her equally disastrous relationship with a boy named Curtis "Amadeus" Sheridan. But the early warning signs were all there: the creeping sense of unease; the feeling she was being watched (the doc had filed that little tic under "paranoid delusions"); and, worst of all, the occasional flicker in the corners of her eyes, of shadowy, blurred things that lurked on the edge of her vision, only to disappear as soon as she turned to look directly at them. And yet, even though those fleeting glimpses of otherworldliness had always tended to freak her out, even though there was every indication that her personal demons were clawing their way back into her psyche after a blessed eight-month, med-free reprieve, she hadn't been able to work up the nerve to tell anybody.

Besides, nobody really believed she could see monsters . . . not even Pan herself.

"Penny for your thoughts, Panda-bear?"

Pan turned to face her mother. Karen Bonifant—she'd dropped the *Zwieback* and gone back to her maiden name after the divorce from David was finalized nine months ago—sat behind the wheel of the 4Runner, lightly tapping the tips of her fingers against the rim in time to the song on the satellite radio: Gorillaz's "Dare." Not one of Mom's favorite group—she still preferred old punk-rock bands like Siouxsie and the Banshees, The Clash, and The Ramones—but every now and then a song came along that she could get into, usually much to Pan's surprise.

It was easy to see where Pan got her good looks from, because Karen had lost none of hers. At forty-three, she could have passed for her daughter's sister— a much older sister, of course. Like her daughter, she had an affectation for wearing rings on all ten fingers, although their tastes differed: Karen's were bands of gold and silver; Pan's were a collection of pentagrams, ankhs, and other mystical symbols. This being Casual Summer Friday at her Web-design job, Karen was decked out in jeans, motorcycle boots, and a white T-shirt—a relaxed look, but still a lot more conservative than her daughter's somber attire.

Pan watched Mom's steering wheel drum solo for a few seconds, then raised an eyebrow. "A penny? That your best offer? And I thought we were done with that 'Panda-bear' stuff. It's *so* embarrassing."

"I thought you liked it when your dad and I called you that."

"I did—when I was five." Pan gestured at herself. "Hello? I'm sixteen now, Mom. 'Panda-bear' was a long time ago."

"Not that long ago," Mom remarked wistfully, then shook her head as though to chase away the pleasant memories. "Anyway, right now a penny's the best I can offer. We *are* living on a tight budget, after all. But I should be able to do better, after I have my meeting with Jerry this afternoon." Jeremy Barron was Karen's boss and the president of BarronQuest.com, an Albany-based Web site design company whose client list included Fortune 500 companies; Karen was one of his top designers. The job her old high school boyfriend had offered was the reason Karen had decided to move back to Schriksdorp—that, and the finalization of the divorce.

"Think you'll finally get that raise you've been asking for?" Pan asked. "It's been—what, three months now?"

"Don't know, sweetie," Karen replied. "I hope so. We sure could use the extra money, now that you're out of school for the summer."

Pan looked at her slyly. "And what would you use it for if you get it?"

"Well, I don't have it—I don't even know if I'll *get* it—so asking me is kind of a moot point, don't you think?" Now it was her turn to raise an eyebrow as she looked over. "Why?"

"No reason," Pan answered, and flashed a disarming smile. Not as disarming as she thought, however. From the look in Karen's eye, it was evident that Mom was already wise to her.

"Oh, I get it," Karen said slowly. "If I got the raise, would I use it to buy something like . . . oh, I don't know . . . say, a car of your own?" She chuckled. "Boy, that learner's permit is just burning a hole in your pocket, isn't it?"

Pan shrugged, trying to appear nonchalant—but yeah, she was dying to get behind the wheel of her own ride. "Just seems a shame letting it go to waste, is all I'm saying."

"Riiiight." Karen paused while she guided the SUV into a lane change. "Truth is, it's not such a bad idea. I mean, I'm more than happy to drive you where you need to go, but with all the hours I'm putting in at work I don't always have the time. And I know how much you dislike sitting around the house." She glanced down at the black sweatshirt Pan wore under her leather jacket: a hoodie with the words I HATE THIS TOWN emblazoned across the front in bright red letters. Just in case anyone still had doubts as to how she really felt about Mom's old stomping grounds. "And then there are things like bills and food and your college fund that have to come first." She shrugged. "Let's see how it goes with Jerry. If he says yes, maybe we can look around for a used one next weekend, just to see what's out there. Then I'll talk to your father—if he can hold off buying trinkets for the store for a little while he might be able to help cover a down payment."

"Really?" Pan's mood immediately brightened—so much, in fact, that she didn't even bother to correct her mother (for, like, the millionth time) that David Zwieback owned a horror museum, not a store. Which Mom knew, of course.

Renfield's House of Horrors and Mystical Antiquities—named after Count Dracula's insane, bug-eating lackey—was her dad's pride and joy. A loving tribute to the movies he grew up watching, the comics and books he liked to read, the toys he collected, the actors and directors, writers and artists he came to idolize. His enthusiasm for creating the ultimate gathering place for horror fans had been absolutely infectious; even Karen hadn't been immune. There'd been a lot of family bonding then; a lot of good times. Long drives to upstate New York in search of antique toys and such. Attending horror conventions to hunt down rare movie memorabilia and comic books. Visiting H. P. Lovecraft's hometown of Providence, Rhode Island, and locations in Maine where some of the Stephen King movie adaptations were shot, and even the mall outside Pittsburgh where George Romero filmed the original *Dawn of the Dead*. That last trip had been part of the best summer ever, three years ago. Unfortunately, that happiness hadn't been destined to last.

"Anyway," Mom continued, "we'll see."

Pan shrugged. "That's okay. I don't mind taking the bus."

"But *I* mind that you do, especially with all the sick freaks running loose in the world. I just don't want anything bad to happen to my little girl."

"Yeah, well, me going out on my own didn't seem to bother you so much when we were living in New York."

"That was different. When you went out, you usually had all your . . . uh . . ." Karen let her voice trail off.

"My friends, right?" Pan asked, unable to keep the edge out of her voice. "I had my friends with me. But I don't have any friends here, and that's why you're worried."

"Hey, it's not like I haven't been encouraging you to make new ones, honey," Karen replied.

"What—in Crapville?" Pan snorted. "Fat chance."

Karen flashed her a stern look. "Well, maybe if you tried cutting back on the attitude you wouldn't be so off-putting to the kids around here. We live in the suburbs, Pandora, not Appalachia. Stop treating them like they're inbred hicks from a Nat Geo documentary."

"Hey, if they were inbred hicks, at least there'd be something interesting about them," Pan countered. "Bunch'a soulless, fair-haired mallrats."

Mom opened her mouth to reply, closed it, sighed deeply, and focused on her driving.

The remainder of the trip passed without further discussion. Karen pulled the SUV up to the curb in front of the main entrance to the Albany Megamall and turned to her daughter.

"Look, sweetie," she said slowly, "I know how tough the past year has been for you, what with the divorce, and moving to a new town, and leaving all your friends behind. But things will get better. I promise."

"I know," Pan replied. "It's just . . . just . . ."

Karen nodded sagely. "Just that you'd like Dad and me to patch things up. You'd like us to be a family again." She flashed a half-smile. "But that's just the nature of the beast, Panda-bear. Sometimes people fall out of love, and it isn't pretty to watch and not everything always works out in the end."

She reached out with her left hand to brush a few strands of jet-black hair away from Pan's face and behind her right ear. There was a gentle tinkle of metal as the ring on Karen's third finger brushed against the three tiny silver hoops in Pan's earlobe. Pan glanced at the ring as Karen pulled her hand back.

Nine months after the divorce and she was still wearing the wedding band. Force of habit, Pan wondered, or because she just wanted old boyfriend and the other guys at work to leave the single mom alone? Or maybe . . .

"Dave and I didn't part on the best of terms—you know that," Karen went on. "And I know how sometimes it feels like the weight of the world is resting on your shoulders. But no matter how bad things ever get, I want you to remember this: We might not be together anymore, but your dad and I love you and will always be there for you. We made quite a few mistakes in our marriage—but you, Pandora Millicent Zwieback, were the one thing we ever truly got right."

The enormous tears that rolled down Pan's cheeks were dwarfed in size only by the lump that formed in her throat. "Mom, I . . ." was all she could manage. Then she threw her arms around her mother's neck and pulled her close, clinging tightly to her in a way she hadn't since she was little. Since the Panda-bear days.

She didn't feel the least bit embarrassed doing it, though, even with all the mall-goers she knew must be watching them. She wanted to hold—no, she *needed* to hold her mother right now. Because the pain and the misery and the sense of loneliness that constantly darkened her thoughts, that weighed so heavily on her heart, were more than she could bear, and the only cure for it was a comforting hug from her mom. That, and to know she was loved.

And you know what? she thought. It felt good. It felt right. It felt . . . like everything would be okay. Like *she* would be okay. And it had been so very, very long since she'd had that kind of reassurance.

Reluctantly, she eased her stranglehold and released Karen, who stared at her, then burst out laughing.

"Now you *really* look like a panda bear," Mom said, pointing to Pan's face.

Confused, Pan reached up with her fingers and touched her cheeks. "Gah!" she exclaimed when she saw the black streaks of mascara on the tips, then started laughing, too. Mom pulled a small packet of tissues from her pocket and dabbed at the dark blotches around Pan's eyes. Pan took the tissue and swiped at the smudges. "Don't worry about it; I'll fix it in the ladies' room."

"And I thought the shoe polish on your head looked bad," Mom said wryly, and smiled.

"It's not shoe polish, it's a cream," Pan explained for what felt like the thousandth time.

"I know, I know . . ." Mom glanced at her watch. "Yipes! I'm gonna be late. I've gotta run, sweetie. But we can talk some more tonight if you want to."

"Yeah. I'd like that," Pan said. She grabbed her demon-decorated messenger bag from the backseat, gave Karen a quick peck on the cheek, and opened the passenger-side door. "Love you, Mom."

"Love you, too, honey. And I'm sorry about the 'Panda-bear' thing. It's just . . . sometimes I forget you're a young woman, now. I don't mean to embarrass you."

Pan felt her cheeks redden. "That's okay, Mom—I know you don't." She glanced around to see if anyone was close enough to overhear them, then leaned forward and whispered, "And, y'know, it's . . . okay if you do it once in a while." She raised an eyebrow and smiled slyly. "Once. in. a while."

Karen chuckled. "Okay, okay, I get the message." She gestured toward the mall. "Now, you be careful in there. And try to curb the spending, all right? We're—"

"On a tight budget," Pan finished for her as she stepped out. "I know."

"Okay, then. I'll see you tonight. If you need to reach me for any reason—you have your cell phone?"

"Right here." Pan reached into her the right hip pocket of her jeans and pulled out the cell for Mom to see. "Have fun with the big kids."

Karen rolled her eyes. "Fun. Right." Pan closed the door and Mom drove away, waving good-bye with her left hand out the window as she pulled into the street.

Pan waved back, chuckling as the 4Runner roared across three lanes of traffic to the passing lane, cutting off two delivery trucks and a minivan. Mom might have been born upstate, but her aggressive driving skills were pure New York City.

A rumble of thunder caught Pan's attention as she walked toward the mall entrance. She turned her face to the roiling, green-tinged sky and smiled as warm, fat raindrops splashed against her eyelashes and the tip of her nose. So it was raining; so the weather was miserable. Who cared? As far as she was concerned, all was right with the world—at least for the time being—and not even a heavy downpour was going to spoil her good mood.

She eased into the throng of dampened inbound shoppers, ignoring the flickering images that danced at the corners of her eyes.

3

The Albany Megamall was the ultimate tribute to consumer excess, wrapped in a three-story façade of polished glass and steam-scrubbed sandstone. Not even the cloudy sky looming above it could dim the pinkish glow the gigantic building seemed to give off. In the five years since its doors had opened, it continually provided the shops at Colonie Center and the Crossgates Mall, not to mention Woodbury Common in Central Valley, with some pretty stiff competition, and showed no signs of letting up. For one thing, you could find most of the items offered by the other places right here, without having to drive all over upstate New York. So the convenience of "one-stop shopping" had a lot to do with the mall's success, as did its large number of parking spaces: acre upon acre of available spots in which to leave your vehicle, with little frustration of getting closed out. Except, as Pan had experienced firsthand, during the weeks leading up to Christmas—then the lots were freakin' madhouses, with the shoppers' bubbly holiday spirit replaced by a frightening mix of total panic and murderous road rage.

But, Pan reminded herself, next Christmas was still months away, so it was a safe bet no one was going to try and stab her with a curling iron over a limited edition gift-pack of scented candles she wanted to give her mom. Not again.

She let the flow of humanity streaming through the wide revolving doors carry her inside. Then, like every other time she'd been here, she paused in the enormous lobby to gaze at the sheer spectacle of the place. From the amusement park in the south wing to the movie multiplexes in the north and east, it was the closest thing to being in New York City's five boroughs—just lumped into one location. Lots to do, lots to see, lots to explore, but right now there were only two stores in particular on which she was focused: the Spencer Gifts shop on the third level for more of that black "shoe polish" Mom so detested (actually Manic Panic's "Raven" brand of color cream); and the art supply depot in the west wing to replace some dried-up oil paints.

After a stopover at the first-floor ladies' room to fix her face, she walked over to the closest escalator that would take her to the second level and stepped on board behind a trio of jogging-suited grannies: mall-walkers out for their daily stroll, no doubt.

That's when her hip pocket suddenly roared with the guttural vocals of the death-metal tune "Incubus Summer." The high-decibel ringtone was guaranteed to cause people to look back over their shoulders to find out what was drowning out The Captain and Tenille's "Do That to Me One More Time" currently blaring from the mall's speaker system.

As if on cue, the grannies turned around and glared at her. Pan sweetly grinned at them as she fished the cell phone from her pocket. She didn't need to check the caller ID, she already knew who it was by the ringtone: her best friend, Sheena McCarthy.

"Hey, jungle queen! What's going on?" Pan said. The nickname was a private joke they shared because Mrs. McCarthy had named her daughter after an old comic book character, "Sheena, Queen of the Jungle."

"Not a lot. Just thought I'd give you a call, see how things are in Craptown."

"Still crappy," Pan admitted, and winked at the old ladies who were giving her the stink-eye. "I'm on my way to check out stuff at Spencer's." There was an odd sound in the background from Sheena's end, like a bunch of people all yammering at once, but Pan couldn't make out what they were saying. "Hey, where are you?"

"I'm in the City." That was New York slang for *Manhattan*. It was a term generally used by people coming from the other four boroughs and not residents of the island, but common enough that everyone knew what it meant. "Standing in front of Burning Souls." That was a former funeral parlor turned performance theater in the Bowery, a popular gathering place for Goths.

Pan glanced over at the face of the humongous clock tower that rose two levels above the mall's main floor. "At ten in the morning, when you're outta school? That's kinda early for you, isn't it?"

"Tell me about it!" Sheena said, laughing. "But Sarkophagia tickets are goin' on sale today and I didn't wanna miss out, so I got on line at seven. There's like a hundred people ahead of me—they camped out on the sidewalk last night!"

"Aw, damn it! I forgot all about that!" Pan moaned. Sarkophagia was one of their new favorite groups—a Norwegian death-metal band praised for their grisly concept albums and grand guignol–style stage shows, the latter complete with simulated human sacrifices and copious fountains of blood. And the dark-haired, muscular lead singer, Leander Faust, was such a complete stud that Pan would have paid to watch him read selections from Dr. Seuss . . . as long as he did it with his shirt off. Pan had played their debut CD, *Incubus Summer*, until it wore out Mom's old Discman, and then replaced it with a bootlegged download—along with a copy of their recent follow-up, *At Midnight I'll Take Your Soul*—for her iPod. Mom never would have paid for a legal iTunes download, not when every song on *Midnight* was flagged with an "Explicit" warning—and with good reason. It covered some real hard-core topics: trepanation—drilling holes in skulls—as an exorcism technique; torture and mutilation; even an ode to cannibalism. It was the kind of music Mom would freak out over if she ever heard it—which, of course, made it even more enjoyable.

A weary sigh pushed past her lips. "This sucks total ass, Sheen."

"Yeah, it's a regular tragedy," Sheen replied sarcastically. " 'Sides, you really think your mom woulda let you come back here for a death-metal concert?"

"Well . . . no," Pan admitted. "But maybe Dad could've . . ." She paused, and thought about that for a second. "No, he wouldn't have gone for it, either." Reaching Level Two, she stepped off the escalator and began threading her way through the crowds. The route to the third-floor escalator led through one of the megasized food courts, no doubt purposely designed that way by the mall's owners to entice shoppers to stop and eat. The greasy odor of fish 'n' chips fought with the smells of fried chicken fat, Szechuan stir-fried vegetables, fresh-baked chocolate chip cookies, and Indian spices for possession of the air above the dining area. It made her stomach rumble hungrily.

"So there you go," Sheena concluded. "Besides, what kinda friend would I be if all I did was to call and torture you with the knowledge that, while you're trapped there in Nature's culture vacuum, I'll be feastin' my eyes all night long on Leeeannnnder?" She giggled.

"Bite me."

"Awww, don't feel so bad, Zee. According to Leander's latest Tweet, they're gonna be playin' Craptown in October."

Pan grimaced. "They're coming to Schriksdorp? Why the hell would they wanna do *that*?"

"I don't know. Maybe they like playing county fairs between major gigs. Or maybe nobody told them what that hole is really like. What, didn't you explain that to Leander in all your e-mails, where you begged him to take you away from that hellish place so you can be his undyin' sex slave?"

"Funny," Pan said dryly, while thinking, *Note to self: Stop copying Sheen on your messages* . . .

"Think Mom'll take your leash off for that one?"

Doubt it . . . Pan grunted. "Maybe. We'll see. So, who's going with you?"

"The usual crowd: Dylan and Lisa, Reyna and Tommy, Tory and Mora—not that any of them was willin' to get up this early to hang out on the line with me. Umm . . . Oh! Uwe's here with me—" Her voice faded for a moment as she apparently turned her head away from the phone to add, "Sorry, babe. Didn't mean to leave you out."

"Ooo-vay Kerr?" Pan replied, intentionally overstressing the first syllable of the Germanic name. "The one who called me a 'lummox' when I kept pronouncing it 'Huey'?"

"Uh-huh."

Pan snorted derisively. "You're *still* going out with that jerk?"

Silence. Then: "I'm gonna ignore that, but only 'cause you're not standin' right in front of me so I could smack the crap outta you."

"Ooh, you're so tough when there's, like, a thousand miles between us."

That got a chuckle from Sheen. "Uh-huh . . . Oh, and my sister Rachel and her boyfriend, Joey, are comin', too. And before you comment on that, no, I'm not happy about it, but Mom and Dad weren't gonna let me go without—quote, unquote—adult supervision. I'm just gonna pretend they're not even there." She paused, then added in a conspiratorial whisper, "I think they're all afraid I might get pulled up onstage and used as a virgin sacrifice."

"Little too late for *that*, don't you think?"

"Oh, nice. *You're* one to talk."

"Hey, at least I don't go bragging about it on my Facebook page."

Sheena sighed melodramatically. "Jealousy, thy name is Pandora."

"Yeah, yeah," Pan replied dismissively. "So, is . . ." She stopped, then unconsciously raised her other hand to nervously chew on the thumbnail. "So, is Ammi goin' with you?" she asked hesitantly.

A *very* long pause; then: "Why would I invite *him*?" There was an unmistakably icy tone in Sheen's voice.

"Well, I . . . I thought maybe you guys had made up by now," Pan said. "I know you and him had stopped talking after he and I . . . you know. But now that I've been exiled to Siberia, I figured maybe . . ." A tiny, forced laugh bubbled from her lips. "I mean, you guys used to be so tight and everything before. I never wanted you to become, like, enemies." She took another nibble along the cuticle, scraping off some of the black polish. "You know?"

"*I don't believe this!*" Sheena snapped, her voice erupting from the receiver with enough force to make Pan flinch. "After all the garbage he put you through, after what he did, you're still pining over that . . . that *asshat*?"

"No," Pan replied. "I'm simply asking a question."

"Yeah, well, don't," Sheena warned. "Ammi's dead to me—and he should be to you, too. *God*, Pan . . . " Her exasperated tone of voice trailed off for a second, then immediately hardened: "You haven't been talkin' to him, have you? Or textin' him or anything? 'Cause I swear to God, girl, if you start that self-abuse crap up again—"

"I haven't done any of that," Pan said earnestly. "I swear. Wiped his numbers from my cell, unfriended him on Facebook, listed his e-mail addresses with the spam blockers—the whole cyber-protection thing. But it's like he dropped off the face of the earth since . . . you know."

"The restraining order your folks took out?"

"Well, before that. Look, I'm not trying to hook up with him again—really. I was just . . . curious."

Sheena *hmmf*ed. "You know what your problem is, Zee? You've been stuck in the boonies too long and the isolation's gettin' to you. You need a new boyfriend to take your mind off your old boyfriend. Seriously—you tellin' me there isn't one fine-looking slab of meat in all of Backwoodsia that isn't even a tiny bit curious about"—her voice dropped to a deep, seductive, Barry White-like growl—"gettin' a little dark-side lovin' from the queen of the damned? Ohhhh, baay-by."

Pan laughed softly. "Hey, believe me, I looked—you know I did."

"Uh-huh—for, like, the first couple months you were up there. Then you turned into a nun or something."

"Yeah, well, that wasn't entirely *my* fault . . ."

"Hey, Zwieback!" a girl suddenly yelled from behind her. "I thought vampires only came out at night. What are you doing out of your coffin?"

Pan closed her eyes and sighed. She recognized that voice, and Nikki Van Schrik was absolutely the last person she'd wanted to run into. Then again, if she'd really made plans to avoid Nikki, she wouldn't have come to the enormous shopping center in the first place; the Dolce & Gabbana shop in the east wing was like the girl's second home. But in a consumer wonderland containing two hundred stores, a half dozen restaurants, and eight-screen movie multiplexes, scattered across three levels that seemed to stretch toward infinity, Pan had figured the odds were more than in her favor that she wouldn't run into Nikki and her gang of suck-ups.

'Course, she always *had* been bad with math . . .

"What's goin' on?" Sheena asked.

"Nothing," Pan replied, a little too quickly. She winced; she never liked lying to her, especially when Sheen could tell when she was being conned. "Listen, I'll give you a call later, okay?"

"Yeah," Sheena said brusquely. She knew Pan was jerking her around, but knowing Sheen, she wasn't going to press. Not right now, anyway. "Talk to you then."

Pan, however, knew she couldn't leave things the way they were—not with her best friend mad at her; she had to put them right. *Besides*, she thought glumly, *what'd you expect for bringing up your ex to the girl who kicked his ass—on your behalf?* "Hey, Sheen?" she said quickly.

Sheen sighed. "Yeah?"

Pan gnawed at her cuticle a bit more. "Look, I . . . I'm sorry if I pissed you off before. I know you're only looking out for me, and I do—I really do—appreciate what you did when all that stuff was going on between me and Ammi. I don't *ever* want you thinking I don't. 'Cause I do. Really." She paused, waiting for a reply, but none came. "So . . . are we good? You and me?" *God*, she thought, *that sounded* so *needy . . .*

"Sure, Vampira, we're good," Sheen replied in a playful tone. "BFF and all that—right?"

Pan grinned. "Yeah."

A flood of voices suddenly poured through the receiver. "Look, I gotta run, too," Sheen said, loud enough to still be heard. "The line's startin' to move."

"Okay. Get some good seats for the show, or Tory's gonna bitch about it for days."

Sheen grunted. "I'm doin' my best. I'll tell you all about it tonight. Love ya, Zee!" There was a tiny beep as she hung up.

"You, too, jungle queen," Pan murmured happily. She closed the phone and pocketed it, then turned around.

One crisis down . . .

4

The Legion of Dullards was in full attendance today, with team leader Nikki Van Schrik in the foremost position, flanked by Travis Warrenfield and Mekai Franklin on her left, and Sondra Branch and Kirsten Richards on her right.

Pan sneered. She'd never get any shopping done today; she could just tell.

Nikki was one of those Schriksdorp "Stepford kids" Pan despised, all blond hair and haute couture and superior attitude—the latter no doubt coming from the fact that it was her family for whom the town was named. Regardless of her ancestry, she was a girl so spoiled and demanding she was almost a cliché, but then Pan could have said the same thing about a number of Upper East Side teens she'd had the displeasure of knowing back in the City.

It hadn't taken long for them to start hating each other: it began a few weeks after Pan arrived at Christiaan Huygens High School back in September. She was coming in a year late—the new kid transferring from the Big Apple—and all the alliances and cliques that started gelling in freshman year had long since solidified. She was the odd girl out, but that was okay in the beginning: her arrival generated a lot of interest. Everyone wanted to ask her questions about life in Manhattan, how she got her look, did she ever run into any celebrities on the streets. Things seemed to be cool.

With everyone except Nikki, that is. Apparently she didn't like getting shoved out of the spotlight, and took steps to re-establish her dominant role in the sophomore pecking order. That's when the rumors about Pan started whispering along the corridors. That she'd moved to Schriksdorp after getting kicked out of school for selling drugs, and her mom was trying to keep it quiet. That she *took* drugs. That she was one of those Goth freaks who drank blood and worshipped Satan. That she tortured small animals and buried the bodies in her backyard. That she was a lesbian—well, that one backfired because all the guys thought it was great (no doubt imaging a little girl-on-girl action between her and Nikki). And though Pan couldn't prove who the source of those rumors was, there was absolutely no doubt in her mind it was Nikki Van Schrik.

The members of Nikki's entourage weren't as bad as their leader, but were still jerks in their own ways. Travis was . . . well, calling him Nikki's latest significant other wasn't quite accurate; she'd never seen them do any real boyfriend/girlfriend stuff, like hold hands. Sex slave, maybe? It would certainly explain why he put up with her. He wasn't a bad-looking guy—although he could do without the frosted tips on the ends of his dark hair (trying a little *too* hard to look like he didn't come from the sticks)—and stood just over six feet tall. From his trim hips and well-developed arms and chest one could tell he worked out, but the fact he was holding Nikki's handbag made it pretty obvious who really wore the jockstrap in their relationship. Pan suppressed a grin. Sixteen years old, and already 'whipped . . .

Mekai Franklin and Sondra Branch *were* a couple, but for the life of her, Pan could never figure out why they hung out with Nikki. Sure, their families were rich and Mekai and Travis were friends, but they never struck her as being on Nikki's level of vanity. The best Pan could come up with was that Mekai went where Travis went and brought Sondra along. And yet the two sixteen-year-olds had to have *something* in common with Nikki to be part of her crew—probably a love of money, and the sense of entitlement it gave them.

As for flaxen-haired, lip-glossed, fifteen-year-old Nikki-wannabe Kirsten . . . well, every bad guy needs a toady, right? Dracula had Renfield, Doctor Frankenstein had Ygor, and Nikki Van Schrik had Kirsten Richards. If the girl had any kind of personality of her own it was hard to tell, because the almost creepy idolization of her alpha-female mistress seemed to be the only trait she possessed. Kirsten was the one who got Nikki's hand-me-downs, whether it was used clothing or used boyfriends, so odds were good she'd be wrapped around Travis's waist before the summer was over, her mistress having moved on to a new conquest.

Pan glared at Nikki. "What?"

It was Travis, however, who responded by gesturing at her clothing. "Hey, Pan, you're lookin' real 'lone gunman' today," he said with a condescending smirk. "Y'know, if you're lookin' for the gun store"—he jerked a thumb back over his shoulder—"it's over by Newville. I hear they're havin' a two-for-one Psycho Chick Sale. Maybe you oughtta check it out."

The group laughed—Nikki obviously forcing her donkey-like braying just a bit louder so she could be heard over everyone else—only to quickly fall silent as Pan took a menacing step forward. She tilted her head down slightly, so she could look at them with her eyes rolled upward, and slowly grinned in her best impression of Jack Nicholson in the movie version of *The Shining*.

"Already got everything I need right here, Travis," she growled, and patted her leather jacket. "Like to see?" She reached under the cracked leather, her smile widening as the group as a whole moved back a couple of steps. Amazingly, none of them turned to run, but Kirsten shrieked as Pan quickly pulled out her hand … to reveal a cellophane-wrapped package of chocolate Twizzlers. She tore off one of the waxlike candy strips, took a big bite, and laughed. "Man, do you losers need to lighten up," she commented between chews.

Nikki's horrified expression slowly morphed into one of intense anger. For a moment, Pan couldn't help but wonder if that was because Nikki didn't like being played the fool, or because she was disappointed the weird Goth chick had failed to live up to her potential as the dangerous whackjob they made her out to be.

"You're *such* an asshole, Zwieback," Nikki muttered.

Pan pointed at her with the Twizzler. "And *you* need to buy yourself a sense of humor, Van Schrik." She smiled broadly and took another bite. "Maybe Daddy can get you one from Sharper Image for your next birthday if you ask real nice. You know—like that boob job he promised for your graduation present you've been telling everybody about."

Nikki's cheeks turned five shades of red. Sondra and Kirsten giggled softly, but a heated glare from their ringleader was enough to shut them up. She might be willing to take a few cheap shots from an enemy, Pan knew, but there was no way Nikki would take any crap from her devoted followers.

Nikki turned back to Pan, and sniffed haughtily. "You know, Pandora, considering the kind of antisocial freak you turned out to be, I'm not surprised your parents got a divorce." She grinned wickedly. "I hear your dad's an asshole just like—"

The right cross snapped her head to the side before anyone even realized Pan had thrown the punch. Nikki spun around once—a complete three-sixty—then crashed backward onto the food court's carpeted floor.

Sondra screamed. Travis and Mekai stepped up, placing themselves between Pan and her human speed bag.

Pan snarled. "You shut up about my mom and dad," she growled, stabbing a warning finger at Nikki.

Nikki raised a trembling hand to her mouth, her eyes growing big as a CD as she saw the blood staining the tips of her fingers. "Oh, my God, I'm bleeding . . ." she choked.

Pan smiled tightly. That wasn't the only surprise Nikki had coming. Once she got to a mirror, she'd find out her left cheek was tattooed with the shape of the pentagram from the ring Pan wore on her right middle finger. It was a pretty deep impression, too, highlighted by the bright-red impact zone where Pan's fist had made landfall. Or would that be "facefall"?

The arrival of mall security ended any further thoughts on the correct terminology. Like most rent-a-cops, they came in two flavors: old and overweight, and young and trim. The old guy reminded Pan of actor Danny Glover, only ten years older and maybe sixty pounds heavier, wearing a light blue uniform shirt that should've been traded in for an XXL a few years back; the badge pinned to his shirt identified him as OFF. ASHMAN. His sidekick was about thirty-five years or so his junior, and apparently the "muscle" of the duo, if the bodybuilder physique was any indication. His shirt was stretched tight across his chest, just like his partner's, but in a far more pleasing way.

"Don't you go anywhere, young lady," Old Lethal Weapon said to Pan, pointing a stern finger at her. "I saw the whole thing." Which was doubtful, considering how packed and noisy the mall was, as it usually was on Fridays. At best, he'd probably heard Sondra's ear-piercing scream and turned in time to see Nikki smooch the floor. Pan, however, knew better than to argue the point. It wasn't like any of Nikki's butt-kissers were about to side with her.

The Incredible Hunk strode over and clasped one of his catcher's mitt-sized hands around Pan's upper arm. He had some grip there, she noted. "You'll have to come with us, miss," he said, and the bass in his voice caused a giddy little shiver to run up her spine.

"Okay," she replied huskily, knowing full well the smile she couldn't force down probably made her look like an even bigger troublemaker—one who was obviously treating this whole thing like it was a joke. She stole a glance at his badge Off. Rivera. For a security guard, he sure was a stud . . .

"I'm going to need you to come along, too, miss," his partner said.

Pan looked over to see that Nikki had pulled herself off the carpet with the help of Travis and Mekai. The boys were holding her up, although it was evident to anyone with eyes in their heads that Nikki was more than capable of standing on her own. She was just milking the situation for all the sympathy she could get, but the angry stare she was directing at the guard wasn't going to win him over anytime soon.

"Why?" she demanded. "I didn't do anything wrong."

"You're full of—" Pan began, but the stern look Rivera gave her made it clear she should keep her mouth shut. "Whatever," she mumbled.

"I'm not saying you did," Ashman said to Nikki, "but we're going to need both sides of the story for our report."

The CD-size eyes reappeared. "What report? Aren't you just gonna arrest her?"

"That's not how it works," Ashman said. "We're security guards. We don't have the power to arrest folks, just detain them till the police arrive. But in a case like this, we don't call them in until we know the whole situation. That's why we need you to come with us to the office."

"But you said you saw everything . . ." Nikki whined.

Ashman winced, like he was suffering a sharp pain; maybe an attack of conscience, Pan figured. "Well, maybe I was stretching the truth just a bit . . ." he slowly admitted. The embarrassment of being caught in a lie was quite evident on his face as he stole a quick glance at Pan.

She didn't bother hiding her smirk.

"So what *can* you do?" Nikki asked sharply. She gestured toward Pan. "That bitch almost broke my jaw!"

"Not even close," Pan replied snidely. "But if you'd like me to try harder . . ."
She took a step forward. Rivera moved to block her.

"Knock it off—both of you!" he barked.

The girls fell silent. Ashman looked from one to the other, sighed wearily, and turned to his partner. "Let me talk to her," he said, pointing to Pan, and gestured to an alcove just off the food court where a bank of wall-mounted pay phones was located. "Miss?" Pan nodded and joined him on the short walk.

"This isn't over, Zwieback!" Nikki yelled after her.

Pan flipped her The Bird without turning around.

At the pay phones, Ashman let Pan enter the alcove first, obviously so she couldn't try and run off while his back was turned. Then he leaned against the entrance. "Before we get the police involved—and believe you me, I'd rather not have to call them, what with all the paperwork and whatnot I'd have to do in filing a report—would you mind telling me what that was all about?"

So Pan told him. He stood there, arms folded across his wide, flabby chest, and listened to her tale, nodding occasionally, frowning often. And when she was done bringing him up to speed, he scratched his jaw for a few moments, putting some real thought into the situation.

"Well," he finally said, "the only thing I can think of doing—without handing you over to the police, that is—is to ask you to leave the mall."

"*What?*" Pan exclaimed. "Oh, come on!" Was this guy serious?

"Just for today," he replied. "Just until the two of you've had time to cool off. I'm not in any mood to deal with all the problems there'd be if she jacked you up in retaliation five minutes after Officer Rivera and I walked away."

Pan snarled. "This is bull—"

"You watch yourself, young lady!" the guard snapped, and thrust a warning finger in her face. "Or so help me, I *will* call the police!"

"But she started it," Pan insisted, pointing in Nikki's direction.

"And *you* finished it. I'd call it a draw, but I'm inclined to think you never gave her the chance to throw the first punch."

Pan started to answer, stopped, shrugged, and looked down at her feet. "Whatever . . ." Then she looked back up, eyes bright with anger. "But why am *I* the one who has to leave?"

"*Because* you're the one who finished it," Ashman replied. His stern expression eased into a gentle smile. "Look, it's not like I'm banning you from the mall forever—just one day." He held up an index finger. "One day. That's all I'm asking for. Hell, a confident young lady like yourself, who obviously knows how to throw down with the best of 'em—you oughtta be able to roll with that easy."

Pan jammed her hands into her jacket pockets and chewed on her bottom lip for a few seconds. She considered her options—not many—then reluctantly nodded. "Fine," she muttered.

"All right, then," Ashman said pleasantly. "You come back tomorrow, and I'm sure everything will have been forgotten. A brand-new day and all that. And to be quite honest about it, miss, I appreciate your willingness to cooperate."

Well, it was either that or a trip to Cop Central, Pan thought. Not really much of a choice. "Can I go now?" she asked brusquely.

Ashman frowned. Apparently that wasn't the sort of response he was looking for. Well, too bad. She might be willing to "cooperate," but that didn't mean she had to like it. If he was expecting a "You're welcome," he was gonna be waiting a helluva long time.

The guard stepped aside, making some room for her to leave.

"*So* not fair . . ." Pan walked forward, making no effort to turn sideways so she could squeeze around him. Let him hug the wall if he wanted her to get by.

It was while she was pushing past him that her hand brushed against his. That's when IT happened.

As soon as they made skin-on-skin contact, it felt as though a million volts were running through her body. Her muscles started to spasm; it became hard to breathe; her eyes rolled back in her head. She couldn't talk, couldn't see; the only sound she heard was a roaring in her ears, like waves crashing on the shore. Dimly, she wondered if she was having a stroke. Or maybe some hidden blood clot had just exploded in her brain and she was about to die.

And then just like that—it stopped. Connection broken the moment Ashman pulled away from her.

Pan gasped and staggered back. She bounced off a pay phone and slid to the tiled floor, then sat there in a daze. "Holy . . . holy crap . . ." she wheezed. There were spots dancing in her vision, and she rubbed at her eyes to clear them.

She heard Ashman kneel beside her, his considerable bulk thudding to a landing a few inches to her left. "Hey, are you all right?" he asked. Whether the note of concern she heard in his voice was caused by genuine interest in her well-being or because he could see himself standing on the unemployment line by tomorrow morning, she didn't care. All she wanted to know was why he'd zapped her with a Taser or a cattle prod or whatever the hell it was. Because she wouldn't say thank-you to him for tossing her out of the mall? Because she'd tried elbowing past him?

She opened her eyes and turned to face him, not certain if she should scream at him for attacking her or give him a pentagram tattoo to match the one adorning Nikki's face. What she saw, however, made her forget all about stun guns and punching out his lights.

He was a monster.

His face—if it could be called that—was a shifting, bubbling mass of boiled-over flesh and festering sores oozing with brackish yellow-green pus. Occasionally, the white gleam of bone shone through, only to disappear as the tide of rotting skin swept over it, then receded, then swept forward again. The eyes were tiny red pinpricks glowing in hollowed sockets, the mouth a lipless slash void of teeth—a pit into which the rivulets of pus and pieces of watery skin pooled and mixed, thickening into a chunk-filled mucus that coated the roof of his mouth and hung down in weblike strands.

Pan's hand flew up to her own mouth; it was a toss-up as to whether she was holding back a scream or trying to keep from spewing that morning's breakfast. A little of both, actually.

"Oh, God," she whispered hoarsely. "Not again . . ."

"Are you all right, miss?" the creature asked. It came out sounding like he had a barrel of molasses poured down his gullet, every syllable pronounced with a thick and heavy and disgustingly gooey accent. He reached out with an equally misshapen hand to touch her forehead—probably to check if she had a fever—and Pan frantically scrambled away. The last thing she needed was another jolt of whatever electrical charge was flowing through his (its) body.

"I'mfineI'mfine," she said quickly. "Really." She stumbled to her feet, keeping plenty of distance between her and Officer Grotesque-o.

Ashman (was that even his real name?) levered himself back to a standing position, and watching him maneuver that prodigious, loose-fleshed bulk almost caused her to lose control of her stomach again. He reached out for her again.

"*DON'T TOUCH ME!*" she shrieked. *Why can't the damn monsters ever leave me alone?*

The guard stared at her, and even through the soupy mess of his face she could tell he was surprised. No, not surprised—totally shocked. *Aw, crap,* she thought. *I didn't say that last part out loud, did I?*

Apparently she had. "Monst— You can *see* me?" Ashman croaked, lowering his voice. "The *real* me?"

She didn't understand what he meant. "W-what . . . ?"

His shock quickly turned to anger. "That's impossible! You're not . . . Who are you?" he demanded, and took a step toward her. "*What* are you?"

"W-what am *I*?" Pan cheeped. "What're *you*?"

Before either one could get an answer, Ashman's partner, Rivera, came into the picture. He clapped a friendly hand on the monster's shoulder. "What's goin' on, Rog?" he asked, and turned his steely gaze on Pan. "Marilyn Manson here givin' you trouble?"

A crowd formed behind the two guards, Nikki and the jerk squad at the forefront, and Pan gasped in horror as she realized there were monsters among them, too. One looked like a deer cut down the center and turned inside out, its bloated intestines hanging like paper streamers from its misshapen antlers. Another resembled a human being with goat legs. And a third was some kind of hideous cross between a skinned rat and a melted toad. It took her a couple of seconds to realize the last one was Kirsten Richards, and that was only because she recognized the particular shade of lip gloss Nikki's loyal minion always wore.

Nonononono! Pan thought hysterically as she squeezed her eyes shut. *OhGod, OhGod, please just let me get out of here!*

Panicked, she opened her eyes and charged forward, pushing past Ashman before he or Rivera could stop her, ignoring the promises of revenge Nikki made as she went by. As she raced for the down escalator, Pan stole quick glances at the people around her. Although (thankfully) not everyone looked like a figment of some Clive Barker fever dream, there were still plenty of grotesqueries that she spotted. Monsters walking in and out of stores, monster parents pushing their monster kids in strollers, monster couples kissing or holding hands—all milling about, browsing and chatting and minding their respective businesses like nothing was out of the ordinary. Just another day at the Albany Megamall. It was as though the gates of Hell had been thrown wide open and all the demons of the pits had crawled out to walk the Earth and—what? Go shopping at Neiman Marcus?

Sure, it was crazy. Sure, it made absolutely no sense. But that's exactly what was happening. And she was the only one who could see it.

Of course she was. After all, wasn't she the one with the hallucinations? The one who was always seeing hideous creatures? And now they weren't just lurking at the corners of her eyes, they were all around her . . . just like old times.

"Oh, God, make it stop . . ." she moaned. A few of the things turned in her direction, and she hurriedly flipped up her hoodie to hide her face. Improvised blinders to prevent her from looking anywhere but straight ahead.

She ran down the escalator and sprinted for the exit, wanting nothing more than to get as far away as possible from the mall and the monsters that infested it. Outside the doors was the real world. The safe world. The sane world.

But as Pandora Zwieback knew all too well, that world was full of monsters, too.

5

Karen had driven about three-quarters of the way across the Patroon Island Bridge, heading west along Interstate 90 on her way toward BarronQuest's offices in Sheridan Hollow, when she sensed that something was wrong. ESP, telepathy, a sudden weight in the pit of her stomach, a mother's instinct for her child's well-being—it all came down to a five-alarm warning that started jangling through every nerve ending. And she knew it had something to do with Pan.

Keeping one hand on the 4Runner's steering wheel, she reached behind and grabbed the imitation Yves Saint Laurent Uptown Tote from the backseat, then dropped it on her lap and began riffling through its contents for her cell phone. A difficult task, given that she had one eye on the morning rush-hour traffic zipping around her and one on the wallet, cosmetics, house keys, credit card receipts, iPod, breath mints, and loose change—among other items—that she scooped out and tossed on the passenger seat, but eventually she was rewarded by her fingers closing around the smooth, plastic rectangle that was her iPhone. Then, with the sort of intuitive driving skills that could only have been honed on New York City streets—or a NASCAR racetrack—Karen stomped down on the accelerator and executed a sharp right-hand turn that carried the SUV across two lanes of traffic toward the nearest exit ramp. She ignored the horns honked at her by the infuriated drivers she cut off and began thumbing through the phone's address book to bring up Pan's number. When it popped up on the screen, she keyed the entry and held the cell to her ear as she guided the 4Runner back toward the bridge's eastbound lanes.

The ringing on the other end of the line seemed to go on forever, each unanswered burring tone making Karen just a little bit more anxious, her mind awhirl with an endless number of worst-case scenarios, until she finally heard: "Mom?"

The tiny, painfully meek tone of her daughter's voice sent an uncontrollable chill up Karen's spine. "Pan, what happened? Where are you?"

There was a loud sniff from the other end of the line—had she been *crying?*—and Pan mumbled, "Outside the mall. In the back, by the loading docks."

Loading docks? Karen's first impulse was to ask *why* Pan was lurking around the back of the shopping mall, but she forced herself to ignore the panicked questions stacking up in her mind. If she didn't maintain her focus, if she didn't stop dwelling on those worst-case scenarios, she'd wind up doing something stupid like plowing through the guardrail, and plunging into the Hudson River was *not* going to help her distraught daughter.

"Pan?" she asked gently. "Are you okay?"

"Um . . . yeah. Just, could you . . . could you come get me?"

Karen wheeled the SUV into the right-side breakdown lane and goosed the engine a little harder. If a state trooper happened to catch sight of her driving so recklessly on a rain-slicked roadway, she thought, well . . . screw it. He'd have to catch her first. She caught a quick glimpse of a sign overhead as the 4Runner practically flew past the slower-moving traffic: EXIT 7 – WASHINGTON AVE – RENSSELAER.

"Stay right there, baby, okay?" she urged. "I'm on my way. I'll be there in a couple of minutes."

"Okay," came the soft reply. And then: "Mom?"

"Yes, honey?"

"Don't hang up?"

It was a plea so heartrending, so unexpected, so . . . unPanlike that for a moment Karen almost dropped the phone and lost control of the 4Runner. Pan had never sounded this helpless in her entire life, not even during the contentious divorce proceedings. Now Karen really *was* afraid something terrible had happened. Still, she managed to regain her composure in time to avoid plowing into the back of a FedEx delivery van in the next lane.

"Pan, I'm right here. I'm not going anywhere," Karen assured her. "I'm just going to put the phone down so I can steer. Okay?"

"Sure."

Despite her inclination to hang on to the phone, Karen hit the speaker button and dropped it in her lap; then she gripped the wheel with both hands. "Still there, honey?"

"Yeah."

"Okay. I'm just getting off the thruway. Give me another minute."

"I'll be here." It was no doubt meant to be a lighthearted remark, but hearing it delivered in such a flat, emotionless tone made Karen's heart skip a nervous beat.

She floored the accelerator, and the 4Runner flew down the exit ramp.

Karen reached the mall in what she thought must be a new land-speed record. Not such an easy—or wise—thing to do, considering that by the time she'd reached the entrance to the parking lot the storm-tossed skies had completely opened up and she'd found herself racing through a torrential downpour that made seeing, let alone driving, difficult at best.

Still, she was soon inelegantly fishtailing her SUV around the back of the megamall. Ahead of her, on the left-hand side, were a half dozen loading bays where big rigs would pull in to deliver the latest shipments of goods for the mall's innumerable stores; they were empty now, with only a few workers lounging around watching the downpour. She didn't see any sign of Pan, though. Had she gone back inside?

Karen picked up the iPhone from her lap and looked around. "Honey, I'm at the loading docks. Where are—"

And then she spotted her daughter.

Pan was sitting in the rain on top of a Dumpster across from the bays, near the chain-link fence that marked the end of the mall's extensive property. The hood of her sweatshirt was pulled up, concealing her face in deep shadow, but even from this distance Karen could see that it, as well as the rest of Pan's clothing, was completely soaked through. And Pan either hadn't noticed . . . or just didn't care.

A tear rolled down Karen's cheek. "Oh, honey . . ."

It's just a bump in the road, it's not the end of the world. It's just a bump in the road,
it's not the end of the world . . .

Pan continually repeated the coping statement Dr. Farrar had taught her to deal
with panic attacks as she stared at her mother's car, uncertain of what to do next.
Go to her? Run away? Rainwater dripped into her eyes from the sodden edges of
her hoodie, but she ignored it. Her attention was solely focused on the shadowy
figure that sat behind the 4Runner's steering wheel. She knew who that figure was,
but the thought of *what* it might be terrified her.

She couldn't handle it if it turned out her mom was a monster, too.

"Oh, honey . . ." Karen's pain-tinged words spilled into Pan's ear from the cell
phone pressed against it. The voice sounded normal enough—no gooey, phlegmy
rattle like what had spilled out of the security guard—but so what? Who said every
monster had to talk like they were coughing up the world's biggest hair ball?

Tightening her grip on the cell, Pan screwed her eyes shut and gritted her teeth.
Pleasepleaseplease, she thought desperately. *Please don't let this turn out bad. I'll*
totally *lose my mind if it does—I just know I will . . .*

The sound of a car in motion caught her attention, and she opened her eyes
to find the 4Runner moving toward her. This was it, then—nowhere to run and
hide; nothing to do but wait for the outcome. A nervous tremor ran through Pan's
body as the SUV pulled to a stop a few feet away. She tried to peer inside, but the
combination of rainfall, overcast skies, and furiously swishing windshield wipers
made it impossible to see if her worst fears were about to be confirmed.

The door opened, and Pan held her breath. Karen slowly stepped out from the
vehicle . . .

And she was beautiful.

No, *more* than beautiful—she literally glowed from head to foot with a golden
light that swirled around her with the brilliance of a sunrise. It played across

Karen's features, highlighting her cheekbones, intensifying the hue of her green-blue eyes, adding a new level of radiance to her hair. This was no monster; it was an angel come to her rescue.

Pan choked back tears of relief. In a day when it seemed as though every conceivable nightmare had crawled out of the depths of the underworld just to torment her, to make her question her sanity, here at last was proof that not everything in the world had turned bad; that like her mythological namesake, after all the monsters had been unleashed, there was still a glimmer of hope for her to grab onto.

And right now, she'd gladly take whatever she could get.

"Mom!" Pan yelled. She leaped from the Dumpster and threw herself into Karen's arms, holding on as though afraid she might suddenly disappear and abandon her to her misery. Karen held on just as tightly, burying her face in her daughter's hair as she kissed the top of Pan's head and offered reassurances. When they finally pulled back to look at each other, Pan couldn't help but laugh—Karen's mouth was smeared with black dye.

Karen, however, didn't see the humor in the situation—the fear shining brightly in her eyes was all too apparent—but she understood the reason for Pan's amusement. She wiped her mouth with the back of her left hand, then used both to gently take Pan's shoulders and push her out to arm's length. Her eyes did a quick head-to-toe scan, as though seeking physical evidence of whatever ailed her daughter. When nothing presented itself, her gaze returned to Pan's face.

"Honey, what's wrong?" she asked.

"Uh . . ." Pan halted. What exactly could she say—*Hey, Mom, this old guy electrocuted me and now I'm seeing monsters again?* No way. She'd be sitting in the Adolescent Unit at the Capital District Psychiatric Center before the day was over, discussing panic attacks and Cassandra complexes and post-traumatic stress with Dr. Farrar for the nine-millionth time. But none of that would solve her problem—it never did—and the minute she admitted what was really troubling her, it'd be right back to the Seroquel and the Klonopin or whatever other antipsychotic meds the doctor might prescribe to "help" her through this setback. Help turn her into a wall-eyed zombie again, was more like it. No thanks.

Karen slipped an arm around her shoulders and steered her toward the 4Runner, a momentary reprieve. "Let's talk about it in the car," she said. "You're soaked to the bone and you'll catch a cold or the flu or something if we keep standing in the rain. Me, too, probably."

Pan shuffled along, one thought stumbling over the other in a race for a plausible explanation to her admittedly bizarro behavior—one that wouldn't immediately cause Mom to start calling her daughter's therapist. She remained silent as Karen guided her into the front passenger seat, then closed the door and ran around to the driver's side. The door slammed shut with a resounding thunk; the roar of the downpour outside eased to a steady drumbeat on the SUV's roof.

Karen shivered and rubbed her arms. "Little chilly." She reached for the climate control knob on the dashboard and a welcome blast of warm air rushed from the vents. Karen smiled gratefully. "Much better."

Pan pulled back her hood and looked past Karen at the creatures that were milling around the loading bays. Were they getting ready to attack—or just curious about the teen head case and her glow-in-the-dark mother? She really didn't want to find out.

"Mom?" she asked, knowing there was a note of mild hysteria creeping into her voice, but being unable to prevent it. "Can we get out of here?"

Karen's confusion was evident. "Sure, sweetie," she replied slowly. Then she turned to look in the direction of Pan's thousand-yard stare, and the escapees from *Pan's Labyrinth* clustered at the docks. When she turned back around, her brows were knit tightly together and her teeth were clenched. "Did those men over there have something to do with you sitting on a Dumpster in the rain?" she asked angrily. "Did they try to do anything?"

Men, Pan noted, not monsters. So, just like always, she was the only one who could see their true selves—if those *were* their true selves. *Gah*, she thought glumly. *Maybe I do need to see Dr. Farrar . . .*

Karen didn't wait for Pan to respond; she opened her door and moved to step out. Pan frantically leaned over and grabbed her arm. "Mom, what're you doing?"

"I'm going over there to get some answers," she replied sharply. "I want to know what they did that had you running out of the mall."

Pan tried to tug her back inside. "They didn't do anything, Mom—really."

Karen eyed her suspiciously. "Really?"

Pan nodded. "I swear." She tugged on Karen's arm again. "Can we just go now? Please?"

Karen frowned. "All right." She closed her door, then wagged an index finger at her daughter. "But you're going to tell me everything on the ride home."

Pan started. "Home? I thought you had to get to work."

Karen shrugged. "I'll call Jerry and tell him I can't make it in—I've got something more important to take care of." She smiled warmly, and reached over to stroke Pan's cheek. "That work for you?"

Pan grinned. "Sure."

"Great." Karen slipped on her seat belt; Pan did the same. "Besides, I can still work from home—a little telecommuting for one day isn't going to throw BarronQuest into turmoil." She shifted gears into Drive and swung the 4Runner around, heading for the parking lot exit.

As the SUV moved past the loading docks, Pan did her best to not look at the demons that seemed to be eyeing her so hungrily.

The issue of what was bothering her couldn't be avoided forever, though. After Karen got them back on the interstate and headed for home, she called BarronQuest to let Jeremy Barron know that she had to take care of a "family emergency." But once that was done Karen sat quietly, no doubt expecting Pan to break the ice.

When that didn't happen, she finally said, "So, feeling better?"

"Yeah," Pan droned, her attention focused not on her mother but on the driver of the red pickup truck in the next lane. The man's features shimmered like she was looking at him through a heat haze—normal one second, grotesque the next. His tangled dark brown beard became a writhing collection of maggots and worms, then turned back to hair; his pustule-ridden cheeks dripped with ooze, then appeared to be as smooth and unblemished as the proverbial baby's bottom. And the more Pan stared, the more the nonscary version of the guy began to take dominance.

A weary smiled tugged at Pan's lips. Maybe—hopefully—the monstervision was wearing off. Maybe she'd finally be able to put the whole nightmarish morning behind her. Maybe—

Karen's cell phone rang—or, more accurately, exploded with the sounds of Cheap Trick's "Surrender": *"Mommy's all right, Daddy's all right, They just seem a little weird . . ."* She picked it up. "Hel—" she began, and then almost dropped the phone as the voice on the other end of the line roared in her ear; to Pan, it sounded like a giant chicken squawking. The 4Runner drifted a little into the right-hand lane, and Pan got a good look at the shock on worm-beard's face as the SUV came close to swapping paint chips with the side of his pickup. Karen compensated just in time and brought the 4Runner back into her lane, ignoring The Bird the pickup driver flipped at her as he increased speed and roared off.

Karen frowned as she raised the iPhone back to her ear. "Who is this?" she demanded. "And I'd appreciate it if you could tell me without blowing out my eardrum . . . Who?" Her eyes widened in response, and she glanced at Pan. "Mrs. Van Schrik?" The look of momentary surprise became one of suspicion. "How did you get my cell-phone number?"

Pan's stomach did a nervous flip. She'd been so freaked out over her psychosode that she'd completely forgotten about her run-in with Nikki Van Schrik and her crew. But Nikki hadn't—big surprise, there—and had turned around and told her mom, and now things were going to get *really* ugly.

"What do you mean, attacked your daughter?" Karen asked, shocking Pan out of her reverie. Her mother's voice had jumped about three octaves.

Pan gulped. Forget ugly—things were downright apocalyptic from the get-go. Most definitely.

"Mrs.—" Karen began, but Nikki's mom cut her off; her voice gushed out of the phone like a flash flood, though Pan couldn't make out any specific words. "M—" Another cutoff, and now Karen was clearly losing her temper; her face reddened, and her right hand squeezed the steering wheel in a death grip.

"*Mrs. Van Schrik!*" she snapped, then exhaled sharply. "I realize how serious this is"—she glared at Pan—"believe me, I do, but right now I'm a little busy trying to keep my SUV on the road in the middle of a rainstorm. But I'd like—" She grimaced, and lowered her voice. "Well, not *like*, but I'm willing to continue this discussion after I get home; I should be there in about an hour. Does that work for you?" She paused to listen. Pan couldn't hear any chicken squawking this time, so Nikki's mom must have lowered her voice to a civilized level as well. "Yes, that'll be fine . . . Yes, I'm sure you have my home number, too," Mom responded sarcastically. "Thank you, Mrs. Van Schrik. Bye-bye."

She ended the call, then tossed the phone onto the dashboard in frustration. "Damn it!" She grunted as she stared out the windshield. "Well, now I know why you were hiding out behind the mall . . ."

"Mom—" Pan started.

"Don't," Karen interrupted, waving a hand to cut her off. "Just . . . don't. Unless you're going to tell me she hit you first, or she did something that made you *think* she was going to hit you, I don't want to hear it." She paused. "So did she?"

Pan looked away. "No." She turned back. "But—"

Up went the hand again. "Stop." Karen sighed. "Pan, I thought I've always been clear about this: just because someone disagrees with you, or insults you, is no reason to beat them up. I'm still making payments on the eyeglasses you broke from the dustup you had with that other girl."

"Becca Seo."

"Yeah, her," Karen replied. "Didn't know designer eyewear could be so damned expensive . . ." she muttered.

"But Nikki was insulting you and Dad!" Pan pleaded.

"It doesn't matter," Karen countered. "They're just words. You know—'sticks and stones' and all that? Haven't you been over that a hundred times with Dr. Farrar already? And Dr. Elfman before her?" When Pan frowned in response, Karen sat quietly for a moment, no doubt trying to think of another approach. "Look, I know you've been having problems with that Van Schrik girl and her friends all year; I know she's been riding you every chance she gets. But you've got to learn to control your temper."

Like you with Mrs. Van Schrik? Pan thought, but wisely didn't say out loud. Instead, she folded her arms across her chest and hunkered down in her seat—total sulk mode, she knew, but she didn't care. "Whatever."

"All right, we'll talk about it later," Karen offered in a softer voice, then added in a sarcastic tone, "Right now I have to go home and get my ass chewed off by the matriarch of one of the most powerful families in the state—you know, the one *Schriksdorp* is named after. I can only pray she doesn't want to press assault charges or sue us into oblivion. Think you can avoid decking anyone else between the driveway and the front door?"

"I'll see what I can do," Pan muttered sourly. She turned away to glare at the hellspawn behind the wheel of the British flag–decorated Mini Cooper puttering along on her side.

Mom's weary sigh seemed to echo in the 4Runner all the way back to Schriksdorp.

6

At a glance, the town of Schriksdorp should have had some appeal for a horror fan like Pan: roiling storm clouds that at times seemed to have taken up permanent residence in its skies; mist-shrouded woodlands; the spooky old mansion that loomed above the town's six thousand residents from atop Ezra's Mountain to the west—both land and home owned by the famously high-brow Van Schrik clan; and a cemetery that dated back to the original Dutch settlement, complete with squeaky iron gates and creepy, potentially inbred grave diggers. (Well, the inbred part was just a guess, but the slovenly, unibrowed Atkinson brothers, Filo and Vance, did look pretty creepy.) Throw in a public library that looked more like a county jail—because it used to be one—and a major Halloween celebration every year, and it should have been a regular Dread Central.

That had been Pan's first impression of the place, as she tried to convince herself that moving to rural America could still have its adventures—after all, 'Salem's Lot and Castle Rock were small-town settings for Stephen King novels and he sure made those places seem exciting. And there was Ray Bradbury, too, with books like *Something Wicked This Way Comes* and *Dandelion Wine* and a ton of short stories—those were all set in small towns. There had to be *something* of interest in Schriksdorp, some little quirk that was so absolutely pants-wetting frightening it would appeal to her freakazoid nature—right?

It was too bad, then, that she'd had to stick around long enough for a *second* impression. There were no ghouls prowling the streets of Schriksdorp, no hobgoblins haunting its back alleys, no devils opening curio shops on Main Street, no great evil—or even Great Pumpkin, for that matter—rising up from ancient burial grounds to cause mischief. Nine months of poking around alleyways, tromping through the woods, and exploring the graveyard had proved that. Schriksdorp was a quiet little town in a quiet little section of upstate New York, where other than the Halloween blowout the most exciting events came in the form of bake sales and county fairs.

Still, there was one good thing about being stuck in Craptown: having her own room in her grandparents' Queen Anne–style home, with its steep, peaked roofs, three-story hexagonal tower, and a porch that encircled the first floor from the front door to the pantry steps in back. Oh sure, there were similar houses scattered around Schriksdorp—the result of a mini population boom in the 1890s—but the Bonifants' was the only one in town painted yuletide colors of pine green and burgundy; as a child, Pan always thought it was like living in Santa Claus's summer home, especially when Grandpa Morgan, with his flowing white hair and beard, used to parade around in his bright red volunteer fireman's pants and shirt. Of course, with Grandma Ellie and Grandpa Morgan now living in Miami, the house was just a big, empty, quiet place, like the town around it.

But never quiet for long . . .

The phone started ringing in the first-floor den as soon as Karen and Pan came crashing through the front door to escape the rain.

"Doesn't waste any time, does she?" Karen sarcastically remarked. She looked her waterlogged daughter over. "You better get out of those wet clothes. We'll talk after Mrs. Van Schrik is done bending my ear."

"Over some mint chocolate chip ice cream?"

The stern expression that had so dominated Karen's features on the drive home softened considerably. Perhaps she was remembering her daughter's rain-soaked, pitiable state in the parking lot, or the forlorn sound of her voice on the cell phone. Whatever the reason, she reached out to stroke Pan's cheek.

"Sounds like a plan," she replied with a gentle smile—which quickly became a fearsome snarl as the phone continued ringing. "All right!" she barked at it. "I'm coming!"

Pan watched her mother stride down the hallway toward the back of the house, to receive her verbal beating, and the guilt weighed heavily on her conscience. Not guilt over laying Nikki out when she so rightly deserved having her clock cleaned—in Pan's opinion, at least—but over dragging Mom into the whole mess. Karen had enough problems to deal with working a full-time job, raising a daughter, and paying the bills; she didn't need any more complications in her life. And yet that was exactly what Pan had given her.

She sighed, wondering if she'd ever figure out all the complexities of teenage life—and not just the ones involving her psychological troubles.

Mom's weary voice echoed down the hallway from the den: "Mrs. Van Schrik, if Nikki was able to tell you all this, then it's *obvious* her jaw wasn't broken . . ."

To Pan, that sounded like her cue to go to her room and change. She tromped up the stairs, her boots thudding loudly against the paisley runner that covered the center of the oak staircase. As she reached the halfway point, Pan looked up in time to see a small head covered in black fur hovering at the edge of the second-floor landing. Bright green eyes regarded her with cool interest.

Pan smiled. Here, at last, was a monster she could handle. "Hey, Vlad," she cooed. "How's my baby?"

The black tomcat mewed softly as Pan took a seat on the landing and reached out to stroke his head. Vlad, however, was apparently in no mood to be manhandled by a soaking wet human, even if she *was* his owner. He jumped back and sniffed distastefully at her outstretched hand; then he turned away and trotted off down the hall, toward a smaller staircase that led to Pan's bedroom at the top of the tower.

Not sure whether to be insulted or depressed by the rejection, Pan rose to her feet and sniffed her hand. She shrugged. "I don't smell anything . . ." she muttered, and trailed after her cat.

Entering Pan's inner sanctum was like stepping into the Schriksdorp franchise of Renfield's House of Horrors and Mystical Antiquities—except this branch was a tad more funereal in its color scheme. The purple wall paint and the black bedding on the mahogany four-poster bed had a lot to do with that, much to Karen's constant angst. This used to be her room when she was growing up.

On the far side of the room, directly across from the door, were tall windows set into three of the tower's hexagonal walls. Beneath the windows were bookcases filled with horror novels and reference tomes, graphic novels and monster toys. Mary Shelley and Bram Stoker, Edgar Allan Poe and H. P. Lovecraft shared space with Stephen King and Sutter Cane, Nancy A. Collins and Pan's current favorite, Marietta Dixon; *Marvel Zombies* and *Dogwitch* sat beside *Where the Wild Things Are* and *30 Days of Night*; the *Necronomicon* and *The Long Lost Friend* rubbed bindings with *The Zombie Survival Guide* and *The Colossal Book of Faerie*. Across the top shelves there were miniature graveyard scenes in snow globes that contained, not snow, but tiny bats that flitted about when shaken, a few Living Dead Dolls, and a Barbie and Ken that Sheena had gothed-up—their blond hair painted jet-black, and their bright summery clothes replaced with black leather-and-lace outfits—as a going-away present for her best friend. And posed in the center, locked in eternal combat, action figures of the Frankenstein monster and the chain-saw-wielding Ash from the *Evil Dead* movies fought Pumpkinhead and Pinhead to the death while the Bride of the Monster, Hellboy, and Vampirella looked on.

Between the door and the windows, on the right side of the room, were the bed and a small desk, the latter's surface buried beneath a scattering of notebooks, sketchpads, and some Goth culture fashion magazines; shoved against the mess was a laptop computer. The bed, on the other hand, had only one thing draped across it: a black cat that gazed impassively at Pan before yawning and stretching out for a good nap. Past the bed and dozing cat was an easel Pan used for her infrequent painting projects; from its wood-framed resting place, a blank canvas stared back at her, waiting for her next moment of inspiration.

On the bedroom's left side was an antique dresser on which sat a jewelry box, a discounted flat-screen television, a DVD player on its last legs, and a small stack of movies. Next to that was a door that opened onto a balcony, which, in turn, connected to a short exterior staircase leading to the laundry room on the second floor.

The walls were decorated with movie posters, rock-star pinups—these days, mainly shots of Leander Faust that she'd downloaded from the Sarkophagia Web site and printed on glossy paper—and a handful of paintings of mythological creatures done by Pan over the years. She was especially proud of the nonmonster portrait that hung above the bed: a group shot of her with her parents, reproduced from a photograph taken during happier times.

The final decorative touch was a lavender glass vase that held a dozen mummified roses, set on a table by the balcony door. A year earlier the flowers had been very much alive and a gorgeous bright red in color; Pan never told anyone, but they were one of the few gifts she'd kept from her time with Ammi. Sheena, she knew, would scream if she ever found out. After they'd died, Pan had kept them—against Karen's frequent requests for her to toss them out—because . . . well, because dead roses went so well with the rest of the décor. At least that's what she kept telling herself every time she tried to put Ammi out of her mind.

Like now, for instance. Pan shook her head to clear it. This wasn't the time to be thinking about her ex-boyfriend—not with all the yelling Mom was doing as she tried to counter whatever Mrs. Van Schrik was throwing at her.

Just to the left of the inside door was Pan's closet, where she went to gather a replacement outfit. On the way she turned on the computer, where her music library was all ready to go. She clicked on the iTunes DJ playlist and smiled as HorrorPops' "MissFit" wailed from the exterior speakers. Pan couldn't help but join lead singer Patricia Day in what now sounded like an anthem to her life in Schricksdork—especially, she noted, when it came to the lyrics about raising her fists.

After shucking off her damp clothes Pan wrapped herself in her favorite floor-length bathrobe—black terry cloth, the back decorated with a huge reproduction of the cartoon head of Jack Skellington from *The Nightmare Before Christmas*—and then grabbed another pair of black jeans and black low-top sneakers. From the dresser she grabbed a Sarkophagia T-shirt emblazoned with a photographic image of Leander Faust in all his bare-chested, smoldering-hotness glory. She ran an index finger along his sculpted two-dimensional abs and shivered pleasurably.

"Oh baby," she cooed, "the things I'd do to you . . ." Then she laughed in embarrassment and tossed the shirt and jeans on the bed. Walking to the door, she paused only long enough to crank up the volume on the psychobilly tune before striding into the hallway.

"*My fist!*" she sang happily as she headed for the second-floor bathroom. "*In the middle of your face! My fist! In the middle of your . . .* "

After a shower and a fresh makeup application, Pan emerged from the bathroom and reentered her room to find Mom sitting on the end of the bed, gently stroking Vlad's head as he dozed in her lap. Apparently he didn't have any trouble with the smell of *her* hands. On the nightstand beside the bed were a glass of water and a little tan-colored pill.

Inwardly, Pan sighed. Eight months of skipping her meds—without Mom knowing—and all it took was one really bad morning to force the antipsychotics back into her life. Stupid monsters.

Karen looked totally drained, as though she'd just fought a war and lost. Even the magical glow she gave off—the one Pan's monstervision was still detecting—had dimmed to a weak shimmer.

Deciding that she'd had enough confrontations for one day, and to give Mom a break, Pan dutifully walked over to the table, took her pill, and chased it down with the water. "Mmmm . . . crazy pills," she said with a grin, and hopped into bed.

Karen smiled weakly. Vlad gave Pan a dirty look for disturbing his sleep, then went back to counting Z's.

"So you and Mrs. Van Schrik are, like, best friends now, huh?"

Karen laughed sharply. "Oh, yeah. She even invited me to join her crocheting group next week—right after she takes her daughter to a cosmetic surgeon to see about smoothing out that pentagram-ring tattoo you gave her." The strain in her voice was all too evident, sarcasm notwithstanding. She shook her head forlornly.

"First that Seo girl, now this Nikki . . . Where did you ever learn to hit like that?" Then her eyes narrowed. "Did your father teach you?"

"Nope." Pan smiled. "Grandma Ellie did."

Karen's eyes widened. "My *mother* taught you how to beat up people?"

Pan shrugged. "You know how she is about girls growing up in big cities. She just wanted to make sure I knew how to protect myself." She raised an inquisitive eyebrow. "What, she never taught you?"

"No!" Karen yelped. Then she blushed and looked away. "Well, she did . . . tried to, anyway." The blush deepened. "I was never really interested in that female wrestling stuff she used to do. It was kind of embarrassing. To me, at least."

"Hey, women's champion six years in a row is a pretty good record."

Karen shrugged, as though trying to cast off an unpleasant memory. "Anyway, Mrs. Van Schrik and I did talk, and . . . well, it could've gone better."

"I kinda figured that from all the yelling you were doing." Pan scooched over beside Mom and draped a consoling arm around her shoulders. "Wanna talk about it over a bowl of mint chocolate chip? Or would the whole pint work better for you?"

Karen grunted. "Trust me, sweetie, no amount of ice cream is going to make this better."

"But that wouldn't stop you from eating it anyway."

Mom sighed and rested her head against her daughter's shoulder. "Well, of course not. But gorging myself isn't going to make our problem disappear. And besides, I'd only feel guilty about eating all that crap after I finished it and spend all day tomorrow trying to find ways to work it off . . . although I understand stress is great for that." Another sigh. "I've certainly got enough of that already . . ."

"But you'd still eat it," Pan said with a grin.

Karen raised her head and turned to flash a warning glare. "Get thee behind me, Satan."

Pan's grin broadened. "Moo-ha-ha," she chuckled in her deepest, most ominous voice. When the only response she got was a tiny, weak smile, she gave Mom a gentle squeeze. "So, how bad is it?"

"Bad. Mrs. Van Schrik would love nothing better than to see you in a jail cell before the day is out, but I think she'd settle for driving me into bankruptcy with a lawsuit."

Pan started. "Seriously?"

"So serious I called Jean Loscalzo the minute I got off the phone with Mrs. Van Schrik." That was Karen's best friend and lawyer, the one who'd represented her in the divorce proceedings. She was very good at her job, but for obvious reasons Pan wasn't too fond of her.

"What did she say?" Pan asked.

"To keep you as far away from Nikki as possible. With any luck, this whole thing might blow over once Mrs. Van Schrik calms down."

"You think that'll happen?"

Karen shrugged. "It's the best I can hope for. I don't know what we'll do for money if she drags us into court." She fell silent and went back to stroking Vlad's head. He purred in approval.

"Okay. So what's the plan in the meantime?"

"Jean thinks I should get you out of town for a little while. 'Out of sight, out of mind' and all that." She paused. "Given what we're facing, it . . . made a lot of sense to me."

It took a couple of seconds for the words to sink in, but when they did the shock she felt was so hard-hitting that Pan almost fell off the bed. "What? You're putting me into exile?" She wanted to add *again*, but knew better than to drag up that old argument.

"Exile?" Karen held up a hand to stop the counterargument that was coming. "Hey, you're the one always telling me how much you hate living here—"

"Not in this house! Not with *you*!" Pan said, well aware of the note of panic creeping into her voice. "Just this town!"

Karen smiled gently. "Well, you can't have one without the other, kiddo. But right now, just to keep the peace"—she reached up to tousle Pan's hair—"hell, just to keep you safe, I need you to do this."

Pan sneered. "You want me to run away."

"No, I'm trying to protect you. I could never forgive myself if something happened because I let you stay and Nikki and her friends decided to get back at you."

"I can take care of myself," Pan said, a touch sullenly.

"I know you can. But I'm trying to resolve this peacefully, and I think the only way to do that is if we remove the temptation for Nikki to cause any trouble."

Pan raised an eyebrow. " 'We'? That mean I get a vote in this?"

Karen grinned. "Absolutely not. I'm just trying to give you the false impression that we work as a unified front, when you're actually living under a dictatorship."

"Thanks," Pan muttered sarcastically.

Karen gave her a reassuring squeeze. "It'll just be for a little while—long enough, say, for Nikki's jaw to heal and her mother to cool off."

"Riiiight. The only thing my going away will do is give Nikki more time to plot her revenge for the day I get back."

"Hopefully it won't turn out that way. I'm sure Dian Van Schrik and I can come to an understanding when I meet with her Monday morning."

Pan's eyes widened. "She invited you to the mansion?"

"Yes. Which means you need to be out of town before then."

"What's the rush? You think something might happen between now and Monday?"

"I just don't want to take any chances," Karen admitted. "From what you've told me about Nikki and her clique I wouldn't put it past them."

"Well, you know what the solution is, right?" Pan asked with a gleam in her eyes. "You take me with you on Monday. And while you and Dian are working things out, Nikki and I can hang in her room, talking about boys and school and all kinds of girly stuff . . . while I'm tossing her sorry ass around the place."

Karen frowned. "And you wonder why I want you out of here . . ."

Pan grinned. "Grandma taught me this wicked submission move—it's kinda like a choke hold, right? But with kidney punches mixed in." With her fists, she acted out throwing a series of crushing body blows.

Mom rolled her eyes in exasperation. "Would you stop? Please?"

Pan swept back the hair that had fallen in front of her eyes and smiled. "So who're you dumping me with?"

"I'm trying to figure that out." Another frown creased Karen's features. "And I'm not 'dumping' you with anybody—it's just a temporary relocation. But based on what you've just been telling me, Mom and Dad are absolutely out of the picture. I don't need her making things worse, like teaching you how to beat people with metal fold-up chairs—"

"Too late!" Pan said with a laugh.

Karen hung her head and groaned.

Chuckling softly, Pan gave her a hug. "I know," she sighed. "I'm just incorrigible."

"No argument there." Karen looked up. "Incorrigible? Where'd you pick up *that* word? Not that it doesn't apply to you, of course."

"Well, how else am I gonna be a writer if I don't learn some big words to throw around?"

Karen glanced at the easel in the corner. "I thought you wanted to be an artist."

"That, too." Pan smiled. "Writer, artist, fighter, lover—I'm all about the multitasking."

"Yeah, well, more creativity, less brutality, if you don't mind," Karen replied. "It'd keep my hair from turning gray before its time."

"Mmm . . . I'll see what I can do," Pan said cheerily.

"*Sigh,*" Karen remarked melodramatically. "And on that note . . ." She gently moved Vlad off her lap and onto the bed, then rose. The cat yawned, stretched, then rolled over and went back to dozing.

"You didn't say where I was going," Pan reminded her. "Or are you just gonna put me in a basket like baby Moses, and toss me into the Hudson River and hope for the best?"

"Oh. Well, Peter and Ginnifer"—that was Mom's older brother and his wife—"are taking the kids camping in Yellowstone on Monday, so they can't take you—"

"*Thank God,*" Pan said. She didn't care for Peter. A Pennsylvania state trooper and a staunch conservative—a bad combination, as far as Pan was concerned—he was always badgering his free-spirited niece to "stop dressing like a freak and embarrassing your mother" (among other comments) whenever they crossed paths. A time or three she'd come close to telling him what he could do with his familial advice, but Mom could always sense a pending explosion and quickly intervened before Mount Pandora blew her top.

"—and Cassie and Allie"—Mom's younger sister and her partner—"are in the middle of having their apartment completely remodeled, so they've been living in a budget hotel for the past three weeks. She said they might be there until July."

"Wow. You must've been dialing like crazy, the whole time I was in the bathroom"—Pan sighed dramatically, the back of her right hand pressed to her forehead in a damsel-in-distress pose—"and all for naught." She laughed as she caught sight of Mom's annoyed expression. "So if your immediate family is out of the running . . ." Her voice trailed off as the list of options ended with only one possible outcome, and she grinned. "Dad?"

"Yes," Mom replied, then held up a hand before her daughter could start celebrating. "Maybe. Nothing's been arranged. I tried his cell, but either he doesn't have it on, or he's forgotten to recharge the battery. Again."

"Yeah, he does that a lot."

"I'll try him again later." Karen wagged a warning finger. "But it's not a permanent arrangement, you understand. Just until things calm down. Trust me— you'll be back here terrorizing the townsfolk before you know it."

"And my return shall be a terrible thing to behold," Pan intoned ominously in a gravelly voice. "Moo-ha-ha."

"Yes, that's *exactly* what this situation calls for—escalating hostilities," Karen said drolly. "Look, come downstairs. I'll make some grilled cheese sandwiches for lunch, and later we can drown our sorrows in ice cream."

"Ooohh, it's a date. Be there in a few minutes." She watched Mom walk out; seconds later, the hall echoed with the sound of stairs creaking as Karen made her way toward the first-floor kitchen.

Pan lay back on the bed and closed her eyes, feeling the medication take effect. It began as a comfortable fuzziness along the edges of her consciousness, then gently billowed out like the softest blanket to wrap her troubled thoughts in soothing warmth. A relaxed sigh eased from her lips, and she slid around to pull Vlad into her arms—which he allowed. She buried her nose in the warm black fur of his neck and laid that way for a little while as Vlad purred contentedly. It was, Pan realized, the first peaceful moment she'd had that day—and one she was reluctant to give up, even if it was medicinally induced. Maybe if she didn't move a muscle, she thought, didn't make a sound, everyone would eventually forget all about her and she could put this god-awful morning behind her . . .

"No, that's not gonna work . . ." she said with a groan. After complaining to Mom about being forced to run from Schriksdorp, she couldn't very well just turn around and try hiding from her problems—certainly not by hunkering down behind a pussycat. Great as pets, sure, but they made for lousy camouflage.

She lifted her head, rested it on her arm, and stared off into space. Food-court fisticuffs, cranky old security guards who shot electricity out of their hands, having a complete mental breakdown in public, sitting in the rain because you were too afraid to go back inside with all those things staring at you, and then being told by your own mother that she was running you out of town—even by Pan's standards that was, like, two weeks' worth of drama packed into one Friday morning . . . and it wasn't even lunchtime yet!

"Well," she muttered, "maybe things'll improve when I get back to the City. Maybe. Hopefully . . ."

7

Morrison Ebenezer Millar took pride in his work. There weren't many people left in the world today who still carried on the sort of tradition he'd inherited from his father, and his father before him—one, unfortunately, that polite society generally frowned upon.

So what if grave-robbing and crypt burglary done for profit were against the moral and ethical codes of civilization, not to mention being highly illegal? A Euro was a Euro, no matter how you earned it, Morrison firmly believed; besides, it wasn't as though any of the dearly departed were really going to have much use for expensive jewelry and finely tailored clothing in the afterlife. Didn't they all get issued wings and big, flowing robes once they were done talking to St. Peter? That's what Morrison used to hear every Sunday as a boy when his mother dragged him to church—or so he dimly remembered from the few times he managed to stay awake during the vicar's droning sermons. If that were true, he figured, then why let all that Prada and Versace, Jimmy Choo and Lucien Piccard go to waste rotting in a coffin?

It'd be a sin, wouldn't it?

And it wasn't as though the people with whom he conducted business really wanted to know where he obtained his merchandise. Straight supply and demand, no questions asked, major credit cards and Paypal accepted, and the less they knew about the origins of their purchased items, the better for all concerned.

Take David Zwieback, his latest client, for instance: an American, with the same last name as that rock-hard cookie you give to teething babies. Sounded like a bleeding great fanboy on the phone, going on about a listing he'd found on Morrison's Web site, The Graveyard Examiner; blathering about Christopher Lee and Peter Cushing and the "incredible" Hammer horror movies they starred in back in the sixties and seventies. It was all tosh, Morrison thought, boring movies starring boring actors who belonged to his dad's generation, running around a bunch of cheap studio sets with wobbly stone walls. He'd seen one of them on ITV years ago: *Taste the Blood of the Brides of Frankenstein Who Must be Destroyed*, or some such nonsense. It put him right to sleep within the first ten minutes, even with the numerous young women in it who displayed their bountiful gifts for all to see in corsets and frilly lace nighties and whatnot. Utter rubbish. Give him a *28 Months Later* or a *Hostel* or even a *Hellraiser* any day. Real blood-and-guts splatterpunk stuff was a lot more to his liking.

Still, he'd put up with the Yank's gibbering—an act which required far more patience than he'd ever displayed in most of his forty-six years on this planet—because, at the start of the conversation, Zwieback had explained he was the curator of a small museum in New York City, looking to add to his collection of the "unusual," and the item he'd found at The Graveyard Examiner was just what he was looking for. Euros had started dancing in front of Morrison's eyes. Museum types, his dad used to say, always had money to throw away on the most frivolous things when the collecting bug bit them. So if all it took to make sure he kept scratching at that bite was to listen to the Yank's incessant chattering, then Morrison was willing to make the sacrifice. For a little while.

He'd had inquiries about Item #179 before, but most interested parties begged off when the discussion turned to monetary matters. In general, oversized shipments from the UK didn't come cheap, and there were other things to consider: freight and handling costs; insurance fees; rush charges; and, in some cases, a little cash incentive given under the table to certain customs officials in order to avoid having any bothersome questions asked about the contents of the order. But, he always pointed out, for a rare antiquity like this, a one-of-a-kind find for an avid collector, the expenses were worth it . . . if the buyer was truly serious about acquiring such a prize.

Zwieback, however, was the first potential customer to actually stay on the line after the sales talk was over, which made him either a top-notch procurer or a prime mark asking to be taken. Whichever he was made no difference to Morrison—the art of the deal was the be-all and end-all of his profession. Client motivations were unimportant.

Still, he'd had to drastically come down in price when Zwieback explained that the museum he ran was no bigger than a storefront. Dreams of an early retirement dissolved like candy floss in a rainstorm; Morrison had half a mind to hang up the phone. But, truth be told, Item #179 wasn't doing him any good gathering dust and taking up warehouse space; he couldn't even remember how or when he'd aquired it. So, a little haggling and the negotiations were swiftly concluded. Payment by credit card went through without a hitch, and a week ago the box had been loaded on a cargo ship bound for the States. And that, as they say, was that for Morrison . . .

Until the three well-dressed thugs showed up in his office this evening.

Two of them—one black, one white—looked like steroid kings, with muscles the size of their heads. The white one had a squarish head, with short black hair, a thick handlebar mustache, and dark stubble that outlined a broad, anvil-like jaw. His sidekick was bald, with a small diamond stud in each ear—expensive baubles, from the look of them—and sported a neatly trimmed goatee. He stared at Morrison over the frames of a pair of designer sunglasses.

It was the one standing between the thugs, however, who looked like real trouble. Hands in his trouser pockets, he was tall and thin, a veritable scarecrow in a fitted Hugo Boss suit—but Morrison could tell he was the one in charge. He practically radiated power.

Who they were wasn't as important a question to Morrison as how long they'd been standing there, watching him—he hadn't heard the door open and close when they came in, though he'd been sitting in the room not six paces from it. Well, he figured, that's what he got for concentrating more on the football scores in the *London Times* than what was going on in his own shop. But when he was done with these three, he promised to have a little talk with Eddie and the other lads in his employ about letting strangers come up to his office unannounced.

So: gangland types who moved with the stealth of ninjas, obviously wanting information of a sort or they wouldn't be here. No worries, Morrison told himself. The best course of action was to act cool, keep the conversation light—and avoid provoking them.

"Something I can do for you gents?" he asked, flashing his winningest smile. The harsh fluorescent lights above did nothing to improve the dingy, nicotine-stained quality of his teeth.

"The box—where is it?" Anvil Jaw snapped. His voice was like a stalling engine, with a Russian accent so cartoonishly thick it was almost laughable.

"Straight to business, eh?" Morrison said coolly. "I can understand that." He leaned back in his chair and eyed his guest suspiciously. "Problem is, Boris, I don't ever remember chattin' you up on the phone—and believe you me, yours is not the sort of voice that'd be hard to forget."

The bruiser snarled; his dental hygiene was even worse than Morrison's. He took a step forward before the scarecrow gently placed a restraining hand on his chest.

"Please excuse Alexi," he said lightly. "He has problems with the language." Morrison nodded, but said nothing. "What he meant to say, Mr. Millar, is that we're hoping you can help us locate a certain object. We understand it's currently in your possession."

Morrison's right eyebrow crept up in a quizzical fashion. "Is that right? And what might this 'certain object' be, if you don't mind my asking, Mister . . . ?"

"Elden. Just . . . Elden." The man turned to his other companion. "Noureddine?"

The black weight lifter reached into the inner breast pocket of his jacket to retrieve a BlackBerry. Using a thin metal stylus, he touched the screen and searched through a number of files before apparently finding the one he wanted.

"It's listed as item one-seven-nine on your Web site," he said, each syllable pronounced slowly and deliberately, as though he liked hearing the sound of his own voice.

Morrison grinned. "Sorry, mate, you're outta luck on that one. Shipped it off just the other week. Guess my Webmaster forgot to take it off."

Elden frowned. "How unfortunate. Might we inquire as to the identity of the buyer?"

Morrison chuckled and shook his head. "Now, what sort of businessman would I be if I just handed out the names of my clients to any interested party?" He shrugged. "Sorry, gents. I work under the strictest level of confidentiality." A sly grin stretched the corners of his mouth, and he winked. "Unless, of course, you'd be willing to discuss the matter on more of a *monetary* level?"

"No," Elden said simply.

"Ah. Then I can't help you. But maybe I can interest you gentlemen in something similar? I get quite a few items like that one just about every week." He reached for the phone. "I'll just call my supply manager downstairs and—"

Alexi slammed a meaty fist onto the phone. The hard plastic receiver cracked into two large pieces. "The box!" the goon bellowed. "Now!"

That was all Morrison was willing to take from this crew. Showing up unannounced and uninvited was one thing; smashing his fixtures was quite another. He shot to his feet and angrily jabbed a finger into Alexi's chest. "Who the hell do you think you're talkin' to, mate?" He leaned to one side to look around the furnace-sized torso blocking his view of the room, and pointed at Elden. "I'm givin' all'a you to the count of three to get the hell outta my office before you lot find yourselves in a world of hurt—you understand me?"

He hadn't meant it to sound like anything other than the threat it was intended to be, but for some reason his visitors found his tone amusing. Elden chuckled; his friends grinned and exchanged a knowing glance.

"Threats, Mr. Millar?" he asked. He shook his head, as though disappointed in Morrison. "My understanding was that you were an intelligent businessman, not some back-alley thug."

"Yeah, well, that all depends on the circumstances, don't it?" Morrison shot back. "You lot show up without an appointment and start snappin' out orders, I got no reason to treat you with respect, or be all businesslike."

The man nodded. "Quite true, quite true. Were our positions reversed, I'd no doubt take a similar stance." The wolfish, condescending smile he flashed stretched the corners of his mouth a bit too wide for Morrison's liking. "But then, I'm not in your position. And let me assure you, Mr. Millar, yours is a very *bad* position in which to be."

Morrison felt a nervous lump form in his throat, but fought the urge to swallow it. The gulping sound he knew would follow would only make his visitors laugh even louder. His gaze briefly drifted toward the door.

"Expecting your men to come running up the stairs like the cavalry charging the redskins in those Yank westerns?" Elden chuckled. "I think you'll be rather disappointed with this ending of *this* film, Mr. Millar. Bit nihilistic in tone. Very un-Hollywood-like."

Morrison wasn't entirely certain what he was talking about, but the way in which he'd said it sent a sudden chill down the spine. And where were his men, anyway? With all the yelling going on in the last few minutes, old Bob should have tromped up to see what was going on. Haltingly, keeping one eye trained on his visitors, Morrison moved across to the big observation window on the far side of the room: a one-way glass through which he kept tabs on activities down on the warehouse floor. Normally when he checked, he could see his men—Eddie, Joel, Bob, and a dozen others—either handling incoming and outgoing merchandise, or at the very least trying to appear busy.

When he gazed down now, the first thing he saw was the blood.

"Jesus wept . . ." Morrison croaked.

It covered everything: walls, floor, and ceiling. Spattered about like one of those Jackson Pollock paintings he'd moved through black market channels two years ago. As far as Morrison could recall, though, Pollock had never used major organs and unspooled intestines for his brushes.

Eddie, Joel, and Bob were down there, but he only knew that because their heads had been mounted on upended tiki torches from a Polynesian bar that had closed six months ago. Their wide, dead eyes stared up at him in surprise. As for the other men, he found it impossible to distinguish what parts belonged to which dismembered bodies, scattered about as they were. It was as though some mad butcher had swept into the warehouse, meat cleavers whizzing around like buzz saws, and turned it into a slaughterhouse—and his men into the special cuts of the day.

Morrison felt the contents of his stomach turn over once, then come roaring up his gullet. He clenched his teeth, damming the flood before it could burst past his lips, and swallowed hard. He wasn't about to lose his dinner in front of this crowd, wasn't about to show them any sign of weakness. His esophagus burned with acidic backwash, and he fumbled in his pockets for a mint. Couldn't find one, unfortunately.

He turned back to face his visitors. They didn't move, didn't speak, just stood there silently. Had they been waiting for his reaction? he wondered. Expecting him to scream, like some terrified girl in a slasher flick? They'd be waiting a long time, then.

"Who are you?" he asked, his voice barely above a whisper, although he had a fairly good idea of their identities. Professional killers didn't go around handing out business cards, but their work spoke for itself. He'd known a few in his time, but he'd never heard of anyone who could do what these three had accomplished: wipe out a roomful of armed men without making a sound.

Maybe they *were* ninjas . . .

"The name of the buyer, Mr. Millar," Elden said.

What happened next was purely instinctual on Morrison's part. He could have gone to the laptop on his desk and opened the file containing the list of recent buyers; it wouldn't have taken all that long to retrieve the information. But professional killers preferred having no witnesses to their gruesome work, and Morrison knew he had seen too much the moment he looked up from his newspaper.

So instead of going to his computer, he pulled out the .40-caliber Glock 23C he carried in a shoulder holster under his jacket—and started firing.

To Morrison, it felt as though he were acting out a scene in that Quentin Tarantino movie, *Pulp Fiction*: that moment when the college kid comes busting out of the bathroom, firing blindly at John Travolta and Sam Jackson . . . and having every shot miss. But this was no movie, and Morrison wasn't scared enough to miss his targets.

Elden took three in the chest. Alexi got one right between his bloodshot eyes. Noureddine received a cut-rate tracheotomy. All three men collapsed to the floor in a heap, but Morrison didn't stop firing until he'd emptied the ammunition clip of all fifteen rounds, and the gun's slide clattered back. Which was when he realized he'd been screaming the whole time.

Morrison lowered his gun hand and stood there, trembling. His eyes watered and his throat tightened from the acrid cloud of gunpowder that filled the room, and his eardrums rang like the chimes at Westminster Cathedral, so much that he couldn't hear his footfalls as he stepped across the office to inspect his late visitors. He frowned in confusion as he took a closer look. There didn't seem to be all that much blood splashed about, considering the damage his shots had inflicted. Heart, head, and throat? He should be slipping around like there was ice on the floor.

No worries, he thought. *Dead is dead no matter how you slice it, right? And if they ain't bleedin' out, that's less cleanup work to deal with.* He glanced back at the one-way glass. *Don't know what I'm gonna do about the downstairs, though . . .*

"Guess you lot weren't ninjas after all," he said with a sneer, although he couldn't quite hear himself. "I mean, ninjas are supposed to dodge bullets, not *eat* them, right?" He laughed nervously, then bent low over the leader. "Well, next time you girls wanna dance a couple rounds with Morrison Millar, you better send over your whole flippin' clan if you wanna do the job right."

And then Elden opened his eyes.

"Oh, I doubt that would be necessary, Mr. Millar," he said. "Three is *more* than enough for the task at hand. . . ."

8

Morrison shrieked and jumped back. Automatically, he raised the Glock and pointed it at Elden's head, only to remember he'd already fired every round. Panicked, he turned toward the desk. There was another clip in the middle drawer . . .

He ran to the desk as Elden stood up, his similarly bullet-riddled companions scrambling to their feet to join him. The scarecrow turned to Noureddine, who was gingerly touching the gaping hole in his throat where the bullet had entered.

"Everything all right?" he asked.

"Give me a second." Blood flowed from the wound at a steady pace, but Noureddine looked more annoyed by the stains it left on his clothes than by the 200-grain hole-puncher lodged in the back of his neck.

As Morrison watched in shock and disgust, Noureddine plunged his index finger deep into the bullet hole and poked around for a bit, turning his head this way and that, then massaging the sides of his throat with his thumb and middle finger. It reminded Morrison of the time he'd gotten a chicken bone stuck in his throat and had the devil's own time of getting the thing loose before he choked to death.

The results were fairly similar, as Noureddine coughed loudly and the compacted lump of metal that had been a bullet tumbled from his mouth in a torrent of red saliva. Instantly, the hole in his throat began closing, as though the wound was healing itself. Noureddine rubbed his neck, and nodded in apparent satisfaction.

"Much better," he sighed, and flashed a wide—an impossibly wide—smile at Morrison.

It was the sight of those teeth that finally began to pull it all together for Morrison, because they allowed him to see at last the monster that lurked beneath the surface. The teeth were sharp and pointed and set in two rows—the kind he'd seen in the mouths of great whites on one of the Discovery Channel's "Shark Week" specials—with the canine teeth a touch longer than the rest. The first thing that popped into his head was that the man must be wearing novelty teeth . . . because stopping long enough to consider the alternative was almost guaranteed to make Morrison lose his mind.

He looked over to Alexi, who was also digging into his own bullet hole. With a grotesque sucking noise, the Russian's index finger and thumb emerged from the bloody tunnel in his forehead, a flattened slug held tightly between their tips. The metal shone bright red in the office's fluorescent lighting. The shark smile he presented to Morrison matched Noureddine's—and now Elden's.

"Gentlemen, I do believe Mr. Millar at last realizes the severity of his situation." Elden chuckled. "What do you think his next course of action will be?"

Alexi tossed aside the bullet. "Gun is empty, so he goes for fresh magazine in desk. Starts shooting again. Results will be same as before."

Elden turned back to Morrison. "And you probably thought I just kept Alexi around for his good looks," he said sarcastically.

The butt of the Glock slipped in Morrison's sweat-drenched hand, and thumped heavily onto the desk. He froze—his other hand mere inches from the middle drawer and the spare clip of ammunition—and stared at his visitors. The three monsters snarled at him, grinding their teeth with a sound like bone saws working an autopsy.

Elden frowned. "Before you attempt to deafen us all with another useless barrage of gunfire, Mr. Millar—at which point we'll have no other choice than to tear your head off for being so unconscionably rude to your guests—I will ask you one last time: to whom did you ship item one-seven-nine?"

Morrison stared at him, his mind suddenly blank. He might not have been frightened before, but he sure as hell was now. Adrenaline and anger had long since drained away; all he had left were trembling legs and a widening pair of sweat stains around his armpits. He was going to die; he was certain of that now.

"You know," Noureddine commented, "I could just get the information from his laptop. I'm sure all his transactions are listed on it."

Elden shook his head without looking at his companion. His eyes were squarely focused on Morrison. "Mr. Millar will provide us with the information—won't you, Mr. Millar?"

"I'm sure he would," Noureddine agreed, "if this tosser was still capable of pulling together a cohesive thought. Just look at him—he's about ready to stain his trousers. Really, Elden, I don't think you're going to get much from him at this point." He gestured toward the desk. "The computer is right there. It would only take me a second or two—"

Elden cut him off with a dismissive wave of his hand, but never turned from Morrison. "It's your decision, Mr. Millar. All you have to do is provide us with the name of the buyer, and we'll be on our way." He nodded toward the window. "Unless, of course, you're more interested in sharing the fate of your former employees . . ."

The threat was just what Morrison needed to tear apart the layers of gauze that had wrapped around his mind. His upper lip curled in a snarl as he glared back at Elden. Going for the ammo clip was out of the question. In the time it would take him to open the desk drawer, drop the empty magazine, replace it with the new one, and ratchet the slide back into position, the creatures would have torn him in half and stuck his head on one of those tiki-torch pikes. So instead of doing what they expected him to do, he decided to try something they wouldn't be expecting. Hopefully.

"Screw this!" he barked, and threw the Glock at the scarecrow—who ducked out of the way, much to everyone's surprise.

Morrison didn't wait around to see what happened next. He tore across the office and was out the door before the . . . things could stop him.

"I don't believe it," he heard Noureddine say, as the ghoul's voice echoed down the corridor. "You take three rounds bang in the chest without batting an eye—but you duck when he throws the gun at you?"

"Yes, well . . . force of habit," Elden replied sullenly.

Anything else they might have said went unheard as Morrison pounded around a corner and raced down the hallway, toward a door marked LADIES. It wasn't a privy, however, but an emergency exit, the sign placed there to keep any police officers—or unwanted visitors, like the three not-so-dead men back in the office— from following him in case a quick departure was required.

A set of steps led down to a door at the rear of the warehouse where he parked his car. He came to a sudden halt on the third step. *No, not that way. They'll be expectin' you to go for your ride; probably got another one'a their crew waitin' for you down there.* The sound of footsteps at the far end of the hall behind him drew his attention back to the "ladies" exit. It wouldn't take his pursuers long to figure out which direction he'd taken, and this time he wouldn't have the comforting feel of a gun in his hand to offset the rising terror he was experiencing. Even if it didn't do a bit of good against those nattily dressed creatures.

The footsteps became louder. The monsters were definitely headed in his direction.

"Upstairs," Morrison muttered, then ran back to the landing and up the next flight of stairs, taking them two at a time until he reached the third floor. He tried to be as quiet as possible, but stairwells made for excellent echo chambers; each footfall against the blue-painted concrete steps sounded like a shotgun blast to his ears.

He reached the next level and eased open the door, just as the one downstairs banged open and slammed against the concrete wall. He froze, not even daring to breathe, as Elden and his sidekicks shuffled around on the landing one flight below.

"*Told* you it wasn't the loo," he heard Noureddine say.

"Yes, well, good for you," Elden replied. "Care to guess where Mr. Millar has rabbitted off to, as long as you're impressing us with your vast intellect?"

"His car, most likely," Noureddine said. He sounded pleased with himself. "Won't get very far, though, with that engine in its current condition—right, Alexi?"

"*Da*," the third ghoul agreed. "Many expensive repairs to make."

"Well, let's not keep Mr. Millar waiting, then," Elden said.

The trio began walking down the stairs at a leisurely pace, as though in no hurry. Apparently confident they'd find their quarry right where they expected. Wouldn't they be in for a disappointment? Morrison thought. He couldn't help but smile at his cleverness.

"Don't know why I can't just look up the bloody listing on his computer . . ."

Noureddine commented in a sullen tone.

The exit door opened, followed by the sound of footsteps on the gravel that covered the parking area. Then the door slammed shut, and Morrison was finally able to breathe again. He stepped into the third-floor hallway, and eased the door closed behind him. Then he jogged along the corridor, toward the front of the warehouse. With luck, he'd be out the door and hotwiring Bob's old Datsun before those three came back to canvass the building.

But when he reached the dirt-encrusted windows over the front entrance, he looked down to find Alexi stalking around. The Russian paused beside each car in the lot to look inside, obviously expecting to find his target behind the wheel of one of them. Morrison cursed. How could that wrecking ball of a man have gotten around to this side so fast?

He was trapped, and it wouldn't take long for them to track him down. What he needed was a weapon, or at least some kind of plan—and since he hadn't been able to solve this particular problem with a gun, he'd pretty much exhausted his readymade supply of ideas. It was a shame, he thought, that his men had been turned into chopped meat—one of them might have made a suggestion he could use. *Now* who could he turn to?

And then it hit him.

"Annie . . ." he whispered. He grinned, nodding in complete agreement with himself. If anyone might have a solution to the problem of the three land-sharks chasing him it would be Sebastienne Mazarin. Monsters were her specialty.

He reached inside his jacket, came out with a BlackBerry. He flipped it open, then paused, his thumb hovering above the touchpad. Damn it, what was her number? They'd had so little contact over the years he'd never bothered to log it in the smartphone's contact list.

She was living in New York, last he'd heard, so at least that was a start. He lightly thumped the side of his head with his fist, like he was testing the soundness of a ripe melon. Apparently that did the trick for jogging his memory, and he punched in the number. The call connected, and the line began ringing. And ringing. And ringing.

"Come on, Annie," he urged through clenched teeth. "Come on, stop washin' yer hair or watchin' yer damned soap operas and pick up the bleedin' phone . . ."

And then a hand gently touched his shoulder.

Morrison yelped and spun around, losing his grip on the BlackBerry. It flew from his hand and bounced off a crate near his feet before slamming to the floor. The impact disconnected the battery pack—cutting off the call—and sent it skidding under a wooden palette that rested against the wall under the windows.

The dark-haired woman hadn't been there a moment ago; he was certain of it. He certainly would have heard her walking up the hallway, even if she'd quietly slipped through the fire-stairs door: every step she took on the three-inch-thick platform soles of her Mary Jane–style shoes would have sounded like sledgehammers in the unnerving quiet.

She was a strange one, dressed in the style of the "Gothic Lolitas" who fluttered around the London club scene. The black minidress with white apron was straight out of an adults-only version of *Alice in Wonderland*, its hem ending a few inches above white thigh-high stockings, the tops of which were decorated with a single black bow. A rectangular headdress of white lace and black ribbons sat atop her head, fixed in place by a large black bow under her chin. Over her left shoulder hung a coffin-shaped black leather purse almost large enough to house her and whatever paraphernalia it contained. The pocketbook, however, didn't strike him nearly as odd as the item she held in her right hand: a stuffed toy bear dressed in a hooded PVC outfit, like some kind of S&M executioner—complete with double-edged plastic ax.

The girl appeared to be in her late teens or early twenties, Asian—Japanese, maybe—with jet-black hair that started at bangs that hung low over her forehead and ended in a cascade of flowing locks at the small of her back. Her skin was white as porcelain, her lips full, her eyes sparkling violet. There was a lot of mischief reflected in those wide, unblinking doll's eyes, Morrison thought, but not a single trace of warmth, of humanity, in them.

"Who . . . who the hell are you?" he croaked.

She tilted back her head in an imperious fashion, so she could look down her nose at him. "I am Lady Kiyoshi Sasaki of House Otoyo," she replied, her tone making it very clear that her title carried quite a bit of weight—no doubt among the other Goths back in Tokyo or wherever—and he should be impressed by it. "And you, Morrison Millar, possess information I have traveled far to acquire."

Morrison groaned. A Japanese woman, leading a pack of killers. He wasn't so far off the mark, it seemed, in thinking there were ninjas involved—monster ninjas with maws like sharks, but ninjas nonetheless. And while the three ghouls were stalking around outside, here he was, face-to-face with their leader, who was glammed up like Dracula's favorite china doll.

The sound of glass breaking down in the lot was quite audible in the silent warehouse. Probably Alexi had grown tired of peeping through car windows and gone for a more direct approach to find his elusive target. Morrison nodded toward the windows behind him. "Come to finish up your lads' work, then?" He tried hard to keep the nervous stutter he felt building under control, but there was nothing he could do to prevent his voice from rising an octave.

She giggled; under different circumstances, it might not have sounded quite so sinister. "You mean those bunglers from House Orlock? I would sooner have the heart torn from my breast than ever be seen in their company." Her lips twisted into a fierce sneer. "I make it a point to never socialize with clans of inferior breeding."

Morrison blinked in surprise. "You're not with . . ." he began to say, then stopped. He might be a little slow on the uptake sometimes, but he was finally beginning to understand what was going on. At least he thought he was. "You're here for the box, too, ain't you?"

Kiyoshi nodded pleasantly. "Such a clever piece of meat," she cooed, although it didn't sound like she was being complimentary—more like she was eyeing a slice of beef in a butcher shop window. "And now you will reveal the location of this item one-seven-nine to me," she continued in a harsher tone, "or House Orlock will be the least of your worries."

She smiled, revealing teeth that were blindingly white—and extremely sharp. The violet irises clouded over, became solid black in color: now they truly *were* doll's eyes that perfectly matched the cold, dead lips of the monster that leered at him from behind the flawless porcelain skin.

Morrison backed away, holding up his hands as though it might actually ward her off. There was no getting out of this situation, of that he had no doubt; at most, he might be able to come out the other end of this nightmare alive. With that clearly in mind, any considerations for the sanctity of smuggler/client privilege were immediately tossed aside as he recalled a time-honored phrase commonly used among his peers in the black marketeering profession: When the chips were down, it was every man for himself.

"L-look, we . . . you don't ha-have t'do this," he said, not caring anymore if he stuttered like a machine gun until his teeth fell out. "I'd b-be happy t'get it for ya. W-we can go t'my office an'—"

Kiyoshi shook her head; the ribbons in her headdress gently swayed back and forth across her cheeks. "By now those idiots will have taken possession of your computer. It will not take Noureddine long to crack your files' encryption codes, and then they will have the information I need. They must *not* be the first to claim the Prize. That honor *must* belong to House Otoyo."

"What prize?" Morrison blurted out, unable to stop himself. He knew what the contents of Item 179 were—but how anyone might consider it a prize of any value was beyond him.

Kiyoshi swept forward like a breeze, cloggy shoes hovering a couple of inches above the floor—which explained how she was able to sneak up on him, he realized— and seized his throat in a delicate, lace-gloved hand. Morrison gasped for air as her grip tightened against his Adam's apple.

"You will tell me where the Prize is," she growled in a voice that sounded as though she had gargled with broken glass and rinsed her mouth with a bottle of drain-cleaner. Very monster-ish in tone, he thought dimly, like those creepy voices heard in movies . . . only those digitally created sounds had never caused him to soil the front of his trousers. "Are you listening, Morrison?"

"Y-yesss . . ." he hissed. "But . . ." He craned his neck upward, trying to draw in what air he could past that crushing hand. "But it's already . . . on a boat . . . to America," he wheezed. "Left . . . a week ago . . ."

"*Where* in America?"

Spots danced before his eyes—spots as big and black as the doll's eyes that seemed to fill his vision. He felt light-headed, could hear his heart pounding in his chest, fit to burst. His voice trailed off to an incoherent burbling.

Kiyoshi loosened her grip and shook him violently by the lapels of his jacket.

Morrison gasped hoarsely as oxygen flooded into his lungs, snapping him awake. "*Where?*" she demanded.

"Don't remember . . . exactly," he croaked. "Someplace in New York . . . but the address . . . on my computer . . ."

The Goth princess smiled sweetly, and gently smoothed out the wrinkles in his lapels. "Of course you remember, Morrison," she said, and reached up with her right hand to playfully thump the side of his head; the teddy bear's ax blade swung out to clip the end of his nose. "The knowledge is stored somewhere in your mind. I shall find it."

"H-how?" he whispered.

"Like this." She tilted back her head and opened her lips wide. Morrison got a good look at the sizable canine teeth she displayed—hanging like stalactites from the roof of her cavernous black mouth—just before they ripped into his carotid artery.

And as the raven-haired predator drank her fill, Morrison dimly realized that the Millar family tradition of profiting from the dead was about to come to an abrupt—and rather messy—end. The proof of that was currently taking a bite out of his neck, wasn't it? Poetic justice, he thought. George A. Romero couldn't have scripted it better in one of his zombie movies.

Then the world dissolved in a bloodred haze.

9

Greenpoint, Brooklyn is, in general, a residential area lined with brownstone apartment buildings, shops, churches, schools, pizzerias, corner delicatessens, and the occasional bodega, and dates back to its first Huguenot and Dutch settlers in the mid-1600s. As with the rest of New York City, change is a constant element, and the neighborhood has seen its share, from farmland to urban sprawl, urban renewal to artistic Mecca. However, the most notable transformation of the borough came about in the late 1990s when Brooklyn gained a reputation for being the trendiest part of New York to live in. It started in the area known as DUMBO—Down Under the Manhattan Bridge Overpass—where artists, musicians, and struggling actors moved to where real estate prices were somewhat more manageable than those in Manhattan. Warehouses transformed into lofts and condominiums; abandoned shops became small, Off-Off-Off Broadway theater companies and storefront churches. When DUMBO eventually became too crowded, neighborhoods like Greenpoint were more than happy to receive the spillover.

But not all of Greenpoint could be converted to living space. Along the border separating Brooklyn from the neighboring borough of Queens—the line of demarcation being the notorious Newtown Creek, a stagnant, often foul-smelling tributary that still bears the title of most polluted waterway in all of New York— is a vast collection of oil refineries, warehouses, junkyards, auto body shops, and factories. And rising majestically into the sky above the constant rumble of eighteen-wheelers and sanitation trucks and delivery vans on Greenpoint Avenue are the bulbous, silver-tiled storage tanks of the Newtown Creek Water Pollution Control Plant, a wastewater treatment facility that sits on land once occupied by a far less attractive city dump. Unfortunately, the construction of a high-tech water treatment unit had come much too late for this industrialized area. For decades, large amounts of petroleum, gasoline, and various dangerous chemicals had already leaked into the ground and the creek through cracks and holes in the aging metal pipes that run underneath the neighboring businesses—leaks that, for the most part, were never repaired. This further contaminated an inlet already treated as something of a trash receptacle by residents on both sides who were less concerned in protecting the environment than in disposing of a broken television or rusted-out automobile.

Yes, this particular section of Greenpoint was far from being a potential homeowner's dream—which made it the perfect location for a goblin pack.

No one seemed to know exactly when the vicious creatures had moved in, but over time their presence had become hard to ignore, especially when the number of brutal attacks and unexplained disappearances in the area increased. And then the half-eaten body parts started turning up.

It was only after the police had failed in its numerous attempts to apprehend the pack—and the body count continued to rise—that it became evident a specialist was required. Off the books, of course, and certainly off the record; the last thing City Hall wanted publicized was the fact that the NYPD wasn't really equipped to handle a bunch of cannibals running wild through the streets of Brooklyn. Or let it slip out that the five boroughs were not just home to one of the world's most ethnically diverse populations, but also to Gothopolis: the largest supernatural community in North America. A community that had been constantly growing since the early days of the New Amsterdam settlement, both in numbers and in the danger they presented to their human neighbors—or, as the goblins liked to call them, lunch.

Gothopolis wasn't its real name, of course, and it didn't have one specific location, but like so many New York neighborhoods that became defined by its residents— such as Little Italy, Chinatown, and Little Brazil—it stuck once people began using it as a convenient shorthand for the City's supernatural populace.

Names aside, as one would expect, with magical creatures ultimately came magical crimes, and the NYPD thought it could handle the situation. But after 160 years of busting up vampire speakeasies that raided blood banks for their cocktail ingredients and black-market butcher shops that specialized in the choicest cuts of human meat, battling werewolves and necromancers and science experiments gone horribly awry, and exposing politicians who truly were bloodsucking leeches, New York's Finest was still no closer to reining in the deadly excesses of the creatures of the night.

That's where the specialist came in.

Her name was Sebastienne Mazarin—Annie, to her friends and family—and when it came to dealing with basilisks and leucrotta and girtabilili there was no one better . . . at least, no one she'd ever met in her four hundred and thirty years of existence. Stalking weirdlings wasn't the most glamorous occupation for someone who, with her raven-black hair, long legs, and curvy figure looked as though she should be strutting a fashion show catwalk rather than poking around behind Dumpsters and peeking into sewer gratings, but such was the life she'd chosen as an independent monster hunter. Besides, as Annie often told her friends, the hours were flexible, she was her own boss, she got to travel the world and meet lots of interesting people—and best of all, she got to kill monsters.

And she *really* enjoyed killing monsters.

It took a few days for Annie to work out the logistics of hunting a group of beasties: checking out what might be their regular haunts, learning what times of the night they usually made an appearance, and locating traces of their spoor to give her something to track. Accomplishing the latter often involved literally sticking her nose in places—and things—that would make most people puke, but eventually her efforts paid off.

She found one of her quarry in a scrap metal yard not too far from the Newtown Creek. He was sitting on the hood of a gutted Chevy Impala, cleaning his nails with a paring knife.

There was nothing fairy-tale attractive about the bloated, gap-toothed, bulbous-nosed grotesquerie that glared menacingly at her as she approached. Like most of his kind, the creature's hair was a dirty, matted affair that vaguely resembled dreadlocks drenched in motor oil; his fingernails were long and dagger-sharp—honed to a point by constantly scraping the edges between his spikelike teeth. The tattered, threadbare clothing that stretched around his girth were probably pickings from a Salvation Army drop-box. His skin was pale, almost deathly white: a lack of pigmentation caused by a subterranean lifestyle mostly spent in sewers, subway tunnels, and underground passages.

As goblins went, he was one of the handsome ones.

"Sweet eventide, La Bella Tenebrosa," the goblin rasped. It was a title she'd picked up along her travels: the beautiful dark one. Generally, it was uttered as a form of respect, even among her enemies. Not in this case, though.

"You have a name, beast?" She wasn't in the mood to exchange pleasantries.

He growled, insulted by her name-calling. "I be Jakloww."

"Well, Jakloww, you know why I'm here. Your people have a treaty with me—and you've broken it."

"Aye. Survive we must, and why live off scraps when the larder be so plentiful?" He gestured past the gates of the scrap yard; across the East River, the Manhattan skyline gleamed a bright pinkish hue in the fading rays of the setting sun. "Old Jakloww thinks there be more than enough to fill the belly of every hungry goblin for years to come."

"Well, that's what the treaty is supposed to prevent." That, and the possibility of an all-out war between humanity and goblin-kind. Annie frowned. "Look, *otario*, you can't just go around eating people because you got tired of gnawing on garbage. Not as long as the humans are under my protection."

"You cannot protect *all* the humans of this city, butcher," the goblin said with a sneer. "Powerful you may be, deadlier even still, of that there is no doubt. Yet you are only one well-gifted meat dog, and there are many weirdlings in the world. Too many, old Jakloww thinks, even for you to handle . . ."

That was apparently a cue for the rest of the pack to come out of hiding.

She'd caught their scent before they stepped from the shadows. There were five of them, each as ugly and foul-smelling as the next, and their fashion choices were as straight-from-the-mildewed-Dumpster as Jakloww's. Four were built just like him: old bulls long past their prime but up for a tussle, if only to show they were still pack-worthy to the elders of the Great Lodge. That might be true for most hunts, when the prey consisted of rats or stray dogs and cats, but when it came to someone who could fight back? They'd probably run for the hills as fast as their stubby, wobbly legs could carry them—if she allowed it.

The fifth grotesquerie was going to be the real problem. Annie had never heard of a goblin growing taller than five feet; their girth and considerable weight compensated for their reduced stature when it came to facing down an opponent. This bruiser, however, was as tall as he was wide—which, by her estimation, put him around seven feet and three hundred pounds, most of it solid muscle. In her current situation, that meant the advantage was his by close to a foot in height (even with her high-heeled boots) and 175 pounds, give or take. The ax he was holding probably outweighed her, too, its handle almost as thick as a lamppost, its double-headed blade sharp enough to slice through her with a single swing. He was younger than the others: a veritable baby-faced killer among goblins who must have passed the century mark. That was troublesome, because a young bull was always out to prove himself, was always willing to take the risks older goblins would never have considered.

And yet, as Annie well knew from experience, risk takers were more often a greater danger to themselves than to others, and that could work to her advantage . . .

"Old Jakloww thinks this will be your last hunt, dark lady. Your head should make a fine trophy; perhaps it will hang above the fireplace in the elders' Great Lodge, so that all can see your time has passed, and the night belongs to us once more. And then tomorrow night, we will fill our larders with the meat of all those tasty humans you can no longer protect."

The other goblins closed in. Hot, fetid breath washed over her face; the odor made her want to retch. It was like standing in a sewer on the hottest day of the summer, with her head stuck in a waste pipe. Only not as fragrant.

Then she was on the move, charging at them instead of running away. Annie's challenging roar was loud enough to make the goblins wince, and it grew deeper in tone with each hurried step. More guttural. More . . . animalistic.

And that was when she *changed*.

The transformation was instantaneous; after four centuries, shape-shifting came as easily to Annie as drawing a breath. One moment, she was a dark-haired woman running down the sidewalk; the next, she was a panther, black as night, leaping the remaining distance to close on her prey.

She went for the young one first; you always took down the biggest dog in the yard before he had a chance to take you down. This piece of wisdom she'd learned the hard way back on Devil's Island, and whether it was on the humid streets of New York or in a rancid cell in French Guyana, it was always the hardest lessons learned that stayed with you, even a hundred years later.

Annie slammed into his chest—the impact sending the ax spinning from his hand as she bore him to the ground—and sank her teeth into his throat so deeply that her top and bottom canine teeth met near his spinal column. Blood—hot, salty, and tinged with the magic of the faerie realm from which all goblins originated—filled her mouth, and she hungrily slurped it down. She purred contentedly as a warm tingle ran through her body. The goblin's eldritch power energized her—a boost to the magick she, too, possessed. Magick that had been her birthright, as much as the ability she'd inherited from her mother to take the form of any creature, whether human or animal . . . like that of a bloodthirsty panther on the hunt.

The young bull gurgled his final breath as Annie released her death grip on his throat and roared in victory. Then her body quivered, shifted, and blurred as she returned to her natural state. She looked over her shoulder to see what the rest of the pack was up to.

The remaining five members had inched their way out of the shadows. Moonlight and the glow of overhead security lamps sparkled along the edges of the blades they wielded—although what "old Jakloww" thought a paring knife might be useful for in battle she couldn't begin to guess. The sight of the youth's blood, smeared across her face and hands, had made them reconsider attacking her; she could see it in the worried glances they flashed her way.

The old bulls looked hesitantly at one another, waiting for someone to work up enough nerve to make the first move. No immediate takers, though.

Annie picked up the young goblin's fallen ax and made the decision for them.

Jakloww screamed when he realized she was coming straight for him.

She was brushing her tongue, trying to get the acidic taste of raw goblin meat out of her mouth, when the bathroom mirror began talking to her.

"So? How did the hunt go?" it asked.

The silvered surface darkened and Annie found herself gazing not at her reflection but at the hawkish features of a Middle-Eastern man. His eyes were black as onyx, his nose long and hooked, his cheekbones sunken to the point of gauntness. For more than two hundred years this specter staring back at her had haunted homes up and down the East Coast since the day it arrived in the United States, terrifying children, shattering lives, driving men and women to the brink of madness. From his native Persian language, his name roughly translated to English as "the dreaded soul-devouring demon in the mirror."

She'd taken to calling it "Jerome."

It was meant as a compliment, she'd explained on more than one occasion. Jerome was the name of a member of the 1980s band The Time who often brought out a mirror during live performances so the lead singer, Morris Day, could check his appearance. Jerome carried a mirror, the spirit lived inside a mirror—it made perfect sense to her. Besides, her attempts at pronouncing the demon's original name in Farsi were painfully embarrassing to hear.

Unfortunately, as she had come to discover, she was the not-so-proud owner of the only looking-glass spirit in the five boroughs that lacked a sense of humor—of any kind. But it certainly knew how to belt out off-key Broadway show tunes and ribald nineteenth-century sailors' diddies when she was taking a shower . . .

Annie spat toothpaste into the sink and reached for the mouthwash. "About as dangerous as Christmas shopping at Macy's at the height of the holiday season—during a red-tag sale."

He frowned. "That bad, eh?"

"Almost," Annie mumbled through a mouthful of Scope, cheeks puffed out as she swished around the mint-flavored antiseptic until it began burning her tongue. She spat it out, then used a hand towel to wipe her mouth and watering eyes.

"Hmm." Their conversation apparently over, Jerome started to fade away, but then abruptly flashed back to a full-strength image. "Oh, before I forget, you had two calls while you were out . . . although why I should be acting as your personal secretary and taking messages is beyond me."

It was beyond her understanding as well. She had an answering machine, a cell phone with voice mail, and an e-mail account; she didn't need a "personal secretary" to take messages. And yet Jerome insisted on tapping into her landline so he could take calls on her behalf. His cure for boredom, it seemed. She'd ultimately decided that if acting as her assistant made him feel useful she wasn't going to stop him.

"It's probably because I don't get out of this dreary home all that often," Jerome lamented. He sighed. "My social life is almost as tragic as yours . . ."

"Oh, you poor thing," she said in mock sympathy, and rolled her eyes. Were all glass-spirits such drama queens, or was it just hers? "So, who called?"

"Well, the first call, I assume, was a wrong number; it rang three times before they hung up. Probably another of those imbeciles who confuse your number with that of the tavern down the street. The other was Alexander."

"Oh!" she said with a smile. "Is he stopping by?"

"No, he's still at that week-long Knights' conference in Denver."

"Oh, right." she said, disappointed. "I forgot about that." That wasn't entirely true—she hadn't forgotten about it as much as blown it off. She'd been to the Knights' gatherings before—they held a get-together every seven years in different cities around the world—but hadn't felt like going this time, even though Alexander had mentioned she was supposed to be the guest of honor. Why she'd turned down the invitation she couldn't say, but at some point in the last decade or so, she now realized, she'd become quite the party pooper. "So, what did he say?"

"He was checking to see if you were getting into trouble while he was out of town. I told him you'd call back after you were done torching every blood bar in Gothopolis." Jerome grinned. "He said he'd be on the first flight home tomorrow morning."

Annie sighed and lowered her head in exasperation. "I wish he'd stop doing that.

I'm not some delicate flower, after all. I mean, I know he likes to worry about me, and it's very sweet, but . . ." She shrugged. "I don't know. Why should he listen to me, right? I'm only his mother."

"Riiight . . . So, what are your plans for the rest of the evening?" No one could ever accuse Jerome of not knowing when to change the subject. He glanced down at the sink, and a gobbet of half-chewed meat sitting atop the drain cap. "I see you've already had dinner," he added in a droll tone.

"Getting out of these bloody clothes, for one thing," Annie replied. She glanced down at her outfit: there were large bloodstains on her white silk blouse, the right sleeve was frayed at the cuff, and the left had been completely torn away at the shoulder, to reveal the slender, deeply tanned arm underneath; the black velvet pants were sliced in a couple of spots; both thigh-high boots sported scuffs and scrapes that dulled the shine of the black leather, and the laces that ran up the front of the left boot had been sliced through near the knee. She'd picked up a few cuts on her arms and face, but most of them had started healing on the drive back from Brooklyn—one of the benefits of possessing a magick-enhanced immune system.

Unfortunately, her clothing lacked such regenerative abilities. She held up the tattered sleeve of her blouse. "I won't be wearing *this* again."

"That makes two this month. Maybe you should try chain mail."

Annie shook her head. "Did that once; it was like strapping a bank vault to my chest. I'll stick with silk blouses." She undid her belt buckle and dropped the wide leather strap on the floor. Her hands paused above the blouse buttons, and she looked up at the mirror. "Do you mind . . . ?"

"Modesty? At your age?" Jerome said huffily. "Very well; I can take a hint. If you want me, I'll be in my mirror, admiring that exquisite dog-on-black-velvet painting you have hanging across from me." He faded from view.

Annie leaned around the bathroom door to watch his progress. There was a brief pale-violet flash of light as Jerome returned to the mahogany-framed mirror that hung in the fourth-floor hallway of her Manhattan town house. "For the thousandth time, it's not a dog, it's a panther!" she yelled.

"Yes, well, then someone should have told the artist that panthers don't wear bright-red neckerchiefs that say 'Rex' on them," Jerome shot back.

Annie grunted. "Stupid demon . . ." she muttered, and slammed the door shut with her foot. She wasn't about to explain that *she'd* been the artist of that piece, painted while she lived in Berkeley, California during the early 1970s, when velvet canvases and black-light posters had been all the rage. *Well, I like it,* she assured herself.

She unbuttoned the blouse and was about to take it off, when a bright-red patch on her left side, just below the rib cage, caught her eye.

Blood. And it looked fresh.

Annie frowned. She pulled a hand towel from the rack on the wall and dabbed at the blood. Under it she found a vertical slit; the area around it was inflamed and felt extremely tender.

"When the hell did I get stabbed?" she muttered. "And with what?" She remembered Jakloww poking her with his paring knife during the five-on-one brawl—but since when could a little thing like that seriously hurt her?

She pressed the towel against the wound, then held it there for a few seconds, but as soon as she moved it away a trickle of blood seeped out from the hole. A chill spidered its way up her spine.

"That shouldn't be . . ." She wiped at it again. Still bleeding. Not as badly as it might have for a normal human under the same circumstance, but her magick-accelerated healing factor should have closed the wound before she arrived home.

But it *hadn't* closed, hadn't stopped oozing blood, and that indicated something was wrong with her immune system. Which meant there was a good chance that on her next hunt—

I could die . . .

For the first time that night, for perhaps the first time in a long while, Sebastienne Mazarin, the "beautiful dark one," the centuries-old destroyer of monsters and nightmares-given-flesh . . . felt afraid. And very, very mortal.

10

"So what is your prognosis, Doctor Noureddine?" Elden asked with a wry smile. Standing at the small bar in his flat at House Orlock's London headquarters, he dropped a pair of ice cubes in a glass, splashed two fingers of Type O-Negative over them, and added a twist of lime. He swirled the drink around a couple of times and took a sip. Adequate, for a nightcap. Not as satisfying as lapping it fresh from the vein, but sufficient enough to help take the edge off a particularly trying evening.

Hunched forward on a leather sofa in the center of the living room, the broad-shouldered African grunted in disgust as he stared at the monitor of the laptop computer that sat on a glass-topped coffee table before him. The iBook, appropriated from Morrison Millar's warehouse office, had so far proven to be infuriatingly difficult when it came to coaxing valuable information from it—not unlike the situation they'd faced with its former owner. For instance: There were three dozen or so open folder icons on display at the moment, each marked with such useless titles as STUFF, IMP. STUFF, and OTHER STUFF—as well as various multiples thereof—set against a grainy wallpaper photograph of a scantily clad blonde lovely. A blowup of a low resolution scan from some magazine or other, though it was difficult to tell whether the girl was a celebrity or a pinup model with all those folders littered across her landscape.

Noureddine exhaled sharply. "I'd say that, as a businessman, Mr. Millar makes a far better Internet pirate." He waved a hand toward the screen and snarled. "Most of the files he has on here are illegal downloads: music, movies, pornography . . ."

Elden snorted. "Charming." Glass in hand, he eased into a leather armchair, leaned his head back, and closed his eyes. "So now we know two of Mr. Millar's more cunning traits: a penchant for stealing copyrighted materials, and an exemplary skill for evading pursuers." He sneered. "Including three of House Orlock's best hunters."

He heard Noureddine snarl in response. It was a sore point for all of them, but especially so for Elden. In three hundred years, no target had ever escaped him, human, animal, or other. Millar was the first—and would be the last, he swore. After all, he had a reputation to protect.

What bothered him more, really, wasn't so much that Millar had managed to slip away from the warehouse without being seen, but that in doing so he had outsmarted his pursuers. And that was just unacceptable. Humans, no matter how clever, were incapable of outwitting even the youngest vampire-child, and Millar was a prime example. The man didn't have two decent brain cells to rub together to run a properly defended black market business, let alone formulate an escape. Hell, he'd damn near wet himself when Elden opened his eyes after being shot. So, no, he didn't think it likely that Millar possessed anywhere near the level of intelligence necessary for matching wits with hunters of the first order.

But what if he had help . . . ?

"Damn it!" Noureddine snapped, followed by the heavy thud of something striking the glass coffee table. His fist, no doubt. Elden slowly opened his eyes and glared at him.

"Have a care, old friend," he warned sternly. "Venting your frustrations is understandable." He bared his fangs. "Doing so with my furniture is not."

"Sorry, Elden," Noureddine mumbled. "Lost my head for a second. Won't happen again." He sat back on the sofa, scrubbed his face with both hands in an exasperated gesture, and exhaled sharply. "I just don't understand it. I've cracked defense department databases without breaking a sweat; tapped into spy satellites without detection so we could keep an eye on the other clans." He waved helplessly at the laptop. "How, then, could some lowborn meat-sack possess the know-how to encrypt files even I can't access?"

"The answer is, he doesn't," Elden replied sourly.

"Then how . . ." Noureddine's voice trailed off, and his eyes slowly widened in shock. "You don't think the little bugger's in league with one of the other houses, do you?"

Elden nodded. "I'm almost certain of it. How else could he have slipped past the three of us? The question is, which house?" Actually, a better question was, if Millar was working for a rival clan, why didn't they already have possession of the Prize? House Bathory certainly would have shouted news of it from the rooftops, braggarts that they were; so would the Karnsteins and the Varneys. He knew House Akinyemi in Nigeria and the Baital clan in India had had no luck; neither had the Ch'ing Shih of Hong Kong. And House Tepes would have dropped hints about their success, in preparation for the big reveal, but there'd been nary a peep out of those Rumanian thugs in the past few months.

But, he now realized, the members of Japan's House Otoyo were just the opposite of their rivals; in fact, they tended to be secretive to a maddening fault. If they were Millar's masters, no one would know they had the Prize until it was put to use—and by then it would be too late to do anything about it . . .

Noureddine pointed at the laptop. "And you think they messed about with the files, too?"

The elder hunter shrugged. "What other explanation could there be?"

"Maybe you two think too hard," Alexi commented from the far side of the room.

His partners slowly turned to face him. The burly Russian was lounging across a love seat, head resting on the padded wooden arm at one end, black stocking feet propped on the other. His right arm was draped over his eyes, as though he'd been trying to sleep. Elden noted it had been some time since his companion had bothered to change his socks—the pointed edge of the overgrown nail on his left big toe was starting to poke through the thinning fabric.

"And what's that supposed to mean?" Noureddine demanded. He folded his arms across his broad chest. His body language made it clear he wasn't all that interested in hearing whatever suggestion his companion was about to offer.

Without looking over, Alexi waved his left hand in the direction of the laptop. "Maybe answer is on machine," he answered in his typically stilted English, "but is hiding in plain sight. So plain you not even realize it there."

Noureddine snorted dismissively. "That's ridiculous. You really think I wouldn't have noticed something like that?"

"I wouldn't be so quick to scoff at him if I were you," Elden suggested. "Alexi might be the brawn of this operation, but he's always proven good enough for one brainstorm a century." He winked. "I'd say he's been long overdue for one."

Noureddine threw out his hands and looked helplessly at his leader. "But it's so . . . so simpleminded!"

Elden nodded. "And it's that simplicity which makes the notion so appealing."

"*Da*. That how it work in 'The Purloined Letter,' " Alexi added sagely.

Noureddine started. "Hold on. You know what 'The Purloined Letter' is?"

Alexi moved his arm away from his eyes so he could look at his shocked inquisitor. "What? You surprised I read Edgar Allan Poe?"

"No," Noureddine replied archly. "I'm surprised you can read."

"*Zasranec*," Alexi muttered sourly in his native tongue.

Elden had a good idea of how that would translate into English, but decided to say nothing. Instead, he gave Noureddine a slight nudge on the arm. "Go on. Try it his way. It's not as though your luck with the damn thing could get any worse."

Noureddine sighed and leaned forward, positioning his hands over the keyboard. "All right. I'll put myself in Millar's place; try to think as he would."

"Steady on, old boy," Elden cautioned mischievously. "No need to endanger your IQ level just to prove a point."

Alexi snorted a piggish laugh. "*Da*! Is already low enough!"

Noureddine let the remark pass without comment and focused his attention on the computer. His eyes slowly closed, and Elden watched as his brow furrowed in deep concentration. He glanced over at Alexi, who'd risen to a sitting position. Elden raised an index finger to his lips, signaling him to remain quiet. Alexi nodded.

"Hang on . . ." Noureddine muttered, and his eyes snapped open. "Something I saw . . ." He dropped his left thumb onto the screen cursor control pad and swept the tiny arrow over to a folder marked Benjy Stuff, clicked to open it, scrolled down to another folder, eBay, and clicked on that. A list of documents, e-mails, and PDF—Portable Document Format—files tumbled open. Noureddine studied them for a few moments, scrolling up and down as he searched for whatever had caught his eye during his first attempt at solving the riddle of Millar's hard drive. He stopped at a Microsoft Excel document labeled JunkDeals and clicked on it.

A spreadsheet filled the screen.

Elden leaned forward to get a better look. "Is this a list of his inventory?"

Noureddine nodded. "And his transactions," he added happily. He looked over his shoulder at Alexi. "Cheers, mate."

"*Pozhalsta*," the Russian replied amiably. He leaned back on the sofa to return to his dozing.

The undead hacker resumed his search. It didn't take more than a few minutes to find the listing he wanted. A final click on the cursor pad, and the information appeared onscreen:

DAVID ZWIEBACK
RENFIELD'S HOUSE OF HORRORS AND MYSTICAL ANTIQUITIES
ASTORIA, NY 11106

Noureddine raised an eyebrow. "Zweeback?"

"It's that bricklike cookie mothers give their mewling infants to gnaw on," Elden explained. He took a second glance at the address and sneered. "Renfield's House of Horrors. How charming. It seems Mr. Zwieback is a collector of sorts. An aficionado of the supernatural, if the name of his establishment is any indication."

"A bleedin' horror fan is what he is." Noureddine flashed a shark-tooth grin. "Well, if that's the case, I'll be happy to give him the fright of his life—just before I end it."

Elden drained his glass and slammed it down on the coffee table. The hunt was on again, and he was eager to pick up the trail. "All right, gentlemen, we have our destination. Inform the New York chapter of our pending arrival and then pack your overnight bags. We're going to New York." He grinned wickedly. "And by tomorrow night, the Prize will at last be ours . . ."

A little over 1,500 miles west of London, high above the moonlit waters of the

Atlantic Ocean, another hunter was echoing Elden's sentiments—for entirely different reasons.

"For too long have the other houses looked down upon the members of House Otoyo," Lady Kiyoshi Sasaki declared at the conclusion of her speech. "For too long have they ignored the strength of our clan. But once the Prize is ours, they shall come to respect us—and fear us, as well."

There was a polite smattering of applause from the dozen house members who had joined her on the private jet for the transatlantic flight to America. Kiyoshi gave a small nod of appreciation and sat down.

She smiled impishly, pleased with the results of her mission at the Kensington warehouse. The hint of evil in Morrison Millar's blood as she drained him had been mouthwateringly sweet, but it was the memories she absorbed from his mind that had provided a more appetizing feast. Millar's subconscious contained not just the name of the ship on which the prize was being transported—the *Demeter*—and the date it was scheduled to arrive in New York, but the address and identity of the meat-sack who'd purchased it. A buyer who would soon enough forfeit his claim to it—not to mention his life. As the late Morrison Millar had.

"Do you really think the other clans will fear us, Yoshi?" asked a timid voice beside her.

Kiyoshi swiveled her seat to the right to face her younger sister, Miyuki, who sat across the aisle from her. To see them, one would never think they were related. Where Yoshi was brooding and often withdrawn, Miyu was radiant and bubbly, although she had her shy moments as well. Where Yoshi could be cruel and snappish and dangerously vengeful, Miyu was gentle and soft-spoken and forgiving. Yoshi the moon and Miyu the sun—sisters of darkness and light, their mother, Shina, had called them when they were children.

And so they remained, even in death.

About the only thing they had in common—other than their vampiric lifestyle, of course—was their sense of fashion, both great admirers of the Elegant Gothic Lolita style that had become so popular among the young women of Tokyo and Osaka. The other clan members—at least those of the sisters' generation—followed their example, choosing leather and lace, satin and velvet over the sharp business suits and latex bodystockings and Japanese school uniforms worn by some of the rival houses. House Otoyo was all about style, the women resplendent in flowing gowns and knee-length pinafores, the men debonair in frock coats and top hats—although not all dressed in such a gender-specific manner. A few of the male members, like Kiyoshi's second-in-command, Hiromi Takami, who was the co-pilot for this trip, preferred a more feminine mode; and Emiko Matsuda, who sat two aisles down from her leader, could have passed for a slim-waisted man at first glance. The clothing wasn't an exact duplicate of Victorian Era attire, of course; no one wanted to be *that* old-fashioned. There were leather corsets and chunky-soled boots added to the mix, and a variety of body piercings and extreme hair coloring to offset them. Nineteenth-century fashion, upgraded and fetishized and filtered through a Japanese visual kei band called Malice Mizer and its cross-dressing leader/fashion icon, Mana, for twenty-first-century couture. And the Sisters Sasaki were two of his biggest fans.

Yet even there they differed. Where the leader of House Otoyo wrapped herself in the colors of night, blacks and midnight blues—Mana's favorites—Miyu favored the hues of morning: pinks and yellows, lavenders and pale blues. Her clothing this night reflected that preference: a long-sleeved, light pink bustle shirring dress trimmed with white lace, the skirt decorated with swirls of embroidered red and pink roses. A pair of pink bows—one at the collar, the other tied at the waist—matched a much larger one that Yoshi glimpsed at the back of the dress. White knee-high socks—also accented with embroidered roses—and pink Mary Jane shoes completed the Sweet Lolita outfit. All in all, very fashionable; the epitome of Elegant Gothic & Lolita style. The oversized, white vinyl Hello, Kitty handbag lying on her lap, however, wasn't; if anything, it was so totally anti-EGL it practically made Kiyoshi's teeth ache. It *really* had to go. It was a childish touch, completely inappropriate for the sister of a venerated clan leader, and just so . . . so . . .

So totally Miyu, Yoshi realized as a warm smile tugged at the corners of her mouth, that she could never order her to toss it away. It would break Miyu's unbeating heart.

She reached out and gently tousled her sister's jet-black hair. "They were always meant to fear us, Miyu. It's just that now they will have no excuse to deny it to themselves."

Miyu nodded in agreement, then smiled sweetly, her slight overbite highlighted by the soft pink lipstick that perfectly complemented the dress. "Do you think we'll have any time to sightsee while we're there?" She opened the handbag, dug through the clutter within, and pulled out a soft-covered guidebook: The *"I Love New York"* *Book of Dreams*. Back in Tokyo it was a bestseller, very popular with teenagers who fantasized about becoming successful artists or dancers or even hip-hop club deejays in the West—goals they never believed they could reach by remaining in Japan. Miyu tapped the book's cover with a bright pink fingernail. "I've never been to New York, and I would *so* love to visit Greenwich Village. I hear the people there dress like in Harajuku—but all the time!"

Yoshi laughed. How typical of Miyu. Here they were in a race against time, competing with every vampire house in the world for possession of the ultimate prize—perhaps even the ultimate weapon, if some of the stories were to be believed— and her sister was more interested in checking out Western fashions!

Well, she considered, it wasn't all that surprising. With her youthful appearance and attitude—in spite of her advanced years—Miyu was very much like the Goth- and punk-influenced teenagers who congregated around Tokyo's Harajuku Station every weekend to show off their unique styles and check out the latest fashion trends in the shops along nearby Takeshita Street. Small wonder, then, that she'd befriended a number of them, although Kiyoshi frowned upon clan members fraternizing with livestock. As she'd explained to her younger sister more than once, you didn't chat up a cow before you turned it into steaks—why should humans be treated any differently? But Miyu enjoyed the company of her lowborn friends, and Yoshi eventually gave up trying. There were more important matters for her to focus on than dissuading her sister of playing with her food.

"Greenwich Village?" She gave a small, noncommittal shrug. "Perhaps, if there is time. But you must remember, Miyu, this is no holiday excursion we are on. The survival of our clan depends on the success of this mission."

Miyu nodded solemnly, the playful attitude of the Goth fashionista quickly replaced by the cool demeanor of a responsible clan member. "I know that,

Yoshi. Just as you know that I'll do whatever you ask of me to make sure we are successful." The hint of a smile curled the left corner of her mouth. "And then we can go sightseeing—right?" She leaned forward to gaze imploringly at her older sister. "Pleeease?"

Kiyoshi snorted a very unladylike laugh, and covered her mouth with her hand. "Very well, Miyu," she conceded with a sigh. "I never have been able to deny you anything; why should this time be any different?" She reached out to pat Miyu on the hand. "You'll have your visit to Greenwich Village—that I promise. In the meantime, why don't you ask Emiko to help you research our destination? I know nothing of this 'Queens' other than it being an area one must travel through on the way to Manhattan from JFK Airport. Find out all you can—*and* whether any of our competitors have chapters nearby."

"All right." Miyu grinned. "And perhaps I can look up information on the Village, too, while I'm at it . . . ?" There was an unmistakably hopeful tone in her voice.

Kiyoshi nodded, then held up a warning finger. "But gather the intelligence on the location first."

"Hai," Miyu said with a quick nod, and rose from her seat.

Kiyoshi watched her sister walk toward Emiko, then swiveled her own seat back around in order to look out the window. At 25,000 feet, the jet was racing the moon across the Atlantic for the American shore, and somewhere behind the moon, running in second place, were the lummoxes from House Orlock. A distant second, if their actions at the warehouse were a true indication of their abilities—or rather *lack* of abilities—as hunters. It should have been impossible to slip past the three of them with Millar in tow, but Kiyoshi had managed it with little effort, while Elden and his cronies stood around, scratching their heads.

Europe's finest hunters, Hiromi had told her. Fierce competitors possessing razor-sharp intellects, he'd said. They'd be hard to outsmart. Kiyoshi snorted in disgust. *As if.* Well, perhaps 'Romi had been expecting some other group of hunters, instead of the bunglers his leader had so easily embarrassed.

Still, the shortcomings of House Orlock meant little to her now. House Otoyo was only hours away from crossing the finish line and claiming the Prize—and once in her possession, Kiyoshi would not hesitate to put it to use. Human or vampire, wyvern or rakshasha: no matter the species, all would finally bow before Lady Sasaki and her clan . . . or be destroyed.

Kiyoshi leaned back in her seat and smiled, pleased with the thought of subjugating an entire world.

But she was getting ahead of herself. First she had to reach her objective; then she could start making plans for world domination. Still . . .

Empress Sasaki. It had a pleasant ring to it, she thought.

Kiyoshi closed her eyes and dreamed of vampiric dynasties.

11

As Morrison Millar had realized shortly before dying, Item 179 wasn't some run-of-the-mill antiquity—not with all the attention it was getting of late. But to the two men sitting in the delivery van that had transported the crate from a cargo ship docked in Red Hook, Brooklyn, to a tree-lined side street in Astoria—a quiet residential neighborhood in the borough of Queens—that's all it really was: just another box, no different from the others they were hauling around on a Saturday morning in June.

Parking the battered yellow van at the curb, the driver—an ox of a man named Guillermo Barcino—paused to stare at the redbrick building that stood before him. Well, not so much at the building itself, but rather at the strange-looking store located on its first floor . . . although strange didn't seem like the most appropriate word to describe it.

"What kinda freak show is this?" he murmured. Yeah, that pretty much summed it up, he thought. A freak show.

Located a block from Kaufman Astoria Studios—home to numerous film and television productions—Renfield's House of Horrors and Mystical Antiquities, according to the sign in its window, promoted itself as a museum dedicated to the bizarre and the strange, the unique and the disturbing. Beneath a hand-carved wooden sign bearing the museum's name, its letters painted to look like they were dripping blood, stood a life-size wax figure of Hungarian-born actor Béla Lugosi, dressed in the tuxedo and flowing cape of the character that had made him an overnight sensation in 1931: Dracula, lord of the vampires. One arm extended toward the museum's front door, the waxen Lugosi stood ready to greet fans of the supernatural, as well as the occasional curious passerby. To the left of the front door was a large display window. Behind the glass could be seen a collection of strange objects: onyx figurines of creatures that were half-human and half-octopod; weather-beaten books bound in covers of faded leather; pins and amulets—some metal, some ceramic—bearing mystical symbols.

All in all, Renfield's House of Horrors was exactly the sort of place in which an avid horror fan could feel right at home.

Guillermo slowly shook his head. "House'a *Weirdos* is more like it," he said with a sneer.

Stepping from the van, he turned back to his partner, Manfred Fletcher. If Guillermo was built like a tank—average height and beefy, with thick arms and a barrel chest—then Manny was his exact physical opposite: tall and wiry, his dark-brown uniform hanging off his thin frame. All too aware of the weight of the crate they were about to haul from the van—having muscled the thing into the vehicle when they picked it up at the docks—Manny had already strapped on a thick weight lifter's belt to avoid injuring his back.

"Let's get a move on," said Guillermo. Manny nodded, grabbed the clipboard next to his seat, and followed his partner to the rear of the van.

As the two deliverymen struggled to unload the crate, the front door of the museum suddenly flew open and a handsome, dark-haired man in his midforties stepped out to join them. His strong, wide jaw tinged blue-black with stubble, he was dressed in black jeans, black denim shirt, and black boots. With an outfit like that he was either the owner of the museum, or a laid-back mortician.

"You got it!" the man said cheerfully. Rubbing his hands together, he strode toward the men. "This is great! Just great! We were just getting ready to open!"

Manny glanced down at his clipboard and scanned the crate's shipping form. "You David Zweebeck?"

"Zwieback," the man replied. "Long 'I' sound." He gestured toward the museum. "I'm the curator of the House of Horrors."

Manny glanced at the storefront, then looked Zwieback up and down. "Figures." He tossed the clipboard into the van and turned back to help Guillermo unload the crate.

After an uncomfortable moment of silence, Zwieback softly cleared his throat.

"You guys need a hand there?"

"Nah," Guillermo grunted. "We got it."

With a groan of wooden slats scraping across the rubber matting that covered the floor of the van, the crate suddenly popped loose and slid out faster than expected. The deliverymen jumped back in surprise as it slammed onto the pavement and stood straight up.

Zwieback hopped forward, placing a hand on the crate before it could pivot into the street. "Guys! Guys! A lighter touch here, okay? This isn't some secondhand couch from the Salvation Army you're dropping off."

"Yeah, sorry," Guillermo said. He reached out to grab hold of the crate. Not that it was really about to flip over, now that it was upright; it was just an attempt to show he had everything under control. Manny aided him in wrestling the crate onto a two-wheeled hand truck. "So, whatta we got, here—you mind me askin'?"

The curator's eyes gleamed with excitement. "It's a coffin."

Guillermo frowned. "A coffin."

"Hey, is that, y'know, legal?" Manny asked, his voice a little high-pitched. His head seemed to turn on a spring as he looked around. Probably expecting cops to jump out of every doorway and bust them for grave-robbing.

"Sure, sure. Everything on the up-and-up," said Zwieback—although he, too, did a quick sweep of the block with his eyes. "But it's not just *any* coffin, you know," he continued. "It's a very special one."

"Oh, yeah? What makes it so special?" Manny asked.

"Well, it's not really the coffin that's special, it's the contents," the curator said cheerfully. "You see, there's an honest-to-God *vampire* inside it."

The deliverymen shared sidelong glances.

"Riiiight," Guillermo drawled as he retrieved the clipboard from the van.

Another awkward moment of silence passed. "So, uh . . ." Zwieback finally said. "How about you guys take it inside?"

Guillermo shrugged. "Just show us where you want it. Wouldn't want all this sunlight and fresh air blowin' up Dracula here."

"Uh . . . yeah," Zwieback muttered. Then he stepped aside to make room as Guillermo and Manny rolled the crate into the House of Horrors.

Béla Lugosi, silent and waxen, seemed to look on approvingly.

"Now what the hell is *that* thing?" asked a voice as Dave trailed along behind the deliverymen and their cargo.

Dave turned to face Tim Merrick, his assistant curator, who was standing behind the admission counter, just to the left of the doorway. At six foot six and 230 pounds, attired in a dark blue New York Giants football jersey and baggy blue jeans, Tim looked more like he should be sacking quarterbacks on a gridiron than selling horror memorabilia in a Queens storefront. But playing professional sports held little interest for him—filmmaking was his passion. And as Tim had explained when he interviewed for the position last year, working in an establishment that honored the movies of classic genre directors like James Whale and Tod Browning was a way for him to stay connected with that passion. It also didn't hurt that the museum was within walking distance of a movie studio and the Museum of the Moving Image, and across the street from a multiplex cinema.

"What—that?" Dave replied, pointing to the crate. He shrugged, trying to act nonchalant. "Oh, just the box from England."

"Really?" Tim's broad grin practically lit up the room. He reached under the counter and came up with their latest theft deterrent device: a two-foot-long iron crowbar with the name Deathbringer spray-painted along its length. "So when do we get to open it?"

Dave chuckled. As a film major at New York University, Tim might be interested more in the art house imagery of a Darren Aronofsky than the grindhouse visuals of a Tobe Hooper, but when it came to objets de bizarro, the twenty-one-year-old African-American was almost as big a geek as his employer. "Soon as these two gentlemen finish unloading," he explained.

But that, he noted with a knowing smile, could take a few minutes. Like all visitors to the House of Horrors, the deliverymen had automatically eased into a slow-footed shuffle once they'd crossed the threshold, stunned—and perhaps a little frightened—by the overall strangeness of their surroundings. There was certainly a lot to see: bookshelves crammed with vintage pulp magazines and comic books, toys, phonograph records, and, yes, even books; glass cases housing rubber masks; framed posters from a variety of movies; a smattering of authentic movie props and costumes. There wasn't an inch of display space that didn't have something crammed into it.

"Pretty impressive, huh?" Dave said to his visitors. "And it's just a little over half of what we've got. There's even more in the basement."

The larger of the two men made a slow turn to face the curator, then shook his head and looked away. "Freak show . . ." he muttered. Then he and his lanky sidekick resumed their shuffling journey to the back room.

Dave closed his eyes and wearily let his head droop. It wasn't the first time he'd heard someone casually dismiss all the hard work he'd put into the museum, but hearing it for the hundredth time didn't make it any easier on his bruised ego than when he'd heard it the first time. He sighed, opened his eyes, and looked over to his assistant, who smiled weakly and shrugged.

"Truly, they are not of our kind," Tim remarked in a lispy British accent that sounded like a rough imitation of Boris Karloff. A *really* rough imitation.

The floor—and just about every bit of memorabilia in the place—suddenly shook from a heavy impact as the deliverymen dumped their burden.

"Okay," the big guy grunted, "that oughtta do it." The thin man grabbed hold of the hand truck and eased it out from under its cargo.

Dave frowned at the battered crate stuck in the middle of his showroom, then realized that he should have directed them toward the metal cellar doors outside the store; now he and Tim would have to drag the thing into the basement.

He mentally shrugged and glanced over to Tim, who held up his right hand and slid his thumb and middle finger against each other, as though rubbing two coins together—the universal sign for money.

As the heavier of the duo pulled alongside, Dave handed him a ten-dollar bill. "Hey, thanks for dragging it in here," he said. "I really appreciate it."

The deliveryman shrugged and pocketed the cash. Then he held out the clipboard, and the delivery receipt it held. "You gotta sign for it."

Tim handed Dave a pen, and the curator scribbled his signature at the bottom of the page. The man detached a pink carbon copy and passed it to him. "Have a nice day," he commented, although his lack of sincerity made it clear he was only saying it out of habit. Then he walked out the door, no doubt grateful to be back in the sunlight and away from the "freaks."

His partner, however, stopped at the counter. "You guys got a flyer or a brochure or somethin'? My boy Alvy's into all this . . ." He waved a hand at the collection around him. "Y'know, this weird stuff." He shrugged. "I'da know. Maybe he might get a kick outta the place."

Dave plucked a green-paper brochure from a stack by the register. "This has all the basic information—the times we're open, stuff like that—and a list of our upcoming exhibits. How old is your son?"

"Ten."

Dave grimaced. "Okay, so maybe you shouldn't bring him around during our salute to Japanese 'body horror' films at the end of the month. It'd probably be too upsetting for somebody that young."

The guy snorted. "Eh. Kids today, they see worse stuff on the TV." He took the brochure and stuffed it in his work shirt's breast pocket. "Thanks. Have a good one." Pushing the empty hand truck, he followed his partner outside. The door slowly closed behind him.

Dave smiled as he heard the delivery truck's engine cough to life. "Think he'll bring his kid by?"

"No," Tim said.

"Yeah, me neither," he replied with a laugh.

Tim nodded toward the latest acquisition and held out Deathbringer. "So, we gonna do this?"

Dave took the crowbar and gazed at his prize. The crate was scuffed and scratched and filthy from its travels, a few of the wooden slats were cracked and splintered, and a small stream of blue packing peanuts flowed from a hole in one corner. He hoped the same battered conditions didn't apply to its contents—otherwise a certain delivery company was going to owe him for a ten-dollar tip.

The phone rang, and Tim reached under the counter to pick up the mobile. "Renfield's House of—" His eyebrows shot up and he looked over to Dave. "Oh, hey, Karen. How you doing? . . . Great . . . I'm good, too, thanks. I take it you're looking for David? . . . Yeah, he's right here."

Dave motioned toward the back of the museum. "In the office," he stage-whispered, and headed in that direction. He shrugged at the crate as he passed it. "Sorry, Dracula, but family comes first." Then he held up the crowbar. "But don't worry, you'll be free soon enough—and then the fun begins . . ."

Dave strode into the office, which was just as cluttered with wall-to-wall memorabilia as the rest of the museum—only not as organized. Rubber masks and plastic Pez dispensers fought for space on an old sofa with antique toys and rolled up movie posters and theater lobby cards; stacks of hardcover and paperback books leaned precariously against dusty mounds of comic books and magazines along the baseboards; a life-sized cardboard figure of Elvira, Mistress of the Dark, gazed out from behind a corner table packed with more books, records, and CDs waiting to be catalogued and put on display. In the center of the chaos stood a battered and scratched wooden desk that had lost its glossy finish a lifetime ago. Its surface was covered with a scattering of vintage horror magazines, as well as a foot-high pile of bills, receipts, and museum brochures. Atop the stack was a plastic bobblehead doll wearing a white baseball uniform and blue batting helmet: a toy version of Mr. Met, the baseball-headed mascot of the New York Mets. And somewhere under Mr. Met's feet, a phone was ringing.

Dave tossed the crowbar on the guest chair in front of the desk and began sifting through the mess; he came up with the phone on the second try. "Hey, K," he said after picking up the transferred call. Then he plopped down into his "boss" chair. "Don't tell me—life in the sticks has finally gotten to you, and you and Pan are coming home."

"Swing and a miss—again," she said playfully, then added soberly, "No, that's not the reason I'm calling. We have a problem, Dave. A big one."

Dave sat upright. "Pan?"

There was a brief pause. "Yeah."

"What happened? Is she okay?"

"She's fine. Physically, at least. The other girl . . . not so much."

His eyebrows did a quick upward crawl. "Other girl?"

Karen sighed wearily. "She got into another fight. At the big mall in Albany, this time."

"Crap. How bad did it get?"

"Bad enough. Do you remember the Van Schrik family?"

"Uhh . . . Oh, sure. They're the ones your town's named af—" He winced. "Oh, she didn't."

"Yup. Punched their daughter Nikki in the face. Left a mark on her jaw from one of those big heavy rings she's always wearing."

Nikki Van Schrik. The name sounded familiar . . . "Isn't that the girl who was giving her all the grief in school?"

"One and the same."

"Well, I hate to say that maybe she had it coming . . ."

"That's not helping," she said curtly.

"Okay, you're right. Sorry. So, they gonna sue?"

"Don't know yet; the mother invited me over there for Monday so we can talk. But the Van Schriks don't screw around—they're the kind who have the phone numbers for a battery of lawyers programmed into their speed dialers."

"I hear you. So, did you want me to give Pan a stern talking-to or something?"

"*You* give a 'stern talking-to' to Daddy's Little Girl?" Karen chuckled softly. "That'll be the day. No, what I need is for you to meet her at Penn Station at noon."

"Penn— Wait. You're sending her down today?"

"I know it's a last-minute thing, but she's in one hell of a mess. And it won't get fixed if she's still hanging around here while I'm trying to smooth things out. You get my meaning?"

"Uh-huh. You have to get her out of town—and fast, before the lynch mob forms. Any idea how long Calamity Jane needs to hide out?"

"Haven't got a clue," she confessed. "Could be a week, could be the whole summer if they really want to make a stink about it."

"Okay. Not a problem." He paused. "There anything else? You said Pan was fine physically. Does that mean what I think it does?"

"Yeah," Karen slowly replied. "Maybe. I'm not sure. After she got into that fight I had to go pick her up, and on the way home she kept looking at the people around us like they were . . . they were . . ." Her voice trailed off into an uncomfortable silence.

A chill crawled up Dave's spine. "You think she's having a relapse?"

Karen didn't answer right away. In his mind's eye, Dave could see her nervously chewing on the end of her right thumbnail, scraping away the polish with her teeth. *Like daughter, like mother*, he thought.

"I don't know," she finally said. "I thought she was doing okay; she hasn't had an episode since school began. But then I found her watching TV in the living room at four this morning, just channel surfing and saying stuff like, 'Nope. Nope. Yup. Kinda figured,' while she stared at the people on the screen."

Dave sucked in a breath. He and Karen knew what that sort of behavior indicated: their daughter's dreaded "monstervision" had returned and she had been using it to determine which actors, to her eyes, were human and which . . . were something else. "Crap. Sounds like she off her meds again."

"I know. I checked her prescriptions and the pill count was right on the button for her taking them every day—"

"But you're not sure she was actually taking them."

"We had a *deal* about her taking them." Karen sighed. "I thought I could trust her this time."

"Hey, now don't go tying yourself in knots. It's not the first time she's faked us out, you know. Remember four years ago, when the haldol magically became a bottle full of Reese's Pieces?"

"I remember," Karen admitted. "I only got suspicious because she was suddenly so willing to take them."

"And now she's learned how to not tip her hand. You know she gets all that cleverness from me," he added, trying to add a lighter tone to the discussion.

It worked. Karen snorted a laugh. "You wish."

"I can dream, can't I? You talk to Dr. Farrar?"

"Nicole and her husband are on vacation in Paris for two weeks, but her office promised she'll get back to me. I'm hoping she can refer a therapist down by you."

He scratched his jaw for a couple of seconds.

"How about Dr. Elfman? She still in business in the old neighborhood? You know Pan always liked her. Of course, that was when she was eleven . . ."

"No, that's a great idea!" Karen said, her mood instantly brightening. "I think I still have Desiree's number in the files. I'll give her service a call."

"No, you'll e-mail her info to me and *I'll* give her a call if you don't hear from Nicole before Monday," he said firmly. "Sounds like you've got enough on your plate already."

"Yeah . . . Thanks, Dave," she said warmly. "But you know, I could just send you a text message after I find it."

He snorted. "Oh, please. You know I can't figure out that texting stuff. I'll stick with what I know." Then he added in an exaggerated old-man voice, "Change scares me, girlie!"

"All right, Grandpa, have it your way," she said with a laugh. "Look, I better go—I have to finish putting things together for the trip. The Amtrak schedule says the Adirondack gets into the City around noon."

"I'll be there. Can I talk to her before you head out?"

"Sure. Hang on." Dave heard the sound of footsteps as Karen walked across a wooden floor—probably crossing from the living room to the main hall of the old house, from all the creaking that was going on. "Pan?" she yelled. Dave pictured her standing at the bottom of the stairs, calling up to their daughter's bedroom. "Pick up the phone! It's your father!" Then she added in a normal tone, "I'll speak with you later, Dave."

There were two clicks on the line—Pan picking up her extension, then Karen hanging up.

"Hi, Dad," Pan said, her voice low and soft. She sounded depressed—and who could blame her, given her current state of mind?

Yeah, Dave thought, *but she wouldn't* be *in that state of mind if she'd just take her pills.* He shook his head. Being angry and confrontational with his daughter was no way to approach the situation, as he knew from experience; in this case it would only strengthen her resolve to not take her antipsychotic medication. The solution was to be upbeat and supportive, and find a subtle way that would have her convincing herself that getting back on her meds was the right thing to do. As his mother used to say, you get more flies with honey than you do with vinegar, so . . .

So. Don't press, don't fight, and don't mention anything about the stability of her mental health, he told himself. *Wait for a quiet moment after she gets to the City to bring it up—and* then *you can drop the hammer on her. But in a supporting, upbeat way, of course . . .*

He took a deep breath, exhaled, and smiled warmly. "Hey, Panda-bear. I hear you're coming up to spend some time with your old man."

"Well, it's either that," she said sarcastically, "or wait around here for the villagers to show up at the door with the torches and pitchforks."

He chuckled. "Been watching Frankenstein movies again, huh?"

"Yeah, well, y'know . . ." He could just about see her shrugging her shoulders on the other end of the line. "Sometimes it's pretty easy to empathize with him."

"Wanna tell me about it?" he asked.

"Not right now," she replied. "When I get home. I *will* tell you this, Dad: Nikki had it coming."

"Cripes, don't let your mother hear you say that. She'll go nuts." Dave winced. Now *there* was a poor choice of word . . .

"I know," Pan said. From her tone, it was easy to picture her rolling her eyes in exasperation. *Like I hadn't thought of that already, Dad. Jeeeeez.* "So, you gonna meet me at Penn Station?"

"That's the plan," he replied. "Mom says you'll be in by noon, so I'll be there. Listen, you better go see if she needs any help with the arrangements. Just do us a favor and try not to deck anybody on the train—okay?"

"I'll try . . ." she said playfully. "Love you, Daddy."

"Love you, too, pun'kin. I'll see you at twelve. Have a safe trip." Dave heard a click as the call disconnected; then he hung up the phone, exhaled sharply, and slumped back in his seat.

Dave reached inside his shirt to pull out a thin gold chain he'd taken to wearing for the last couple of months, even though he wasn't a jewelry sort of person; at the end of it dangled a gold wedding band. Nine months later and he still couldn't part with it.

"Never gets any easier, does it, K?" he muttered. "But things sure were a hell of a lot better when we were together . . ."

A knock at the door stopped him from sinking into an even deeper funk. Tim popped his head into the room. "Everything okay, Dave?"

"Yeah. Couldn't be better." He shoved the ring back under his shirt and forced a tight smile. "Pan's coming to stay with me for a while. Kinda short notice."

"But, that's a good thing, right?" Tim asked as he entered the office. "I mean, you haven't seen her since . . . when was that?"

Dave thought about it for a couple of seconds. "Her Sweet Sixteen." He grunted. "Almost two months ago. God . . . seems like forever."

Tim nodded sympathetically, then jerked a thumb over his shoulder in the direction of the museum proper. "So, we gonna open that thing . . . or do you wanna wait till Pan gets here?"

A Cheshire-cat smile crept onto Dave's features, and he sprang to his feet. "Hey, that's a *great* idea, Tim! We can leave it for after she gets here, and make it a surprise for her—like Halloween and Christmas, all smushed together!"

Tim chuckled. "Yeah. Hey, what Goth chick *wouldn't* want her very own monster?"

12

What Goth chick wouldn't want her very own monster? Well, Pan for one—monsters she already had in abundance; if anything, she could have done with a lot less of them. Unfortunately, standing on the platform of the Albany-Rensselaer Amtrak station as she was, surrounded by gooey-faced weekend travelers, insect-headed baggage handlers, and mutant children, it was pretty clear a reduction in the monster population wasn't about to happen anytime soon—certainly not with a three-hour railway trip ahead of her. And yet she stood her ground, refusing to let them get to her, although it was taking every bit of courage she had to not repeat her spaz-out in the mall. The real challenge, though, was in boarding a train that, to her heightened eyesight, would look like the Transylvanian Express.

The sunglasses she was wearing helped, coupled as they were with a weather-beaten, black New York Mets baseball cap, its frayed-edge visor pulled down low to rest on the thin metal frames. With that much artificial shade, it was almost impossible to see her sleep-deprived, bloodshot eyes.

Almost—but not entirely.

She swallowed nervously. As much as she hated her meds because of how woolly-headed and uncoordinated they often made her feel, right now she felt the overwhelming need for a bit of medicinal support . . .

No, she decided with a firm shake of her head. *I'm not going back.* She'd been off her meds for months, she'd been handling her problem just fine without them (except for the ghost images at the corners of her vision—and those were only annoying, not scary), and if it hadn't been for Electro, the Teen-Shocking Security Guard, she'd never have suffered that stupid relapse. In a big public setting. Right in front of Nikki Van Schrik.

Still would've punched her in the face, though . . .

Thank goodness that highbrow troll didn't know anything about her mental misadventures. If she did it wouldn't take long for the Tale of the Madwoman of Schriksdork to get around town, and then Pan wouldn't be able to set foot outside the house without being treated like a complete pariah.

Well, *more* of a complete pariah than she was right now . . .

As for riding the Ghoul Train, the trick was in not letting her fellow passengers know she was aware of what they really were during this latest psychosode. That perception would level off, of course, once her brain finally unscrambled itself and the monstervision faded; it always did. Although, she had to admit with some concern, this particular episode was taking a lot longer to reach its conclusion than normal. Her previous psychosodes usually lasted either a few minutes or a few hours, depending on her level of stress; this one had passed the twenty-hour mark by the time she and Mom had left the house for the station, and showed no signs of ending.

Maybe just *one* pill? Just to calm her nerves?

I am not *going back on the meds. I can get through this—it's just gonna take a little more time. Besides, you dope,* she added with a tiny, smug grin, *you left all of them in your room, remember? Too late to get them now, with the train coming.*

Standing beside her, Karen tilted her head down to speak quietly into her daughter's ear. "How you holding up, sweetie?"

"Oh, you know." Pan flashed a lopsided—and incredibly forced—grin. "Couldn't be better."

Karen quietly studied her for a moment, no doubt taking note of Pan's fidgeting and the way she kept glancing at the people around them. She gently swept back a lock of hair that had crept out from beneath the baseball cap, and tucked it behind Pan's ear. "Maybe this wasn't such a good idea . . ."

"I'll be fine, Mom. Really."

"I know," Karen agreed, although she didn't sound all that certain.

Pan lowered her sunglasses just enough so she could peer over the top of the frames. She regarded her mother's worried expression. "The question is, will *you*?"

A comforting smile lit Karen's features; even the soft glow that Pan could still see around her brightened considerably. She draped an arm over her daughter's shoulders and hugged her. "I'll be fine, too. It's just another bump in the twisty-turny road called parenting. Happens all the time." She flashed a steely glare at Pan. "Some roads are just twistier and . . . *bumpier* than others."

"I'm sure I have no idea what you're talking about," Pan said dryly.

Karen sniffed dismissively. "Anyway, I'm certain Mrs. Van Schrik and I can work something out. She seems like a reasonable person . . . once you get past the screaming and the death threats."

The throaty roar of a train whistle in the distance signaled the approach of the Amtrak local to New York. Pan noticed the worried look creeping back into Karen's eyes as she gazed down the tracks toward the Adirondack. Deep frown lines marred her beautiful features as she seemed to look right through the train and past the horizon toward—what?

"Mom? Maybe I should stay. You know—in case you need backup."

Karen's gaze slowly turned back to her, the thousand-yard stare still in effect until worry eventually gave way to amusement as Pan's words sank in. "Oh, I think I can handle one outraged mother by myself. I survived that encounter with Mrs. Seo after your other fight, didn't I?"

"Yeah, but she only put down the rolling pin after you offered to pay for Becca's glasses."

"Well, at least Mrs. Van Schrik isn't a restaurant chef." The whistle roared again as the train reached the platform. Karen pointed an index finger at her only child. "You, on the other hand, need to be on that train. Your father's expecting you, and now that I've had time to think about it . . . well, maybe it's not such a bad thing for you to spend some time with him."

Pan's eyebrows rose in disbelief. What exactly had her parents been discussing this morning before Dad talked to her? Maybe they were having second thoughts about the divorce? Mom was still wearing her wedding ring, after all. Dad, too, probably; he had been the last time she'd seen him. And if there was a chance her parents might get back together, maybe a trip to New York wasn't such a bad idea—just to keep the wheels greased on Dad's end.

Yeah, Pan concluded, *I could do that . . .*

The train crawled into the station, and the waiting travelers flowed around Pan and Karen toward the edge of the platform.

Pan flashed a weary smile. "Time to go, huh?"

"Yeah," Karen replied, a trifle hoarsely. She reached out to pull her child into a heavy-duty hug, which Pan returned in kind. Then Mom abruptly stiffened. "Oh, I almost forgot!" She stepped back and reached into her handbag, from which she extracted a small parcel: a black plastic bag wrapped around something thick and soft. She handed it to Pan. "I picked it up last week at that café you're always dragging me into at the megamall."

Pan's eyes sparkled as she spotted a corporate logo printed on the bag: a cartoon drawing of a bright-red demon slurping down a steaming cup of coffee. "Latte's Inferno? Sweet!" Like Starbucks, it was an international chain of coffeehouses, only the Inferno catered to an edgier sort of clientele—although considering the sparse Goth community of Albany and its neighboring counties that clientele usually consisted of Pan and the occasional wannabe who'd wandered in from the Hot Topic three doors down. But at least the baristas were friendly enough.

"I know I shouldn't be rewarding you after that trouble yesterday, but . . ." Karen shrugged. "What can I say? I'm just a softie."

Pan unfolded the bag and pulled out the gift it contained: a black T-shirt emblazoned with a cartoon drawing of the dark-haired head of a devil-girl—Latte's rebellious daughter, Lilitu. Her angry glare, bruised right cheek, and Band-Aid-covered nose gave the impression she had just come from a brawl at the T-shirt factory—and was daring any and all takers for a second round. The fact she was defiantly sticking out her tongue was proof of that. It was a shirt that practically screamed attitude.

"A My Lil' Hellion shirt?" Pan glanced at her mother. "So . . . what're you trying to say with this, Mom?" she asked wryly.

"I'm sure I have no idea what you're talking about," Karen replied.

"Uh-huh," Pan said. "Well, I love it anyway, hidden message and all."

Mom nodded toward the bag. "There's something else in there, too."

"Oooo, another present?" Pan asked with a grin. She reached in and hit a hard plastic object—two of them, in fact, both round and cylindrical. And they rattled. Her lips immediately twisted into a frown.

She peeked in and found two light-orange bottles with big white screw-on caps; wrapped around the bottles were equally large labels with her name printed on them—along with recommended dosages.

Her meds.

Pan sighed.

"You were so busy packing for the trip I guess you forgot to include these, too, huh?" Mom said with a knowing smile. "Good thing I remembered."

"Yeah," Pan grumbled. "Thanks."

"Honey, you know you have to take them if you're going to get better."

Pan forced a smile. "Yeah, I know . . ." It wasn't entirely true, though, and they both knew it. The meds were more a stopgap measure, a way of grounding Pan when her psychosodes became overwhelming; of calming her down when she feared she was losing control. But a decade of psychotherapy had taught her one simple truth: Colds and flu you could "get better" from. Monstervision was forever.

"Besides, we had a deal, remember? You take your pills on time, and I keep my supertalented artist in paints and canvases." She hesitated. "You *have* been taking them on time, haven't you?"

On any other day, the lie would have slithered past her lips without hesitation: *Of course I have, Mom. Duuh. What do you think?* But today she found it difficult to be glib about the situation. "Well . . ." she muttered, and let her voice trail off. She didn't need to say more.

Mom nodded; she'd been expecting that answer. "Well, since I've been keeping up my end of the bargain, I'd appreciate it if you'd honor your commitment to your poor harried mother and take them this time. Please? Medicine doesn't come cheap, you know."

"Okay," Pan replied, ignoring the momentary pang of guilt she felt from breaking their deal. This new lie came a tiny bit easier, because how would Mom ever know if she wasn't taking them? She'd be up here, while her daughter was all the way down in the City.

Unless, of course, Mom had mentioned her suspicions to Dad when they spoke this morning. That would totally suck, because it meant he'd be on Panda-bear watch. She'd have to figure out a way to get around that . . .

"All aboard!" yelled the conductor from a set of doors in the next-to-last car. "Next stop: Hudson!"

Karen grabbed the handle of Pan's rolling suitcase and began pulling it toward the train. "You have your cell phone?"

Pan patted the right front pocket of her jeans as she kept pace. "Got it right here—like always." She pointed to the suitcase. "And the charger's in there. I'll give you a call after Dad picks me up."

"Okay. Oh, and please, please don't spend the entire trip talking to Sheena, okay? I can't afford all the roaming charges I'll get hit with if you girls start yammering away. You'll have plenty of time to talk when you see her."

Pan grinned mischievously. "How about texting?"

Karen grunted. "Same difference. Save the phone for important calls; try reading a book. Or do some sketches to pass the time—you haven't touched a canvas in weeks. Maybe you'll get some inspiration from the trip."

"Yeah. Maybe." *Although you sure didn't like what I was sketching the last time I had a major psychosode . . .* Pan thought wryly. She did her best to avoid staring at the briefcase-wielding monstrosity that pushed past her. Thankfully, all that Axe bodyspray he'd hosed himself with cancelled out the eye-stinging, odorous vapor trail he left behind . . . a little.

They hugged one last time as Pan stood inside the doors. "Love you, Mom," she murmured.

Karen kissed her on the cheek. "Love you, too . . . Panda-bear." With a mischievous grin, she hopped back, and the doors slid closed before Pan had a chance to warn her again about using that childhood nickname. As the train pulled out Mom cupped both hands around her mouth and yelled, "And stay out of trouble! I mean it!"

An impish smile tugged at Pan's lips as she waved good-bye. "You, too, Mom," she replied softly. "You, too . . ."

She turned from the doors to look around the crowded car for a seat. The Montreal to New York City–bound Adirondack was normally packed on weekends, and this time was no exception. Luckily, though, she spotted an empty aisle seat at the back and made straight for it—only to come to a dead halt when she realized who was occupying the window seat.

The Axe Man looked up from his copy of the *Albany Democrat-Herald* and flashed a quiet, gooey smile at her. In what appeared to be a chivalrous gesture he yanked his briefcase off the seat and placed it on the floor, then motioned for her to sit. The sweep of his hand sent a wave of putrefaction rushing up her nostrils.

With a deep sigh, Pan stored her suitcase in the overhead luggage rack, plopped down in the available seat, jammed in her iPod's earbuds—and wondered how long she could hold her breath before she passed out from the smell.

13

"Despierta, dormilóna," a gruff female voice whispered in Annie's ear.

Annie groaned, then buried her face in the pillow and rolled over on the army-issue cot. "Five more minutes," she muttered.

"No, that's what you said a hour ago. I let you slide then 'cause I had a bunch'a *touristas* from North Dakota buying stuff, but naptime's over. Now get up." A thick finger prodded Annie in the left bicep for a few seconds, but when that did no better in rousing the huntress than the verbal commands had, the entire hand came sweeping down—to loudly smack against Annie's denim-covered behind.

That got her up, all right.

"Ayy!" she yelped. Rubbing her sore rear end, she sat up on the cot and looked at her attacker. "What'd you do that for, Izzy?"

"'Cause you don't wanna get up, that's why!" Isadora Maldonado snapped, her *Boricua* accent heavily tinged with New York attitude.

"What time is it?" Annie asked around a sizable yawn.

"Five to twelve. You wanna grab some lunch?"

Annie started. *"Twelve noon*? Oh, my God. How long was I sleeping?"

"'Bout two or three hours. You looked like you could use it." Izzy jerked a thumb over her shoulder, in the direction of the floral-pattern curtains that served as a makeshift door for the storage room in which the two women were arguing. "But now I got my grandson Javier stopping by. He's a young boy, you know, with all those hormones running through him at his age, and I don't need him getting impure thoughts from staring at your *culo* while you're counting sheep." She tilted her head to one side and studied Annie's backside. "I mean, that could be, like, a all-day project . . ."

"You're saying *I've* got a big ass?" Annie snorted. "Pot, meet kettle . . ."

Izzy proudly drew herself up to her full five-foot-four-inch height and turned a hip to display her sizable rump, which was accentuated by the white summer dress she wore. Even at the age of sixty-two, with hair more silver than black and a lifetime of hard work etched on her features, Isadora Maldonado could still turn a head or two. "Sure I got a big ass—but at least I still know how to put it to work!" She playfully swayed her hips, which got a chuckle from Annie. "You used to, too, you know."

A weary smile pulled at the corners of Annie's mouth as she tugged on her running shoes. "Those were the days, huh?" she asked. "You and me, a couple of hippie chicks driving around in a Volkswagen minibus, following the Grateful Dead from city to city, the country caught up in that whole Summer of Love. And then there was Monterey and Woodstock, and all those concerts we went to in the seventies, and . . . and then . . ." Her voice trailed off as she realized where her comment had been going. Embarrassed, she turned away to stare at her feet.

Izzy seemed to realize it, too. With a gentle touch she took hold of Annie's chin and raised her head. "And then I started gettin' old," she said warmly. "You can say it, Annie—I don't mind." She chuckled. "After forty years I'm kinda used to it by now—you know?"

Annie opened her mouth to speak, but couldn't think of what to say. What *could* she say? Izzy spoke the truth—the 1960s and early '70s were a pleasant memory, to be sure, but for her that all happened over four decades ago. For Annie, who'd been alive for ten times that number of years, it was almost a blink of the eye.

"Um . . . yeah . . ." she muttered. "Well, anyway, I, uh . . . I would've gotten up . . . eventually," she remarked, quickly changing the subject, and patted the cot. "It's just that this was the first really peaceful sleep I've had in . . ." She paused for a moment, then shrugged. "I don't know how long."

Izzy, bless her, wasn't going to press the issue about Annie's evasiveness. She understood. Instead she grunted and said, "No wonder, with all that running around you do every night. When was the last time you went to the movies, or one'a those Broadway shows? You used to love going to those!"

Annie nodded wearily. "I know. It's just that—"

"Or on a date!" Izzy interjected. "I ain't seen you with a man in a dog's age!" She flashed a knowing grin. "No wonder you're all wound up tighter'n a watch spring."

"Izzy!" Annie exclaimed. She turned to look away as the blush of embarrassment warmed her cheeks. Her friend probably wasn't too far off the mark, now that she thought about it . . .

"You know it's true," Izzy said softly as she led the way through the curtains.

"Maybe. But what can I do, Izzy? It's not like I can just take a month off and hope somebody else will handle the mess. There *is* nobody else!"

Izzy grunted and waved her left hand dismissively, causing the dozen thin metal bracelets that encircled her wrist to ring like wind chimes. "That's just your ego talking, o high an' mighty La Bella Tenebrosa. 'Course there is. What about the Knights? You're always helping them out; let them pick up the slack for a change."

Annie shrugged, reluctant to admit that Izzy was right. "Well, sure, they could help out, but they've got more important things to do than hunt goblins in junkyards."

"*One* date," Izzy snapped, holding up a meaty index finger for emphasis. "It ain't gonna kill you." The finger whipped downward to point at a large, squarish lump under the left side of Annie's plain black T-shirt. "But *that* kinda crap sure as hell will."

Annie lifted the hem of her shirt and gingerly touched the gauze dressing that was taped over the stab wound she'd received the night before. The skin beneath was still tender and inflamed, but with Izzy's careful ministrations the wound had finally closed. Annie's advanced healing factor would take it from there.

The monster hunter smiled. "Hasn't killed me so far," she quipped. "I mean, it's not the first stab wound you've treated, right?"

"Ha!" Izzy snapped. "That's not what I was hearing when you woke me up in the middle of last night!" She loudly clasped her hands together and twisted her face into a comically pained expression. " 'Oh, Izzy, I got stabbed and the cut won't close! I'm bleeding all over!' " She pressed the back of her left hand against her forehead and pretended to swoon. " 'Oh, I think I'm gonna pass out! What am I gonna do? I don't wanna diiiiie!' "

"I did *not* sound like that!" Annie said, exasperated. She nervously chewed her bottom lip as she tried to remember the phone conversation. Had she really sounded that frantic over such a minor injury?

Well, maybe a little . . .

"Regular little drama queen," Izzy commented. She folded her arms across her chest and glared at her friend. "And no, that ain't the first stab wound I fixed on you—but keep running into enchanted blades like you did last night and we'll see how funny you think this is."

"Is that what it was? No *wonder* the damn cut didn't close!"

"Yeah, magick people getting shanked with magick knives—never a good thing when you're the one on the receiving end of it. You just lucky I made some new comfrey poultices the other day that can treat that kinda crap."

At the mention of the herbal curative, Annie gazed around the tiny botanica that had been Izzy's alternative medicine store for the past fifteen years. There was no sign above the front door to identify this establishment, only a window filled with religious paraphernalia—statues of the Virgin Mary, Buddha, the Pope, and a multitude of saints (and, for some reason, Gandalf from *The Lord of the Rings*); tall red, yellow, and green candles in cylindrical glass holders decorated with portraits of the baby Jesus, the Archangel Michael, and other icons—and yet people from all five of New York's boroughs, and beyond, knew exactly where to find Izzy's West Thirty-sixth Street hierberia. Its floor-to-ceiling shelves were stocked with all manner of potions and herbal remedies—most concocted by Izzy herself—as well as the individual ingredients for customers to make their own. Whether they suffered from broken bones or broken hearts, there was something for everyone to be found here, and that included those patrons who believed in more spiritual means to cure their ailments. Catholicism, Buddhism, santeria, espiritismo—if the religion existed, Izzy probably had an oil, an amulet, or a charm that would be perfect for the dutiful, yet budget-conscious, worshipper.

She also knew her magick inside and out, so if she said the knife was enchanted . . .

"Goblins with magick-enhanced knives," Annie muttered. "Great. Like they weren't dangerous enough already . . ."

"Just be glad he didn't know how to use it proper," Izzy replied. "If he'd got you in the heart"—she slapped the edge of a fist against her own chest—"you and me, we wouldn't be talking now."

Annie flashed a smile. "Well, thank you for the help, Isadora. I owe you— again."

"You wanna pay me back, take a night off." Izzy shook her head. "You been working yourself to death hunting monsters for what, five hundred years—"

"Four hundred." Annie wiggled a hand in a measuring gesture. "A little over."

"Whatever. If you don't slow down and rest, you're gonna die—and then how you gonna save the world?"

"Izzy . . ." Annie began.

"No! Either take a few days off, or I'm gonna slip something into your food that'll knock you out for a week!" Izzy slowly unveiled a blood-chilling grin. "You still like eating them pineapple cheesecakes?"

Annie grinned just as broadly—and far more threateningly. "You know, I don't just eat sweets . . ." she growled softly, and licked her chops.

Izzy stepped into a combat-ready position. "Oh, yeah? Well, bring it on, Hungry Hungry Hippo—I'll give you something to choke on . . ."

The ringing of the bell above the front door interrupted their trash talk, and into the shop walked a tall, handsome Puerto Rican youth decked out in blue jeans, spotlessly clean white Nikes, and a blue pin-striped replica of a New York Yankees white home jersey. His black hair was short and stylish, his face clean-shaven and acne free. As with most youngsters his age, the air around him fairly crackled with youthful energy; with her enhanced abilities Annie could literally see it flowing around him in coruscating, multicolored waves. For a sixteen-year-old, Javier Maldonado was growing into quite the man, she thought. From what Izzy had told her, he was becoming a regular heartthrob at his Bronx high school, although he had yet to set his sights on any particular girl. But both women knew *that* wouldn't last for very long . . .

"Hey, ladies," he said brightly as he turned off the hip-hop tune that was blasting through his cell phone's earbuds. A small yank of his fingers on the thin plastic cord and the buds popped out of his ears to drop onto his palm. He shoved them and the phone into one of his pants pockets.

"There's my boy!" Izzy said, and hurried over to envelop him with grandmotherly affection. He had to bend forward so she could wrap her arms around his neck to give him a hug.

"Hey, Javier," Annie said. She smiled as his cheeks reddened. He might have the looks of a lady-killer, but he could still be an awkward teen when it came to interacting with attractive older women. Like when he was being mauled by his grandmother in Annie's presence, or—*yup, there it was*— when he realized she was aware of the quick, sly glance he'd directed at her chest before he met her gaze. The look of shock and embarrassment on his face was just so damned cute she could never be upset with him. Besides, most boys were like that at his age. It was only when they grew into men and the furtive glances became prolonged stares that the ogling truly became a major annoyance.

Javi slipped free of Izzy's embrace and took his time smoothing out the wrinkles in his jersey. Trying to regain his composure, obviously, since he made it a point to avoid Annie's gaze. "So, what're you ladies up to? From outside it looked like you were gonna throw down."

"Oh, your grandmother was just trying to get me to take a vacation," Annie replied. "She thinks I work too much."

"And she, of course, wasn't listening," Izzy said huffily.

Annie shrugged. "Hey, why start now?" She grinned, then before Izzy could object, quickly added, "I'm kidding, Izzy. I really do appreciate the concern—you know I do—and I'll think about what you were saying. Okay?"

Izzy reached out to tenderly stroke her old friend's cheek. "Annie, you're gonna kill yourself if you don' get some rest. Take one night off—just one. I promise you, the city'll still be here tomorrow. Please."

"All right. One night." With a smile Annie wrapped her arms around Izzy's ample waist and pulled her into a tight hug. "Oh, Izzy," she cooed, "what would I ever do without you?"

"Probably pester one'a your kids into fixing your wounds," Izzy replied good-naturedly, returning the embrace. "But none'a them would put up with your crap."

Annie stepped back, then tilted her head to place a gentle kiss on her forehead. "And that's why you're my best friend."

"Because I *will* put up with your crap."

Annie grinned and winked at Javi. "Well, sure. Why else?" Laughing, she pirouetted out of Izzy's reach before she could land a playful punch, and reached behind the counter to retrieve her bag: a black Tumi T-Tech–brand Adventurer backpack—an otherwise expensive accessory if not for the wonders of New York's and New Jersey's outlet malls. Just because she acted like a modern-day Professor Van Helsing didn't mean she had to carry around an old medical bag.

She swung the backpack onto her right shoulder. "Say hi to the family for me," she called back as she headed for the door.

"I will," Izzy replied. "And you go find yerself a man!"

"*Yeessss,* Mother," Annie said dryly. With a cheery wave she exited the botanica.

Izzy's parting comment stuck in Annie's mind as she slipped on a pair of Christian Dior Aventura sunglasses and walked toward the corner of West Thirty-sixth Street and Eighth Avenue. As much as she hated to admit it, her old friend was absolutely right—it *had* been a dog's age since she'd been on a date, let alone experienced any sort of stable relationship.

Thankfully, any further introspection was interrupted by a familiar voice calling, "Hey, Annie, wait up!"

Javi came jogging down the sidewalk with all the long-legged grace he usually demonstrated on his high school's baseball team as a premiere base stealer. In one hand he clutched a small brown-paper bag.

"Izzy told me to give this to you," he explained, pointing to the grease-stained package. "It's another poultice. She said to swap out the one you got in a couple days and replace it with this." He held out the bag, which she accepted and dropped into her backpack. "So, why do you need poultices?" he asked, then quickly added, "I mean, if you don't mind me asking."

Annie shrugged. "It's for a wound Izzy fixed up." She glanced at the passersby streaming around them and added in a conspiratorial whisper, "I got stabbed by a goblin last night."

His eyebrows shot up. "For real?"

She nodded. "It happens, sometimes."

"So, was it, like, a magic knife or something?" Now it was *her* eyebrows' turn to do an upward crawl, above the frames of her sunglasses. Javi grinned. "Well, you being magic-based I figured it'd kinda make sense, being vulnerable to stuff that's got that same magic vibe. It's like Superman, y'know? The only thing that can kill him are chunks of his home planet."

"Kryptonite, right? Yeah, it's something like that." Annie smiled. "You're very perceptive, Javier."

"Oh, yeah? Maybe perceptive enough to take along the next time you go hunting?"

"Ahhh," Annie said knowingly, and chuckled. "The lure of adventure, is that it? Trust me, Javi—it's not all it's cracked up to be. You've got to stop listening to your grandma's wild stories."

Javi snorted. "You kidding? I been hearing her stories since I was four! Why would I want her to stop now?" He started ticking off points on his fingers. "There was—what? The wendigo in Canada, the gerjis in Malaysia, the Blatant Beast in England, the mani . . . mano . . . that graboid thing in New Mexico . . ."

"The manitoukinebic? She told you about that?" Annie grimaced. "Oh, God. The damn snake nearly swallowed *both* of us before stupid me remembered to detonate all that C4 Izzy tossed down its throat . . ." Her voice trailed off as she noticed the gleam of excitement in Javi's eyes. She was making her final hunt with her best friend sound way too enticing for an adventuresome teen. "But that's exactly why you *can't* go along with me," she quickly added. "The kind of work I do is just too danger—"

A familiar tingle suddenly prickled the frontal lobe of her brain, and she froze. Wouldn't you know it? she thought. Here she is, trying to discourage Javi from following in his grandmother's footsteps, and that's *just* the moment she has to get the warning sign of a supernatural presence in the area—and one nearing her location, given the growing strength of the sensation. It had started as a mild tingle, but now it felt as though a swarm of angry bees was buzzing in her sinuses—and she *really* hated bees.

Javi noticed her unease. "What? What's going on?"

The screams were all the answer he needed.

Just ahead of them the block-long New Yorker Hotel rose high above the pedestrian-congested sidewalk of West Thirty-fourth Street. Painted a brilliant white with blue trimming, the hotel was hard to miss among the cell-phone stores, fast-food eateries, and discount clothing shops that filled the area. It was also the only establishment that had a Sumatran orang pendek currently crashing outward through its front doors. Tourists and doormen, bellhops and cabdrivers alike dove for cover as shattered glass and broken metal rained down on the sidewalk.

The orang pendek wasn't very large, no more than five and a half feet tall, but it was as powerfully built as some of its larger primate relatives, which made it just as dangerous. Luckily, though, the creature seemed more concerned about hanging on to the large garbage bag its arms were wrapped around than in lashing out at the tourists who were now unwisely thrusting digital cameras and cell phones in its face to snap pictures. It howled with indignation.

Here is Kong, the Eighth Wonder of the World . . . Annie gazed with some sympathy at the primate. Flash photography and wild animals—never a good combination, in movies or real life. But some people just never learned until they had a limb torn off.

The creature was covered in short golden-brown fur from the top of its flat-topped head to its ankles, ending just above the strangely inverted feet that were a common trait among its kind—nature had provided this particular species with backward feet in order to confuse hunters tracking them. But what really made the animal so unique was that it shouldn't exist; like the goblins from the previous night, the orang pendek was a mythological creature. And corralling supernatural beasties was Annie's responsibility, no matter what Isadora said—even if the beastie in question, like this one, looked more frightened by the humans surrounding it than the humans were by it.

The primate quickly looked around, as though confused by its surroundings, but Annie knew what that frantic head turning truly meant—like her, it could sense the presence of other weirdlings. And when its gaze finally settled on her, its eyes widened in terror. With a high-pitched shriek, the orang pendek turned away and ran as fast as its reversed feet could take it.

Slipping the remaining backpack strap over her left shoulder, Annie smoothed down her T-shirt and exhaled sharply. "So much for a day off . . ."

"Oh, come on," Javi said. "How much trouble is a monkey with a garbage bag gonna cause?"

Her lips curled into a small, disapproving frown, Annie removed her sunglasses and glared silently at him.

"Yeah, okay," he finally admitted, and jerked his thumb in the direction of the botanica. "But Izzy ain't gonna like it."

"She won't like it only if you plan on telling her." Annie stared at the devilish smile Javi flashed at her in response. She knew what *that* expression meant; she used to see it all the time when his grandmother was her constant companion. The lure of adventure, the thrill of the hunt—sometimes its siren call was too powerful for certain individuals to ignore.

She held up a warning finger. "Okay—but just this once. And you better keep up."

And then she was charging after her prey, following as it ran hell-bent through congested midtown traffic, across Thirty-fourth Street and down Eighth Avenue, toward the Madison Square Garden sports arena—and the entrance to Pennsylvania Station.

Javi grinned and broke into a run. After all the stories his granny had told him about her best friend, after all the dangers the two women had faced, *he*, Javier Maldonado, was finally getting his own chance to chase monsters at the side of La Bella Tenebrosa.

Now all he had to do was ignore the impure thoughts that kept popping into his head as he allowed her shapely *culo* to lead him into potential danger. . . .

14

Never had a three-hour train trip passed so agonizingly slow, and that was entirely the fault of the Axe-drenched turd in the next seat. He didn't get off the train anywhere between Hudson and Croton-Harmon as Pan had hoped, and it didn't appear that the next stop, Yonkers, was his destination either—not from the noisy slumbering he was doing. No, it became clear he was going to ride all the way to New York City, and eventually it was Pan who had to leave, grabbing her suitcase from the luggage rack and abandoning her seat for the metal-floored landing between the Metroliner's cars. Not the safest or most comfortable place to sit, but here the air wasn't tinged with the stench of her former seatmate's body odor and there was room to spread out. As Pan knew from experience, the closer the train rolled toward Manhattan the more crowded it became, until it was standing room only for the final leg of the trip. And packed train cars meant increased levels of BO—and that was *before* you factored in Axe Man's unique scent (did that guy even *know* what a shower was?).

The other advantage to ditching the cattle car was that she now had the privacy to take off her sunglasses and put away her Mets cap—no monsters to hide from here—and make a couple of important cell-phone calls: one to Dad, just to make sure he'd be at Penn Station when she arrived; and one to Sheena to let her know the Sucktown exile had ended and there should be—make that better be—much rejoicing in the streets of Queens. Unfortunately, Sheen only grunted in response, being too busy having her throat nuzzled by her Germanic love toy, Uwe, while Pan was trying to have a conversation with her best friend.

Stupid Huey.

The remainder of the trip was spent doing pencil sketches in an art pad of the monsters she kept seeing—though (thankfully) with lessening frequency as the hours passed—while zoning out to an iPod filled with a week's worth of songs performed by Leander Faust and his goth-rock peers. Add to that one of Mom's chicken salad megasandwiches on pita bread and a couple of bottles of Diet Pepsi from the café car, and it wasn't such a bad way to pass the time. It would have been even better if she hadn't noticed El Stinko stealing glances at her through the window in the door after he'd woken up from his nap. Talk about creepy . . .

"Next stop: Pennsylvania Station, New York City," the conductor's voice blared through the speakers mounted inside the cars. "Please remain in your seats until the train comes to a complete stop at the platform."

Of course, that sort of command always had the opposite effect on travelers, so it was no surprise when passengers in the cars on both sides of her started heading for the landing. And somewhere in the middle of the pack was her gross seatmate. Pan caught a glimpse of him openly staring at her as he tried to force his way down the crowded aisle. This was seriously starting to freak her out—was the guy some kind of perv?

She didn't wait around to find out. As soon as the train came to a halt and the doors opened she jumped off and bolted toward the end of the platform, then ducked behind one of the concrete pillars that supported the ceiling. Cautiously, she poked her head out to look back. As she suspected, her odious admirer was gazing around, searching the crowd for a sign of his elusive quarry. When it became apparent that he'd lost her, his shoulders slumped in defeat and he joined the rest of the passengers in riding the escalators up to the lobby of the Amtrak terminal.

Exhaling sharply with relief, Pan slid back into hiding and checked her cell phone—unfortunately, being this far underground meant no signal, so calling Dad about her situation was impossible. But according to the phone's clock the train had arrived fifteen minutes early, so odds were good he wasn't even in the station yet. She chewed on her lower lip while planning her next move, then decided to wait a few minutes before going upstairs. That should give her creepy stalker time enough to leave . . . unless, of course, he hung around to see if she was still in the area.

Well, one thing at a time, she thought. *Kill some time first, then see what happens.* Satisfied with that course of action, she reached for her iPod's earbuds, which hung around her neck. A couple of Sarkophagia tunes would help make the time go faster while she waited . . .

She never got to listen to them, though, because just as she untangled the earbud cord, a flat-headed monkey dropped from the roof of the last train car and landed on the platform about twenty feet in front of her.

A monkey holding a garbage bag.

It was really sort of beautiful—the monkey, not the trash bag—once you got past the scared look on its face. Golden-brown fur, gold-flecked eyes . . . the backward feet were kind of strange, but after what Pan had been seeing in the past twenty-plus hours they barely fazed her. The garbage bag, however . . . well, she couldn't even begin to figure that one out. Maybe it couldn't afford luggage.

It stared right at her, and Pan smiled warmly and slowly raised her hands to show she was no threat. "Hey, it's okay," she said in a calm, soothing voice. The last thing she wanted was to say or do anything it might interpret as a threat—those long monkey arms could probably rip her in half.

With a look of pure terror lighting its eyes, the monkey hugged the bag tightly to its body and shrieked at Pan, then leaped away. A little bug-eyed with shock and a lot frightened by that hair-raising shriek, Pan could only watch, slack-jawed, as the trash monkey somersaulted off the next platform and then bounded down the tracks toward the darkness of the train-tunnel system.

"Well . . . *damn,*" Pan whispered hoarsely when she finally found her voice.

The approaching sound of sneakers slapping concrete a few moments later yanked her thoughts back to her own current problem—namely, the smelly perv she was trying to avoid. Had he come back downstairs to search the platform, heard her yelling, and was even now racing toward her hiding spot? She snarled, and balled her hands into tight fists. If this creep thought he was going to find some scared little girl cowering against a pillar, he . . . well, he should've gotten here a minute earlier. Now, she'd beat the stink off of him.

The footsteps thudded loudly from around the pillar. Bellowing a loud war cry, Pan leaped out to confront her stalker . . . and then froze in midscream.

It wasn't the walking turd—not unless he had the ability to morph from a balding middle-aged slimeball into a dark-haired teenage stud. And that would be totally gross.

He stood close to six feet tall and was kind of wiry, but in a muscular way; he looked like an athlete, maybe on a high school track-and-field or baseball team. The latter probably, she decided, given that detestable Yankees jersey he was wearing, but considering his chiseled good looks she was willing to overlook his poor taste. For now. And in spite of his serious character flaw, she was grateful that the monstervision didn't present him as an escapee from Hell. He looked totally normal. And totally hot.

"Uh . . . hey," he said, looking both surprised and confused by her sudden appearance. He had *great* eyes . . .

"Hey," she croaked.

"Umm . . . Are you, like, looking for a fight?" God, he even *sounded* good-looking . . .

She started—"Huh?"—and then realized she was still in a combat-ready stance, fists raised to deal out some major stink-beating. "Oh," she muttered, and dropped her hands. "Sorry. Thought you were somebody else."

His mouth slowly formed a *very* pleasing, kinda sexy smile. "Well, then, I'm glad I'm not whoever it is that's gonna get their ass kicked." He put out his hand. "I'm Javi. And *you* are . . . ?"

"Oh!" She cleared her throat. "Uh . . . Pan. I'm Pan." His palm was warm and a little calloused when she took it, his grip firm and confident. No weak-wristed greeting here—this was a man's handshake. Was she grinning like an idiot? She couldn't tell, but he seemed to like her reaction just fine. Which was the reason it took the greatest of efforts to release his hand.

His gaze swept across the platform, then out toward the tunnels. "You didn't happen to see a—"

"A monkey with a garbage bag? Kinda hard to miss."

"Yeah, me and my friend Annie were chasing it, and we got separated." He shook his head. "That thing is *fast*, man."

The grin fractured. "Annie? Is she, like, your girlfriend?"

Javi snorted a laugh. "Hells, no! She's one'a my grandma's friends. I'm just helping her out."

One of his grandmother's friends? That meant she was probably a senior citizen. Excellent! The broken grin instantly healed.

"Look, I better get after her," Javi said. "Annie has this habit of getting into all kinds'a trouble, and I'm like—"

"Robin to her Batman?"

The dazzling smile he flashed made her heart do a tiny pirouette. "You into comics?"

"Uh-huh," she managed to gasp.

"Sweet. Me, too." He started to move down the platform in the monkey's direction, then turned around and walked backward while he continued speaking. "Hey—maybe I'll see you around, okay?"

"Umm . . . Okay. Yeah! That'd be great!" she squeaked.

And then he was gone, racing down the tunnel in pursuit of the trash monkey.

Pan leaned against the support pillar and blew out a breath. It'd been such a long time since a boy her own age had looked at her with anything but scorn that she'd almost forgotten what it felt like to be appreciated by one. Or how to properly react to it without getting all tongue-tied and blushy. But the quickening of her pulse, the sudden inability to catch her breath, and the prickling of gooseflesh along her arms all reminded her of what that old sensation was like—and could be again, if she was willing to listen to her heart.

And yet, in spite of her hopes, her old fears also resurfaced and she couldn't help but wonder if he was just being polite when they spoke, that he wasn't truly interested in her. Maybe she'd been too afraid of what she might find to look past that bewitching smile—insincerity, maybe, or even worse: pity.

Besides, she thought, *Javi's probably already got a girlfriend, who's pretty and sexy and tall and . . . and a Yankees fan, too. A guy like him's probably got six girlfriends, one for every day of the week with rotating schedules for Sundays. I mean, just look at him! Somebody that hot doesn't want some gawky midget vampire chick hanging around. That'd be crazy . . . right?*

. . .

Please don't let it be crazy . . .

Logic dictated that she head right up the escalator to the waiting area and see if her dad was there, and forget all about trash monkeys and teen hotties; she already had enough complications in her life to last the whole summer. But then she thought about the scared-but-aggressive expression on the creature's face, and that cute/sexy smile Javi had flashed her, and Pan just *knew* she couldn't simply walk away and pretend none of this happened. Besides, she wouldn't be able to live with herself if Javi wound up getting torn apart over a bag of garbage while she stood around, doing nothing.

She shrugged. "Well, I wanted to kill some time, right?" she asked the empty platform. Then she picked up her suitcase and hurried off after the handsome monkey hunter.

The fact he was a total stud had *absolutely* nothing to do with her interest in the matter.

. . .

All right, maybe a little . . .

A few hundred yards ahead of Pan, Javi slowed his high-speed charge to a cautious walk, creeping from one pool of shadow to the next as he moved between the weakly glowing work lights strung along both sides of the tunnel. He paused to check his surroundings. Even with the stench of human and animal wastes that mixed with the odors of diesel fuel and rotting garbage in this confined space he easily picked up the scent of the orang pendek—Annie had told him it would be a citrusy tang made even more distinctive by the flood of sweat generated by its mounting fear. She hadn't been kidding; it smelled like an orange juice factory had exploded down here.

He realized, of course, that being on his own wasn't the smartest decision he could have made. He wasn't a professional hunter—hell, he'd never been trained for it! Annie and Isadora always tried to discourage him from joining the legendary La

Bella Tenebrosa in her battles against the creatures of the night, and had refused to teach him even basic monster-fighting skills, so all he possessed were a head full of his grandmother's tales of epic derring-do and a burning desire to have some adventures of his own. But honestly, whom was he trying to impress with this recklessness? Grandma Izzy? She'd tear his head off if she ever found out he was doing something this stupid. Annie? Amateurs who willingly placed themselves in harm's way—like he was doing right now—never impressed her. They only pissed her off.

That cute Goth chick, Pan, back on the platform?

Yeah, he had to admit, that probably had a lot to do with it. She had a really great smile, and those eyes of hers—

A can rattled against the tracks a few yards ahead, the sound almost lost amid the rumble of another Amtrak train passing through a nearby tunnel. Javi froze.

"Annie?" he whispered hoarsely, but a flash of golden-brown fur in the dim lighting indicated it wasn't his friend.

He crept forward and halted at the base of a metal staircase; a rusty, grime-encrusted sign on the wall beside it identified the steps as an emergency exit to the street. Javi frowned. It was really dark at the top of the stairs; for all he knew, the thing could be waiting for him up there.

"Aw, hell, it's just a monkey with a garbage bag . . ." he muttered, and started his ascent—

—to go reeling back as a dark figure leaped down at him from the shadow-draped landing above. The monster's ear-piercing screech was only slightly higher in pitch than the startled cry Javi let out in surprise.

The orang pendek's backward heels plowed into his chest, driving the breath from his lungs and catapulting him off the steps, into the air. The back of Javi's head struck a wooden railroad tie, and he collapsed in a heap across the tracks.

He never saw the creature land beside him and pick up a discarded steel bar—nor heard its victorious scream as it prepared to crush his skull.

15

Just up the tunnel, Pan was beginning to have second (and third, and fourth) thoughts about wandering around an active train yard in pursuit of a boy chasing a monkey. It wasn't her business, after all, and who was to say the monkey wouldn't get all homicidal with her if they crossed paths again?

She knew why she wouldn't turn back, though: she wanted to see Javi's sexy smile directed at her again. The rest of him wasn't bad to look at, either. *I'm pretty sure this isn't what Sheen had in mind when she said I needed to find a new boyfriend—*she mentally shrugged—*but what the hell.*

She struggled to drag her roller suitcase along the track bed, but the bag kept wobbling as the tiny wheels on its base snagged on the wooden ties, bounced off mounds of garbage, and slid through sticky puddles of glop that smelled like pee and rancid hot sauce. Or were those monkey droppings?

And just think, she ruminated with a deep frown, *yesterday in Sucktown I was actually missing all this . . .*

A scream delivered in two-part harmony suddenly echoed off the walls from just around the curve in the tunnel, and Pan froze. A couple of seconds later it was followed by the sound of something heavy crashing to the ground. Like, *human body* heavy.

Pan swallowed hard and pressed against the wall, hoping the combination of the tunnel's dim lighting and her black apparel made her close to invisible. It was pretty clear that one of two things had just happened: either Javi had caught the trash monkey . . . or it had found him first. Probably the latter, if the victory screech that now pounded her eardrums was any indication; she doubted Javi had that kind of vocal range. In which case, maybe it was time to head upstairs and see where Dad was—he'd get really pissed if she went and got herself killed, too . . .

And yet, if she had now made the decision to retreat, why then were her feet still moving forward?

Because I'm an idiot, that's why—and I should know better. I must've watched hundreds of slasher movies where girls are always doing something stupid, like walking into dark tunnels or basements and getting their heads chopped off 'cause they were just asking for it . . . but here I am, doing the same thing anyway. Over a Yankees fan. She grinned. *Sheen's gonna be* so *jealous when I tell her about this . . .*

Taking a deep breath to steady her nerves, she stepped onto the track bed and walked around the bend. The creature immediately looked up; even in the low lighting Pan could see the steel bar it held. Javi was lying motionless across the tracks; from this distance it was impossible to tell if he was breathing.

"Javi?" she called. "Are . . . are you okay?"

Nothing. Pan felt her heart in her throat. He couldn't be dead, could he?

Thankfully, no. Just as she started to give up hope, Javi groaned softly, muttered something unintelligible, and drifted back into unconsciousness. But his response caused the monkey to turn its attention back to the boy. It raised the improvised weapon and prepared to deliver its deathblow.

Pan jumped forward. "No, *wait!*"

The monkey spun in her direction. And snarled.

She slowly held out her hands and began speaking in a gentle tone. "Hey, there, fella. Remember me—back on the platform? You know—the one not chasing after you?"

The trash monkey glanced at her, then Javi, then back to her. Its low growl made the hairs on the back of Pan's neck stand on end . . . yet she continued to move forward. The animal watched her advance.

"Now look, you're absolutely right," she agreed. "It was totally wrong of people to go chasing you for stealing garbage, but just because Javi was trying to catch you is no reason to beat his brains out. You know—that whole 'two wrongs don't make a right' thing. Right?"

The monkey paused, but Pan couldn't tell if that was because her argument was making sense to it, or because the calming tone she was using was having a positive effect. Either way, she noticed some of the fire dwindling in the creature's eyes as she drew nearer, and then breathed a tiny sigh of relief as it lowered the bar.

Pan smiled encouragingly and reached for the weapon. "That's it," she cooed. "We're all friends here. No reason for anybody to get hurt, right?"

The tension in the monkey's body seemed to drain away and it opened its palm, offering the rebar to Pan.

And that was when Javi's missing partner had to go and ruin the moment by yelling, *"What the hell is going on?"*

Pan turned to face the speaker . . . and then quickly had to turn away or risk going blind. "Gah!" she yelped.

To her supersensitive eyes the woman was lit up like the sun, a thousand times—maybe even a million times—brighter than the glow Pan had seen around her mom; so bright it hurt to look directly at her. She scrambled through her jacket pockets for her sunglasses and hurriedly slipped them on. That only cut the brilliance to a hundred times brighter, but at least now she could look at the woman without her retinas burning out.

She was amazingly beautiful—how could anybody generate that much light and *not* turn out to look like some runway model?—in her midthirties and wore tight blue jeans, a black T-shirt, and scuffed-up running shoes; when she strode down the tunnel, it was with the grace of a ballerina. A thick mane of jet-black hair cascaded around her shoulders and flowed down to her waist. Her skin was the color of light caramel, which offset the brilliance of her hazel eyes. Seeing her, Pan couldn't help but feel like the world's plainest, most awkward girl.

Was *this* Annie? Javi's grandma's senior-citizen friend? If so, it meant either there was a cosmetic surgeon out there who could work miracles with facelifts and implants and Botox, or a mad scientist who knew how to transplant old-lady brains into supermodel bodies. Or maybe she was an android . . .

The creature shrieked at the newcomer, clearly spoiling for a fight. Pan, however, wasn't interested in being caught in the middle of a fight to the death. Before the primate could close its paw, she snatched the bar away and held it behind her back.

"No," she said sternly.

It snarled at her, no doubt annoyed that she'd confiscated its toy. Pan took a step back.

"I said, *no*." Did her voice sound firm enough? She hoped so.

Annie stepped in front of her. "You better listen to her," she ordered the creature. "You're in enough trouble as it is."

The monkey's shoulders drooped in defeat.

"What's it doing down here, anyway?" Pan asked.

"Hiding from me," Annie said without turning around. "Before that, it was foraging. But orang pendeks are supposed to do that only late at night, so they don't scare anyone." The trash monkey screeched at her in response. "Oh, blah blah blah!" she snapped. "You know the rules, and you broke them! Don't start making excuses!"

Pan started. "Excuses? You mean you can actually understand what that thing is saying?"

"Well, of course I—" Annie began to reply. Then she looked over her shoulder at the girl. "Excuse me, but . . . who *are* you? And what's with the sunglasses?"

"Her name's Pan, Annie," came a weak reply from down by their feet. Javi moaned, grabbed the top of his skull with both hands, and slowly sat up. "I don't know nothing about the shades." He gazed at her in confusion. "Why *are* you wearing sunglasses?"

"It's a long story," she said evasively, then dropped the rebar and knelt beside him. "You okay?"

"Yeah, yeah, I'm fine," he muttered sullenly. "I just feel kinda stupid."

"You could've been feeling kinda *dead* if this girl hadn't shown up," Annie said brusquely.

"Huh?" He gazed from Pan to the trash monkey, then back, and spotted the steel bar near her feet. "Did you just save me from getting a pounding?"

Pan smiled shyly. "Uh . . . yeah. It looked like you could use some help."

Javi pointed to the weapon. "Well, if he was gonna brain me with that, I'd say you were right. You took it away from him?" She nodded.

And there was that sexy smile, the one she'd hoped to see turned her way again.

"Wow. You're one badass chick."

She felt her cheeks warm. "Let me take a look at you." She quickly moved behind Javi to prevent him from seeing the return of her idiot grin, and delicately brushed aside the hair around an egg-sized lump on the back of his head. "You've got a good-sized knot here, but I don't see any bleed—"

And then, as she lightly touched the bump, tiny sparks flew out of her fingertips and across the injury.

Javi jumped. "Whoa! What was *that*?"

"Sorry! Sorry!" Pan said quickly. "I think it was, like . . . I don't know, static electricity or something." What else could she say? She didn't have a clue as to what just happened.

It was more than a simple static discharge, however. As she watched in disbelief, the lump became smaller; three seconds later, it was gone without a trace.

Javi sighed pleasurably. He looked over his shoulder at her and smiled. "Hey, that felt pretty good. What'd you do?"

"I . . . I . . ." An image of the mall security guard, and the electrical shock he'd given her, popped into her mind. What she'd just done—it couldn't have anything to do with that . . . could it?

"Who are you?" the guard had said. *"What are you?"*

She felt eyes boring into her and looked up. Annie was studying her. Intensely. Like she was assessing a potential threat. Pan swallowed nervously.

Thankfully, the scrape of backward feet along the track bed diverted the huntress's attention. She turned back to her quarry, who had tried slinking away.

"Where are *you* going?" Annie said harshly. "We're not done." She glared at the creature. "You monsters—you think you own this city, but you're wrong. I *allow* you to live here; don't ever forget that." She gestured toward Javi. "You were going to kill my friend. How much longer do you think you would have lived if you had?" Her hand moved toward Pan. "You're just lucky this girl showed up to save you, otherwise I'd be picking your entrails out of my teeth for the next two days."

Pan's eyebrows rose. Annie couldn't really have said *monsters*, could she? No, it had to be *monkeys*; she must have misheard it. Regardless, there was a more immediate question that came to mind. "Umm . . . can I ask you something? You said he was foraging, but that orange pendants—"

"Orang pendeks," Annie interjected. She pronounced it slowly, for Pan's benefit.

Pan shrugged. "Whatever. You said they aren't allowed to do it until after dark."

"Right."

"So, my question is: Did you ever think about asking *why* he was stealing garbage in the middle of the day?"

Annie snorted. "No. And why should it matter? He broke the rules. That's all I'm concerned with."

A flash of gold at the top of the emergency exit stairs caught Pan's eye, followed by a glimpse of a timid little face that was the spitting image of the full-grown creature. "Well, maybe this time you *should've* been concerned about something else," she said, pointing toward the miniature orang pendek as it scampered down the stairs.

"What . . . ? *Oh.*" Annie's eyebrows nearly levitated right off her forehead as she spotted the baby, which was the size of a toddler but probably weighed in excess of forty or fifty pounds. The adult primate moved quickly to scoop it up before it wandered too close to the huntress.

"You see?" Pan said to Annie. "He was just trying to feed his kid, but you had to go all *Fugitive* on him."

Annie gave her a quizzical look.

"She means the movie," Javi explained as he rose to his feet. "Y'know, the one with Harrison Ford and Tommy Lee Jones?"

"Oh," Annie said. She shrugged. "All right, maybe I did go running off half-cocked. It's an occupational hazard."

"Yeah, well, maybe you should find a new occupation," Pan said.

Burbling happily, the little orang pendek disentangled itself from its parent and jumped over to Pan, wrapping its spindly arms around her in a friendly hug.

"Ew! Monkey stink!" Pan yelped as she held the baby at arm's length. "Now I'm gonna smell like . . ." She paused, then leaned toward it and took a cautious sniff. "Huh," she remarked in surprise. "Actually, you smell pretty good." She pulled the baby back to her chest, took a deep whiff of its fur, and looked at Annie with a smile. "It's kinda like the potpourri my mom buys."

Annie nodded. "It's their diet. They usually eat flowers and vegetables. Makes their poop smell like sweet basil."

"Ugh. T-M-I," Pan slowly replied with a grimace.

The baby suddenly scrambled out of Pan's arms and climbed onto her shoulders, where it began poking around her jet-black locks. "Hey, what's it doing?"

"Looking for bugs," Annie replied. "They eat those, too."

"I don't have any—" Pan scowled as she tried to look over the top of her head at the little primate. "Hey, I just washed it yesterday—all right?"

"Well, if we stay around here much longer that won't be the case," Annie cautioned as she gazed into the surrounding darkness. "These tunnels are *crawling* with vermin. If we don't leave now, your parents will have to get you deloused before they let you go home."

"Yeah, my . . ." Pan's eyes widened in shock. "Oh crap—my dad! He's probably going nuts, wondering what happened to me!" She hurried over to the orang pendek and handed over his baby. "Hey, it was really nice meeting you—kinda." She jerked her head in Annie's direction. "Sorry about the misunderstanding. It won't happen again."

"Don't make promises I won't keep," Annie replied.

Pan sighed dramatically. "You are *so* not helping . . ." With a friendly pat on the baby's head, she took Javi by the arm and began leading him back up the tunnel, tossing a casual "You coming?" at Annie as she passed her. She glanced back in time to see Annie pointing to her own eyes with her index and middle fingers, then turning her hand to direct the fingers at the adult primate. "Oh, my God, are you *serious*?" Pan chided her. "You're pulling that I'm-watching-you crap—on *monkeys*?"

"Just so he knows I'm serious." With a final warning glance at her former quarry, Annie moved to help Pan with her burden. "Let's go."

Pan shook her head in exasperation. "*So* lame . . ."

None of them looked back to see if the orang pendeks were watching their departure, but a clatter of feet on metal made it clear Dad was already vaulting up the staircase.

"Damn monsters," Annie muttered with a sigh. "And Izzy wonders why I never get enough sleep."

There—she'd said it again! *Monsters*. And this time there was no mistaking it for another word. The questions now were, why did she keep saying it . . . and why did Javi act like her saying it was perfectly normal? It had to be a codeword for something.

"Hey, at least this one didn't stab you," Javi said.

"Yeah, there *is* that . . ." Annie agreed. "But only because he was more focused on crushing your skull."

Javi shuddered. "Oh, yeah . . ."

"So, the two of you do this a lot?" Pan asked lightly, gesturing in the direction of the now-absent trash monkey and his kid. "Go chasing after *monsters*?" She waited for them to join in on the joke.

But they didn't.

"I don't, but Annie does it *all* the time!" Javi replied. "Monster hunting twenty-four/seven/three-sixty-five."

Annie snorted. "Not *all* the time."

"Damn near close to it, according to Grandma Izzy."

"She likes to exaggerate. But so what? I'm doing my part to keep people safe, and even *you* have to admit I *am* the best in the business."

"Oh, absolutely. You're kinda like Wolverine from the X-Men," Javi replied, then added in a gruff voice, " 'I'm the best there is at what I do, darlin' . . . an' what I do ain't nice.' "

Annie nodded. "As good a description as any, I guess."

They were totally, *totally* serious.

Pan's skin prickled with goose bumps. Maybe these two were as crazy as she was . . .

"Now, I have a question, Pan," Annie said as they stopped to retrieve the girl's suitcase. "What's with the sunglasses?"

"Oh. Well, it's . . . uh . . ." Pan stepped away from Javi and moved closer to Annie so she could whisper. "See, I've got these really sensitive eyes and . . . well, it's . . ." She swallowed, then blurted out, "It's 'cause of all that light pouring outta you. It's giving me a headache."

Annie started. "You see *light* pouring out of me?" The words echoed loudly along the tunnel.

"Umm . . . yeah." Pan's cheeks burned with embarrassment as she stole a glance at Javi. *So much for the potential new boyfriend,* she thought. *Any second now, he'll start running as fast as he can to get away from the weird Goth chick—even if she did just save his life.*

Still, he didn't seem weirded out or in any hurry to leave. He actually looked intrigued.

And then Annie completely knocked her for a loop.

"So this light . . . is it as colorful as the one I see around you?" she asked. "Because you're glowing like a rainbow."

Pan gasped. "Wh-what?"

"I didn't want to say anything before; I figured you'd think I was crazy. But since you brought up the subject . . ." Annie looked over to Javi. "You wouldn't *believe* how beautiful she looks."

"You don't have to tell me that," he said.

Pan spun around to face him. "You mean, you . . . you can see it, too?"

"Nope," he said. "But I don't need a rainbow to tell me what I already see." He meant it, too; she could see it in his eyes. There wasn't a trace of pity or scorn in them—just complete sincerity. And total interest.

He thinks I'm beautiful. ME.

If she hadn't already felt light-headed from Annie's glowing-rainbow talk, she might have started spinning around in circles and giggling with joy . . . except badass chicks were supposed to be cooler than that. She settled for giving her idiot grin free rein.

"You didn't know about your aura?" Annie asked. "After you healed Javier I assumed—"

"She what?" Javi interjected. He gingerly touched the spot on his head where he'd banged it on the track tie, and seemed confused by what he found—or rather didn't find. "Hey, I thought you said I had this huge bump back there," he said to Pan.

"You did." Annie took him by the shoulders and turned him around so she could examine the injury. "It's gone, now. Completely healed. Good job," she added with a wink to Pan.

"Uh . . . thanks," she mumbled.

"And *you* did this." Javi looked amazed.

"I-I don't know," Pan stammered. "I guess. There were these sparks when I touched it, and then . . ." She let her voice trail off and shrugged.

Annie gently placed a hand on her shoulder. "You've never done this before, have you?" Pan shook her head. A smile dimpled the corners of the monster hunter's mouth. "A newbie, huh? I haven't met one of those in a while. Well, then we *really* need to talk."

"I don't know . . ." Pan said hesitantly. After all, hadn't she been thinking these two were nuttier than she, with all their talk of monsters? Just because Annie was saying all the right things now—or at least things Pan wanted to hear so she didn't feel like such a total freak—it didn't mean she was any saner than she had been a minute ago. And yet . . .

"Oh, I know *that* look," Annie said. "You think the glowing woman who yells at monkeys and talks about healing and rainbow Goths and monsters is a complete nutjob." She flashed a warm grin. "I get that a lot."

"A *lot*," Javi emphasized.

Annie frowned at him. "Quiet, you." Then she turned back to Pan. "But there's a part of you that thinks, just maybe, I'm telling the truth—right?"

Pan drooped her head. "Well . . ."

Annie laughed. "That's what I thought. I bet you have all *kinds* of questions."

"I think I might have one or two of my own," Javi remarked, and winked slyly at Pan.

"Then let's sit down somewhere and talk." The monster hunter picked up Pan's suitcase and began leading her charges back to the platform. "So, Pan, do you and your father have any plans for lunch?"

16

Lunch would have to wait, as Pan discovered when she, Javi, and Annie arrived in the Amtrak waiting area. As soon as they stepped off the escalator they were greeted by her worried-looking father . . . and a coterie of New York City transit cops, all of whom appeared to be extremely annoyed. Thankfully, only a few looked like escapees from a Heironymus Bosch painting, with demonic faces and gooey flesh. Still, given Pan's last scarifying run-in with a uniformed officer, it was understandable—at least to her—that as they drew near she automatically stepped back.

"Hey, Dad," she said lightly. "Got your own bodyguards now?"

Dave Zwieback, however, was clearly in no mood for jokes. "Pan, where the hell have you been?" he asked sharply. "I've been going frantic, wondering what happened to you. I tried calling you for the last twenty minutes. Why didn't you pick up?" He glanced at his daughter's companions. "And who are your friends?"

"Uh . . . Annie, Javi, this is my dad," she said, awkwardly making the introductions. "Dad, this is Annie and Javi. I . . . um, I don't know their last names. We just met."

Dave nodded at them—"Hey. How's it going?"—but seemed to be in no mood to shake hands.

"And about the calls . . . well, there's no signal down there," she continued, pointing toward the platform one level below. She pulled her cell from her pocket and looked at its screen. "Wow. Fifteen messages? Yeah, I didn't hear *any* of them coming through."

"And when I had you paged over the loudspeakers three times?"

"Didn't hear it." A follow-up quip about the normally poor quality of New York public address systems—through which every announcement sounded like a combination of static, feedback, and cats fighting in a burlap sack—never made it past her tongue, however, when she noticed the fearful look in her father's eyes; he really *had* been terrified that something ugly had happened to his only child. And seeing him so openly display that level of unease made her feel a bit like . . . well, a jerk for being so lighthearted about the situation.

"Sorry, Dad," she muttered. "Didn't mean to freak you out."

Dad stared at her for a few moments, and Pan fully expected him to launch into a full-blown lecture on the dangers of irresponsibility. She'd heard similar ones; right now she probably deserved it. But then his jaw unclenched, his tightly drawn lips flowed into a warm smile, and he held open his arms. "C'm'ere, you."

Pan happily slid into his embrace and hugged him back just as hard. "Miss me?" she asked.

She felt him kiss the top of her head. "Always, Panda-bear," he mumbled into her hair. Then she heard him sniff a couple of times. "Is that a new shampoo? Smells like your mom's potpourri."

Pan laughed. "That's what *I* said . . ."

Their reunion was cut short, however, as a heavyset male cop pushed through the line of dark blue-uniformed men and women standing behind Dave. He was in his late fifties, with short-cropped gray hair swept back from a sizable forehead; from the short-sleeved white dress shirt he wore, accessorized with a gold badge on the left breast pocket and two gold bars on each epaulet, he seemed to be the guy in charge. What really caught Pan's eye, though, was his tie clasp: a small cloisonné pin in the form of a sword in a star. The pin was round, with a design running around the edge that looked like a braided golden rope; inside that was a sky blue field in which a white seven-pointed star was centered; and in the center of the star was the golden hilt of a silver sword, the blade pointing downward. She didn't recognize the symbol. The Knights of Columbus, maybe? Sure, that had a sword—but no, it had an ax and an anchor in it, too. She remembered that from the school dances she used to attend at the KoC assembly hall in Woodside—there was a big reproduction of the symbol hanging on the wall just above the entrance.

"Is this the runaway, Mr. Zweeback?" the cop demanded, disrupting her thoughts.

Pan's eyes widened. "Runaway?" She looked to her father. "Dad?"

Dave pulled away from her and turned to face the commanding officer. "I *never* said my daughter ran away, Captain Hobbes. I just said I couldn't find her. And it's Zwie*back*—long 'I' sound."

Hobbes grunted and turned to face Pan. "Well, if you didn't run off, little girl, then you sure as hell better start explainin' where you an' yer boyfriend there disappeared off to fer the last twenny minutes."

"*Boyfriend?*" Pan and Javi said in unison, then gazed at one another.

Damn, she thought, he sure looked supercute when he smiled like that . . .

"I had my men search that whole damn train from front to back," Hobbes continued, "an' you weren't on it—or the platform, neither. An' because o' us havin' t'turn the whole station upside down lookin' for you, now we got trains backed up all over the Northeast Corridor." His eyes narrowed. "I think we better take you in for questionin'. There's no tellin' *what* kinda mayhem the two'a yas was causin' down there in the tunnels, but I'm gonna find out." He glanced at Annie. "Sorry— the *three* o' yas."

"Apology accepted, Captain," she said with an amused smile. "But I'm afraid you won't be questioning anyone."

That certainly got him to direct his full attention to her. "Oh, really," he replied gruffly. "Says who?"

"Says me." She stepped over to him, pointed to his tie clasp, and leaned forward to whisper in his ear. Pan couldn't hear what was being said, but the effect that Annie's words had on the transit cop was instantaneous. His head snapped back like he'd just received a tremendous electrical shock (*And don't I know all about those?* Pan thought), and his jaw dropped.

And then to everyone's total surprise, Captain Hobbes started to genuflect at Annie's feet—in front of his own men, right in the middle of Penn Station! She placed a gentle hand on his shoulder and put the brakes on his descent.

Hobbes lowered his gaze and muttered in a conciliatory tone, "My lady, I didn't know . . ."

"Don't worry about it," Annie said. "No harm done." She nodded toward Pan and Javi. "These two were helping me with a small problem. It's been resolved. Sorry to have troubled you, Captain."

"No trouble at all, my . . . ma'am," Hobbes said.

She smiled pleasantly. "Thank you. Now if you'll excuse us . . ." She turned to Pan, Dave, and Javi. "Coming?" Then she strode right through the line of transit cops as they cleared a path for her. Javi fell in step behind her.

Dave picked up his daughter's suitcase and draped an arm around her shoulders. "Uh, thanks for your help, Captain," he said.

"Yeah, look . . . sorry fer the trouble a minute ago." Hobbes winked at Pan as she passed. "Keep up the good work, there, young lady."

"Er . . . okay," Pan said, not having a clue about what just occurred. Then again, everything she'd experienced in the past twenty minutes had her so off-balance it was difficult to keep up with new surprises. And Annie seemed to be *full* of surprises. A monkey wrangler and aura expert who could talk to the animals like Dr. Doolittle, then turn around and scare a cop with just a few words? Who considered herself a *monster hunter*?

Who *was* this strange woman?

They found Annie and Javi outside the West Thirty-first Street entrance on Eighth Avenue.

". . . and oh, man, did you see the look on his face when you told him who you were?" Javi was saying to Annie. "It was priceless!"

Annie chuckled. "Poor man. I felt sorry for him." She caught sight of the Zwiebacks approaching—"Oh, here they are!"—and offered her hand to Dave as he drew near. "Sorry about the drama, Mr. Zwieback. I'm Sebastienne Mazarin. But 'Annie' is fine."

"Dave," he said as they shook hands.

She gestured to Javi. "And this is my friend, Javier Maldonado."

"Javi," the teen said and offered his own hand.

"So, anyone care to tell me what the hell is going on?" Dave looked at the trio of adventurers, but his gaze settled on Annie. "You told that cop Pan was helping you with something, but she said you'd just met." His eyes narrowed in suspicion. "Just what have you got my daughter involved in? And what exactly did you say to that transit cop that made him back off? He was so in awe of you I'd swear he was about to start kissing your feet."

"Oooo, *everybody* has questions for me today . . ." Annie smiled. "David, I'd be happy to answer them, but not on an empty stomach. I was hoping you and Pan would join us for lunch. There's a great little café a few blocks west of here, and I always do my explaining better when I eat." Her smile widened. "My treat?"

The Oberon Café, as Annie told her three companions after they'd settled into a booth near the front windows, used to be an Irish pub called the Harp & Fiddle until the wave of gentrification that had swept across Manhattan for decades finally crashed upon the shores of Tenth Avenue and Thirtieth Street at the turn of the twenty-first century. Almost overnight this section of the city's West Side metamorphosed from an industrial conglomeration of factories and warehouses to yet another trendy neighborhood of art galleries and boiler room nightclubs so exclusive you had to know somebody who knew somebody just to find out the clubs' secret locations. And even then there was no guarantee you'd be allowed access.

The Harp & Fiddle had eventually succumbed to the twin knockout punches of New York real estate: skyrocketing rents, and a property owner who wanted a "classier" joint that would appeal to the area's hipper apartment dwellers. And so after forty-three years, the Harp & Fiddle underwent a major renovation, to emerge as the Shakespearean-themed Oberon Café, named after the king of the fairies in *A Midsummer Night's Dream*. Now instead of the Guinness stout and Irish whiskey cake they used to serve to factory workers and meatpacking district butchers, it was family-friendly items like lattes and a chocolate-syrup-drenched sundae with the lame, punny name of A Midsummer's Ice Dream. But according to Annie, they still made one hell of a burger.

After stowing Pan's suitcase in the trunk of Dave's car—which was parked in a lot across from Penn Station—the foursome had headed west, Dave and Annie engaging in small talk while Pan and Javi exchanged pertinent information—cell numbers, Facebook pages, her DeviantArt page, and the like. By the time the group reached the café the teens had already made plans to follow-up their conversation once Pan got settled in at home. Even better, Annie's megawatt glow had lowered to a soft shimmer, which meant either she had a dimmer switch in that old-lady-android body, or Pan's eyes had become accustomed to the light she was giving off. Whatever the reason, Pan was finally able to take off the sunglasses.

It was Dad who got the *real* discussion going again, once their orders arrived. He and Pan sat on one side of the booth, her leather jacket between them, while Annie and Javi sat on the other. "So, *what* were you doing in the tunnels with my daughter while I was going frantic?"

"I guess you could call it animal control," Annie said. "There was this orang pendek—"

"It's like a monkey, only with backward feet," Pan interjected.

Dave's eyes went saucer-wide. "You were chasing after a monkey? Pan, those things are dangerous! What were you thinking?"

"Nah, this one was okay, Dad," Pan said as she added ketchup and mustard to her well-done bison-meat burger topped with pepper jack cheese. "It turned out he just wanted to get some food for his family. Oh! And he had the cutest little baby monkey with him!" She paused. "Okay, maybe not so little, but it was still really cute."

He gazed at her bare arms. "It didn't bite you or anything, did it?"

Pan rolled her eyes. "I'm *fine*, Dad."

"She was *very* helpful, David," Annie said. "I doubt I would have been so . . . diplomatic handling the situation. And, just to put your mind *somewhat* at ease, I didn't recruit Pan. She . . . volunteered to help out."

Dave eyed his daughter. "Color me surprised," he said wryly. "So, what was the outcome? I didn't see any monkeys when you came up to the waiting area."

"Well, they're not really monkeys, but they *are* primates," Annie replied. "And they sort of live in the tunnels."

His eyebrows shot up. "And the MTA allows that?"

No, not the Metropolitan Transit Authority, Pan thought, remembering Annie's speech to the adult orang pendek: *"You monsters—you think you own this city, but you're wrong. I allow you to live here; don't ever forget that."*

"They've . . . learned to live with it," Annie said.

"That have anything to do with you?" Dave asked. "Like the cop who acted like you were the Second Coming of Christ?"

"Oh, that," Annie said dismissively. "He was just overreacting to what I told him."

"Which was . . . ?"

"Private," she replied firmly.

His right eyebrow cocked in a half quizzical, half amused manner. "You said you were willing to answer my questions."

"Up to a point. Ever heard the expression a 'need-to-know basis'?"

"Uh-huh. And I guess genuflecting cops fall under that category?"

"Exactly. But I *will* say I've got a good working relationship with most law enforcement agencies. Does that help?"

He paused for a moment, then slowly smiled. "Up to a point."

"Don't worry about it, Dad," Pan said, "everything worked out. We didn't get arrested, the orange pendants got their food"—she grinned broadly—"and I got mine!" She took a huge bite of bison and cheese. "And we all lived happily ever after," she mumbled.

"Don't talk with your mouth full," Dad warned, and turned back to Annie. "So, do you spend a lot of time chasing these . . ."

"Orang—" Annie began to say around a mouthful of hamburger so rare you could practically hear it moo, then stopped to grab a paper napkin from the dispenser near her arm and used it to wipe away the blood and grease dribbling down her chin. She swallowed and said, with an embarrassed grin, "Sorry. Orang pendeks. And no, it doesn't happen very often."

"That's not what *I've* heard . . ." Javi chimed in. Annie stared daggers at him, and he laughed.

Dave took a bite of his club sandwich, chewed it slowly as though he was mulling something over, and said, "Aren't orang pendeks supposed to be mythological creatures?"

Annie halted in midbite and stared across the table at him. She looked impressed.

Pan just smiled knowingly; mythology was one of Dad's favorite subjects.

"We've got a ton of occult and paranormal reference books at home," she explained. "Dad used to read *The Encyclopedia of Monsters* to me at bedtime, when I was a kid."

Javi took a gulp of Coke. "Weirdness sorta runs through your family, huh?" he said to Pan with a smile. She grinned.

"They're from . . . Sumatra, right?" Dad continued. "The orang pendeks. Have backward feet and flat heads?" He stared harder and drummed the fingers of his right hand on the Formica surface. "Something else . . ."

"Their poop smells like sweet basil?" Annie offered.

He looked up and smiled. "That's it!"

Pan groaned and held up her bison burger. "Uh, hello? Eating?"

"So, they're really real." He shook his head in amazement as Annie nodded. "Wow. I guess you *do* learn something new every day."

Annie smiled at Pan. "I like your father, Pan. He's very knowledgeable."

She snorted. "Not about everything. Trust me."

"Oh, really?" Dave asked as he playfully elbowed her in the arm. "And how would *you* know?"

Pan grinned at Annie and Javi. "For my fifth birthday he gave me the DVD of *Watership Down*."

Annie gasped, and in doing so choked on her burger. When she finally recovered, after a brief coughing fit and liberal gulps of iced tea, she looked at Dave. "Oh, my God. You didn't."

Dave sighed and reluctantly nodded his head.

"You never read the book?"

He shrugged. "Nope."

Her eyes widened in horror. "David, that novel's bloodier than a grand guignol performance. And the movie . . ." She shook her head. "I can't believe you'd give that to a child."

"Yeah, well, it was a big surprise for *all* of us when I put it on," Dave muttered, his cheeks reddening with embarrassment.

"I'll say," Pan chimed in. "I think half the kids at the party are *still* in therapy."

Blood Feud 153

Annie chuckled as she watched Dave squirm in his seat. "Wow. Just"—she gave another disapproving head shake—"wow."

"Well, how was I supposed to know?" Dave countered. "I mean, it was a cartoon with *bunnies* on the cover! Bunnies! How could something with bunnies on it be bad for a kid?"

Pan laughed. "Can you believe it? And *he* used to be an English teacher!"

"Yeah, but that was a lifetime ago," Dave replied, and turned back to Annie. "I run a museum these days."

"A museum? First a professor, now a museum director. You're a man of many talents, David."

Dave's ears reddened; they always did when someone complimented him. "Well, first off, I was never a professor. I taught high school English. And it's not a 'museum' museum, like the Natural History or the Met, or anything like that. It's a storefront in Queens."

"But it's a really cool place," Pan added enthusiastically. "Renfield's House of Horrors and Mystical Antiquities. It's named after—"

"Dracula's assistant. I've read the novel," Annie said. "I'd love to see it."

Dave's eyebrows rose. "Really?"

"Absolutely. Where's it located?"

Dave dug into his jeans' left front pocket and pulled out a faux leather wallet decorated with a cartoony drawing of the Wolf Man's head. "You ever heard of Steinway Street in Astoria?" Annie nodded. "We're about two blocks west of that"— he opened the wallet and fished out a mangled black business card—"down the block from the Museum of the Moving Image." He handed cards to Annie and Javi. "Sorry about the beat-up condition. I keep forgetting to have more printed."

"Good thing I showed up, then," Pan said. "To remind you of important stuff."

"Hey, I picked you up, right?" Dad countered. "*That* was pretty important. Give me *some* credit."

Annie studied the card for a moment, then tucked it away in her backpack before pulling out a small cosmetics bag and moving to slide out of the booth. "If you gentlemen will excuse me, I need to use the ladies' room. Care to join me, Pan?"

"Huh?" Pan saw Annie widen her eyes and jerk her head toward the back of the diner; apparently she wanted to talk in private. "Oh. Sure." She grinned mischievously. "I mean, after a hard day of monkey chasing there's nothing better than a good pee."

That got a hearty laugh from Javi. Dad, of course, didn't find her remark nearly that funny.

"Hey, remember back at Penn Station I said how much I missed you? Well, the foul-mouthed pirate is the part of you I *didn't* miss."

"Yaarrr," Pan growled playfully, then gave him a reassuring pat on the arm before she opened her suitcase to retrieve her own neon-skull-decorated makeup bag. "Gotta take the good with the bad, Dad. Isn't that part of the whole parenting thing?"

"I suppose . . ." Dave sighed and looked to Annie. He waved a hand toward his daughter. "For *this* I almost got arrested?"

"Yes," she said with a gentle smile. "And you'd do it again in a heartbeat."

He smiled warmly as he gazed at Pan. "Yeah," he said quietly. "I would."

Pan blushed, surprisingly at a loss for words, and slid out of the booth. "Be right back, boys."

"We'll be here. I'll give Mom a call, let her know you got in safe." He glanced at Annie. "Relatively safe. And speaking of Mom . . ." Dad held up the worn leather jacket at arm's length, studying the flame-painted sleeves and the metal bat hanging on the left shoulder. "Isn't this her motorcycle jacket?" Then he suddenly looked concerned. "She didn't sell the Harley, did she?"

Pan shook her head. "Nah. She just got a new jacket." The red, 1972 Harley-Davidson Electra Glide (with sidecar) that currently sat in the garage back in Schriksdorp had been passed down to Mom by her own father; she'd die first before she gave up her hog.

"Oh, good. I know how much she loves tearing up the road in that thing." He turned the jacket around to admire the painting on the back panel. "Verrry nice. You still got the touch, kid."

"Thanks."

"*You* painted that?" Javi asked. "That's awesome!"

"Thanks," she said with a wide grin, then turned to Annie. "Let's go."

"Before you start blushing again?" she asked playfully.

Embarrassed, Pan hurried past her. "Could we *please* talk about something else?" She walked briskly down a narrow hallway to the rear of the eatery, with Annie in tow.

"Certainly," the huntress replied. "And I know *just* what we can talk about . . ."

"Your father doesn't have your gift, does he?" Annie asked once she'd closed the ladies' room door. "I noticed he didn't mention anything about glowing auras."

"That's supposed to be a gift?" Pan snorted. "Not from where *I'm* standing." In fact, it was a whole new level of weirdness in her already bizarre life that she could have done without . . . although that healing thingie she did with the bump on Javi's head was kind of interesting. She wouldn't mind learning more about that.

"Well, of course it's a gift." Annie checked her hair in the mirror, teasing a few wayward strands back into place with her fingers. "In the Olde Tongue it's called the inner sight. It lets you see a person's true nature . . . among other things." Satisfied with her primping, she dug into her bag and extracted a packet of tissues, then began removing her lip color. "And the more comfortable you become with who you are and what you can do, the more control you'll have over it."

"So then you mean it's normal to see stuff like frog-headed girls, or guys with split faces who look like Leatherface from *Texas Chain Saw Massacre* just worked them over, and they have blood and pus oozing down their cheeks, or like little kids with daggery teeth that looked like they chewed their way outta Mommy's womb?"

Annie grimaced. "Is *that* what you've been seeing?" She finished the tissues and pulled out a mini-toothbrush and a small bottle of mouthwash. "That's . . . pretty messed up." She set about cleaning her teeth.

"You're tellin' me . . ." Pan leaned against the sink and stared at her reflection. The traces of dark circles under her eyes gave her a mildly cadaverous appearance. Under normal circumstances she might have thought it ghoulishly attractive.

Annie spat toothpaste into the sink and reached for the mouthwash. "But David doesn't see any of that."

"Dad wouldn't hide that kinda thing from me—not with the sorta problems I have. Something like that would be way too important. So, no." She flashed a tiny smile. "Besides, he sucks pretty bad at keeping secrets."

Finished with the mouthwash, Annie began reapplying lipstick. "And your mom?"

"The same. Although . . ." She shook her head. "Never mind."

Annie turned to face her. "No, please tell me."

Pan drew a deep breath and slowly released it. "Yesterday I saw a glow around her—like yours, only not so bright. I didn't say anything about it—I mean, how could I, right? But she looked so beautiful . . . like an angel or something." She sighed. "I don't know. None of this makes sense, and I was screwed up *before* all this new stuff happened."

"What do you mean?"

Pan stared at the sink basin. How, she wondered, do you explain a decade of demonic visions and cartoonishly monstrous imaginary friends; of children who shun you and boyfriends who abandon you when they find out what you see; of being told you're crazy, long enough and often enough by so many people that you eventually convince yourself you *must* be crazy? How do you do that?

And then she realized it all boiled down to one simple statement:

"When I was six, I started seeing . . . monsters."

Pause for Annie laughing in 3 . . . 2 . . . 1 . . .

"All right. And?"

Pan looked up. There wasn't a trace of insincerity in Annie's expression. She was listening attentively, waiting for the girl to continue. Still, Pan snorted derisively. "Oh, yeah, that's right. You're the big monster hunter. Of course *you'd* believe me."

"What's wrong with that?"

"Because monsters are just a bunch of myths and legends. They're not real, they're just figments of the imagination. Everybody knows that."

" 'Everybody.' " Annie smiled, clearly amused by Pan's statement. "Do you mind if I ask who put that *ridiculous* notion in your head? Because that line you just gave me sounded pretty rehearsed."

It was, in a way. Dr. Farrar spouted it at least once every session. "My therapist. And it's *not* ridiculous."

Annie looked horrified. "You've been seeing a psychiatrist?"

Pan frowned. "You miss the part about me seeing monsters when I was six?"

"No, I didn't, but . . . well, that's just wrong," Annie said emphatically. "I mean, you going to a shrink. It's wrong. You don't need"—she sneered—"therapy. You're perfectly fine."

"Ha! I don't think the American Psychiatric Association would agree with you."

The huntress grunted and leaned against the door, pondering her next move. She looked as though she might be at it for a while, so Pan focused on touching up her own makeup and fixing her hair. Between running from the perv on the train and having a baby monkey poking around her scalp for snacks, she'd come out of Penn Station looking a total mess. And Javi had said she looked beautiful? Like this? Yikes.

She took a handful of large cotton balls and a bottle of Sea Breeze from her bag, prepared to strip off the layers of foundation and powder and eye shadow and start over. *If you thought the sleep-deprived cadaver was something, Mr. Maldonado, give me fifteen minutes and I'll show you what beautiful really looks like . . .*

"Hey," Annie said, "what if I could prove that supernatural creatures are real?"

"You gonna turn into a werewolf or something?" Pan asked wryly.

"I could," Annie said with a sly smile, "but to do it right here in a bathroom, when it's just the two of us? No. That wouldn't prove my point, would it? You'd just think you were—"

"Having another psychosode?"

"Exactly. So, if I can prove they exist, would you be willing to give up your therapist?"

"It's not really my decision, you know—I'm pretty sure Mom and Dad might have something to say about it. But . . ." Pan smiled. "Okay, Ms. Monster Hunter. Prove it."

17

"So, *what* exactly are we doing here?" Dave asked Annie. "You said you wanted to show us something, but I'm not sure what I'm supposed to be looking for."

That question was also on Pan's mind, as she gazed at their surroundings. After lunch, Annie had led the way across Tenth Avenue and under the deck of the High Line, an elevated railway built in the early 1930s that, in recent years, had been converted to New York City parkland. Yet, as pretty as the High Line was nowadays, the area below it remained just as seedy and unattractive as it had been before the transformation, dominated by parking lots that stank of exhaust fumes and spilled motor oil, long-abandoned buildings of crumbling brick, Dumpsters piled high with trash, and boarded-up construction sites whose plywood-barrier walls were covered in graffiti. Beyond the underbelly of the High Land, though, was Chelsea, a vibrant neighborhood of art galleries and nightclubs, museums and theaters that Pan and her friends had loved to explore before her move upstate; on one occasion they'd even snuck onto the High Line back when it was an abandoned, rusting hulk overflowing with wild plant life. Those were some really good times.

And so, being as familiar with this part of Manhattan's West Side as she was, Pan couldn't imagine where Annie might be taking them to prove her claim that monsters were real. Maybe she kept the evidence in one of the storage facilities over by Eleventh Avenue?

"Before I answer your question, David," Annie said as they walked along West Twenty-ninth Street, "let me ask *you* something first. I know it's going to sound pretty strange, but just bear with me."

"All right, Socrates," Dave said lightly. "Go on."

"Have you ever heard of . . . Gothopolis?"

Pan halted; so did her father. Javi just grinned.

Oh, no way, Pan thought. *This* was going to be Annie's method of convincing her she was sane? By giving a history lesson on a mythical neighborhood? She frowned, uncertain whether she should be amused by the great "monster hunter's" lame attempt to prove her point, or outright pissed that Annie considered her naïve enough to believe in an old fairy tale.

Pan had stopped believing in those a long time ago.

"Gothopolis?" she replied. "Sure, we've both heard of it. All my friends have, too." Then she added in her spookiest voice, "It's the place where monnnsterrrrs dwellll."

She noticed Dad flinch when she said *monsters*; he and Mom always reacted that way whenever she made jokes about her "condition." They didn't consider it something to laugh about.

"It's an urban legend," Dave said. "A neighborhood where supernatural creatures have supposedly lived since New York was a Dutch colony. It's a nice story, but there's never been any proof of it." He gazed at his daughter and offered a weak smile. "You have no idea how I wish it *was* true."

"See, that's the first misconception," Annie said. "That it's one particular area, when it's so much bigger than that. I mean, it's called Gothopolis for a reason."

Pan looked to Javi. "*Polis* is Greek for 'city,' so . . ."

"City of gothic creatures," he replied. "I know. Annie's told me all about it." He flashed a sly smile. "Sounds like your kinda place."

"So you're saying—what?" Dave asked Annie. "That it's not just a neighborhood, it's more like a city in a city?" He shook his head. "Impossible. I think someone would have noticed it by now."

"Oh, but they have. *You* have." She swept her arms out. "The proof is all around you, right now. You've just never paid attention."

"The proof is all around us," he said with a frown. "That monsters are real."

"Exactly!"

He stared at Annie for a couple of seconds, then looked at Pan. "Honey, did you . . . ?"

Pan stared at her feet. "Yeah, I told her," she muttered. "I mean, after the monkey thing I figured, what'd I have to lose—right?"

"Aw, Panda-bear . . ." he said softly, and draped an arm around her shoulders. He gave her a supportive hug.

"What am I missing?" Javi asked Annie.

She put an index finger to her lips, shushing him, then turned back to Dave. "I know you think I'm interfering, David, but I'm just trying to help."

"*How*?" he snapped. "By messing—" He stopped when he saw people turning his way. If there was one thing a New Yorker couldn't pass up, it was a front-row seat for a public argument. He stepped closer and lowered his voice: "By messing with my daughter's head? She has enough problems without a complete stranger trying to tear down years of counseling, talking about invisible monster towns."

"That's *another* misconception," Annie remarked. "That just because you can't see Gothopolis, it doesn't exist."

"Because it *doesn't* exist, damn it! I don't care if there's a million orang pendeks running loose in the subway tunnels, that's no proof of anything. Gothopolis does *not* exist! Just stop it!" He turned to Pan. "C'mon, honey, we're going."

Annie gently placed a hand on his arm. "But you looked for it, didn't you?" She nodded toward Pan. "For her."

Dave opened his mouth, but no words came out. Pan watched the fire in his eyes start to diminish, then smolder away. He flashed her a tiny smile.

"Yes," he finally said. "Her mother, too."

Pan started. "W-what?"

Annie gestured toward the High Line. "Maybe we should sit down."

"Yeah. That's a good idea," Pan said numbly. "I could use a seat."

They sat quietly on a bench, Pan on one side of Dave, Annie and Javi on the other. Around them the High Line was alive with Saturday afternoon activity: couples young and old strolled hand in hand down the garden-lined walkways; children darted about, giggling and shrieking happily, as their parents struggled to keep up with them; tourists clustered along the railings, snapping pictures of the Manhattan skyline to the east and the Hudson River to the west; pigeons and starlings and house sparrows flitted here and there, landing to pick up crumbs of food before quickly returning to the air; a pair of multihued butterflies glided by on their way to a liquid lunch of wild-flower nectars.

Her thoughts awhirl, Pan stared at her father as he hunched forward and gazed at his feet. Mom and Dad had never mentioned anything to her about searching for Gothopolis; in fact, Dad had always shrugged off any mention of the place as a joke. To now learn that they'd actually made an effort to locate it, *for her . . .* she didn't know what to say.

"No matter how bad things ever get," Mom had told her outside the megamall, *"I want you to remember this: We might not be together anymore, but your dad and I will always be there for you."*

Not just "will always." *Had* always been there for her.

Pan reached out and took his hand. Dad turned his head to smile at her, then sat back and laid a gentle hand across his daughter's shoulders.

"Okay. You have to understand," he at last said to Annie, "Karen and I were desperate. When Pan began seeing things, we didn't know what to do. And when it got worse—the visions, the constant terror . . . The doctors diagnosed her as a"—he glanced around to make sure no one was eavesdropping, then lowered his voice—"a paranoid schizophrenic."

Pan winced and looked at Javi. They'd met only a little while ago and had seemed to hit it off right away—but now Dad had to go blurting out the one thing guaranteed to make Javi think she was a total freak! Pan sighed. So much for a potential new boyfriend . . .

And yet he didn't run off in fright, or roll his eyes, or make snide comments about her condition, or stare at her like she was a miserable, wretched, crazy girl. Rather, he looked as though he wanted to hug her and tell her everything was okay. At least she *hoped* that was the meaning behind the concerned look he was giving her. Maybe she was just reading too much into it.

"Can you imagine that?" Dad continued. "At the age of six! Karen had to watch her every minute while I was at work, or she might hurt herself trying to escape from the . . . the monsters. And there was nothing we could do to help her! Do you have any idea how frustrating that is?"

"I do," Annie said quietly.

"The first time we had to . . . had to admit Pan overnight for observation it just about killed Karen."

God. Poor Mom . . . Pan recalled something of those days, but over the years it had all blurred together in a haze of shadowy bogeymen, white-coated doctors, and heavy medication. Perhaps it was better, she thought, that she not remember the details of her parents' early struggles in dealing with her mental illness; they were certain to break her heart.

Dad paused to take a breath and calm down. "And then I remembered the stories about Gothopolis, and I started researching everything I could find on it, followed every lead, checked out I don't know how many neighborhoods in all five boroughs, and . . . nothing. And after every path I followed hit a dead end and I started to give up, Karen stepped in." He smiled warmly at the memory flooding back. "She didn't believe it for an instant—at least that's what she kept telling me—but she did what she could, picking up where I left off. It gave us a purpose, I guess, something to do so we didn't feel like we were failing Pan."

"Oh, Dad . . ." Pan whispered. "It wasn't your fault."

Dad gave her a squeeze. "On the surface, I think your mom and I know that, honey. But deep inside"—he tapped on his chest—". . . well, I'm not sure we'll ever be able to convince ourselves it's true."

"Maybe I can help with that, too," Annie said.

"Oh, just . . . stop, all right?" Dave said brusquely. "We've all been through enough. Stop trying to make things worse."

"I'm trying to make things *better*—for both of you. And your ex."

Dave started. "How . . . ?"

She pointed to his left hand. "No wedding ring."

Pan gasped. With everything that had been going on today, the last thing she would have ever thought about was Dad's hands. She hadn't spotted the naked ring finger—but her new friend sure as hell had. And they both knew what it signified. No ring meant he'd moved on. There'd be no going back; no reconciliation with Mom. She started to pull away from her father.

Dad noticed her reaction. "Hang on a second." He reached under the collar of his T-shirt and pulled out a thin gold chain; dangling from the end was his wedding band. "I've got it right here—see?"

Her eyebrows rose. "Oh."

"I guess I'm still in the . . . I don't know. I guess you could call it the mourning phase—even if it *is* nine months later," Dad admitted as he stared at the ring. "I didn't think it was appropriate to keep wearing it once the divorce was finalized, but I didn't want to just chuck it in a drawer at home. Too many good things came out of that marriage." His right hand swept over to gently brush her cheek. "And one *very* good thing, of course." He jiggled the chain. "So I compromised." He tucked the ring back inside his shirt. "Crisis averted?"

Pan relaxed. "Yeah."

Dad grinned and tousled her hair. "We good, now?"

"Yeah. We're good." A warm smile eased over Pan's lips as he pulled her into a hug she gladly returned. Maybe, she thought with a tinge of excitement, there *was* still a chance to put things right between her parents.

"So, where's your proof about Gothopolis?" she asked Annie as she sat back.

"Now, honey—" Dad began.

"No, Dad, let her talk. I mean, you and Mom couldn't find it, but since Annie says the proof is supposed to be all around us, I'm guessing she knows something you don't. And I wanna hear what it is. But don't worry, I'm not gonna get my hopes up. Besides, if it turns out she's just talking out of her—"

"Watch it," he warned.

". . . backpack, what harm's it gonna do to *me*?" She cocked her left eyebrow in a wry expression. "I mean, *really*, Dad."

He gazed at her for a couple of seconds, then sighed heavily. "All right."

She turned back to face Annie. "So?"

"Well, based on what David just told me, I *could* say that you've been seeing evidence of Gothopolis's existence for the past ten years and just didn't know it—"

"But you won't," Pan said sternly.

"—but I won't, because that would be a cheat. What you need is someone—not me—to confirm that what your inner sight shows isn't a hallucination." Her gaze drifted toward Javi.

"And how would I do that?" Dave asked.

"Ah." Annie smiled warmly. "I was hoping you'd volunteer."

So had Pan; still, it came as a surprise. "Really, Dad? But after what you just said, I thought . . ."

Dave smiled. "Honey, I might think your friend here is full of crap, but . . . but I can't deny there's still a part of me that hopes she's telling the truth. I'd like it to be true . . . I *want* it to be true, if for no other reason than to finally give you peace of mind. That's all your mother and I have ever wanted for you."

Pan tried to answer, but her throat had suddenly gone dry. She swallowed hard and croaked out, "Th-thanks, Dad."

Dave patted her knee, then turned back to face Annie. "Let's get one thing straight, first," he warned. "You make things worse for my daughter in any way, you better run like hell."

She nodded. "I understand. But I assure you, David, I *am* only trying to help."

"We'll see." He sat up straighter on the bench. "Okay. What do I have to do?"

"Keep an open mind, for one—"

"I can do that."

"—and believe in what you see."

Dave paused. "I can keep an open mind." He winked at Pan.

"Good enough," Annie said with a laugh. "Now, I need you to concentrate." She swept her hand outward at the city. "Look beyond what your mind is telling you is there."

Dave sat forward and narrowed his eyes. "What am I supposed to be looking at?"

Annie patted him on the shoulder. "Believe me, David, you'll know it when you see it. Just . . . try not to scream too loudly when you do, all right?"

He looked up at her, mild panic in his eyes. "*What?*"

She waved him off. "Concentrate." Then she stepped over to crouch beside Pan, who was suddenly wondering if having a hidden city of monsters revealed to a mental patient already haunted by those very same creatures was such a good idea.

Annie smiled. "Having second thoughts?"

Embarrassed by how well the huntress could read her expression, Pan looked down at her feet. "Kinda sorta," she muttered.

"Well, don't—you're doing the right thing," Annie said firmly. "Now, I know your first instinct is to hold back, to try to ignore what your inner sight reveals, but you need to let go of the reins just this once."

"*What?*" Pan shook her head. "No way. You don't understand—I . . . I can't handle it if I don't block it out."

"You *can*." Annie took the girl's trembling hand and gave it an encouraging squeeze. A tingle of electricity danced around the tips of their fingers. "It's all right, Pan. I'm right here with you. You don't have to be afraid—not any longer."

A tiny, pained smile curled Pan's lips. "Yeah?" she said softly. "That'd be nice . . . not being afraid anymore."

"Then trust me," Annie urged. "Trust yourself. You *do* have the strength to face your fears—you know you do. All you have to do is—"

"Keep an open mind?"

Annie nodded. "And believe."

Pan grunted. Annie made it sound so easy, facing her fears, but Pan had been trying to do that for years and "easy" was the last word she'd ever choose to describe the experience. And yet . . . she found she couldn't say no to this demonstration. Like her father, there was a part of her that wanted—no, *needed*—Annie to be telling the truth. Because otherwise Pan was just the crazy girl who one day would probably grow up to be an even crazier woman—and that terrified her more than the monsters.

Pan closed her eyes. She inhaled deeply to steady her nerves, then slowly exhaled through her nostrils. "O . . . okay."

She felt Annie lean in close to whisper in her ear:

"Hold your breath. Make a wish. Count to three."

Pan held her breath.

She wished—prayed—that something special was about to happen.

She counted to three, then opened her eyes.

And the world rippled.

18

The ripple effect lasted only a couple of seconds, but it was as though a curtain had been pulled aside to allow sunlight into a darkened room. Colors seemed more vibrant, the auras of park visitors (especially her own) glowed brighter—even the monsters looked more monstery! Everything was in such incredibly sharp detail she could see that the butterflies that had flitted past her earlier were actually teeny-tiny faeries.

Pan's jaw dropped. Is this what trusting in her inner sight—in herself—was really like? It was all so scary and silly, confusing and exhilarating and magical, she didn't know what to think, except . . . how beautiful the world suddenly was.

Slowly, she turned to face Annie, who grinned.

"Welcome to Gothopolis," the huntress said.

"It's . . ." But then Pan shook her head. "No," she said firmly. "It can't be. It's just another psychosode." An epic one, sure, she thought, but what would you expect from someone who'd been off her meds for months?

Disheartened, she looked toward her father. He was still staring straight ahead, still giving it his best shot. Yet it was only a matter of time before he had to admit defeat; before they both had to face the truth that his daughter *was* the crazy girl everyone said she was.

Annie squeezed her hand. "Don't lose faith now, Pandora. It's *not* a hallucination. Give him a minute. The transition always takes longer for someone who doesn't have your—our—gift of inner sight."

"Oh, give it up, Annie," Pan said sharply. "Dad was right—this is all a bunch'a crap."

As if to affirm her disbelief, he said, "So, when is something going to happen? I feel like I'm about to burst all the blood vessels in both eyes from staring . . . so . . ." His voice suddenly trailed off; then his head began a slow tilt to the right. "Hey, does anybody else see that?"

"Oh, here we go . . ." Javi said softly.

"What is it, Dad?" Pan asked.

"I don't know. There's this kind of . . . shimmering—like a heat haze, you know?"

Pan swallowed nervously. "Is it like everything's . . . rippling?"

"Yes! That's exactly what it's—"

And then he yelped.

"I think the something he was looking for just happened," Annie murmured to Pan with a sly smile, then in a louder voice she asked, "Yes, David? You were saying . . . ?"

"Oh, my God," he whispered hoarsely. Then he started laughing. "Oh, this *can't* be happening . . ." His gaze settled on a black-haired man and woman standing by the railing on the opposite side of the park—although to Pan's eyes they didn't appear to be human. They looked more like—

"Holy crap!" Dad exclaimed. "Those people over there—they have dog heads!"

Annie sighed. "Damn it . . ."

Pan's breath hiccupped. Apparently they weren't human to Dad's eyes either . . . "D-Dad?" she croaked.

"Pan, are you watching this?" Dave continued excitedly. "They're people—with dog heads! Or would that be dogs with people bodies . . . ?" He turned to face her—and right away, she could tell.

He really *was* seeing it, too.

Seeing the world through *her* eyes.

"Oh, my God, you're glowing," he said in astonishment. "Like a rainbow . . ." He gazed at Annie. "You, too! Oh, man, this is so amazing!"

"Calm down, David," Annie whispered hoarsely.

"Yeah, okay, but you and Pan . . ." He pointed at the dog-people, who snarled at the unwanted attention. "And . . . and *them* . . ." he added, his voice rising in pitch. "Do you see them?"

"Stop that." Annie stepped in front of him, to block his view of the creatures. "Yes, David, I *know* they have dog heads. They're Cynocephali, from the island of Macumeran. They *all* look like that." As Dave leaned to his right to get another look at them, she moved to block that as well. "What did I tell you about screaming?"

"I *wasn't* screaming," he said firmly. "I was making an observation."

"Well, now you're making a *scene*, so lower your voice." Annie waved a hand in front of his face as he tried again to see past her. "And would you *mind* not staring at them? It's rude." She looked over her shoulder at the couple. "Sorry!" she called out, and gestured toward her three companions. "Tourists."

"Hey, you take that back!" Javi said.

The couple turned their muzzles up and sniffed disdainfully, then returned to their conversation. Unfortunately, Dave's "observation" seemed to have made at least one of the dog-people self-conscious about their appearance. The female Cynocephal purposely tilted her head down so her shoulder-length hair (mane?) obscured her face. Pan felt a little sorry for her.

Which came as a total surprise. Why should she feel any empathy for a monster, considering the almost constant state of terror creatures like that had put her in for the past decade? If anything, she should have felt utter contempt for it.

But she's not really a monster, is she? Pan gazed at the mixture of humans and thingies strolling by. *Now that I can really see them, a lot of them aren't total monsters. They're just . . . weird-looking.*

Weird, but not all that different from the unsuspecting humans around them, she realized. Monster children squealed in delight as they chased one another around, just like human kids. Monster couples held hands—or paws—and kissed, just like their human counterparts. Love and laughter and even self-consciousness about one's appearance were apparently the same for both species; the only true difference was that she could see the creatures for what they really were.

Maybe, she had to wonder, not all monsters were bad?

Pan pulled at her lower lip in contemplation. She'd have to think about this . . .

Dave looked to his right, and his jaw dropped. "Is that an akkiyyini?" Pan followed his line of sight to a quartet of musicians. Three humans on trumpet, acoustic guitar, and accordion were burning through what sounded like some kind of up-tempo New Orleans jazz number, while providing the rhythm on an improvised drum— actually a large, white, overturned plastic bucket—was a skeletal ghost in a Knicks basketball jersey. Dave pointed farther down the walkway, at a pair of flattish, blue-green, manta-ray-like creatures that floated above the park. "And those are jenny hanivers!" He laughed. "This is fantastic!"

Annie sighed wearily; her shoulders slumped. "Could you *please* stop embarrassing me like this? You're a New Yorker, aren't you? Try acting like one, and not like some moon-eyed—"

"Tourist?" Javi asked in a snarky tone.

She nodded—"Exactly."—then rolled her eyes when she saw him frowning. "Oh, go put a Band-Aid on your wounded ego, would you? I mean, honestly . . ."

Dave turned to face Pan. She noticed he was using the thumb and index finger of his left hand to massage the spot right above the bridge of his nose. One of his sinus headaches coming on? she wondered. "Honey, this is so . . . I don't know what to say."

"*I* think you've already said more than enough," Annie said brusquely. Pan fidgeted on the bench. She didn't want to ask him this, but she was so used to having things go wrong in her life that she had to know for sure. "You . . . *are* really seeing stuff, aren't you, Dad? I mean, you're not just saying all this to make me feel better, right?"

He looked stunned. "Make you . . . ? I think the better question is, are you seeing what *I'm* seeing?" He winced slightly as he pointed at the Cynocephali. "Like those dog-people over there."

"*Stop doing that,*" Annie growled.

"Yeah, I see them," Pan replied softly.

"I'm not imagining them, am I?"

"Hope not," she said with a pained smile. " 'Cause that would make us *both* nuts."

"Which you're *not,*" Annie interjected.

"And the glowing thing? You're doing that, aren't you? And . . ." He blinked a few times, then widened his eyes as though he was trying to refocus them. ". . . and over there." His pointy finger stabbed toward the wild flowers. "What I thought were butterflies . . . aren't those faeries?"

She nodded. "Uh-huh."

"So then how can you ask if I'm just doing this to make you happy, if we're *both* seeing the same weird things?" He leaned close. "They *are* weird, right?" he whispered conspiratorially.

She chuckled. "I'd say so."

"Okay, then." Dad held her hands. "Pan, it's just . . . are these the kinds of things . . . is this . . . This is what you've been seeing all these years?"

She nodded mutely.

"I . . ." His mouth opened and closed silently for a few moments as he struggled to find the right words to properly express his astonishment; eventually, he just settled for: "Wow." His Cheshire grin surfaced. "I think I might be jealous."

Pan blinked back tears and squeezed his hands. "Thanks, Dad." Then she turned to Annie.

"So . . ." the monster hunter said. "Now that your father has so loudly and embarrassingly confirmed your inner sight and come to realize that Gothopolis *does* exist . . . Proof enough that supernatural creatures exist?"

"Yeah," Pan said breathlessly. "Yeah, I guess it is."

She wasn't crazy, she realized—not now, not ever. The monsters she saw, the specters that danced at the edges of her vision, they were real; they always had been. And—

And then she started crying. She couldn't help it, couldn't stop it. After years of therapists and counselors and treatments, of being scorned by adults and ostracized by childhood friends, of doubting herself, of doubting her *sanity*, it was as though a lever in her brain had been pulled, allowing the floodgates of the dam she'd constructed around her heart to open wide and release all the pent-up anger and frustration and fear and loneliness she'd been holding in for so very long. Coming all at once, it terrified and overwhelmed her, both physically and emotionally, but at the same time it felt . . . wonderful. Like her soul had finally been set free.

"*Hey.*" Annie drew the sobbing girl into a reassuring hug. "It's okay, Pan, it's okay," she whispered.

"I . . . I'm *not* crazy," Pan muttered huskily.

"Of course you aren't, baby," Annie purred softly.

"But . . . but the doctors, and all the school counselors, and the other kids . . .

and . . . and . . . *they* all said . . ." She buried her face in Annie's shoulder.

"They were wrong, Pandora; they were all wrong. They just didn't have your gift." Annie hugged her tighter. "My God, child, has no one ever told you how special you really are?"

"M-Mom and Dad did . . . they tried . . . but . . . but it's been so *hard* on them . . ."

Annie rubbed her back, soothing her. "I'm sure it has been, sweetheart. They love you, they support you, but they just didn't understand what you were going through—but, how *could* they have known?" She pulled Pan away a little, so they could see each other's eyes. "But *you've* always known, haven't you—how special you are?"

"N-no," Pan replied, wiping at her runny nose with the heel of her hand.

Annie placed her hands along Pan's cheeks and used her thumbs to brush away the girl's tears. "Of course you did; deep down inside, you *know* you did. All you ever needed was someone to tell you you were right." She leaned forward to press her forehead against Pan's. "To tell you that the magick that's all around you . . . *is inside you*, too." She gently kissed the spot where their heads had touched. "I'm sorry I wasn't here for you sooner."

Pan hugged Annie with every ounce of her strength. "Thank you," she whispered.

"It was my pleasure," Annie said. "But I think you have somebody here who'd enjoy sharing this moment with you even more than I do."

Pan turned to find a misty-eyed Dad staring at his hands. He looked completely heartbroken as he looked up. "Pan, I . . . I am so sorry," he said, his voice thick with emotion. "For ever doubting you, for ever giving up, for . . . everything." His breath hitched. "Oh, God, all those things we put you through . . ." He started to turn away, as though afraid of causing her any further pain.

She gently laid a hand on his arm to stop him. "No, Dad, please. It's okay—really."

He turned back to face her and she fell into his embrace, absorbing the love that radiated from him and returning it twofold.

"Love you, Panda-bear," he murmured.

"Love you, too," she replied, so overjoyed that she didn't even remember to admonish him for using her childhood nickname. Then she turned back to the woman who'd opened her heart to a brand-new world. "Thanks, Annie. I mean it."

Annie reached out to brush some hair away from Pan's eyes. "As I said, it was my pleasure. You two going to be okay, now?"

Pan looked up at Dad and grinned. "Yeah. I think so."

Annie smiled. "Glad to hear it."

"Now we just have to figure a way to give Mom the good news." Dave looked to Annie. "You wouldn't want to take a little trip upstate and explain all this to my ex, would you?"

"Is she as open-minded as you?"

"About most things—except me," he said with a laugh.

Then his face contorted in pain, and he began rubbing his temples. "Ow! Ow, ow, ow." He winced and closed his eyes. "Damn," he gasped. "Where did *that* come from?"

"Sinus headache?" Pan asked.

"More like a migraine, it hurts that much." He opened his eyes and looked surprised. "Hey, where'd everything go?"

"Everything?"

He waved a hand around. "Your glow, the monsters . . ." He glanced across the way at the Cynocephali. "The dog heads! They're gone!"

"Actually, they're *not* gone," Annie replied. "Everything you saw is still right there. It's just that your vision went back to normal."

"See, you're not supposed to stare at that stuff for too long," Javi explained. "Otherwise it screws you up something fierce."

Pan stared wide-eyed at him. "You could see all that, too?"

He shook his head. "I didn't bother looking this time, but I know what you and your dad were talking about. I've seen it."

"Javi can look for only about a minute," Annie said with a sympathetic pout, "otherwise he gets terrible headaches."

"Yeah, last time I tried going longer than that I had to stay in bed for two days with the lights off. Missed a big game 'cause of it, too. Coach Patterson was *really* pissed at me."

"That sucks," Pan commented.

Annie nodded in agreement. "On the other hand, David, considering how long you were gazing it's pretty clear you have a higher tolerance for pain."

Dave moaned. "Tell that to my vibrating skull."

"The effect should fade in fifteen minutes or so." She dug into her backpack and pulled out a bottle of ibuprofen, then dropped two tablets into Dave's palm. "These will help in the meantime."

"Thanks." He tossed the tablets into his mouth and swallowed. "But what *was* that?"

"A friend of mine who works at NASA calls it a perception filter: a psychological barrier that nudges your subconscious so that you see what's in front of you—but don't *really* see it. That's just his way of dealing with it. Rocket science he can understand—but magick?" She shook her head. "It's a little too fanciful for his rational mind. Truthfully, I think it scares him." She smiled. "Ever wonder how New Yorkers can look right at the strangest things and take them completely in stride—or ignore them altogether?"

"Magic?" Dave said.

"Magick," Annie said with a grin. "With a K. Real old-world stuff. It's a spell. The greatest spell ever woven."

"And who did the weaving?"

"Are you familiar with the name Peter Stuyvesant?"

"Wasn't he, like, the first governor of New York?" Pan asked.

"His actual title was Director General," Annie replied, "but you're close enough."

Dave started. "What're you saying—the guy was a warlock or something?"

Annie placed an index finger to her lips in a secretive gesture, and smiled knowingly. "A story for another time." She swung the backpack on her right shoulder and glanced in the direction of Manhattan's southern tip. "Right now, I have to be on my way. I need to head home and work off that hamburger I had for lunch. I feel like such a pig." She glanced at Javi. "And *you* better get back to the botanica. Izzy probably has some errands for you to run." Her eyes narrowed in suspicion. "And don't forget about your part of our agreement, Javier Maldonado, or orang pendeks will be the *least* of your worries."

He laughed off the threat. "Got it." Then he shook hands with Dave. "It was great meeting you, Mr. Zwieback."

"Same here," Dave said. "Although I have this sneaking suspicion we'll be running into each other sooner rather than later . . ." He glanced slyly at his daughter.

Pan blushed and turned away. "Quit it, Dad . . ."

Under the burning gaze of a watchful parental eye, Javi wisely shook hands with her. "Talk to you soon, okay?"

"Okay." Was she grinning like an idiot again? Probably . . . but this time she didn't care.

With a final wink at her he yelled, "Later, Annie!" over his shoulder and raced off to help his grandmother.

Annie chuckled. "He's a good kid."

"Yeah, I guess," Dave said morosely. "Too bad he's a Yankees fan." He looked at Pan and frowned. "Traitor."

She flashed him a Cheshire grin, then turned to Annie. "Hey, are you busy tomorrow?"

Annie paused. "Not so far," she replied slowly. "Why?"

"Well, I was just thinking maybe you could come by the museum tomorrow? I can show you around—we have so much stuff you wouldn't believe—and then we can sit down and talk some more about my—"

"Superpowers?" Dad asked playfully.

"—whatever it is I can do. I mean, you didn't even explain what happened with me and Javi back in the tunnel!"

Dad's eyebrows shot up as he glanced at Annie. "Do I want to hear this?"

"It's not a big thing, David," she said dismissively. "All she did was use a bit of healing magick to fix a bump on his head. But don't worry, it's pretty low-level stuff—she's not turning into Harry Potter. Healers aren't sorcerers. They're more like . . . extreme biofeedback specialists."

"*I'm* a healer," Pan said in disbelief. "Get out."

"Trust me, Pandora—I've been around healers long enough I can spot one a mile away. And you *are* one."

Pan shook her head. "No way. I mean, I can't even figure out how to take those little tabs off of Band-Aids without everything getting stuck together in a clump."

"And yet you *did* treat Javi's injury," Annie pointed out. She smiled warmly. "I guess we *do* have a lot to talk about, huh?"

"I'll say . . ." Pan muttered.

"All right, then tomorrow it is"—she glanced at Dave—"if that's all right with you."

He shrugged. "Sure. Glad to have you. To tell you the truth, I could use a little more in-depth analysis myself about what just happened here. How's two o'clock sound?"

"I'll see you at two, then," Annie said. She pointed to her knapsack. "And if anything comes up I'll give you a call. I have your card." She shook Dave's hand and gave him a friendly air kiss, hugged Pan, and headed off.

Dad watched her departure a little too long for Pan's liking. The easy, sensuous sway of Annie's hips as she walked probably had a lot to do with holding his attention. No, strike that—it had *everything* to do with holding his attention.

"You know, if you like her butt that much you could always take a picture of it with your cell phone," she commented sarcastically.

"Yeah, if I could ever figure out how to work the damn thing. Sure would look nice as my computer wallpaper . . ." He flashed a wicked smile her way. "Moo-ha-ha."

She elbowed him in the ribs. "Hey! Get your *own* evil laugh."

Dad chuckled and threw an arm around her shoulders. "C'mon. I saw a Mr. Softee truck parked down on the corner. I think in light of today's revelations a little ice-cream celebration is in order."

Pan sighed contentedly. She couldn't remember the last time she'd ever been so totally happy; probably not since before the monsters came lumbering into her life.

And speaking of monsters . . .

As she and Dad walked past the Cynocephali couple, Pan met their heated gazes—and gave them a friendly little wave.

It wasn't until she'd crossed Twenty-eighth Street that Annie became aware of the tingling sensation in her side—right on the spot where her goblin-inflicted wound was located. That couldn't be a good sign.

She groaned softly, imagining the hell Izzy was going to give her for undoubtedly reopening it during the pursuit of the orang pendek. Stepping into the doorway of a building to get out of the flow of pedestrian traffic, she gingerly lifted up the hem of her T-shirt to take a look, dreading what she might find. Sure enough, there was a splotch of blood soaking the bandage . . . but not as much as she'd expected. Using a fingernail, she poked at the edge of the tape securing the bandage until the adhesive finally loosened, then pulled the dressing back to examine the wound.

Except the wound was gone.

Annie scratched her chin, trying to imagine how that could have happened. Then she recalled the minuscule crackle of electricity that issued from Pandora's fingers when the two held hands on the bench.

She looked back in the direction of the High Line, and a tiny smile quirked her lips. "*Definitely* a healer."

Tossing aside the bandage, she headed for home with a bit more spring to her step, never noticing the camera lens trained on her from across the avenue . . . or the man who'd been taking pictures of her—as well as of Pan and her father—ever since the Penn Station incident.

Pan's creepy seatmate from the train chuckled as he stared at the last shot displayed on the screen of his digital camera: a not-so-flattering close-up of Annie's face as she grimaced while peeling off the bandage.

"Very nice," he commented, then quickly reviewed the long sequence of shots he'd gathered: Pan on the train; the confrontation with the transit cops; Annie and

David conversing during the walk to the diner; Annie kissing him on the cheek. Some were a little blurry, but the majority was usable.

He stowed the camera in his briefcase and went in search of a cybercafe. He still had a report to e-mail before the day was over, and a very demanding client who was eager to read it.

19

"So, this is our target," Vincenc remarked, pointing to the photograph of the dark-haired woman that was displayed on the laptop screen before him. "The legendary Sebastienne Mazarin. After hearing all those stories about her over the years and never running into her, I was starting to think she was just a myth."

"I've heard those stories, too," Sionek replied. The powerfully built, mahogany-skinned vampire was splayed bonelessly across two cushions of a sofa on the far side of the room, while his teammate Dusana rested her head on his chest and curled up against him. He lovingly ran his fingers through her dark brown tresses. "The werewolf purge of France in 1712," he continued, "the Leviathan killing in 1843 Tokyo, the Black Tom explosion that incinerated Lord Ruthven in 1916 . . . the list goes on and on. They say she's like a force of nature—unstoppable, unpredictable, and completely destructive."

"Whoever 'they' are," Zuzana commented sarcastically as she paused in her examination of the tastefully decorated suite in which the strike team had gathered. Unlike some of the more glamorous, far wealthier vampire clans, House Karnstein could not boast of having an expansion chapter in every country; thus it oftentimes became necessary to rely on the kindness of allies to provide room and board. In New York that meant the Czech Consulate on Manhattan's Upper East Side—a little home away from home for a band of human and undead warriors planning their next mission.

And waiting for night to fall.

The vampiress turned to address the couple, particularly her younger, human sister. "I don't put a lot of trust in old wives' tales. Mazarin probably just has one hell of a good publicist."

A shiver ran through Dusana's lithe frame. "Still . . . maybe we should have been hoping she *was* a myth."

Stretched out on the love seat across from Vincenc, Jenessa Branislav nervously picked at a loose thread hanging from the throw pillow that she hugged against her chest. "No," she said in an unusually quietly tone. "She's no myth, I can assure you."

Vincenc's shoulders tensed in response to the disturbingly timid sound of his team leader's voice. On or off the battlefield, Jenessa was herself a force to be reckoned with, always full of life—even in undeath—and brimming over with self-confidence. But after her initial exuberance at learning the identity of their next target, after the initial high she'd been on from draining the priest's blood, her personality began undergoing a subtle change, boldness and confidence eventually giving way to nervousness and doubt. She clearly was dreading the next phase of the mission. He'd first noticed it on the flight over; it was even more evident as zero hour approached. And if House Karnstein's most respected warrior lived in fear of an immortal monster hunter, then what chance might any of her elite soldiers really have against their intended prey?

From behind him, Zuzana leaned over his shoulder to get a good look at their adversary. The frosted tips of her shoulder-length chestnut hair whispered harshly against the coarse stubble of his ever-present five-o'clock shadow. "Huh. She's a lot prettier than I expected . . . I mean, for a four-hundred-year-old crone. I guess being a shape-changer *does* have its advantages."

Vincenc grunted dismissively. "And you're *sure* she's the one the priest back in Mariz said had the Prize, Jenna?"

She pulled at another loose thread. "None other."

He exhaled sharply through his nostrils. "I'm gonna need a really big gun for this mission, aren't I?" he asked wryly.

"Maybe even two," Jenessa softly agreed. A trace of her old self appeared in the playful smile that briefly curled the left side of her mouth.

He sighed heavily—"Fantastic."—and rose from the chair, gesturing for Zuzana to take his place. He left open the file he'd been studying, as well as the Flickr-stream collection of photographs that were linked to it. "Have a seat. I want everybody to familiarize themselves with the target before we head out."

The vampiress plopped down onto the cushion. "And how do we do that when she can change her appearance?" she asked curtly.

"Because for all her shape-changing and multiple false identities," Vincenc replied as he pointed to the computer screen, "she apparently has *one* face that she likes more than the others."

Jenessa knew that was true enough. The high-resolution images collected in House Karnstein's private Flickr album stretched back over hundreds of years from modern-day digital-camera shots to nineteenth-century tintypes, from early eighteenth-century engravings to late sixteenth-century portraits. Fashion and hairstyles morphed with the passage of time; the settings glimpsed in the backgrounds became less pastoral and more metropolitan as the centuries passed; but the flawless beauty of the woman in the pictures remained the one constant in an ever-changing world.

Zuzana ran an index finger over the cursor pad to scroll through a succession of photos, and shrugged. "Seems like cheating, though"—she waved her hands around from her head to her waist, as though performing an awkward dance move—"being able to move things around and smooth them out when you start to show your age. If you really think about it."

"Which I *don't*," Dalibor quipped from the other side of the room, a champagne flute of chilled blood in one hand and an apricot kolaci—a Czech pastry—in the other. "I have better things to do than consider the beauty secrets of someone who'll be dead before the night is over." He grinned and tilted his glass toward his teammates in a mock toast. "Here's to slaying the vampire slayer. May her dying screams echo across the deepest pits of hell for all eternity."

Jenessa gazed over her shoulder at him. "Enjoying the buffet, Dalek?" she asked with a smile. She'd noticed the gusto with which her friend and confidante had thrown himself at the food—prepared to their specific needs by the consulate's culinary staff—almost as soon as they'd entered the room.

"Oh, *abforutery*," he replied around a mouthful of kolaci before swallowing. "You should try the blood sausage, Jenna—it's really outstanding. The type-A's are particularly sweet."

"Yes, well, try not to overindulge, dear," she said archly. "Nobody likes a fat vampire."

"*I'm not fat!*" he snapped, his voice rising almost to a bloodcurdling screech. "Of *course* you're not," Jenessa replied soothingly. She glanced over to Vincenc and winked. Always yanking her old friend's chain, was Jenessa. Even in her current state of depression, she never tired of doing it.

"Wow," Zuzana suddenly remarked. "Okay, so according to the file Mazarin was born in 1560 or thereabouts in Brazil; her father, Paul Mazarin, was a French explorer; her mother, Amaru—no last name—was a . . ." Her eyebrows rose in surprise. "An Amazon warrior?"

Vincenc snorted derisively. "Nonsense."

Jenessa shook her head. "That report was compiled from reliable sources. It may sound crazy, but every word of it is true."

"But I thought the Amazons were all Greek," Vincenc commented.

"Well, what would *you* call a female warrior who lives in the Amazon rain forest?" Dalibor interjected.

"*My next meal!*" the group said as one, then laughed uproariously. It was an old joke—the question changed with each telling, but the punch line remained constant.

The humor faded quickly when Zuzana saw the next line of biographical text. "Oh. Her mother was a shaman, too?"

"Magick," Krystof said with a snarl. The human brushed aside the fringe of blond hair that normally obscured his left eye long enough for Jenessa to see the anger that flashed in both dull brown orbs. "I *hate* magick."

"Well, she had to get her transformative powers from *some*where, didn't she?" Dalibor said. "But better she be a magician's daughter than an actual magician herself—fewer complications for us that way."

Zuzana went back to her reading. "Expert marksman, world-class swordfighter, munitions expert, and martial artist; Miskatonic University doctorate in teratology—"

"That's the study of monsters," Jenessa interjected for Dalibor's benefit.

"—and a master's degree from Serazawa University in Tokyo in kaijuology,"

Zuzana continued.

"The study of *giant* monsters," Dalibor said before Jenessa could explain it first. "That one I know." He shrugged dismissively. "Not much call for that kind of specialist these days. Probably looks good on her résumé, though."

"Our girl sounds like a regular jack-of-all-trades," Dusana remarked, easing out of Sionek's embrace. "Or would that be a jill-of-all-trades?"

"She's been both, according to this," Zuzana replied, gesturing toward the file. "Apparently she likes to experiment. Switches genders a few times every century, to see how the other half lives." She paused, then her lips curled in disgust. "Ugh. That's just creepy."

"Well," Jenessa said quietly, "I only saw her as a woman, that . . . that one time." She shivered and lightly placed a hand across her collarbone. Almost three decades later and she could *still* feel the metal teeth of the rusty saw as they ripped into her throat; as "the beautiful, dark one" pinned down her limbs with wooden stakes and began cutting off her head while Jenessa screamed and screamed and screamed . . .

"But that's all in the past, Jenna," Dalibor said gently in her ear, his calm voice slowly easing her from the grasp of the terrifying memory. "She'll never hurt you again."

She felt the reassuring pressure of his hand squeezing her shoulder, and looked up to see the equally reassuring smile he so obviously labored to maintain as red-tinged tears clouded his eyes. He'd been witness to her dismemberment that night so long ago, had even suffered two shattered legs and a punctured lung while coming to her defense. A vain effort, of course, but appreciated nonetheless. After a team of surgeons in the employ of House Karnstein was finally able to reassemble her body parts—scattered as they had been across ten miles of Prague alleys and sewers—she'd repaid Dalibor's loyalty the only way she knew how: by turning him.

Well, she always *had* been awkward in making thank-you gestures . . .

Jenessa patted his hand. "Yes, Dalek, all in the past," she murmured, and sighed heavily. "And yet she is always lurking in the deepest shadows of my thoughts . . ."

Dalibor smiled impishly. "Well, I know of one thing that's guaranteed to chase away those shadows." He reached inside his expensive Brooks Brothers jacket and pulled out an impressive-looking weapon: a Mark XIX Desert Eagle handgun. He held out the titanium gold-finished .357 Magnum, inviting her to take possession of it. "You always feel better after you've shot something . . ."

Jenessa laughed softly and accepted the offering. "Oh, Dalek, you know me so well."

He nodded sagely. "And while you're blasting the hell out of the target range in the underground garage, I'll lay out your armor for tonight's mission."

"Oh, very well," Jenessa playfully groaned. She slid her legs off the love seat and gracefully rose to her feet, then turned to face her loyal assistant. "But . . ." she added in a warning tone as she poked his chest with the barrel of the gun, "you must swear to put on your own armor before we head out."

"But it's so confining . . ." he whined.

"Lay off the kolachi and it won't be," she chided him. "I *mean* it, Dalek. Fashion be damned this time."

He pouted at her for a few moments, then replied sullenly, "I'm *not* fat."

She smiled gently. "We can discuss it later—after we've completed the mission. But right now . . ." She ejected the ammunition clip from the Desert Eagle, checked to see that it was full, slammed it back into the pistol grip and ratcheted back the slide to chamber a round. "Right now I feel like blowing holes in something. And then I expect all of you to join me at the target range—say, in twenty minutes?"

"We'll be there, Jenna," Vincenc said.

Jenessa turned to Zuzana. "Print out some of those photographs so we can tape them up on the targets." Then she flashed a wicked little grin. "One's aim is always better when one has the right incentive, you know." She glanced at Vincenc. "Be sure to bring a big gun."

A rare smile stretched the corners of his mouth. "Maybe even two."

Jenessa laughed heartily. And then, with a dramatic flip of her flame-colored locks, she strode from the room with all the swagger and self-assurance of a true warlord.

It was only after she had turned the corner at the end of the hallway, when she was finally out of her team's sight, that the swagger became a weak-kneed shuffle, that self-assurance gave way to doubt . . . and fear. The handgun suddenly felt as heavy as a boulder, and Jenessa dropped it on the paisley runner; it thudded softly against the thick carpet.

Softly groaning, she pressed her back against the nearest wall and slid down it to sit on the floor. Trembling fingers fluttered across the base of her throat, tracing the path of a ragged scar that existed only in memory; her ears rang with the echoes of screams that never seemed to fade.

She exhaled sharply, and laughed nervously as she dabbed at red-rimmed eyes with her fingertips. *Look at the big, tough warrior,* she chided herself. *Still scared of the bogeyman at your age, even when you've been one yourself for . . . what, over a century?* She shook her head. "Ridiculous."

And yet she *was* scared. If it were in her power she would pack her bags right this instant and board the first flight home. Let someone else lead the charge. Vincenc was more than capable of standing in for her, just this once.

But that could never be; the council of elders would never allow it. Nor would her personal code of honor. As strike-team leader, as House Karnstein's fiercest warrior, she was expected to lead her troops into battle—and, in this situation, to face her personal demon head-on. If her clan were to gain any advantage over the other treasure seekers in this race for the Prize, it could only be accomplished by forcing Mazarin to give up its location before the others learned of the monster hunter's involvement. There could be no delay.

And besides, she reflected, she could never abandon her soldiers, her "children," on such a dangerous mission. They depended on her wisdom and guidance, trusted her to bring them home safely. What kind of mother-figure would she be if she turned her back on them just when they might need her the most?

A heavy, weary sigh shook Jenessa's body. There was no escaping her duty, or her destiny. She would lead her team, and confront the monster that haunted her dreams. And if the ancient Watchers truly looked over their undead children, as she'd been taught to believe, she would survive the night.

Gathering her strength, Jenessa pushed off from the wall and gracefully vaulted to her feet, tumbling in midair to reach down and pluck the Desert Eagle from the carpet before softly landing on her toes. Then she set off along the hallway, bound for the staircase that would lead her down to the garage.

Dalek was right. She always felt better after practicing her marksmanship, and right now her mind's eye was forming a very specific target: an image of Sebastienne Mazarin, with the bright-red dot of a laser-targeting sight centered on her forehead.

Jenessa only hoped that, when she faced the real thing, she'd have the courage to pull the trigger.

20

"*I! LIIIIVE!!*" Pan screeched into her cell phone, in a high-pitched nasally voice that was meant to imitate the creepy Hungarian accent of the late movie actor Peter Lorre—only it came out sounding less like the evil Dr. Einstein from *Arsenic and Old Lace* and more like the hyperventilating Chihuahua from the old *Ren and Stimpy* cartoons. She grinned at her father, who appeared to be too busy piloting his car—a classic, light blue 1964 Chevrolet Impala—through the midday traffic on the Queensborough Bridge to comment on the quality of her performance. A wise choice, she thought.

"So I hear," Mom replied drolly through the speaker. "And it only took two and a half hours after your train got in for me to hear from you."

Pan winced. "Eep. Sorry, Mom."

"Apology accepted. The trip down go okay?"

"Yeah, no problems," she said, pushing aside the mental image of the perv on the train. "But, oh, my God, Mom, I have something so amazing to tell you, you are *not* going to believe it!"

"Don't tell me," Mom said. "Your father's closing the museum and moving to the sticks, to pursue the life of a gentleman farmer."

"Swing and a miss—again," Dad said genially. "Actually, Karen, Pan and I do have some news—"

"Like, big, world-changing news!" his daughter interjected.

"—but it's something you and I really can't discuss over the phone. You need to see it for yourself."

"See it for myself?" Mom asked. "And how do you propose I do that?"

"You come down," Pan said quickly. It was an opening she couldn't pass up—not if she was going to get her parents back together.

"Oh, now honey," Mom said, "you know I have that meeting with Mrs. Van Schrik on Monday—"

"So come down tomorrow. Mom, we *really* need to talk about this."

There was a pause, then: "Dave, this isn't about some weird thing you bought for the museum, isn't it?"

"Oh, nonono. Absolutely not."

"You are *such* a terrible liar."

"No, it really isn't, Karen. Not this time."

"But it's something great, Mom," Pan added. "But you gotta come down so we can tell you all about it. What do you say? You come down, we all have lunch, and we show you the big surprise. I swear you're gonna love it!"

"I don't know, sweetie . . ."

Pan looked to her father for help. There had to be *some* way to convince her to get on that train. From the devious smile on his face, it was apparent he'd already thought of the perfect incentive.

"Hey, Karen, would it help if I sweetened the deal with an offer of cinnamon buns from that Italian bakery in Middle Village? You know, the *fresh. warm. gooey* ones you always drooled over, just thinking about them . . . ?"

There was a sound from the speaker that was either a soft hum on the line, or Mom's sweet tooth whining. "You're a fiend, Dave."

"And it only took you—what, twenty years to figure that out?" He winked at his daughter. "We'll see you at Penn Station at noon."

Mom sighed. "All right, you win. But they better be *fresh* buns, right out of the oven."

"They'll only stay fresh—and uneaten—if you don't dawdle," Dad replied, "so don't miss your train. And I'm not lying about that."

"Fiend. Love you, Panda-bear."

"Love you, Mom!" Pan said and hung up. She smiled contentedly. With her mother coming down from Schriksdork, the next step of Project: Parental Rebonding was about to begin in earnest . . . whatever step that might be. She really hadn't thought that far ahead . . .

"So," Dad said slowly, "what do we do now? I mean, honestly, kiddo, what Annie showed us changes *everything.*"

"I know!" she said, so full of energy she felt like jumping out and running ahead of the car. "Oh, my God, do you know what this means, Dad? No more therapists, no more meds—" She squealed. "And when Mom sees for herself . . ."

Dad, however, had to play killjoy. "Slow down, honey, it's not as easy as you make it sound. It's not like Mom and I can just call up Dr. Farrar and tell her, 'Hey, Nicole, thanks for all your help, but you know all those monsters Pan says she's always seeing? Turns out they're real. And you know how we found out? Because a woman who says *she hunts those monsters for a living* showed us.' " He gave her a sidelong glance. "Two seconds after we hang up, she'd be on the phone to child protective services to get you the hell away from us. And then your mother and I would undergo all sorts of psychological exams."

"Oh, I know all about *those.*" She smiled and affectionately patted his shoulder. "But don't worry, Dad. I'll come visit you and Mom every Sunday in the rubber room."

He frowned. "Not. Funny."

Thankfully, before he could continue spoiling her good mood her cell's "Incubus Summer" ringtone began roaring. She checked the incoming number and grinned as she answered. "Hey, jungle queen! All done with your Teutonic *luuurve* machine so we can finally have a civil conversation?"

Sheena sighed. "*Soooo* jealous. It's sad, really. But I guess it's to be expected, when you're livin' among hillbillies."

Pan noticed Dad gesturing to her. "Hang on a sec, Sheen." She hit the mute button. "What?"

"Do me a favor and don't tell your friends about what happened today—all right? Even Sheena. I know you two are like sisters, and she'd probably think what Annie did was fantastic—"

"Well, *yeah.*"

"—but I haven't completely wrapped my head around all these big revelations; I'm sure you haven't either. We need some time to absorb it all, so just wait until after we've talked to Mom and gotten her reaction before you start telling everybody you're okay. All right?"

Her immediate thought was, *Oh, now why did he have to go and say that? I wanna scream it from the rooftops! I wanna post it on the 'Net! I wanna tell everybody, You see? YOU SEE, all you doubters and haters? All you asshats who called me a freak and a loser? I always said I wasn't crazy AND I'M NOT! I have irrefutable proof of that now, and you can all suck on it!*

What she said, however, was: "My silence doesn't come cheap, you know."

"Oh, come on—you just had Mr. Softee!" Her stern gaze, however, didn't waver.

Dad sighed. "Okay. Fine. Cookie Mintster at the Stone Cold Creamery?"

"Deal!" Okay, so her skill at negotiations was as poor as her father's ability to lie well—so what? Later tonight she'd be gobbling up the perfect ending to what had turned out to be a perfect day. Pan clicked back on. "Sorry about that, Sheen. So what's up? Gonna stop by the apartment to celebrate my triumphant return?"

"Can't tonight," Sheen replied, the disappointment evident in her voice. "Nana Hildy's in town to show off her latest husband—probably before his pacemaker shorts out and she gets all *his* money, too—"

"Be nice," Pan said warningly.

"—and Mom insists I have to join them all for dinner. In, like, a *girly dress*, for God's sake!" She snorted. "Probably afraid Nana'll cut me outta the will if I show up just bein' myself."

"Probably afraid all that funereal black you usually wear will scare off husband number . . ."

"Six—no, five. But there'll *be* a sixth. Eventually."

"And staying on her good side could be a good thing. You *have* told me a bunch of times she's the richest McCarthy of them all—or whatever her married name is now."

"Azzi. He's Lebanese." Sheen paused. "Supposedly it means 'silkworm.' "

"Mmmm," Pan purred throatily. "Sounds sexy. Azzi the *luuuv*worm."

"Excuse me?" Dad chimed in. She ignored him—it'd take too long to explain.

"Umm—ew?" Sheen replied. "You mind not puttin' stuff like that in my head, 'specially when I'm about to eat? Now I'm gonna keep havin' visions of old people havin' sex—*BLAAARGH!*"

Pan could practically see her best friend holding a hand over her mouth as she fake-barfed, and she laughed. "So listen, after you're done purging tonight from watching all those senior citizens bumping uglies in front of you—"

"*BLUUH! STOP, damn you!*"

"—you gonna have any time to get together tomorrow? Or will you still be kneeling at the altar of the porcelain god, offering up tasty meat chunks and undigested corn to its gaping watery maw?"

Silence for a moment, then: "What movie'd you get *that* from?"

"I didn't. I just made it up. I've been working on my writing."

"I thought you wanted to be a painter," Dad remarked.

"I'm a Renaissance woman, okay? I'm allowed to have a wide range of artistic interests."

Sheen grunted. "Whatever. So, yeah, I'll be free. What'd you wanna do?"

"Well, Mom's coming, and this really strange woman I ran into at Penn Station is gonna stop by. I thought you'd like to meet her."

"Oh, yeah? So, *how* strange? Like, crazy-old-lady-living-with-thirty-cats-in-a-run-down-house strange?"

"Even better: beautiful-supermodel-hunting-monkeys-in-the-Amtrak-tunnels kinda strange."

Sheen whistled. "Wow. You just meet *all* the innn-teh-restin' people. Did you punch *her* in the face, too?"

"We're not that close yet," Pan replied with a laugh.

An unintelligible female voice squawked in the background. Sheen groaned. "Look, I gotta go. Mom wants to 'help' me pick out an 'appropriate' dress for tonight."

"Bet it's that cute pink summer one still hanging in the back of your closet."

"Then I'll just have to kill myself before anybody sees me in it, won't I?" A louder and shriller, yet still untranslatable remark—her mother again—had Sheen yelling back, "All right, Ma! Gimme a minute!" She sighed heavily. "I'm livin' in hell."

Pan laughed. "See you tomorrow." She hung up and waggled the cell between her thumb and middle finger. "Sheena," she explained.

"I heard. She coming over tonight?"

Pan frowned. "Can't. She's got family stuff."

"Aww, that's a shame," he replied as he pulled up to the curb in front of the museum.

Pan raised an eyebrow. "The museum? I thought we were going home."

"I left Tim minding the store while I went to pick you up. Thought maybe it was time to relieve him." He smiled slyly. "I also thought you might want to check out the new aquisition. I've been saving it for you."

"*Really?*" Pan grinned lopsidedly as she lowered her head between her shoulders and bent forward a little at the waist. Pandora the Hunchbacked Assistant. "Then it would be . . . my . . . pleasure . . . master," she wheezed, rubbing her hands together in anticipation.

Dad grimaced and opened his door. "Y'know, you really need to work on that Peter Lorre imitation . . ."

21

"Hey, *I* know that hunchback!" Tim Merrick bellowed in an exaggerated tone as Pan lumbered through the doorway. "But what's she doin' loose in the daytime, goin' around scarin' decent folk? There's kids around!" Indeed there were—a group of teenagers all dressed in gothy fashions, and all known to Pan. There was acne-cursed Dylan Rodgers, tall and lanky, his curly hair worn short on the sides with the top swept forward over his eyes. Right beside him was his girlfriend, Lisa Danziger, just as tall but even lankier, her always-unruly blond hair tied into unbraided pigtails on either side of her head. Reyna Gonzalez stood just to the left of Lisa; she adjusted the mad-scientist goggles perched on the top of her short dark hair as she greeted Pan with a brace-covered smile. Next to her was her boyfriend, Tommy Guerrero, heavyset and dark-eyed, with just the slightest trace of a mustache forming. Moira Thornton poked her head out from behind Tommy's broad shoulders, her auburn hair tumbling around her freckled face in waves. Bringing up the rear was Moira's girlfriend, black-and-pink-haired Tory Kwon, who at four foot eleven would be shorter than Pan . . . if she didn't constantly wear shoes with four-inch-thick soles.

And standing in the center of the pack in all her purple-haired glory, sporting a grin as wide as a Zwieback Cheshire-cat smile, was the group's bespectacled leader. Today she'd opted to show off her Rubenesque figure in a black 1950s-style rockabilly dress with a fitted bodice and flared skirt, wide fishnet stockings, and black pumps. Coupled with her coiffed hair and perfect makeup she was, as always, the epitome of Goth chic.

"Welcome home, Vampira," Sheena McCarthy said.

Pan squealed and rushed forward to hug them all. Then she lightly punched Sheen's broad chest with her fist. "You bitch! You lied to me!"

"Watch the language . . ." Dad said in a warning tone from his position by the sales counter.

"Oh, what—I was supposed to tell you I was really here and not in my house?" Sheen replied, adjusting her black tortoiseshell glasses. "Where's the surprise in that, Zee? Duuuh."

Pan glared at her father. "You knew all about this, didn't you?"

He smiled. "Well, that text message stuff is like a foreign language to me, but I'm not so completely helpless that I couldn't send one to Sheena while you and Annie were in the ladies' room at the restaurant." He caught her look of disbelief. "Okay, so maybe Javier helped me figure it out . . ."

"I hate you," she said in mock anger.

Dad shrugged. "Eh. I'll learn to live with the pain."

She turned back to Sheen. "So, no dinner with Nana Hildy?"

"That's actually tomorrow night." Sheen pouted. "Still don't wanna go, though."

Pan chuckled. "Poor baby. So that wasn't your mom yelling at you to get ready, then? Sounded a little like her."

Sheen gestured toward the redhead. "No, that was Moira."

"Shayna!" the freckle-faced girl brayed. "Git offa dat phuune an' git drayssed fer yer saintly ol' nan what's cuumin' ovah ta dah huuse!"

"Why? Why do you always keep doin' that voice?" Sheen demanded, her hands on her hips. "My mom does not sound like some old Irish washerwoman!"

"Well, she is Irish, isn't she?" Moira countered, her natural voice still tinged with the lilt of the Emerald Isle from which she and her parents had emigrated a few years back. "An' she works at a Laundromat, now doesn't she?"

"Yeah, but . . ." Sheen paused for a moment to think it over. "Yeah, okay. I get it. But knock it off, wouldja? She's not that old."

"I'll be sure t'keep it in mind for next time, dearie." The sarcasm was unmistakable.

Pan nudged Sheen with an elbow. "So? Where's yo' maayynn?"

"Uwe's gotta work. His boss wanted him to help out gettin' ready for some big

wedding banquet they're havin' tomorrow at the catering hall." She smiled impishly. "But he sends his love."

Pan snorted. "Yeah, I'll bet. I'm sure there's a b-word in there somewhere you
forgot to pass along."

"Mmm . . . could be." Sheen grinned. "But he said it in a *really* endearin' way."

Dad clapped his hands together, once. "So, we all heading off to Pizzeria Uno to
celebrate the prodigal daughter's return . . ." His Cheshire-cat grin slowly appeared.
". . . or are you interested in seeing something really cool?"

"What's goin' on, Mr. Z?" Dylan asked. "Tim was talkin' 'bout some mystery box
you got in the cellar."

"Yeah," Lisa added. "He said it was gonna be the next big exhibit."

"You better believe it!" Dad grinned broadly. "After all, how many museums
do you know that can boast having the skeleton of an actual, honest-to-goodness
vampire?"

Pan's eyes went as wide as dinner plates. "What?"

"Squee!" Tory exclaimed, and hopped in delight. "For real?"

"For real," Dave replied.

"Wait a minute," Pan interjected. "Where'd you get a vampire skeleton from?"

"Uh, Transylvania?" Dylan said. "Duuh."

Lisa gave him a sharp nudge in the ribs with her elbow to shut him up.

"C'mon, Dad," Pan continued, "there's no such thing as a *real* vampire . . .
although, sure, it would be pretty cool to see one. But there's never been any actual
evidence of one."

Dave grinned. "Ah! So says Count Draaah-cuu-lah's child bride," he said in a
heavy-tongued mangling of an Eastern European accent. It was almost as painful
to listen to as her Peter Lorre imitation. "Und who vould know bet-tah den sooch
an authority, yeeess?"

Pan sighed. "Daaadd . . ."

He shook his head. "It's no bull, Pan," he said in his normal voice. "Got the
certified paperwork and everything from the seller, signed by a mayor or burgo-
master or whatever his title was in the Czech Republic, back when it was still called
Czechoslovakia. It's all legit, far as I can tell."

"And this Count Skeletor," Reyna said. "We're gonna be the first ones to see it?"

Dad nodded. "Uh-huh."

"Not to mention I'm gonna record the whole thing as my next short-film project," Tim said. He reached under the sales counter and came up with a large, bright yellow polyethylene carrying case. With a flourish he undid the metal clasps and opened it to reveal a professional—and very expensive-looking—camcorder. "All locked and loaded and ready to roll."

Dave looked to his daughter. "So? How's that for a surprise?"

"Sweet!" Pan said. "Gonna make me famous on your YouTube channel, Tim?"

"More like *infamous*, knowing you," Dad remarked.

Pan regally tilted back her head and looked down her nose at him. "You say that like it's a bad thing."

Dad sighed. "You're right—I should know better," he said, glancing toward Tim.

Tim chuckled. "Daddy's Little Girl."

"From *hell*," Dad added.

"Yes," Pan agreed. "And right now Daddy's Little Hellspawn needs her suitcase."

"And why is that?" Dad asked.

She grunted in exasperation and gestured toward her clothing. "Well, I mean . . . just look at me!"

"Huh? You look fine."

She rolled her eyes. "*Such* a liar. I'm a total mess and I've gotta go change. I've gotta redo my makeup, fix my hair, put on something nice . . . I'm not gonna let Tim immortalize my big moment on the 'Net looking like . . . like I just spent time chasing monkeys in a train tunnel! It'll be up there forever for all the world to see! For all my friends to see!"

"They already see," Dave pointed out, nodding toward her crew. "And they haven't said anything about your appearance."

Sheen grinned maliciously. "Yeah, but that's only 'cause we're too busy laughin' at the hobo"—she tapped her chest—"on the inside." The others pointed at Pan and snarled in disgust as they hissed, "*Hobo . . . hooohh-booohh . . .*"

Pan pointed to her friends as she faced her dad. "You see? They're *laughing* at me!"

"But only on the inside," Sheen reminded her—with a smirk.

"How am I supposed to live with that?"

He stared at her for a moment. Then his left eyebrow slowly cocked in preparation for the sarcastic remark she could practically see forming in his mind.

"Oy," he replied, lightly slapping his cheeks with his fingertips in a false gesture of concern for her fragile ego. "Such a tragedy."

Pan, however, was having none of it. "Yes! Yes, it would be! You should *want* your only child to avoid becoming a public disgrace! What kinda parent are you?"

"The long-suffering kind, apparently . . ."

She pointed to the door. "Go! Get me my stuff so I can fix this!"

" 'Only child . . .' " Dave sighed heavily, and began shuffling toward the door. "This is the last time I hire hunchbacked assistants," he remarked to Tim. "Buncha prima donnas . . ."

"Go!" Pan ordered. "*You're* the one with the car keys."

"Going, I'm going . . ." he muttered.

The door swung shut behind him, and Pan turned to face Tim. He looked highly amused. "What?"

Tim shrugged. "Just couldn't help noticing you got him trained well."

"Of course." Pan flashed a wicked grin. "And now, Timothy," she intoned in her deepest, most ominous voice, "at last you know the true power of being Daddy's Little Girl . . ."

" *'Cause we. are. the. FIIIEEEEND CLUUUUUB!*" Pan wailed, head thrown back, as she and the crew sang along with The Misfits and danced on the steps leading to the museum's basement floor.

Not the easiest thing for her to do in four-inch heels—especially given the fact this was only the third time she'd ever worn her "girly shoes" since buying them (why bother wasting a good pair of pumps in Sucktown, right?) and her sense of balance was just slightly better than that of an elephant crossing an icy lake—but sometimes the price you had to pay for being glamorous involved taking risks. And if that meant she had to walk around for the rest of the night with her arms constantly windmilling to keep her upright, then so be it.

First, though, she needed to stop fooling around on the rickety wooden steps and reach the cement floor without doing a face-plant . . .

"You know this thing is running, right?" Tim asked as the song on the CD player faded, and pointed with his left hand to the camcorder that rested on his right shoulder. He was watching her through the viewfinder.

"Of *course* I do," Pan replied. "Why d'ya think we just sang our theme song? *I* think it'd be a great opening for the film."

He chuckled. "Only one director on this picture, babe. You can choreograph dance numbers all you want, but *I'm* the one calling the shots."

"You are *such* a dictator." Pan frowned and glanced at the stairs. "You're not gonna keep rolling if I fall and break my head, are you?"

Tim gave a half-shrug. "I can edit that part out."

"Great . . ."

"Or you could use it for a gag reel," Sheen replied with a grin. "If you can make it look painful *and* funny, Vampira, he could probably get ten thousand hits on YouTube right out the gate."

Tim nodded. "Girl has a point."

Pan pouted as she grabbed the banister for support. "You're all a bunch'a sadists."

"Hey, *you're* the one looking for immortality." He lowered the camera and held out his free hand. "C'mon."

She gratefully took hold and let him guide her down the steps.

"Whoa." Now that she was standing in the full light of the overhead fluorescents, Tim gave her appearance a look-over and nodded in approval. "That's some outfit you got on there. I like the hair, too."

Pan grinned. "Really?" She did a slow pirouette to show off her little black sleeveless dress, which was decorated with a multitude of white skull-and-crossbones appliqués. Combined with high heels and black pantyhose, dark eye makeup, black lipstick and nail polish, she certainly couldn't be mistaken for a boy—or even a teen, for that matter. In fact, she appeared to be in her early twenties. Daddy's Little Girl, all grown up.

"Well, the makeup's a little much," Tim replied, "but that's just me." He glanced around at her friends—"I know you Goths like to go all out with that stuff."—then turned back to her. "But you look really hot." He suddenly winced—"Damn. I mean, *nice*."—and glanced toward the top of the staircase, and the open door that led to Dave's office. He leaned forward and whispered, "Don't tell your dad I said that, okay? He'll think I'm some kinda pedophile."

Pan chuckled. "No, he won't. He's met your girlfriend Sherri, remember? A bunch of times. And she's really beautiful." She shifted uneasily on her feet. "I mean, I'm like the total opposite . . ."

"Aw, don't be so hard on yourself, Corpse Bride." Sheen draped an arm around her best friend's shoulders. "You *do* look hot. Like, freakin' supernova hot. Ain't nothin' wrong with admittin' that to yourself . . . even if your biggest admirer *is* an older, pervy dude."

"*Nice*," Tim muttered.

Tory pulled out her cell from her handbag. "You want me to, like, call *Dateline NBC*, just in case?" She flashed a wicked smile at Tim. "Maybe we got, y'know, a predator they need to, like, catch."

Tim's eyes narrowed as he turned toward her. "Yeah . . . let's, like, *not* do that, okay?"

"Yeah, Tory," Pan said, "the museum doesn't need *that* kinda publicity. Besides, we've got bigger things to deal with."

"Like what?" Tim asked.

She wheeled around on her spiky heels—just barely managing to keep from toppling over—and pointed to the large wooden crate lying in the center of the basement. "Like . . . *what's in the box?!*" she yelled in a whiny, high-pitched voice. "*C'mon, tell me! What's in the box?*"

"Ooh, wait a minute," Tommy said. "I know that line." He screwed his eyes shut, thought about it for a couple of seconds, then opened them. "Uh . . . Brad Pitt in *Seven*. Just before he found out it was Gwyneth Paltrow's head."

"Uh . . . *spoilers*?" Moira groused.

"Very good," Reyna said. "Most folks don't remember that one."

"Well . . ." He tapped the side of his head. "I'm a reg'lar human encyclopedia. My head's filled with all kinds'a things like that."

Reyna snorted. "Too bad remembering my birthday's not one'a them."

"How we doing down there?" Dave called from the top of the stairs. In one hand he held the set of keys he'd used to lock up the museum; in the other was Deathbringer, the crowbar he kept under the sales counter.

"Hey, Dad!" Pan struck her best *America's Next Top Model* pose, back arched, one hand on her hip, the other resting on the side of her head. "What do you think?"

His eyes snapped open, big as the proverbial saucers. "Oh, my God . . . you look like a . . . a . . ."

Pan immediately lost her fashionista vibe. She straightened up, her black lips curled into a fierce snarl. "Be *very* careful about the next word you utter."

Dave's mouth hung open for a few seconds—apparently his immediate follow-up comment had gotten caught in his throat on its way to alienating his daughter—before he finally answered: "Princess. I was gonna say 'princess.' " He closely inspected her. " Where'd you get that thing?" His eyes narrowed. "Does your *mother* let you walk around Albany in that?"

Pan rolled her eyes. "Not a chance; she banned fun when we moved to Dorksville. The dress was a present from Sheena—"

"Oh, *there's* a surprise . . ." he muttered.

"Hey!" Sheen yelled in mock anger. "I'm standin' right here!"

"—but *you* paid for the shoes." When his eyebrows shot up almost to his hairline—because, clearly, he didn't remember ever purchasing stilettos for his only child—Pan added, "I mean, with some of the child-support money. Your daughter's gotta have clothes, right?" She smiled. "Aren't they fantastic? I found them for half price at Payless."

"Yeah, great," he said dourly, turning his head to break eye contact with her. "Just . . . change back to your other clothes when we're done, okay?" he asked quietly. "Maybe wash off all that makeup?"

She knew why her dad was suddenly so combative—the hurt look that had come into his eyes was evidence enough. The dress and makeup gave her an older appearance and had presented him with a startling glimpse of the not-too-distant future, where his little girl had become a young woman. A sobering reality for any father, to be sure.

Still, having spent close to an hour with Sheen and Moira and Reyna in the tiny bathroom upstairs, getting all glammed up for her big video moment, she wasn't about to cave in so easily. She folded her arms across her chest and tilted back her head so she could sniff haughtily at her dad. "I'll think about it."

"Girl's just trying to fit in with her friends, Dave," Tim explained. "And she *did* just come home after a year of living among the country folk."

"That's right!" Sheen added. "City girl needs to es-press huhself!" She grinned at Tim.

He slowly shook his head, as though disappointed with her. "Sheena, babe, you are *much* too white to try saying it like that . . ."

That got a laugh from Moira—as did the reddening color of Sheen's cheeks as they glowed with embarrassment. Pan gave her best friend's arm a little comforting squeeze.

"Seriously, Mr. Z," Tommy said, "one night of Pan gettin' her freak on isn't gonna kill you . . . right?"

"No," Dave grunted, then slowly nodded his head in reluctant agreement. "Okay . . . but only for tonight. Tomorrow morning I want her freak off, the Queen of the Damned gone, and my daughter back. Deal?"

Pan's mood brightened immediately. "Deal!" She turned to Tim. "Now get that camera rolling, Mr. Director"—she grinned wickedly and held out her hand for Deathbringer—"and gimme that crowbar! I wanna see Gwyneth's head!"

22

Gwyneth Paltrow's severed head wasn't inside this particular box—Pan checked, just to be certain—but the oversize coffin she found buried underneath a Dumpster-load of protective excelsior more than made up for her initial disappointment. At first. Then she took a closer look at it, and the enthusiastic smile she'd been sporting while tearing her way into the crate was instantly sandblasted from her face.

"Uh . . ." was all she could think of to say.

Sheen inelegantly nudged her aside to see for herself. "Oh, my God. It's a piece'a crap!"

That it was—a plain, unfinished pine box about three feet wide and seven feet long that appeared to be so thin and fragile that one tap from the crowbar might shatter it into kindling. As vampire storage units went, this was about as impressive as a cardboard box.

"Well, *that* was anticlimactic." Lisa picked strands of packing material from her hair—she'd been digging through the stuff with the same fervor as Pan, and was now covered with white cedar shavings—and frowned at Dave. "The way you were talking about it, Mr. Z, I thought this was gonna be some megadeal."

"It *is* a big deal," Dave countered. "The box isn't important, it's what's inside."

"Well, if there's nothing but a bunch'a dog bones in there," Sheen said, "I'm leavin.'"

"I *like* dog bones." Tory poked her head over the lip of the crate, her eyes sparkling with the glee of a kid gazing through a candy store's window. "Bird bones, too." She grinned at Pan. "I'm building an ossuary behind my house."

Moira nodded. "A thing'a beauty, i'tis. It's gonna look amazing when she's done."

"Well, dog or vampire, only one way to find out if I got my money's worth," Dave said, and Pan handed him Deathbringer. "Everybody stand back, okay? This coffin looks so delicate, for all I know it might explode when I touch it."

"Groovy," Dylan purred in his best Bruce-Campbell-in-*Army-of-Darkness* voice. Lisa chuckled and gave him a peck on the cheek.

As the group moved away Dave slid the thin edge of the crowbar between the lid and one of the sides, and began to lift. The ancient wood groaned.

"Don't hurt the dog bones!" Tory jokingly pleaded with him. Moira draped an arm over her girlfriend's shoulders and held her hand to offer support.

There was a loud snap, like rifle fire, and the first loosened nail shot straight up, clanged off the heating pipes overhead, and buried itself in one of the brick walls—just inches from Pan's head.

She eased out of the crouch she'd dropped into and stared at the rusty, six-inch-long missile that had impaled a few strands of her hair. She gulped. "Well, damn . . ."

Dad dropped the crowbar and hurried over as she untangled herself from the nail. "Honey, are you okay?" He gently took her face between his hands and inspected her for injuries.

With all her friends watching.

Pan blushed with embarrassment. "Dad . . . *Dad* . . ." She eased his hands away. "I'm fine. Really. Just a little scare—nothing to freak out about. Just . . ." She waved a hand toward the crate. ". . . go unpack your vampire dog, or whatever it is."

"You sure?" She nodded emphatically. "Okay." He walked back to the box—glancing back once to make certain she really was all right—and resumed his work.

Pan caught sight of Tim, whose camera was still rolling. "I suppose you got all that?"

"You bet," he said. "Very heartwarming. Audiences love that father-daughter bonding stuff after a big scare."

"I *wasn't* that scared," she insisted. When he responded with a knowing grin she grunted, "Whatever . . ."

The rest of the nails gave easily, and the pine box neither shattered nor exploded. All that remained was the removal of the lid. Dave took one end, Tommy the other. "Here we go . . ." Dad said, and Pan felt chills running up and down her spine as the anticipation built. "Ladies and gentlemen, feast your eyes on Renfield's newest attraction: the vampire prince!" And with that, he and Tommy yanked up the lid to reveal—

"Whoa!" Sheen said. "Now *that's* a vampire!"

It *was* a skeleton, just as advertised—*and* with a metal-tipped stake running through the center of its chest! The creature appeared to be about six and a half feet tall and was dressed in faded, tattered black velvet pants and knee-high leather boots; neither age nor the grave had been kind to the materials. Around its waist hung a wide leather belt, fastened by a large metal buckle of a bat with its wings spread.

"Oooh," Pan cooed, reaching out to stroke the buckle. "Me likely. That would go *so* well with the bat on my jacket."

"Hands off the merchandise," Dad warned.

Tommy swept away the bits of excelsior that obscured the vampire's shoulders, then started. "Hey! Where's his head?"

"What?" Dave replied, then began digging around the packing material. "I am gonna be *really* annoyed if this . . . No, wait. Found it!" He came up with a skull that looked pretty fearsome—the rows of sharklike teeth did a lot to give that impression. Dave turned the cranium upside down and examined its base. "Looks like somebody cut his head off," he said with a grin, then delicately placed it back where it belonged. "There we go. Good as new."

The basement suddenly filled with the clicking of digital cameras as the crew pulled out their cell phones and began snapping pictures. Pan scrambled to do likewise. She took a tight close-up of the buckle—that would be her phone's new wallpaper. She still wanted the real thing for her wardrobe, though.

"Whoa! Whoa!" Dave said to the group. "Now before you get all crazy spreading the word around the Goth community, *nothing* goes on the 'Net—no Web sites, no Facebook pages, no message boards—until I formally announce the exhibit. Okay? And that might not be for a few weeks."

The news blackout was met with a chorus of disappointed groans. Even from Tim.

"Look'it the size'a him!" Moira said, gazing into the coffin. "He's a giant!"

"Nah," Tommy said. "I seen wrestlers just as big as him on *Monday Night RAW*. I bet the Undertaker could kick this guy's butt."

While Moira and Tommy debated the skill sets of World Wrestling Entertainment's roster of superstars, Pan turned her attention to the skeleton. The clothes certainly looked old enough to be real, as did the bones and the stake—but could it really be a vampire? She didn't see any possible evidence other than the stake in its chest, but there *was* something sticking out from the back of the rib cage that looked suspiciously like a . . . wingtip?

" 'There were giants in the earth in those days,' " Reyna quietly intoned beside her. " 'And also after that, when the sons of God came in unto the daughters of men, and they bare children to them.' "

Pan smiled gently. "Your mom been reading the Bible at you again, Rey?"

"Not since the last exorcism," Reyna replied sarcastically, then shrugged. "Nah. Some things just stick with you from Sunday school—y'know, back when I was just a *little* devil girl." She gestured toward the skeleton. "The Book of Genesis mentions these blood-drinkin' giants that was supposed to be the offspring of angels an' human women. 'Cept the women didn't have any choice in whether or not they wanted to do it with Lucifer or whoever an' the other boys."

Pan's eyebrows rose. "Angels raping women? Shut. *up*."

"I am *totally* serious. I mean, the Bible doesn't come right out an' say it, but the History Channel had a show on it last month that explained *everything*." Reyna smiled knowingly. "Why d'ya think they call those dudes *fallen* angels, Zee?"

Pan shook her head. "Wow. I never heard that before." She glanced at the skeleton. "You think maybe he's one of those giants?"

Reyna took a few moments to re-examine the "vampire prince." "Nah. Those dudes was s'posed to be really tall—like, Godzilla tall. This dude's way too short." Her eyebrows slowly rose. "You don't think . . ."

Pan shrugged. "I don't know. Maybe. It's no weirder than him being a real vampire. But I know how to find out . . ." She reached down and began tugging at the wingtip.

From across the basement she heard Dad nervously call out, "Uh . . . honey, what're you doing?"

"Just testing a theory."

She heard his footsteps approaching. "Okay, but could you test it on something that *isn't* an expensive relic you're about to irreparably damage?"

"Nope." The rotting velvet pants were caught on the bony projection, so she tugged harder—

And then the coffin really *did* explode. Not into pieces, but the sides of the box snapped off their nails and went flying in opposite directions as everyone scrambled for cover. When the dust settled, Pan found herself sprawled across Reyna, who at some point in their dive for safety had managed to pull the mad-scientist goggles down over her eyes.

"*What the hell was that?!*" Sheena yelped from her perch on the top of the stairs.

"Looked like some kinda booby trap—I think," Dylan said. He was protectively huddled over Lisa in a corner. "Y'know, like in the *Saw* movies."

"I swear to God," Sheen replied, "if some little puppet comes ridin' out on a tricycle, I am runnin' outta here an' you can all fend for yourself!"

"Well, you're in the wrong spot for running away," Dad remarked. "I already locked the front door and set the burglar alarm, so the only way out is through there"—he pointed across the basement to a short flight of concrete steps leading to a pair of metal cellar doors that opened on the sidewalk, then jerked a thumb over his shoulder toward the shadowy far end—"or out that way. But the door back there only leads down a maintenance tunnel to the Greek diner on the next block." He grinned malevolently. "For all I know, Jigsaw could be waiting in there for you."

Sheen stamped her foot in frustration. "*Damn* it!"

"Don't worry, jungle queen," Pan said as she rose to her feet. "No puppets here, and no booby traps. Just a skeleton with some really big wings . . ."

That they were. Well, not full-fledged wings; just their bones. The feathers that presumably once covered them had molted away long ago, leaving behind a skeletal framework that began at the creature's shoulder blades and ended with the outermost tips almost scraping the walls on both sides of the basement. That meant the angel or vampire or whatever it was had a wingspan of twenty feet or more.

"Oh, my God!" Sheen cried in mock horror. "Somebody killed Hawkman!"

Dad sighed. "That is gonna be a *bitch* to get up the stairs, now."

"Watch the language," Pan warned. She winked slyly at him when he targeted her with a parental frown. "So, Dad, you sure the guy that sold you this said it was a *vampire*?"

"That's what he had on his Web site." Dave shrugged. "I don't know. I mean, what else could it be? Maybe Count Chocula here had vampire-bat wings."

"No, those're, like, bird wings," Tory said. "You see the ulna bones just below the radius? Those are, like, what hold the feathers in place. Bats have those too, but they're, like, smaller." She held out her hands, pointed downward, and spread out her fingers. "And bats have, like, these long metacarpals—y'know, the short bones on top?—and phalanges—the longer ones, like, on the bottom. Y'know, like the spines on a Chinese paper fan." She pointed to the skeleton. "His wings, like, don't have those." Her short lesson on anatomy was met with blank stares. "What? I *told* you I collected bird bones for my ossuary."

Moira gave her an encouraging hug. "Isn't she just the smartest person ya'd ever wanna meet?" she said proudly.

"So if it ain't a vampire, then what is it?" Tommy asked.

"Pan thinks it's a fallen angel," Reyna said.

As one, the group turned to face her. Pan flinched.

"That's it—we're all goin' to hell," Sheen quipped as she came down the stairs. "I call shotgun!"

"I never *said* it was an angel," Pan said to Reyna, with more than a hint of annoyance. "*You're* the one who put the idea in my head."

"Not a vampire . . ." Dad groaned. "So it really *is* a fake."

"Sorry, Dad; I tried to warn you, y'know. But hey, look on the bright side: If this is a real angel and not some tossed-out haunted house prop with fake wings glued on, I'd say you got a major bargain. I hear that fallen angels are the new vampires."

"I thought zombies were the new vampires," Tommy said, then scratched his chin in contemplation. "Or maybe that was werewolves . . ."

Dad snarled. "Doesn't matter. All I know is I'm getting my money back."

"I don't understand," Lisa said. "Why can't you just put it in the museum anyway, Mr. Zwieback? You paid for it, you should be able to do whatever you want with it."

"Yeah, you'd *think* so, Lisa, but I'm pretty sure the Pope wouldn't appreciate me putting Gabriel here on display and charging admission." He glanced at Pan. "Or your mother, for that matter."

"So where does that leave us?" Tim asked.

Dave snorted. "You mean where does that leave *me.*"

Tim shrugged. "Hey, I was trying to sound supportive. But now that you bring it up . . ." He rolled his eyes toward the ceiling and pointed at his employer. "It's all on him, God—okay? Just so we're clear on this."

Dave grunted. "Nice."

Pan stepped toward the skeleton, drawing upon every ounce of deductive reasoning she'd ever acquired from all the Nancy Drew mysteries she'd read as a little girl. "Okay, Dad, so let's just say for the sake of argument it's true you got suckered into buying the skeleton of an angel—a real, dropped-from-heaven-here-come-the-End-Times angel—and the guy *knew* it was an angel when he sold it to you. That brings up three *huge* questions that need to be answered."

"And those would be . . . ?" Dad asked.

"Where'd *he* get it from? Why was he willing to get rid of it?" She pointed to the stake protruding from the creature's broken chest. "And who'd be crazy enough to go stabbing an angel?"

23

Ebon wings spread wide behind him, the handsome, dark-skinned angel hovered over her, his fighting hand gripped tightly around the sword's hilt.

"I am already damned!" *Zaqiel roared, and raised the sword above his head.* "But I will not suffer alone!"

The blade swept down, and—

Annie awoke, screaming. She flung out her hands to catch a sword that wasn't there, and in doing so tumbled off the living room couch. Her left elbow banged against the edge of the mahogany coffee table as she crashed to the carpeted floor, and she howled in pain.

It took some minutes for her heart to stop its jackhammer pounding, for her body to stop heaving with uncontrolled gasps; even longer for the burning tears to cease their flow. Almost two centuries gone, and still she couldn't put the events of that night behind her.

The night the world almost came to an end.

The night her world *had* come to an end. Or so it had felt, at the time.

She sat up and wiped her runny nose on the frayed left sleeve of the old sweatshirt she wore, then used the right to dab at her bleary eyes. Her elbow throbbed painfully with the fiery tingling of the funny bone she'd bruised, so she rose from the floor and shuffled down the hall into the bathroom for some ibuprofen, all the while wondering why her psychotic ex-boyfriend (well, this particular one, anyway) should force his way back into her dreams. It probably had to do with that oversized hamburger she'd had for lunch settling on top of her goblin entrée from last night; too much red meat in her diet always screwed up her sleep cycle.

Guess I'll be eating salad all next week, Annie thought glumly. *Except I* hate *salads so much . . .*

As she swallowed two of the pills, the face of Jerome appeared in the medicine cabinet mirror above the basin. "All done serenading the neighborhood for one evening?" he asked coolly.

Annie snarled as she massaged her elbow. "Leave me alone," she mumbled. "Go haunt the mirror in the rec room."

"You know," he continued, blatantly ignoring her, "it's a good thing you live all alone in this dreary old building, otherwise—"

"*I said, leave me alone!*" she bellowed.

"Fine," he said brusquely, and faded away. Then he instantly reappeared, his expression now one of concern. "Are you all right?" he asked gently.

She forced her lips to form an awkward smile. "I'm fine, Jerome. I just had a bad dream. I'll get over it." She sniffed loudly. "I always do, you know."

Jerome frowned. "Well, if this is how you appear when you're 'fine' . . ." He paused, and if he'd possessed shoulders instead of just being a floating head, he would have shrugged. "Well . . . I've seen you look better."

This time her smile was genuine. "Why, Jerome, coming from you that's almost a compliment. I'm touched."

He sneered. "Savor it while you can." And with that he departed, either returning to his mirror home in the main hallway, or—hopefully—following her advice to spend some time in the basement's rec room.

Annie flexed her left arm a few times. Her funny bone had finally ceased throbbing, so either her recuperative power had kicked in, the ibuprofen was working . . . or she was still feeling the healing effect from that strange Goth girl.

Pandora Zwieback. Who also had the odd-but-not-as-strange father.

The handsome, *divorced* father . . .

"*Stop that,*" she told herself. And yet she couldn't help considering a next step—perhaps inviting David out for a drink? Or lunch, for just the two of them. That might be better, as a start. It was dangerous territory in which to tread, though. She'd just made friends with Pan; had agreed to teach her better control over her abilities. Why run the risk of turning the girl against her by making a play for David?

The answer was obvious.

"I ain't seen you with a man in a dog's age!" Izzy had said.

"You live all alone in this dreary old building," Jerome had commented.

That's all it came down to, when she really thought about it. Companionship, maybe even a full-fledged relationship. Lord knew she hadn't had one of those in years. She was lonely and sad and tired and . . .

"Old," Annie muttered as she examined herself in the mirror. She fingered some of the gray hairs that had sprung up among the black, and felt the weight of four centuries settle heavily on her shoulders.

She grunted, then pulled herself together and stood erect. Her life might border on the pathetically hermitic—just ask her friends—but there was still something she could do about her hair color. Annie drew upon the mystical energies that allowed her to shape-shift; two seconds later, the gray hairs were black once more.

Now if only finding a way to invite David Zwieback out on a date, without angering his daughter, could be as simple . . .

From the fourth-floor bedroom of her town house Annie could see that West Twenty-first Street was quiet, for a change: no clubgoers yelling and laughing as they drunkenly stumbled down the block in search of the next party; no SUVs cruising by, the bass of their stereo systems so loud it rattled apartment windows; no succubi trawling for horny men eager to risk their souls for a good time. She looked west, toward Tenth Avenue and the High Line across the street. The park was vacant now—a glance at the digital clock on her cable-TV box told her it was well past three o'clock in the morning—but she could discern movement in the shadows below the mile-long metal platform.

A trio of disheveled figures scuffled back and forth in a kind of stiff-legged dance; a large bag lay at their feet. Homeless men fighting over possessions? A mugging? Unfortunately, with the shadows under the High Line as dark as they were, vague shapes were all she could see . . . unless she adjusted her eyesight.

Her hazel eyes closed for a moment; when they reopened they'd not only changed color to an amber hue but also physically transformed, becoming larger and circular in shape. Now she was gazing through owl eyes, with all the benefits of the best night vision in the animal kingdom.

All the better to see you with, my dears, Annie thought with a smirk. Yes, this was *much* better. Now she could clearly tell what was going on down there.

The trio wasn't homeless men or muggers, but zombies tearing into a garbage bag. Annie scratched her head. There were no fresh beef outlets remaining in the meatpacking district south of her location—most of the old butcher shops had been replaced by high-end boutiques and dance clubs—so what else might appeal to the rotted taste buds of walking corpses?

The bag ripped apart, and the answer to Annie's question came in the form of discarded bake goods—donuts and pastries spilled onto the sidewalk, and the zombies hungrily devoured them with the same relish normally displayed by their more carnivorous brethren.

Sugar zoms—that's what Javier called them. Annie chuckled. It always sounded like the name of a breakfast cereal.

Scooping up the last bits of pastry the corpses staggered back under the High Line in the direction of the West Side Highway, and she followed their progress . . . until her gaze settled on a black van that the zombies lurched past. It was parked far enough away from Tenth Avenue to avoid being displayed under the corner streetlights, and that made her skin prickle. Unmarked black vans parked discretely anywhere in New York were suspicious to begin with, in a city sensitive to terrorist attacks. But an unmarked black van with tinted windows, discretely parked across the street *from her home* in the middle of the night, went beyond suspicious.

She was being watched.

It wasn't the first time she'd been under surveillance—you can't live for four hundred years and *not* call attention to yourself now and then—but given her current state of agitation it wasn't the smartest action for whoever might be inside the vehicle. It made her strongly inclined to go stomping across the avenue and cure them of their Peeping Tom ways in a most unpleasant manner.

That is, if there really *were* Peeping Toms. She couldn't see through the window tints—not even owls possessed vision *that* sharp—but she had no doubts they were there, watching her every move.

Unless, she suddenly realized, the occupants had already exited the van—and were now preparing to strike.

"That is just damned creepy," Dalibor commented as he observed Annie through the electric-green fuzz of his night-vision binoculars. "I think she can see me."

"Are you still in the van?" Jenessa's voice crackled through his headset.

"Yes. I'm even huddled behind the driver's seat, as you instructed."

Jenessa sighed. "Then she can't see you. She's a huntress, Dalek, not Supergirl. She doesn't have X-ray vision."

"But she's staring right at me with these giant round eyes, like . . . like a barn owl's!" A shiver ran down his spine. "I didn't see those in any of her pictures! It's unnatural!"

"Of course it's unnatural," his commander replied. "She's a shape-shifter. She can have any kind of eyes she wants." Jenna paused. "Owl eyes, you say. That means she's using improvised night vision to check out the van." There was a tiny scraping sound through his earpiece—Jenna grinding her teeth. "Damn it, she knows something's up."

"We're all in position," Vincenc said through the open channel. "What's your pleasure, Commander?"

"Take her down," Jenessa said firmly. "Now!"

The first explosion blew the locks on the front door; the second—a much larger charge—sounded as though it had completely disintegrated the door that led to the roof. Attacks from above and below to cut off her exits—she'd been expecting that . . . although it didn't make much sense, when their target was a shape-changer who could become a bird or a bat and fly away. But then the shattering of the back windows in her reference library one floor below announced the arrival of a third strike team, and Annie knew she was running out of escape routes. Now she'd have to fight.

Good, she thought with a malicious smile. *Because you idiots have certainly caught me in the right mood for one . . .*

She blinked her eyes back to their normal size and color and hurried to the walk-in closet at the rear of the apartment-sized boudoir. The racks and racks of designer clothing, shoe trees full of pumps and flats, and shelves of expensive handbags meant little to her at the moment; she had her eye on the gun cabinet mounted on the wall behind her Versace collection.

The Model 500 Smith & Wesson X-frame drew her attention for a moment, but she shook her head—too big, too loud, and the recoil was a bitch to deal with; not quite the perfect handgun for a running battle. She settled for a Sig Sauer P229, and stuck it in her jeans' waistband. No need to check for ammunition—she always kept her handguns cleaned, oiled, and fully loaded. Still, she slipped a few extra clips of 9mm rounds into her pockets; she had a feeling she'd need them. Along with the Sig she grabbed a Hawk Bullpup semiauto shotgun, and rammed in its box of twelve-gauge shells.

Now she was ready to entertain guests.

Armed for bear she stepped out of the closet, only to hear glass breaking. She glanced toward the front windows, in time to see what appeared to be a small, black aerosol can land near her feet.

Flashbang! she realized, and dove behind the bed just as the stun grenade erupted with a burst of blinding magnesium light and ear-damaging sound. Then something far heavier than grenades crashed through the windows: yet another strike team making its entrance.

Great. Five minutes ago I was pining for companionship, she thought. *Now I could do with some serious alone-time.* She popped up from cover and blindly fired the Hawk, and was rewarded with the pleasing sound of someone crying out and hitting the floor.

She rolled to her feet, slightly disoriented, and staggered into the hallway, massaging the base of her head with her left thumb to try and alleviate the flash-bang's skull-vibrating effects. Unfortunately, ringing ears, spot-dappled vision, and a severe loss of balance weren't the sorts of things an improvised shiatsu massage could fix on the run.

Yet even with her head feeling as though it was wrapped in layers of cotton, she could still sense vibrations through the soles of her slippered feet. Thick boot heels pounded on the parquet wooden floor behind her and up and down the town house's main staircase. Her attackers were closing in, fast.

Rec room. Get to the rec room.

Annie lurched toward the stairs, and heard muffled yelling behind her. Instinctively, she dropped to the floor as bullets slammed into the stairs leading to the roof. Had she been an instant slower, her brains would have been splashed across the walnut steps. She glanced back to see a redheaded woman reprimanding a woman with chestnut-brown hair; their bodysuits were so tight-fitting they both appeared to have been dipped in black latex. The light of a nearby table lamp gleamed along the edges of the women's razor-sharp teeth.

Vampires, Annie realized.

Red had a hand on Brownie's machine gun and was forcing the barrel down, to point at the floor. Annie strained to hear what was being said, but all that made it past her flashbang-deadened ears was:

"***uzana, I *** no headshots! *** want *** alive!"

Annie scrambled to her feet and leaped over the railing, to land on the third floor, then glanced up to see a pair of flashbangs tumble down the stairs after her. She swatted them over the banister just as another black-garbed figure charged up the steps from the second floor. The look of astonishment on his face, just before the grenades detonated and knocked him back downstairs, was priceless, but Annie didn't stick around to savor it; she was already charging down the hallway toward the rear of the building to reach the back stairs.

With her now-limited hearing she hadn't understood much of what was going on, but based on the language in which Red had chastised her teammate, the strike force was apparently from the Czech Republic. Annie frowned. She hadn't been in that country for twenty or thirty years—so why was House Karnstein suddenly looking to settle old scores?

Probably another change in clan leadership, she thought. *Every time a house gets a new administration, I'm usually at the top of their to-do lists. You'd think after all these years of constant failure they'd find something new to occupy their time, but no . . .*

At least these thugs weren't on a termination mission; they'd been ordered to capture her. That was encouraging—it meant kill shots were forbidden. The intruders would have to be cautious about where they aimed; she, on the other hand, didn't have to be quite so discriminating.

Then again, she thought dourly as she reached the secondary staircase, *just because they can't shoot me in the head doesn't mean they can't use the rest of my body for target practice.*

As if to prove her point, a barrage of gunfire sounded from below as she started her descent. Bullets raked the wall near her feet and she threw herself down the steps to avoid being hit, only to strike her left elbow against the wall at the bottom of the staircase. The shotgun went flying from her hands.

She tumbled onto the second-floor landing and looked up to see another latex-dipped intruder approaching, this one a blond-haired male. He brushed aside a fringe of locks that had drifted over his left eye.

"I've got her," he reported in Czech into the microphone on his headset. "Rear staircase, second floor." While he trained his rifle on his target he listened to the response of his leader—possibly the redhead, given her display of take-charge attitude upstairs—and then frowned. "Of *course* she's alive, Jenna. She can't tell us where the Prize is if she's dead, right?"

The prize? Annie had no idea what that was supposed to be—A weapon? A book of magick? A map?—or why these soldiers thought she knew its location, but this "prize" couldn't be anything good if their search for it involved pumping her full of lead in order to get answers.

Heavy footsteps above and below told Annie that Blondie's teammates were closing in on their position. He leveled his rifle—an FN P90 submachine gun, she noted—at her. "Do not move," he growled in heavily accented English, "or I will shoot you again."

Annie snarled. Like *she* was going to take orders from a group of thugs trashing her home. The contours of her face blurred as she triggered a transformation. Her features became scaled . . . sharply angled . . . *reptilian.*

Blondie's eyes widened in surprise—"W-what . . . ?" he gasped—and he unconsciously lowered the rifle. It was a momentary lapse in judgment, just a fraction of a second long as he let emotion get in the way of his military training, but Annie took full advantage of the opening—and attacked.

Contrary to belief, spitting cobras don't actually spit their venom—they build up air pressure by contracting the muscles in the venom gland and then fire it through holes in their fangs. But one thing is true about these snakes: when they release their venom they always aim for their target's eyes—as Blondie discovered firsthand.

He screamed and dropped the rifle as he raised his hands to try and wipe away the poison. Annie surged forward, pulled the Sig from her waistband, and put two rounds in his head.

Annie watched his blood soak into the hall carpeting. When it became apparent he wasn't getting up, she muttered, "Huh. I guess not *all* of you are vampires . . ."

Then a woman shrieked, *"Krystof!"* and Annie whirled, instinctively firing at the source. The two women from her apartment staggered under the barrage, but didn't fall.

She bolted down the hallway as Red returned fire, gouging holes in the walls and flooring. Annie ran toward the front of the house as she reloaded, then remembered the male team member she'd greeted by deflecting a pair of stun grenades into his face. He was probably somewhere around here—

"And speak of the devil . . ." she muttered as the dark-skinned man came running at her. He was a big one, over six feet tall and built like a football linebacker, with dreadlocks that fanned out behind him like a cape.

And was that a grenade launcher he was aiming at her?

The building shook from the roar of an MGL-140 being fired in close quarters. Annie dove to the floor as the small missile flew down the hallway; the rear staircase exploded into kindling. Angry yelling let her know Red and Brownie had been momentarily incapacitated by the blast, but they'd be back in the hunt within moments.

Before the warrior could reload, Annie fired back. Bullets raked his legs, chest, and neck, knocking him off his feet and forcing him to drop the launcher. But all that did was make him angry, not dead—he, too, was a vampire.

She tried to leap over him, but powerful hands grabbed her left leg as she passed and slammed her to the floor; razor-sharp fangs ripped through the pant leg and sunk into her flesh.

He started to feed.

"Son of a—!" Annie clubbed him on the top of his skull with the butt of her gun. It took three blows before he lifted his head to flash a gore-drenched smile at her—and then she emptied the Sig's ammo clip into his face.

He shrieked and released his hold on her leg; Annie hobbled away. The point-blank fire would only stun him for a little while, and then he'd be back for a second helping of her blood. The rest of his team would no doubt join in; now that she'd eliminated one of their own all bets were off they'd still want to take her alive.

A brown-haired girl was coming up the stairs just as Annie reached the second-floor landing; her features and chestnut-colored locks suggested she was related to the woman with the predilection for lethal headshots. Unlike her cousin-maybe-sister, however, she looked completely unnerved by the sight of their target speed-hobbling toward her. She gave out a tiny squeak of surprise and started to raise her rifle.

Annie didn't give her time to aim. Without breaking stride she shifted to panther form and leaped on the intruder, momentum carrying them back downstairs. The girl took the full impact of their descent—on her neck, which snapped as she and Annie tumbled off the steps and crash-landed in the first floor's grand foyer.

Disbelieving, lifeless eyes stared back at Annie as she reverted to normal.

The huntress—breathing hard from the exertion of a transformation she *really* shouldn't have triggered in her weakened state—reached out to part the girl's lips.

No fangs.

Another human sympathizer, she noted with some surprise. *When did the clans start making* them *field operatives?* She shook her head. *Wonder, later. Rec room, now. There are three more of them to deal with.*

Make that four. As she headed for the stairs leading to the basement, the pounding of boot heels caught her attention and she turned to see a bald-headed, fanged man with a thick five-o'clock shadow—and a huge serrated knife.

Annie spun, blocking the knife hand to give herself an opening, and executed a high kick that would have done a Radio City Rockette proud; the heel of her slipper slammed into the intruder's jaw and staggered him. She followed that by dropping to her knees and knocking him off his feet with a sweeping leg kick. Then she jumped over the banister and down the steps before he had time to recover.

Her timing couldn't have been better. The town house shook with a barrage of gunfire that tore into the wall just above her head—the survivors of the strike team launching a concentrated attack, just a fraction too late. Annie sprinted to the rear of the basement, past a pool table, entertainment center, and well-used furniture toward a thick steel door set into the brickwork.

The rec room.

To the door's right were a security touchpad—into which she typed her access code—and a retinal scanner that only identified her if she shifted her left eye to resemble that of a jaguatirca. Someday, she had rationalized, the wrong person might get her access code, but there was no way they'd ever think of using a spotted leopard's eyeball to open the final lock. The scanner did its work, and there was the clang of heavy locking bolts disengaging. The door swung open and she stepped inside.

A contented sigh eased past Annie's lips as she gazed at the row upon row of weaponry that filled her personal armory: guns big and small, blades of all varieties, and enough ammunition and explosives to make her the lifetime pinup queen for *Solder of Fortune* magazine. Let those vampiric hit men try to kill her now. She was ready for them.

What she *wasn't* ready for, though, was the mournful wailing that echoed down from the grand foyer.

The arriving vampires had undoubtedly come across the body of the human girl lying at the bottom of the stairs. Annie could identify the pitch of both male *and* female voices in the cries, which meant that two of the soldiers had some connection to the dear departed. One of them was probably Brownie, given the family resemblance. The other . . . a boyfriend or lover, perhaps? Certainly not a husband. Vampires weren't the marrying type.

"Well, what did you idiots *think* would happen when you broke into my house—that I *wouldn't* fight back?" she muttered harshly as the wailing continued. "You want to play soldier, you accept the risks—*and* the losses. I learned that a long time ago . . ."

"So, is it *your* turn to blow up the house, now?" asked a familiar voice. "I know how much you enjoy redecorating."

Annie turned to find Jerome gazing at her from a wall-mounted mirror on the other side of the room. So he *had* taken her advice after all and come down to haunt the rec room—that was a surprise. Another was that she was actually glad to see him.

"Jerome, be a dear and do a quick reconnaissance of the house. I need to know how many unwanted visitors I still have to deal with."

"You yell at me, and suddenly I should act like the security camera system you've always been too cheap to install?"

She batted her eyelashes and forced on her sweetest smile. "Please?"

He sighed. "Oh, very well . . ."

It took him less than a minute to return from his floor-by-floor search of the building. Having a spirit that could travel from one reflective surface to another in the blink of an eye was as good as, if not better than, having a security camera network—which was the reason she'd never had one set up. Not that she'd ever tell him that. He'd probably demand a salary.

"You have four intruders coming down the basement stairs," he reported, "very angry and armed to the teeth—"

"Fangs. They're vampires." She grabbed a two-foot-long machete, ignoring the guns, and picked up a small device that resembled a remote control used for locking a car's power doors. She had something special in mind for her unwanted guests.

"How charming," Jerome replied. "Other than those four the town house is clear . . . except for the fire on the second floor, the two corpses, and all the property damage, of course."

"Of course." She drew a deep breath, exhaled sharply, and headed toward the door, donning a special pair of safety glasses along the way. "Stay here. I won't be long."

They were waiting for her when she stepped out of the rec room. Red stood in front of the pool table; her three teammates were fanned out behind her, ready to open fire. The bright-red dots of four laser-targeting sights clustered tightly on the center of Annie's chest.

Brownie and Dreadlocks wiped at the bloody tears they'd spilled for their fallen comrade, and it seemed as though it was taking them an incredible force of will to maintain their positions. No doubt they wanted to take revenge, but loyalty to their commander kept them from breaking ranks. The bald man was stoic—all business, prepared to take action the moment it was called for. Red, however, appeared a little unnerved by her target's presence, even with three machine guns backing her up. And something more—she looked vaguely familiar . . .

"*Dobry vecer,*" Annie said pleasantly. *Good evening.* "*Mluvíte anglicky?*" *Do you speak English?*

"Yes," Red said.

"Great, because my Czech is terrible." Annie snarled. "So here's the deal, then: I'm giving you one chance to leave. Go now, and I'll forget about killing all of you. For tonight."

Red placed her finger on her gun's trigger. "We're not going anywhere without the Prize." Was there just the slightest hint of a tremor in her voice . . . ? She nodded toward the rec room. "Is it in there?"

"Not unless the prize is a really big gun. Is it?"

"Of course not—as you know very well!" Red snapped. "Well, if it isn't here, then where is it? I know you have its location."

"The only prize I know of is the one Publishers Clearing House gives away in their contests," Annie replied. "Otherwise, I don't have a clue what you're talking about." *Not that I'd tell you if I did,* she added silently.

"Jenessa," Baldy chimed in, "you mentioned the old priest said it had another name. Maybe she knows it by that."

Jenessa. Her name sounded familiar, too . . .

"Oh, yes," Red agreed. "He called it the Devil's Heart."

Annie gasped. "No . . ." she whispered.

The Devil's Heart. That wasn't the prize's real name—somehow the meaning of the original words had gotten lost over time—but she recognized it immediately.

The Devil's Heart—or, more accurately, the devil who stole *her* heart.

In better days, it was the phrase she'd used to describe Zaqiel.

In her mind's eye she again saw the sword he raised high in the air, then the blade sweeping down toward her head, then—

She swallowed hard, ignoring the icy hand of dread that clutched at her spine. "So you've been to St. Adalbert's church." Jenessa nodded. "Well, if it's the Devil's Heart you're after, then I take back what I said before." Annie peeled back her lips in a vicious sneer. *"You die right now."*

She punched a black button in the center of the remote control. There was a whine of energy building and the oak paneling along the center left side of the basement walls slid apart in the space of a heartbeat, exposing a twenty-foot-long row of glass tubes that glowed brightly.

Tanning bed bulbs.

"Hope you brought your sunscreen," Annie said, and dropped to the floor.

The flash of light lasted mere seconds, but considering the bulbs had been designed to release an enormous amount of ultraviolet energy, seconds were more than enough to turn UV-sensitive vampire commandos into smoldering corpses.

With one exception.

Jenessa thrashed about on the carpeted floor, screaming as she tried to extinguish the flames that had consumed her exposed face; the air around her stank with the odor of charred flesh, burned hair, and melted latex.

Annie strolled over to inspect the mortally wounded creature. "Not dead yet?

So, a special breed of vampire, then. Or something in between—like maybe a dhampyr . . . ?"

Jenessa's hands dropped away from her face, or rather what remained of it. The skin and hair had mostly burned off, leaving a gore-covered skull dotted with patches of roasted flesh and spattered with the dripping remains of a poached right eyeball. Teeth ground together in a lipless snarl, and a look of pure hatred shone in a left eye that was lacking both lashes and lid.

"Dhampyr . . ." Annie's eyebrows rose. "Now I remember you! Jenessa Branislav. Thirty years ago—in Prague, wasn't it? You were that hit woman House Karnstein sent after me." She frowned. "Didn't I chop you into little bits and scatter them across a wheat field?" She shrugged and raised the machete. "Doesn't matter. I'll do a better job of it this time . . ."

Jenessa whimpered as she caught sight of the two-foot-long blade.

A volley of submachine-gun fire suddenly roared in the basement and bullets ripped into Annie's chest, slamming her against the rec room door. She crashed bonelessly to the floor, the machete slipping from her fingers. A torrent of blood darkened her sweatshirt, then coursed down to pool in her lap.

"Just you wait . . . until I . . . get up . . ." she hissed in her final breath. Then her head drooped onto her chest and she lay still.

Jenessa looked toward the stairs to find Dalibor standing there with an FN P90 clutched in shaky hands. Dalek never *had* been comfortable with guns, even when he was human; in fact, he looked to be on the verge of tears. But then she realized he wasn't crying because it was the first time he'd shot an enemy—he was crying for *her*.

"J-Jenna?" he croaked. He dropped the rifle and ran to her side. She tried to respond, but he gently stroked her burned cheek and told her to shush. Bloody tears slipped down his cheeks, to patter softly on her teeth. The still-smoking hunk of meat that used to be her tongue slithered out to hungrily lap up the droplets.

He glanced at the huntress. "She's not dead, is she?" Jenna shook her head and a dusting of flaked skin spilled across her shoulders. "Then we'd better leave before she wakes up. We don't need *her*. We'll find another way to locate the Prize—I promise. And the Watchers help anyone who tries to keep it from us."

24

Today is the first day of the rest of your life.

That was one of Grandma Ellie's favorite sayings, usually uttered as encouragement in response to some major event experienced by a family member or close friend. The last time Pan had heard it was after Mom and Dad's divorce had been finalized. Mom had spent a day crying her eyes out, and Grandma had said it to try and cheer her up. Until this morning Pan had never really understood the phrase, but around four A.M., as she lay in bed unable to sleep, its meaning suddenly became crystal clear.

A fresh start. A new beginning.

Annie had given her that, and so much more. Opened her eyes to a bright, magical world ready to be explored. Put an end to the constant fears about her sanity. Made her understand how special she truly was.

And so, just a little before five o'clock, Pan had gone up to the roof of Dad's apartment building to welcome the new day—and her new life.

Now she sat on the top of the roof's stair access shed, waiting for dawn to break as she munched on a chocolate chip Eggo; her other hand held a coffee mug that was an open-top facsimile of the head of Boris Karloff as the Frankenstein Monster. She thought it appropriate, considering the shape of her unruly bed hair, its two-tone locks stuck out in weird clumps and angles from all the sculpting gel and hairspray Moira and Reyna had used for her makeover. Last night she might have been the Queen of the Damned, but this morning she was the Bride of Frankenstein—although she was pretty sure Bride actress Elsa Lanchester would never have greeted the sunrise in an oversize Sarkophagia T-shirt, a pair of shorts, and fuzzy green monster-feet slippers.

She heard footsteps ascending the stairs, and looked down. Between her feet she saw a sleepy Dave Zwieback stagger out onto the roof, dressed in jeans and a rumpled Mets T-shirt. Knowing Dad, once he'd rolled out of bed and discovered her missing, he'd thrown on whatever was handy and lurched out of the apartment to find her.

"Pan?" he said through a yawn.

"Mornin', Dad," she said around a mouthful of waffle.

He looked up, startled to find her looming over him. "What're you . . . Never mind."

"You're up early." She shoved the last of the Eggo in her mouth and wiped crumbs off the front of her shirt, then loudly slurped French Vanilla coffee out of Karloff's skull.

"I got up to check on you and saw an empty bed. Something like a missing daughter tends to keep me awake—know what I mean?" He yawned again and waved a piece of white art paper. "Then I found your message." It wasn't a words-on-the-page kind of note she'd left taped to his bedroom door, but a color-pencil sketch of a rainbow-hued woman standing on a mountaintop, her arms outstretched to greet a sun that was peeking above a purplish horizon. She knew that, to Dad, the message would be clear: your daughter is on the roof, watching the sunrise. His ability to decipher the meanings of her drawings was why they made such a killer team in Pictionary. "What's the occasion?" he asked. "You've never been a morning person before."

"I was a different person before." She patted the gray-painted wood. "Come join me, Father," she said in a passable British accent. "We'll watch the sun rise."

"All right," he grumbled. "Gimme a minute." Rubbing the last grains of sleep from his eyes, he shuffled over to the bottom of the sloped covering. Then he tucked her sketch in a back pocket of his jeans and awkwardly climbed up. "Couldn't just set up a couple of camping chairs, could you?" he asked as he settled in beside her, then pointed to the roof. "It'd be a lot more comfortable down there."

Pan shook her head. "I wanted to get the best view."

"Well, you can definitely see everything from up here," he agreed.

Five fifteen on a Sunday morning, and the Sunnyside, Queens, neighborhood around them was slowly beginning to wake up. Birdsong filled the air, the sound occasionally interrupted by the rumble of passing trains on the elevated tracks along Queens Boulevard to the north and the roar of vehicles on Greenpoint Avenue to the south. Over on Forty-seventh Avenue lights snapped on in a few apartments as, outside, a man walked his dog past a trio of bicyclists headed in the opposite direction. A pair of mourning doves flitted by, getting an early start on their day. Across the street, a woman rummaged through the trash cans in Thomas Noonan Jr. Playground, in search of soda cans and bottles to add to the mountainous collection she'd piled into garbage bags lashed to the shopping cart beside her. And in the east the rays of dawn softly brushed a lavender-hued sky with the first strokes of gold and red.

Dad leaned forward to examine Pan's face. "You get any sleep?"

"A little bit." She didn't need to see the bags under her eyes to know they were there, but she'd been too wired—was *still* too wired—from yesterday's revelations to lie down for very long. And that was before Javi texted her around midnight, which led to a three-hour "conversation" that her keypad-stabbing thumbs were still aching from. But Dad didn't have to know about that.

He draped an arm across her shoulders. "Well, how about after this you sack out for an hour and then we'll go get some breakfast. What do you say?"

"Sounds like a plan." She tried—and failed—to stifle a yawn, and rested her head against his shoulder. Then she abruptly sat up. "Oh! Don't forget about the cinnamon rolls for Mom."

"The bakery will be the first stop after breakfast. Forget them?" He snorted. "I'll never hear the end of it if I don't have her bribe in hand when we pick her up."

"Good." She went back to using his shoulder for a pillow.

They sat quietly, watching a massive flock of chattering starlings swoop in perfect formation across the sky.

" 'I will make you brooches and toys for your delight,' " Pan said, " 'of birdsong at morning and starshine at night.' " She looked up to find Dad's eyebrows rising quizzically. "Robert Louis Stevenson."

"I know," he said approvingly. "Something you read for school?"

"Nope, on my own." She sat up and saw the expression of mild disbelief on his face. "Really, Dad, it's not all Stephen King and Nancy Collins. I *do* like to read other stuff."

"I know. I'm just yanking your chain." He drew her close and kissed the top of her head. "Such a romantic, my little Panda-bear."

She blushed. "Yeah, well . . ." She tried to hide her embarrassment by gulping down the rest of her coffee.

"So, now . . ." He reached back and pulled the sketch from his pocket, then unfolded the paper and held it up to the lightening sky. The warm colors she'd chosen for the drawing shone even brighter. "This, I like a lot. It's so different from your usual dark stuff. Very colorful. Very . . ." He smiled. "Dare I say, lighthearted?"

Pan grinned.

"It's a new style," she said. "For a new *me*."

25

A change in art style was only the first step. An hour of sleep, followed by an invigorating shower, and now she *felt* like a brand-new woman. A hungry one, too. One waffle at sunrise did not a breakfast make.

"How we doing, honey?" Dad called out.

Pan stepped from the bathroom wrapped in a terry cloth robe, a towel wound around her hair. " 'We' are doing just fine. But give me twenty minutes and we'll be spectacular."

"Twenty minutes? You know we're just going down to the diner on the boulevard to eat, right? You don't have to look like a supermodel; I'm sure they'll still serve you pancakes and sausage."

"Yeah, but after we eat we have to drive out to Middle Village to get the cinnamon buns, and then head into the City to pick up Mom. I wanna show her the new me." Her eyes narrowed as she examined his chin. "I notice you shaved this morning." Then they widened in surprise as she took in his black jeans and dress shirt. "And you ironed that shirt!"

Dad shrugged. "I just thought it'd be nice if I looked a little more respectable for this big day."

"Uh-huh," she said with a sly grin. She knew he was dressing up for Mom.

His gaze settled on her makeshift turban. "Hey, are you staining my towels with your shoe polish?"

She rolled her eyes. "It's not shoe polish, it's a *cream*. And your poor towels will be fine. Besides, I had to get all that gunk from last night out of my hair."

"Uh-huh." He pointed at the towel. "Put that ink blotter in the laundry hamper with my clothes and I'll have to kill you."

"Then I'll use my new magical superpowers to come back from the dead," she replied as she walked past him. "Or, better yet," she added as she flapped her bathrobe sleeves, "I'll just haunt you from the grave. *Forevvvvverrrr.*" She floated down the hallway on her tiptoes, heading for her room.

The apartment that Dad had moved into after the divorce wasn't nearly as spacious as the three-bedroom co-op the family had occupied in Woodside—an area where Sheena and Moira and their respective parents still lived, among a constant influx of Irish, Hispanic, Middle Eastern, and Korean immigrants—but was functional enough for one person living alone. That would change, of course, once Pan got her parents back together.

It would *have* to—otherwise they'd be tripping all over each other, she reflected as she wound her way through an obstacle course of horror memorabilia intended for the museum: boxes with titles like JAPANESE BODY HORROR SHOW and SCREAM QUEENS scrawled on them in thick black Magic Marker; a plastic bag full of toys, with a large, pale green SORT AND CATALOGUE THESE!! Post-it stuck to it; and stacks of novels and used reference books. About the only nonhorror items David Zwieback put on display in his home—other than family photos—were New York Mets collectibles: framed copies of the *New York Daily News* and *New York Post* celebrating the 1986 World Series win that hung above the living room couch; the shower curtain in the bathroom; the wall clock in the kitchen.

The mash-up of the sports and horror worlds carried over into Pan's room as well. There were black sheets and pillowcases on a bed covered with a Dark Chemical Wedding duvet that was emblazoned with the image of an angel-winged nymph embracing a dragon-man. Next to the bed a Mr. Met plushie sat in a straight-back chair by a small writing desk crowded with her laptop, monster toys, and family photos taken at Shea Stadium, the Mets' former home before it was torn down. And just as with her room back in Schriksdorp, framed paintings hung on the walls, although these were her early works, from childhood crayon portraits to tween-years painted landscapes.

Her parents never threw away *anything* she drew—not even the framed piece that Dad had hung beside her closet: a kindergarten–era finger painting of Clifford the Big Red Dog tearing into Barney the Dinosaur with bloody fangs (her first controversial work of art!). In some ways their packrattiness was totally embarrassing—few artists actually enjoy seeing their old, "primitive" works on display—but in others it was really touching.

Pan dug through her suitcase to select today's clothes. After all the excitement yesterday, plus the mystery-skeleton unveiling and the pizza party that followed, she hadn't gotten around to unpacking. Black jeans formed the foundation, of course. Add to that a pair of black and orange Converse sneakers and the latest addition to her wardrobe: the Lilitu T-shirt Mom had given her just before she boarded the train.

She held up the T with the thumbs and middle fingers of both hands and stared at the attitudinal devil girl with the tongue sticking out, then shrugged. "I don't know why *anyone* would think of me when they see this . . ."

Then her lips twisted into a little pout. The bat-shaped belt buckle that the skeleton wore would go *so* well with this outfit, but Dad was adamant it remain part of the relic, especially if he had to pack up the whole thing and ship it back to England. Locked away in a crate for another bazillion years—that would be *such* a waste of a great piece of jewelry! And it wasn't like Boney McAngel was ever gonna miss it. But . . . no.

Pan sighed heavily. Life could be so unfair sometimes.

Twenty minutes later, as she was putting the finishing touches on her makeup, she heard him say, "What the hell?"

Pan walked over to his bedroom and leaned against the doorframe. Dad was seated at the small desk beside the bed, hunched over his laptop. "What's wrong?"

He looked up from the computer and stared at his gothed-out daughter. "Hey, where's the new Pan? Still looks like the old one to me."

" 'New' as in a more positive attitude, Dad, not a physical transformation." She pouted. "There's nothing wrong with the way I look."

He smiled. "Never said there was, honey." Then he began crooning, off-key, " 'Don't go changin', to try and please me . . .' "

Pan moaned. "*Please*, Dad, it's too early for Billy Joel tunes." As far as she was concerned, it was *always* too early for Billy Joel tunes—especially if Dad was going to slaughter them with his bad singing.

He snorted. "You kids today. No appreciation for the classics."

Ignoring his comment, she said, "Besides, Mom gave me this shirt yesterday. I want her to see me wearing it." She smoothed out the T so he could have a better look at the devil-girl face printed on the front. "Doesn't it look great?"

"*You* look great."

She grinned. "Thanks. So what was the cussing about?"

Dad pointed to the laptop. "I just got an e-mail from Morrison Millar, the guy who sold me the vampire . . . angel . . . whatever it is. Apparently he's popped into town just for today and wants to talk about the . . . thingis."

"Gonna tell him you want your money back?"

"Thinking about it." Dad shrugged. "I don't know. Maybe you and your friends are right and I should put it on display."

She pointed an accusatory finger at him and snarled. "You *dare* tempt the wrath of God?"

"Meh. More like the wrath of your mother." He reread the e-mail. "Says here he sent the message from his BlackBerry, but he didn't leave a number. So much for calling him back." He sighed—"Fine."—and began typing a reply. "Mr. Morrison," he said out loud as he stabbed at the keys with his two middle fingers. "Sorry for not getting back to you sooner, but I'll be at the museum later this afternoon if you'd like to stop by. Hopefully you'll be able to answer some questions I have—like why you're trying to rip me off."

Pan started. "You didn't really write that, did you?"

Dad looked up and laughed. "No, of course I—" He glanced at the screen. "Oh. Wait. Yes, I did." He started quickly pounding one particular key on the board. "Delete, delete, delete . . ." A few dozens taps later, he reread the last sentence and nodded. "Okay, *now* I didn't." He clicked on the mouse. "And . . . send." Then he rose from his seat. "Okay, that's done. Ready to go?"

She pointed at the computer. "Did you include directions for getting to the museum?"

"My signature has a link to that page on the museum's Web site."

Her eyebrows shot up. "Wow. Look at you, all cyberliterate and stuff."

"Not so much," he admitted. "Tim helped with that."

"Like Javi with the texting yesterday? Sounds like you've got a whole tech-support team working for you, now."

"I suppose. You know it *kills* me to have to rely on a Yankees fan for help," he said wryly. "You traitor."

Pan blushed. "Oh, stop." She started to leave, then turned back. "Oh. Sheena's coming by in a few minutes."

Dad looked confused. "When did you talk to Sheena?"

"We were texting while I was putting my face together."

"And where was she?"

"In church with her mom and dad. She said to tell you Jesus says 'hi.' "

"Texting in church." Dad grunted. "And you say *I'm* tempting the wrath of God."

She tilted her head to one side, as though confused. "I'm sorry. Remind me: *which* of you left the bones of an angel lying on the museum's cellar floor just so you could eat pizza?"

"Well, we *all* did that . . ." he began, then shrugged. "Okay, it was me. My museum, my transgression." He looked toward the ceiling. "Forgive me, Lord."

"You are *so* getting left behind when the Rapture comes," she said with a wicked smile, then rolled off the doorframe and headed back toward her room.

"But you know what, Panda-bear?" Dad called after her. " *'I love you JUST the way you ARRRRE!' '*

Pan clapped her hands over her ears. "Stop! You're a terrible parent!"

Thankfully, the doorbell rang a few seconds later, interrupting Dad's torturous concert. Pan hurried to open the door before he launched into another selection.

It took her a couple of seconds to realize she was looking at Sheena. Her purple hair was pulled back into a neat ponytail and tied with a white Scrunchie. Her makeup was shockingly conservative: a hint of blush, a light amount of eyeliner, and soft pink lipstick to match her nail polish—not a gothy black or bloodred in sight. And her outfit consisted of a pair of white pumps . . . and a white, floral print summer dress. With lacy frills along the hem.

"Oh. My. God." Pan grinned. "Hi, Summer Fun Barbie!"

Sheen held up a warning index finger. "Okay, first? Shut up. And second? What, you never saw me get dressed up for church?"

"Not in a long time." The grin broadened. "You're so *purdy*." She stepped aside with a flourish, bowing low as she swept her arm to the side in a wide arc. "Enter, O glamorous harbinger of spring, and grace this humble domicile with your flowery presence!"

"Bite me." Sheen stomped inside and looked around. "So, where's the monkey chaser?"

"We're meeting Annie later. Where's Ooo-vay? Not a churchgoer?"

Sheen sighed. "Poor baby's exhausted from all the running around his boss had him doing yesterday. And today he's working a double shift for the wedding banquet."

"Aww, that's a shame," Pan said impishly. "So, you eat breakfast yet?"

"Nope. We usually go to IHOP after church, but when Mom told me Nana Hildy was gonna meet us there with hubby number five, that's when I gave you a holler and told them I had to bail."

Pan slowly smiled as she remembered who Sheen was talking about. "Oh, yeah. Azzi the *luuuv*worm."

Sheen grabbed her stomach and lurched toward Pan as though she were about to throw up. "*Urp!* Here comes last night's pizza . . ."

Pan gave her a gentle shove—"Back off, Barbie."—then pointed to her devil-girl T. "Mom just gave me this shirt. Go point your spew someplace else."

"Whatever," Sheen muttered.

"So, anyway, Dad and me were gonna go to the diner for breakfast, then out to the bakery in Middle Village—"

"The one with the killer cinnamon buns?"

"Uh-huh. And then we're driving into the City to pick up Mom so she can meet Annie." Pan had told Sheen a little bit about the mysterious woman and Javi and their adventure in the tunnel, but had honored her promise to Dad to remain silent about Gothopolis and her "superpowers." It was killing her, though. Sheen had stuck by her through all the bad times, from monstervision to monstrous relationships, when others had turned their backs. Keeping a secret as big as this one from her didn't seem fair. Pan *so* wanted to tell her best friend the fantastic news.

Well, she thought, before the day was over both Sheen and Mom would know everything. The question was, how would they react to it?

Sheen held up the black bag she was carrying: a Hell Bunny-brand tote decorated with mummies and warning signs. "All right, look out—I need to change outta this ridiculous dress before I get the urge to watch a *Gossip Girl* marathon." She tromped down the hallway and closed the bathroom door behind her.

"Hurry, O goddess of spring!" Pan called out. "A glorious new day awaits!"

26

"Abso*lutely* glorious," Karen agreed as she took another bite of her gooey cinnamon bun. "God, I missed these," she added around a mouthful of pastry. "As much as you missed me?" Dave asked playfully.

Karen snorted, used a paper napkin to wipe away a drop of cream cheese frosting that had fallen on her Harley-Davidson T-shirt, and turned to Pan. "So, how are you doing, sweetie?"

Pan laughed. "I'm good, Mom. Real good. Amazing, even." She took a bite of her own bun and smiled as she observed the waves of aureate light that undulated around her mother. They weren't as bright as she'd perceived them on Friday, which probably meant Annie was right: the more comfortable she became with the person she now was—or, rather, had always been—the more control she'd have over her gift.

Gift. It was still hard to believe that something she'd considered a curse for so long could turn out to be so wonderful. And yet . . .

Her gaze drifted outward. After meeting Mom at Penn Station Dad had driven them all back to Queens, to picnic at Gantry Plaza State Park in Long Island City. Now, following a meal of deli sandwiches and salads, they lounged on wooden deckchairs, enjoying the view of midtown Manhattan across the East River. Mom and dad ducks, bobbing with the tide near the piers, watched a group of kayakers paddle by; their babies, meanwhile, were engaged in an animated discussion with a green-skinned, blue-haired mermaid. Down by the river's edge, a quartet of water sprites playfully flitted above the reeds lining the bank. A shirtless red troll—or whatever it was—jogged along the asphalt path that wound through the park, bobbing his head to the tune leaking out past his iPod earbuds. And high overhead, a pair of sylphs—air elementals—drifted along, hand in hand, on the light easterly breeze. However, other than those magical creatures, the rest of the people around her remained boringly normal to her eyes. It was no longer a world *filled* with monsters, she realized, just one with its fair share of them. She could handle that.

Today is the first day of the rest of your life, Pan thought giddily. Still, this was *so* gonna take getting used to . . .

She turned back to her mother. "So, how's my baby?"

"Vlad?" Mom shrugged. "Eating, sleeping, commandeering your bed—you know, the usual. I asked Mrs. Mueller to watch him until I get back." Ilsa and Willard Mueller were an elderly couple who lived two doors down from the Bonifant home in Schriksdorp. Unfortunately, no one thought of her as "Mrs. Mueller"; to the people in the neighborhood she was—

"Ilsa the Cat Lady?" Pan said. "The one with, like, a hundred cats? You're letting Vlad stay with her?"

"He'll be perfectly fine. And it's not a hundred, it's more like . . . fifteen. Maybe twenty. Besides, it's not the first time he's visited her, you know."

"Yeah, but that was before we got him fixed . . ."

Mom swallowed the last bite of cinnamony goodness and wiped her mouth. "So, what's the big surprise so important you couldn't tell me over the phone?"

Pan exchanged glances with her dad. Should they tell them now?

"We wanted you to meet someone first," he said to Karen. "She's . . . I guess you could call her a specialist in her field. She's *definitely* someone who can explain the situation better than I ever could." He glanced at Pan and winked.

Mom saw that. "You mean you found a *new* therapist? What happened to Dr. Elfman? I thought you were going to call tomorrow."

"Dr. Elfman?" Pan asked. "I haven't seen her in, like, forever. Why would I go see her?"

Mom turned to her daughter. "Before I put you on the train, Dad and I were talking about finding someone down here to continue your therapy. He suggested Dr. Elfman. I thought that was a good idea, since you two used to get along so well."

"I guess . . ." Pan said noncommittally. Of course, after the events of yesterday the last thing she wanted to do was see another therapist, but then she remembered Dad's warning about what might happen if her sessions came to an abrupt end, and decided it would be better for everyone if she just went with the flow. For now.

The air suddenly filled with the loud but muffled strains of Cauldron's "Into the Cauldron" emanating from Pan's jacket. It was the ringtone she used for any numbers not listed in her address book.

Pan dug into her jacket pocket and pulled out her cell. The number on the screen had no caller identification, but she answered it anyway. "Hello?"

"Pandora? It's Annie Mazarin."

"Oh, hey, Annie! Me and Dad were just talking about you."

"Dad and I," Dave said. Once an English teacher, always an English teacher.

Pan rolled her eyes. "Okay, okay, Dad and I. Hang on a second, I'll put you on speaker." She pressed a button and placed the phone on the table in the center of the group. "You're still coming over, right? My mom's here—she's dying to meet you. Say hi, Mom."

"I am?" Karen leaned toward the phone. "Hi . . . uh, Annie."

"Hello, Mrs. Zwieback!" Annie called out.

Mom flinched, just a hair, and did her best to ignore her ex's Cheshire grin. "Karen is fine."

"Hey, Annie, how'd you get my number?" Pan asked. She imagined the great monster hunter possessing some supernatural ability to read minds over immeasurable distances, or glean such information from staring at the microwave radiation emanating from cell-phone towers.

"I asked Javier for it. He's here with me right now."

"Hey, Cookie!" Javi yelled from the background.

Pan blushed and tried to avoid making eye contact with her tablemates—Sheen in particular. "Hey, Javi," she said with a grin.

"I just wanted to call and tell you I'm running a little late today," Annie said. "Some people broke into my town house last night, and I've got half the city agencies *plus* my insurance agent poking around, assessing the damage. It's a big mess."

Pan started. "Oh, my God! Are you okay?"

"I'm fine. The people who broke in . . . not at all." There was an almost playful tone to Annie's voice. She didn't sound like the victim of a home invasion, all rattled and breathless and tearful, but more like someone who'd taken care of the problem herself—and enjoyed doing it. "What time is it?" Annie asked.

Dave checked his wristwatch. "Heading toward one thirty."

"All right, I should still be able to meet you at the museum at two. I've got the directions from the Web site on my cell." There was a loud crashing sound in the distance, and Annie yelled away from the phone, "Blake, I told you to be careful! What? . . . Yes, I know there's a big hole in the back wall—the RPG did that when it exploded." Back on the phone, she said, "Look, Pandora, I have to go before my insurance agent falls into my backyard. I'll see you in a bit."

"Okay, Annie," Pan said. "Bye!" She clicked off the phone.

"A town house in Manhattan," Dave said. "She must be *loaded*."

"Oooh, I think somebody just found an investor for the museum," Karen said playfully.

His jaw slowly dropped. "Hey, that's not a bad idea . . ."

"Oh, brother . . ." Karen turned to Pan. "Is this Annie the specialist your father was talking about?" When her daughter nodded, she added, "A specialist in *what*, exactly?"

For a couple of seconds Pan considered dodging the question, but knew that Mom wouldn't give up until she had some kind of answer. So she gave her one: "Monstervision."

Mom looked surprised. "Really? You mean she's dealt with cases like yours?"

"Oh, yeah. Tons. She's, like, a total expert."

Mom glared at Dad. "And you first met her when?" There was a stern tone in her voice that made it clear she didn't like her ex consulting with a new therapist without her involvement.

"Turn off the heat vision, Superwoman," he said. "We met her only yesterday, and that was completely by accident. But she definitely knows her stuff. That's why I asked you to come down, so we could talk to her together."

Mom backed off. "Oh. Okay. Well . . . good work, then."

He shrugged. "I do what I can."

"And this Javier?" Mom asked Pan. "Is that her son?"

Pan shook her head. "No, Annie's a friend of his family. He helps her out with stuff."

"Like chasing monkeys in Penn Station," Sheen added.

Mom's eyebrows rose. "Chasing monkeys? What's *that* about?"

Pan glanced at Dad.

"She's gotta hear the story sometime," he said.

Mom glanced from one to the other. "Do I *want* to hear this story?"

"Probably not," Pan replied with a smile, "but it's a *really* good one."

In the broadest of strokes she told Karen the story of encountering the orang pendek and saving Javi's life, capped off by Annie's arrival on the scene and the experience of having a baby monkey pawing through Pan's hair in search of bug-snacks. Then Dad chimed in with his tale of involving the police in his search for their daughter, and ended with the spectacle of a genuflecting transit cop. All mentions of auras and healing touches and Gothopolis were carefully edited out—although keeping those secrets from her mother was almost as painful for Pan as holding them back from her best friend. As far as she was concerned, Annie couldn't meet with them soon enough so the whole truth could be revealed.

Karen sat quietly for a few moments, absorbing all the details of the adventure. Finally, she said, "That's the last time I let you ride the train alone."

"Mom!" Pan cried. "Nothing happened!"

"A lot happened. You were just lucky that nothing *bad* happened."

"Yeah, I guess . . ." Pan muttered, a tad sullenly.

Karen turned to Dave. "So, wait—what is a therapist doing chasing after wild animals?"

"I didn't say Annie was a therapist, hon," Dave replied, "I said she was a specialist." When he saw her heated glare ratcheting up to full strength again, he added, "Look, it's like I told you: She can explain the situation a whole lot better than I ever could. Just hang on a little bit longer."

"You know I hate mysteries, Dave," she grumbled, "but if you and Pan insist on giving me vague answers, then, fine. I'll wait. But not all day, and your friend Annie better spell everything out." She sighed wearily, then turned to her daughter with a smile. "So, tell me about Javier."

"Well, he lives in the Bronx with his parents and little sister, but they've got a weekend place up in Westchester," Pan said, then quickly added, "Oh! And he plays shortstop for his high school baseball team, and he's totally obsessed with *HALO* and *Splinter Cell*, and he likes to read *Spider-Man* and *The Punisher*, and he knows about Goths 'cause his mom watches *NCIS* and there's this Goth chick on it, and—"

"And he's a nice kid, but . . ." Dave grimaced. "He's a Yankees fan."

"Oh, dear God," Karen said in mock horror. "You let a *Yankees* fan get near your daughter?" She raised an eyebrow. "How scandalous."

"It is," Sheen remarked, and frowned at her best friend. "Hey, thanks for leaving out *that* part when you told me about him last night, Zee. You know how Yankees fans are—they'd rather forget how to breathe than go a day without remindin' Mets fans they're better'n us."

"Javi's not like that," Pan said. At least she *hoped* he wasn't.

"I'm warnin' you right now," Sheen said, "the first time new boyfriend starts crowin' about all those World Series championships, I'm gonna beat him with a shovel."

Pan laughed. "So I'll hide all the shovels." She turned to her father. "Anyway, Tommy's a Yankees fan. So's Lisa. And you're okay with *them*, Dad." Truthfully, though, it wasn't so much that Dave was okay with her friends' loyalty to the Bronx Bombers as much as he quietly, painfully tolerated it for her sake.

"That's because neither of *them* makes his daughter blush with excitement when she talks about them," Mom said with a knowing smile.

"Huh?" Pan reached up and touched her cheeks. They were *really* warm. She smiled awkwardly.

"And what's up with that 'cookie' stuff?" Sheen asked, her eyes narrowed in disapproval.

Pan blushed. "It's . . . y'know, like a nickname."

"A nickname based on what?" Dad asked.

"I think *I* know . . ." Mom replied in a singsongy voice.

Sheen gasped. "Oh. My. God. He's making a joke about your last name!" She stared at Pan in horrified confusion. "What the hell, Zee? You *never* let anybody do that!"

"Yeah, I know, but . . ." Pan shrugged. "I don't know. I think it's kinda cute."

"So do I." Mom looked at Dad and grinned. "Isn't that right, Cookie McMets?"

Dave grunted. "Well, it's official. Now he *has* to die."

Sheen started to rise from her seat. "Lemme go find a shovel."

Pan put out a hand to block her. "Stop it. Javi's a nice guy. You're gonna love him, I swear."

Mom eyed her. "You seem to know an awful lot about this boy you just met yesterday."

"Uh . . . yeah," Pan said. "That's 'cause we . . . did a lot of texting last night. After Dad went to bed."

"Well, thank God my cell-phone plan includes unlimited texting, huh?" Mom said sarcastically.

"Yeah, 'cause those late-night booty calls can go on *forever*," Sheen remarked.

Mom trained her heat vision on the girl. "I beg your pardon?"

Sheen hurriedly stuffed the last of her bun in her mouth. "Nom nom nom," she said with a pastry-contorted grin. "Who, me? I didn't say nothin'."

Mom nodded. "Let's keep it that way."

"So . . ." Dave looked at his watch. "On that awkward note I think we better pack up and head over to the museum to meet Annie."

An idea suddenly popped into Pan's head. "Hey, you know what, Dad? I bet Annie might know what that skeleton is."

"Skeleton?" Karen gazed at her ex. "Another one of those world-changing surprises the two of you were promising?"

Dave grinned. "You know me, hon: I like to buy my surprises in bulk."

"A therapist—sorry, 'specialist' familiar with Pan's sort of problems, who can also identify dead bodies? That's not a surprise, it's a *CSI* spin-off series." Karen grunted. "Your friend Annie better have a *really* good story to tell. . . ."

27

Unfortunately, it wasn't the sort of story Mom wanted to hear . . .

"So we're *back* to this Gothopolis nonsense?" she said hotly.

"Would you *please* just hear her out?" Dad asked. "Trust me, Karen, I was the same way as you before Annie proved her point."

"I *knew* sending her down to you was going to be a big mistake," Mom snapped. "God almighty, Dave, our daughter's with you all of one day—one day!—and *already* you're trying to ruin ten years' worth of therapy by digging up this . . . this fairy-tale crap again? What is *wrong* with you?"

"Hey, you used to believe in that 'fairy-tale crap' yourself, you know," he countered.

"And then I grew up," she replied. "I guess you still haven't."

Dad apparently didn't have a comeback for that one.

Standing outside Dave's office at Renfield's House of Horrors, Pan shifted nervously on her feet. She'd had a strong feeling that Mom would have a negative reaction when Dad and Annie tried explaining the situation; she just hadn't expected it to be so . . . volatile.

Obviously aware of her best friend's unease, Sheen reached out and gave Pan's hand a reassuring squeeze. "Just like old times, huh?" she asked with a pained smile.

"Yeah," Pan replied softly.

Sheen moved in close and lowered her voice to a conspiratorial mutter. "So, what haven't you told me about A-Rod yet?"

Pan shook her head to dispel the dark thoughts that had been forming as Mom continued her tirade inside the office. "Huh?"

"You know . . ." Sheen nodded her head toward the front of the museum, where Javi was thumbing through the pages of some horror graphic novel he'd pulled down from a shelf.

Pan knew what Sheen was trying to do—distract her from the war being fought on the other side of the closed office door. Still, she was grateful for the change of subject. "Oh, Javi? I told you, he was the one I kept from getting his head bashed in by the orange pendant."

"And you met him only yesterday, and you spent all night texting, and already you're fallin' for him—right?" Sheen held up a warning finger. "Don't try and deny it; I saw your eyes get all sparkly when he showed up. Plus your face turned beet-red."

Pan thought about saying it was all a figment of Sheena's overactive imagination; that it'd be ridiculous for something like love at first sight to happen to her— her, Pandora Zwieback, the queen of bad relationships. But then she thought of Javi's smile and the way it made her feel, how just being *near* him made her feel, and realized she'd only be fooling herself by denying the accusation. She slowly nodded, which brought an exasperated sigh rushing from Sheen's lips.

"Aw, Zee," she moaned softly, then lightly placed her head against Pan's and gave her a gentle squeeze. "I know I told you the other day you needed to get yourself a man, baby girl, but you can't keep leadin' with your heart like this. Not after the last time."

"Wait. You mean the one time I actually take your advice you're gonna give me grief about it?"

"I . . . I just don't wanna see you get messed up again," Sheen said in all seriousness.

Pan exhaled sharply. "He's not like Ammi," she insisted.

"Really," Sheen replied drolly. "And you know this after one day because—how? Your new superpowers make it so you can peer into the depths of his soul?"

"Kinda sorta," she replied.

Pan grinned. Sheen hadn't seen any display of her "superpowers," hadn't even been shown how to look past the perception spell yet, but she had accepted the explanation of Pan's magical gifts without argument. Whether she actually believed the incredible tale, however, was a completely different matter. Still, magic spells and healing touches aside, it was evident she was overjoyed that someone had finally confirmed what she'd been insisting for years: that her best friend wasn't crazy.

Except when it came to boys, that is . . .

"I'm tellin' you, Zee," Sheen continued, "this guy ain't a good fit. I can feel it." She glanced over her shoulder to examine Javi. As though conscious of her heated gaze boring into his back he turned around, nodded once pleasantly, and flashed her a smile before returning to his reading. "Sure, he's all self-confident and kinda studly . . . I mean, if you're into the muscular, good-lookin', athletic type—"

"Which I am . . . now."

"And I can see how that pretty-boy smile of his would make you feel all . . ." She smiled shyly, placed the tip of her index finger against her lips, and giggled idiotically—clearly making fun of the tongue-tied embarrassment Pan displayed when Annie had arrived with Javi in tow. ". . . inside."

"Quit it . . ." Pan growled.

"But I mean, for God's sake, Zee, he's a *Yankees* fan! That'd be like sleepin' with the enemy!" Then the blood practically drained from her face. "Oh, God. You slept with him, didn't you?"

Pan started. "*What*? No! I just met the guy! Besides, between the monkey wrangling and the whole vampire-angel thing last night, where exactly was I supposed to find the time to do *that*?"

"But you're lettin' him riff on your name and stuff . . ."

"Maybe 'cause I really like him? Ya think? So . . . deal with it, jungle queen. Anyway, what're you—my mother?"

Sheen widened her eyes completely; a grotesque, sickly smile contorted her purple-colored lips. "Why, yeessss, Coraline," she said in a raspy voice. "I'm your Other Mother. And you should *always* listen to your Other Mother."

Pan snorted at the movie reference and elbowed her friend in the ribs. "Dork."

"Yeah, the dork who's gonna kick lover boy's ass if he gets outta line," Sheen said in her normal voice. She took another quick glance at Javi, then shook her head in resignation. "Okay. Fine. I'll allow it."

"Gee, thanks," Pan replied sarcastically.

Sheen chuckled. "Y'know, now that I think about it, I guess you coulda done worse."

Pan eyed her suspiciously. "How so?"

Her best friend wiggled her eyebrows and smiled. "Lover boy coulda been a *Phillies* fan."

The office door suddenly flew open and Karen came charging out. Annie was right behind her.

"Mrs. Zwie—" Annie began to plead, only to stop in midspeech as Karen turned to glare at her. "Karen, I mean. If you'll just give me a chance to guide you through the process—"

"You mean hypnotize me, or whatever it is you did to convince my daughter that all the hard work her therapists have put in to help her is just a bunch of crap?" She gestured toward Annie's well-endowed chest. "It's obvious how you won *Dave* over."

A stunned silence descended over the museum.

Pan sucked in a sharp breath between her clenched teeth. Behind her, she heard Javi drop the graphic novel on the floor.

"Daaamn . . ." Sheen whispered.

Annie snarled at Karen. "Oh, don't even *go* there."

"Hey! Hey, now!" Dave yelled as he followed the two women out. "Ladies! Ladies! Could we at least *try* and keep this conversation civil? There are children present, you know."

"Children?" Sheen yelped angrily. Pan gave her arm a tiny squeeze, indicating she should shut up. Thankfully, Sheen took the hint.

Javi sauntered over to join the group. "Hey, Annie, why don't you just do that thing you do? You know . . ." He fluttered his hands in front of his face, like a magician performing a trick. "That thing."

Annie frowned. "Javier . . ."

"What? It'd put an end to all the yelling, wouldn't it? C'mon, it'll take you two seconds. Go on—*show* her."

Sheen leaned over to Pan. "What're they talkin' about?" she muttered.

"I have *no* idea."

Karen cast a suspicious eye toward Annie. "Show me what?"

"Well, like Pandora I have certain . . . talents," Annie hesitantly explained.

Karen snorted derisively. "Sure, you do. I already know what *your* talent— *OHMYGOD!*" she screamed, and jumped back.

Sheen did likewise, as did Pan. The girls hugged each other in fright.

Annie had disappeared; in her place stood a completely different woman.

Correction: not *just* a completely different woman.

Another Karen Bonifant.

She was an exact duplicate: same clothes, same height, same hair, same face— right down to the one-eyebrow-cocked sarcastic expression Mom had been wearing before she'd come face-to-face with her double. As the original stared at her with openmouthed astonishment, Karen 2's lips curled into a grin.

"Yes, Karen?" she said in Annie's distinctive voice. "You were saying . . . ?"

For the first time since Dad and Annie had dropped the Gothopolis bomb on her, Mom was speechless.

Pan disentangled herself from Sheen, to find Javi standing close by. Smiling warmly, he opened his arms.

"Me next." When neither girl responded, he raised an eyebrow. "What—ain't you, like, those 'free hugs' chicks I see walkin' around comic book conventions?"

Pan gave him a playful little shove. "Jerk." Then she cautiously stepped forward to reach out with an index finger and poke the doppelgänger in the shoulder.

"How . . . how did you do that?" she asked.

"I'm a shape-shifter," Annie replied matter-of-factly. "Watch this." She demonstrated her mimicry even further by performing a rapid series of metamorphic changes—from cynical mom to panther, to some kind of ugly monster- thing wearing an Adidas track suit, to a duplicate of Dad, to a golden-haired orang pendek, and finally to a familiar-looking Goth chick. "Pretty neat, huh?" faux- Pan said with a Cheshire grin.

"I'll say!" The real Pan turned to Karen. "Hey, Mom, check it out—instant evil twin!"

Mom, unfortunately, didn't appear to see the humor in this bizarre situation. In fact, she looked a little ill. Even the glow Pan saw around her had turned a sickly pale yellow.

Pan blanched. "Mom?"

"That's not . . . I need to sit down," she said weakly. Dave and Pan rushed forward to grab her before her knees gave out, then he led her toward the office.

Annie reverted to her normal supermodel self as the couple walked past. "Karen, I'm *really* sorry for shocking you like that. I just thought it would help you understand Pandora's situation better."

"It's okay, Annie," Dave said. "Just give us a minute. Karen and I need to . . . absorb this." He looked the monster hunter up and down. "How come you didn't mention this yesterday?"

Annie flashed a shy smile. "I don't like to show off."

"Uh . . . right." He turned back to guide Karen into one of his guest seats.

Not knowing what to say herself, Pan turned to Sheen for a comment.

"*That* was awesome," Sheen said with a grin. She threw an arm around her friend's shoulders. "See? I always *said* you weren't nuts."

"I know," Pan replied. "Thanks, Sheen—for everything. You've always been there for me."

"And I always will be, Zee," her friend said, then added with a wicked smile, "Especially when your choice in boyfriends totally sucks." Then she turned to the monster hunter. "Ooh! Do me next!" She clasped her hands together in a begging gesture. "Pleeeeease, Annie?"

The shape-shifter chuckled. "All right, all right."

"Yay!" She turned to Pan. "I'm gonna have my own evil twin, too!"

"Yeah—except *you'll* be the evil one."

Sheen took her friend's chin between thumb and forefinger and gave it a tiny squeeze. "Oh, Vampira, you say the *nicest* things," she cooed, then released her and turned back to Annie. "Okay, let's see!"

As Sheen squealed with delight at meeting herself, Pan followed her parents into the office. From the expression on his face, Dad obviously thought that after yesterday he'd be prepared for whatever came next, but Annie's transformation had shocked him as much as it had Mom.

"How you guys doing?" she asked in a gentle tone.

"I . . . honestly have no idea," Mom said. "That was a trick—wasn't it?"

Pan smiled. "Not unless my type of crazy suddenly got all contagious."

Karen looked horrified by the joke. "Oh, Pan, don't . . ."

Pan rushed forward and placed her hands on Karen's shoulders. "Mom, no, it's okay. Really. And the therapy *did* help—I don't think I could've ever made it this far without Dr. Elfman or Dr. Farrar. " She smiled. "Or you and Dad. It's just that . . . things have changed—for the better, I mean."

Karen didn't look convinced. "Sweetheart, I don't want you pinning your hopes on fairy tales."

"But that's just it—it's *not* a fairy tale." Pan wiggled her eyebrows. "Want me to show you? It's really cool. Please?"

"Give her a chance, K," Dave said with an encouraging smile. "I'm telling you, it will absolutely *blow* your mind." He held up his fists near the sides of his head, then opened them as he mimicked the sound of an explosion.

"Great," Mom said dryly. "But do I *want* my mind blown?"

"Oh, yeah," Pan said, grinning. "You do. You really do."

Karen looked from daughter to ex-husband, and back again. It was clear she wanted to say no, but in the end she sighed wearily and shrugged. "All right. Blow my mind, then."

"Sweet!" Pan stepped back about five feet. "Okay, now I want you to concentrate on me. Look right at me."

"I'm looking," Mom said.

"No, I mean *really* look—like you're trying to see through me."

"It helps if you lean forward and squint," Dad offered. "That's how it worked for me."

Mom sighed again but did as suggested. "Okay, I'm *really* looking," she said, eyes narrowed.

"Are you trying to see through me?" Pan asked.

"Kind of hard to do with that devil girl's face staring back at me. Nice T-shirt, by the way," she added with a wink.

"*Mom,*" Pan said, exasperated. "C'mon, now."

"Fine, fine." Mom returned to leaning and squinting.

"You see anything?"

"The only thing I'm seeing is a heat haze in this room because it's too damn hot in here and your father didn't think to turn on the air-conditioning."

A heat haze? Pan gasped. Wasn't that how Dad had described the barrier when he'd started looking through it?

"That's it, Mom!" she yelled. "You're doing it!"

"Doing what?"

"You're seeing past the perspective thingie!"

"Perception filter." Dad looked impressed as he turned to Mom. "Wow, hon, you did that pretty—"

Karen gasped. "Pan! You're . . . you're *glowing.*"

"—fast," he concluded. *"Damn."*

"Of course I'm glowing—just like you are," Pan said, smiling. "Oh, Mom, you look so, *so* beautiful, it's . . . You look like an angel."

"That's what *I've* always thought," Dad said.

Karen blushed; to Pan's eyes her aura turned a rosy hue.

"Can you see me glowing, too?" Karen asked her ex.

"Not at the moment, because I'm not trying. But I know what you're both talking about."

"If you look too long you get killer headaches," Pan explained to her mother. "Dad got hit with one yesterday."

He nodded. "Yeah, and I'm not looking for a repeat. But before that? I could see Pan's aura, I could see Annie's, I could see . . . a lot of strange things. Believe me, Karen, Lite-Brite auras are just the tip of the supernatural iceberg."

Karen shook her head. "I don't know—it's all still hard to believe."

"I know exactly what you mean," Pan replied with a playful smile. "It's like finding out you and Dad went hunting for Gothopolis when I was little."

This time Karen's aura blushed a deep red. "He told you about that, huh?"

"Oh, yeah." Pan crouched down and took Karen's hands. "You have no idea how much what you and Dad did means to me, Mom. Thanks."

Karen squeezed her daughter's hands. "Well, you're my Panda-bear—there's nothing I wouldn't do for you."

"Then please, Mom, keep an open mind. Do *that* for me. As freaky as all this stuff is—and yeah, it's *totally* freaky—I gotta tell you: I like being Magic Girl a whole lot better than thinking I'm losing my mind."

Karen reached up to touch Pan's face. "And this is how it's always been for you? Seeing auras and . . . and healing bumps on heads?"

"Annie and I told her everything," Dad explained.

"Oh. Okay." Pan shook her head. "No, not the healing stuff; that didn't start happening until yesterday. Before that, it was . . . well, you know how it was."

She grinned. "But wait until you hear the *whole* story."

When they emerged from the office fifteen minutes later, after Pan had brought her parents up to speed on her run-in with the mall guard and subsequent monstervision overload, she felt as though they were a family again. At least that was her perception of how well things had gone in there; she could only hope Mom and Dad felt the same. It would give her something to build on later.

Their guests had managed to keep themselves busy during their absence. Annie was examining some of the movie posters hanging on the walls. Sheen and Javi, meanwhile, had their cell phones out and were engaged in some serious texting or Tweeting—more than likely not with each other. All three turned to face Pan and her parents.

"Everything all right?" Annie asked.

"Couldn't be better," Pan replied with a grin. "I even showed Mom how to look past the spell."

"Do I get to look past the spell, too?" Sheen asked. "Whatever that is?"

"I'll show you later," Pan said. "You are *so* gonna freak."

Karen, looking mildly embarrassed, walked over to the huntress. "Uh, look, Ms. Mazarin—"

"Annie."

"Annie. I'd like to apologize for what I said earlier. About . . . you know."

"The girls?"

Karen laughed. "Yes, them. It was uncalled for, and I'm sorry."

"Well, then, apology accepted. Besides . . ." Annie smiled. "I've heard worse. *Believe* me."

Javi looked to Annie. He seemed confused. "Who are the girls?"

"Never mind," she replied. "You'll understand when you're older."

Pan turned to her father. "Hey, Dad, what about the skeleton?"

Karen groaned. "I thought we were done with the world-changing surprises for one day. I'm worn out from all this *X-Files* stuff already, and I still have a long train ride back to Albany to look forward to."

"It'll just take a minute, Mom. Promise."

Karen nodded wearily. "All right. Bring on Skeletor."

"What's this about, now?" Annie asked.

"C'mon, I'll show you." Pan turned and led the troupe back into the office and toward a door in the rear that led to the cellar. "See, Dad bought this weird-looking skeleton and we took a look at it last night. The guy he bought it from said it was a vampire—"

"Oh, for the love of God . . ." Mom muttered. Dad wisely avoided making eye contact.

"—but my friend Tory said the wings on it are all wrong. She said they looked more like bird wings than bat wings."

"Reyna thought it was an angel," Sheen pointed out.

Pan opened the basement door. "Yeah, that, too. So I was wondering if maybe *you'd* know what it is, Annie."

The huntress shrugged. "Identifying dead bodies isn't really my area of expertise. I mean, I can *try*, but I'm not a forensic pathologist or anything like that."

Dave gave Karen a nudge. "So much for your *CSI* spin-off series."

"It has this totally gorgeous belt buckle that would go *so* well with some of my outfits—if certain people would let me have it."

"Hey! Don't make me start singing Billy Joel again," Dad warned.

"Whatever." Pan flicked on the lights, then stepped to the side and made a showman-like sweep of her arm toward the new acquisition. "So, Annie . . . have you ever seen anything like this before?"

As she stepped onto the landing, to say Annie was surprised would be the understatement of the year; to say the skeleton horrified her didn't begin to describe her reaction.

"*NO!*" she screamed, and jumped over the railing to gracefully touch down on the concrete floor. "Oh, my God, no . . ." she moaned softly as she gazed at the creature's remains.

"Annie?" Pan asked. "What's wrong?"

A haunted look came into the shape-shifter's eyes as she stared mutely at her young friend.

"Do you know what that thing is?"

Annie slowly nodded.

"Zaqiel . . ." she whispered hoarsely. "It's Zaqiel. . . ."

28

Sebastienne's senses were as sharp as the tempered steel she clutched in her sweaty hands. She could hear the rumble of the volcano on which she stood, the groans of the dying around her, the clash of weapons in the distance, the shrieks of nightmarish beasts stomping across the fiery landscape in search of prey—and the screams of their victims; she could smell the nostril-singeing odors of musky sweat and burnt flesh, coppery blood and voided bowels, amid the sulfurous odor of lava flows and superheated ash.

She could see the faint, bloodred moonlight that peeped through the rising pyroclastic cloud, to sparkle along the bat-shaped belt buckle worn by the beautiful, dark-winged man standing before her. His amber-colored eyes gleamed brightly as he smiled at her.

"Oh, for the love of God," she screamed, *"would you just die already?"*

Zaqiel took a moment to glance down at the sword protruding from his bare, sculpted chest before turning his attention to the beautiful woman attempting to shove the remaining two feet of steel through his rib cage.

"I hope you won't take this the wrong way, dear Sebastienne," the angel commented glibly, "but if this is how you *normally* show affection to your lovers, I'm beginning to understand why you live alone."

"Go to hell, Zaqiel," she sniped. "Or go back to heaven, if He will have you—I don't care which it is. But your madness ends here. Tonight." Gripping the hilt with both hands, she threw her weight against the sword, grunting loudly from the exertion as she tried to force the blade deeper. The night air echoed with the nerve-jangling rasp of metal scraping against bone.

"Do you want me to say it tickles more than the whisper of your sweet breath caressing the nape of my neck?" he asked with an infuriatingly playful grin, which quickly evaporated into a sneer. "It doesn't, actually. It's rather quite painful."

"Good," Sebastienne snapped through clenched teeth. "I'm just getting started."

"No, I rather think you've had enough fun for one evening," Zaqiel said. "You can stop now."

Her only response was to dig her boot heels into the earth and push even harder on the weapon. Sweat beaded on her temples as she strained, but the blade wouldn't penetrate any farther.

"No, really," he insisted. "Stop."

"Shut up and die," she growled.

The fallen angel sighed melodramatically—and then smashed her across the face with a backhanded strike. Caught off guard by the savage blow, Sebastienne lost her grip on the sword and staggered back a few feet before crashing to the ash-covered dirt on her rear end. Too dazed to move, she could only sit and watch numbly as the former prince of heaven wrenched the blade from his chest. The wound healed instantly.

Zaqiel hefted the blade in his left hand—his fighting hand—and nodded appreciatively. "Good balance . . . well crafted," he commented, "but not a very effective weapon against the Almighty's favorite children—"

"The Almighty's *rejects*, you mean!" Sebastienne countered. "Admit it, Zaqiel, that's what you really are—you and Lucifer and all the other traitors He cast out! You're an embarrassment to your creator. That's why he banished you Watchers to that stinking pit for the rest of eternity—so He wouldn't have to look at you anymore . . . so He wouldn't have to remember you ever *existed*." She flashed a wicked smile. "Forgotten by all . . . mourned by none."

Zaqiel's lips pulled back in a snarl; a flash of lightning in the pyroclastic cloud gleamed off razor-sharp fangs. She'd hit a nerve with that remark, her caustic words doing far more damage to him than her useless sword ever could. She hoped they left a ragged scar on his heart, as his betrayal had left on hers.

"Perhaps you are right," he growled. "But I escaped the crucible, did I not? While God looked the other way and busied Himself with offering salvation to his monkey-children I regained my long-denied freedom—unlike my brothers who still beg Him for release!" He pointed up toward the rim of the volcano. "And now I have returned to free them!"

Zaqiel strode toward her, his fighting hand gripped tightly around the sword's hilt. "And yet who should arrive at my hour of triumph, to disrupt my plans? The lowly *beast* I had the poor judgment to choose as my lover—and who now has turned on its master. A mongrel that doesn't know whether it should be human or animal!" He sneered. "And you have the temerity to speak of *me* of God's rejects."

Sebastienne blinked back the tears that threatened to spill down her cheeks. Her words might have cut his heart, but his tore at her soul. "Damn you, Zaqiel . . ." she whispered hoarsely.

"*I am already damned!*" the angel roared, and raised the sword above his head. "*But I will not suffer alone!*"

The blade swept down, and Sebastienne screamed.

But then from out of the smoke and ash and hellfire charged a raven-haired avenger—her clothing tattered, her skin spattered with blood and dirt—to block the killing blow with a spear whose burnished iron tip glowed with preternatural energy.

According to legend, this was the same weapon once owned by a Roman soldier named Longinus—who in 30 A.D. used it to stab Jesus Christ as he hung from a cross.

Legend also said this ancient relic was the only true defense against the fallen ones, although that had never been put to the test. Still, the questionable potency of a weapon mattered little when it came to matters of the heart—for a mother protecting her only child, *any* weapon is potent enough if one has the skill to wield it properly.

And on the killing field that night, none wielded them better than the warrior-shaman named Amaru Mazarin.

As powerful and deadly as her attack was, however, Zaqiel neither lost his footing nor relinquished possession of his sword as he countered her flurry of spear thrusts—until the iron point swept through an opening in his defense to rip across his unprotected chest. He shrieked as blood geysered from the wound, and fell to his knees gasping for breath. The look of horror that contorted his handsome features almost brought a smile to Sebastienne's lips—but then she remembered the sword strike that would have cleaved her head in two had her mother not intervened, and the smile quickly faded.

"Well, at least we know this thing really works," Amaru said as she gazed at the spear. She flicked it to shake off the blood that glistened along its tip, then pointed the iron head toward her foe. "And now I know how to kill you."

Zaqiel snarled. "But that knowledge only helps if I don't kill you first."

With a mighty thrust of his wings he flung himself at her. Once more the battlefield echoed with the clash of sword and spear, only this time it was Amaru who stumbled back under the assault. Forced into a defensive position by her airborne enemy, limited to blocking his sword strikes and unable to bring the iron point to bear, she could only give ground and wait for another opening.

Seeing her mother in peril, Sebastienne quickly eyed the carcasses strewn around her; there had to be a weapon she could—

The double-headed ax caught her eye. One blade was coated with drying blood; the other was buried deep in the skull of an obese, green-haired troll who would never see his bridge-home again. She leaped over the corpse of a mountain giant— whose throat she'd torn out when he'd tried to stop her from reaching her angelic ex-boyfriend—and grabbed hold of the thick, rawhide-covered ax handle with both hands. It wouldn't budge.

A sharp cry pierced the night air, and she turned to see her mother splayed on the ground. Blood gushed down her left arm, and she was using her right hand to try and stanch the flow. Zaqiel had struck an artery, and unless Amaru's supernatural healing factor was given enough time to close the wound, she would bleed to death.

The fallen angel, though, wasn't about to give her an opportunity to mend. He kicked aside the spear and closed on his prey. Already weak from blood loss, Amaru kicked at the ashen soil, trying to push herself away from the sword strike that was soon to fall, but there was no escaping her would-be executioner. And yet he seemed to be in no hurry to deliver the deathblow; apparently he wished to savor this kill.

Sebastienne yanked on the ax handle, but the troll's thick head refused to give up the weapon. She slammed a foot down on the corpse's shoulder to pin it to the ground and heaved with all her might. Slowly, the ax began to move.

Desperation adding strength to her limbs, she closed her eyes and pulled, screaming at the troll that he would not deny her this chance to save her mother.

There was a loud *pop!* and suddenly she was staggering backward as the ax came free and swung over her head, with her fingers still wrapped in a stranglehold around the handle. She righted herself before the ax's momentum could send her tripping over the body of the mountain giant behind her, and grinned, pleased with her success—

Until she noticed that the troll's head was still attached to the blade. She'd pulled it right off his body—along with part of his spinal column, which hung down like a bony, gore-spattered tail.

"Eeewwww . . ." she said, grimacing.

Her disgust was short-lived, though. There would be plenty of time later to be nauseous—after she rescued Amaru.

"You leave my mother alone, Zaqiel!" Sebastienne screamed, and held high the ax—troll head and all—as she charged.

The angel turned from his fallen enemy to confront this new threat. At first he seemed surprised at the notion of his ex-girlfriend racing across the plain, brandishing an ax with somebody's head stuck to it, but he got over that quickly enough and flew to meet her halfway.

Sword and ax crashed together, although not with the metallic clang one would expect; it was more of a squishy sound, like that of an overripe melon being smashed with an iron bar.

Zaqiel stared at his sword, now wedged in the troll's head as tightly as Sebastienne's ax blade. "Well . . . this is unexpected."

"You know what else is unexpected?" she asked.

He frowned. "Wh—"

The toe of her boot stabbing into his groin at lightning speed was *very* unexpected. And painful, to be sure. It didn't completely incapacitate him, but it caused him to moan and stagger back.

"That's for calling me a lowly beast," she said with a snarl.

He spun on his heel, and before she had a chance to dodge out of the way, his right wing smashed into her face, breaking her nose and tossing her twenty or so feet away. She landed face-first, her mouth filling with the bitter taste of blood and ashes.

"And *that* is for calling *me* a reject," he replied smugly—then gasped as the double-edged blade of a mortuary sword pierced through his chest from behind.

"And *that* is for hitting my daughter, you bastard." Amaru drove the weapon into his back, all the way up to the hilt. Her clothes were covered in blood, but apparently Sebastienne's attack had provided her with ample time to recover her health and strength—as evidenced when she sadistically gave the sword a half twist to force the angel to drop his troll-embedded weapon.

Sebastienne staggered to her feet dazed and aching, and took a weak step toward the combatants. She almost tripped when her boot heel rolled across the top of a wooden shaft half buried in the ashes; it took her a moment to realize she'd stepped on her mother's spear. Picking up the weapon, she gazed at the iron tip and felt the power radiating from it.

"The Spear of Longinus . . ." she whispered in awe.

A low, deep groan pulled her attention back to the battlefield. By twisting and turning the mortuary sword, her mother had driven Zaqiel to his knees, and the pain he was experiencing was obviously agonizing. Ebon wings flapped helplessly as he struggled to rise.

"Remember the first day we met, Zaqiel?" Amaru asked. "I said I'd kill you if you ever laid a hand on my child—and I always make good on my promises."

Zaqiel snarled. "Just . . . not . . . today."

She snorted derisively. "Try saying that without a head."

With a roar of anger, she yanked the sword from his back and spun in a circle, putting all her strength into a two-handed swipe guaranteed to decapitate him.

Zaqiel's movements were a blur. As the blade swept around, he spun to the side and smashed his left wing into Amaru, knocking her off-balance—even as his hand closed around the ax handle.

"*Mother!*" Sebastienne cried and, spear in hand, raced to help.

Amaru stumbled to regain her footing, as the angel rose up and swung the ax. There was the crunch of steel against bone, and the female warrior's sword clattered to the ground—along with the hand that still held it.

She screamed.

Zaqiel flashed a shark-tooth smile. "Try saying *that* without a head." He reared back to deliver the fatal blow, but then the gleam of a metal object hurtling toward him caught his eye—a split second before the iron tip of the ancient spear skewered his chest.

"*DIE, YOU BASTARD!*" Sebastienne roared as tears rolled down her cheeks.

Blue-tinged lightning crackled around the spearhead, then exploded outward to envelop his body, and now it was the angel's turn to scream, in an even louder and higher pitch than that voiced by the woman he'd intended to kill. His ebon wings burst into flame, the fire quickly spreading to char his skin from head to toe. Blood and pus seeped from the cracked flesh as he cried out until his throat was raw . . . but he did not die. Not yet.

The ax fell from his hands so that exposed finger bones could scrabble uselessly to remove the spear tip, but Sebastienne wasn't about to allow him any opportunity to free himself. She ran forward, grabbed the spear with both hands, and threw her full weight against it, driving Zaqiel backward until she'd pinned him to the ground.

Exhausted, she leaned against the spear, as much to remain on her feet as to prevent him from rising. Not that she needed to worry. Zaqiel struggled, but there would be no escape for him this time—from either death, or the wrath of the woman who'd given her heart to him.

"*Why*, Zaqiel?" she demanded. "Why did you do all this? I *loved* you!"

"What do *you* know of love?" he growled through cracked and bleeding lips. "My brothers and I thought we were loved . . . until He turned against us." He limply waved a hand toward the volcano. "Do you see? *This* is how your 'kind and just' God punishes those he loves—with anger; with scorn; with eternal damnation. There is no such thing as 'love,' Sebastienne—it is a deception, a falsehood devised by a merciless Creator to distract his monkey-children from ever learning of his unspeakable cruelties."

She shook her head. "No," she insisted, and looked over her shoulder, to find her mother wrapping the stump of her wrist in strips of her blouse. There was no restorative healing for that sort of injury; Amaru would live out the rest of her days with only one hand. She was a warrior, though, and would find a way to carry on regardless of setbacks; she always had. Suddenly aware that there were eyes on her, she glanced up to see her daughter—bloodied, bruised, and gore-soaked—standing over their enemy. Amaru smiled, elated at the victory and never prouder of her child.

Seeing her mother's approval reenergized Sebastienne; her aches and exhaustion seemed to melt away as she straightened her back and stood tall.

"You are wrong, Zaqiel," she told the angel. "There *is* love to be found in the world—true love."

"Such as the one you had for me?" He barked out a laugh to clear his mouth of blood. "Sad, little fool."

Every hate-filled word he uttered was like a dagger ripping into her soul, but the tears that fell onto the remains of his once-beautiful face were not of anger, but of loss—for the happiness they had enjoyed, for the intimacies they had shared, for the eternity she had planned to spend with him. Memories and dreams and hopes forever destroyed by his actions this night.

And yet, she could not find it within herself to hate him.

"Then I am not the only fool, my prince, for the love you showed for me in return *was* true . . . before it was stolen away by all-consuming hatred. I know it was—as do you." She glanced at the ax lying by her feet, and dislodged the troll's head with a kick that sent it rolling into the mists; then she bent down to retrieve the weapon. "Does that make me sad? Undeniably. But even sadness, like love, must sometimes end . . ."

Without the added cranial weight the ax should have felt lighter, but it rested even heavier in her grip than before. Perhaps the balance was off, she thought. Or perhaps it was the newly added weight of a heavy heart that made it so difficult to wield the deathbringer as she prepared to end this long, nightmarish day.

"Damn you, Annie . . ." he whispered hoarsely.

"I am already damned, Zaqiel, for you have torn my soul asunder and broken my heart—yet still I care deeply for you. In truth, I imagine I always shall. But know this, my angel," she said, smiling warmly through her tears. "What I do now is done through love, not hate. You have suffered a great deal in your life—more, perhaps, than I shall ever know—and my only wish is to end your constant torment. May this finally bring you the peace you have long been denied."

The ax rose above her head. "Rest now . . . my love."

The blade swept down, and Sebastienne screamed.

The Devil's Heart, Annie thought. *Well, at least I kept House Karnstein from finding him . . .*

There was a sharp tug on her left elbow. "Hey, Annie, you okay?"

The dark-haired shape-shifter snapped out of her reverie, and stared at the girl standing beside her. "Umm . . . what . . . ?"

"I asked if you're okay," Pan replied. "You kinda went"—she placed an index finger against the side of her head, and swept it away to point into the distance—"way out there somewhere for, like, a couple minutes."

"No, I'm fine. I was just . . ." She took a deep breath, then exhaled sharply and pointed to the skeleton. "It's Zaqiel."

"Yeah, that's what you said just before you wandered off into Flashback Land, or whatever. So, what's a Zaqiel?"

"A part of my past, come back to haunt me." Annie looked up to Dave, who was coming down the stairs, accompanied by Sheena and Javi. Karen had apparently decided to remain on the landing. "Where did you get these remains?"

"I bought them from a dealer in London."

"Was his name Morrison Millar?"

"Yeah," Dave said. "You know him?"

The huntress groaned. "Of *course* he'd be the one to sell it—that *bundão*. Well, that's the last time I hide something in one of his warehouses." She pointed at Zaqiel's remains. "How much do you want for him?"

Dave started. "Excuse me?"

"The skeleton and the spear—I'll buy them from you, right now. I'm even willing to pay three times whatever it was that Morrison took you for."

"That sounds fair," Karen said.

"You don't even know what I paid for it," Dave said.

She glared at him. "Do I *want* to know?"

He stared at his ex for a couple of seconds, then turned back to Annie. "That sounds fair."

She nodded. "All right. Let's go up to your office and I'll write you a check. Then I'll make some calls. I can have it hauled out of here in a couple of hours."

"And then what're you gonna do with it?" Pan asked.

"Seal it away forever," Annie said gravely. Before some idiot tried to resurrect Zaqiel and bring about the Apocalypse—again.

269

"So this Spear of Longitude thing—it's really . . . real?" Pan asked. Annie had given them most of the details of her bloody breakup with Zaqiel after the group had returned to Dave's office, and she'd made some calls to whoever was supposed to haul away the skeleton.

"The Spear of Lon-*gi*-nus," Annie replied. "And yes, it is. Obviously. I mean, you *saw* it poking out of Zaqiel, right?"

"The spear Jesus was stabbed with," Karen said drolly, each syllable dripping with disbelief, "stuck in the chest of a fallen angel. By you. Before you cut his head off."

"You know, Karen, when you say it like that, it sounds *completely* irrational," Annie said good-naturedly.

"You think?"

"I see your point," Annie said with a laugh. "But when you've been doing this for as long as I have . . ." She shrugged. "Well, you get used to the irrational."

"Hey, y'know," Javi chimed in, "in the old Justice Society of America comics, they used to call the Spear of Longinus 'the Spear of Destiny.' "

"Yankee nerd says, 'Whaaat?' " Sheen mumbled into her chest.

"What?" Javi asked, then frowned when he realized what she'd tricked him into saying. "Oh, nice."

Sheen flashed a false and totally insincere smile at him—which earned her a soft elbow jab in the ribs from her best friend, who was sitting between the baseball rivals on the couch.

"So, when exactly did all of this happen?" Dave asked Annie. "You and the angel and this war you were fighting. Because I don't remember anybody covering it on the networks, and I think something like what you described would've at least gotten a mention on *PBS NewsHour*."

Annie smiled timidly. "Let's just say it predates *PBS NewsHour* and leave it at that—all right?"

He raised a quizzical eyebrow. "This one of those never-ask-a-lady-her-age situations?"

"Something like that."

"Okay." Dave held up his hands in surrender. "I know better than to go near *that* topic." He winked at Karen.

A chime suddenly rang in the office, followed by an unusual voice:

"Vun! Two! Three! Four! Four o'clock! Ah-ah-ah!"

Everyone looked up toward the Sesame Street clock that hung above the door: a cartoony drawing of the Count stared back from the clock face. The purple Muppet-vampire's arms pointed to the hour.

"Is that really the time?" Annie asked, and looked to Javi. "We've got to get back. The city's probably marked my entire building for demolition by now, the way the housing inspectors were talking this morning."

"Yeah, but Alexander's there, so no chance of that ever happening," he remarked. "And Dad said he'd give you a call if there were any problems, didn't he? And he hasn't called the whole time we've been out."

"His dad's a contractor," Pan explained to her parents and Sheena. Javi had mentioned it during their late-night texting session.

"Right," Annie said to Javi, "but still . . . just thinking about all those strangers parading through my home, poking into everything?" She grimaced. "It creeps me out."

"Says the woman who cuts the heads off angels," Karen said wryly.

"Hey, we all have our ick factors," Annie replied. "Mine is invasion of privacy. I tend to be a very private person."

"And what does *that* person look like?" Karen asked.

"Well, like— Oh." Annie slowly smiled. "You mean with the shape-changing. Very clever."

Karen shrugged. "I have my moments."

"Before I go . . ." Annie grabbed her backpack from the floor and rummaged through it, eventually coming up with a checkbook and a pen. She quickly filled out one of the checks and handed it to Dave. "This should cover everything."

"But I didn't tell you what I—" A glance at the amount shut him up. "Yeah, that oughtta cover it . . ." he said in quiet astonishment.

"Great." Annie rose from her chair and swung the backpack onto her shoulder. Everyone stood up as well. "The deliverymen should be here around five. If there are any problems, give me a call." She shook Dave's hand, gave him an air kiss, and turned to Karen, whom she hugged. "It was a pleasure to meet you, Karen. You're lucky to have such an extraordinary daughter."

Karen turned and smiled at Pan. "That's what *I've* always thought."

As Dave led the way to the front door, Pan slid up alongside Annie.

"Walk you two to the subway?" she asked, all too aware that everyone knew the real reason she was volunteering; the glance she stole at Javi only confirmed it. She didn't care.

"Actually, my car's parked over by Kaufman Studios," Annie replied as Dave opened the door. "But you're more than welcome to escort us—isn't that right, Javier?"

"Oh, *absolutely*," Javi said, grinning. Then he caught sight of Dave frowning at him. The grin quickly disappeared. "I mean . . . sure. Thanks, Pandora." He waved meekly at her father—"Good seeing you again, Mr. Zwieback."—and made a beeline out the door.

"Hey, Annie, can we stop at a hardware store on the way?" Sheen asked as she followed the huntress, then smiled wickedly at her best friend. "I gotta pick up a shovel . . ."

"Quit it," Pan growled.

The door closed behind them.

Dave hung his head low. "A Yankees fan," he muttered. "Why did it have to be a Yankees fan . . . ?"

He sighed heavily and headed to the office, where he found his ex had moved to the couch and stretched out across the cushions. "Comfy?"

"Comfy, but confused as all hell." A worried expression contorted Karen's lovely features. "Dave . . . with everything that went on here today—"

"Are we doing the right thing, letting Pan hang around with Annie?" He took a seat on the corner of his desk. "I've been asking myself that same question since yesterday and . . . I think it might be okay."

Her eyebrows rose. "Really?"

"I said *might*. I mean, I think it's great that someone was finally able to tell us what was happening to our daughter—"

"As bizarre an explanation as it is. And certainly not anything we could ever tell her therapist."

"Granted. But if Annie can help Pan come to terms with the things she can do— hell, if she can help *us* come to terms with the things Pan can do—then I think it's worth the risk."

"Up to a point."

"Up to a point."

"Whatever *that* will be."

Dave shrugged. "We'll figure that out when it comes. Right now, all we do is take it a day at a time and see how things develop."

"I suppose . . ." Karen sighed heavily, then nodded toward Annie's check. "So? How much did you get for Skeletor?"

The old Cheshire-cat grin surfaced. "Let's just say that after I recoup my expenses, we could make a very healthy cash injection into Pan's anemic college fund." The grin faded. "Unless you're in a real bind right now and need the money, that is. Are you?" Karen fidgeted in her seat. "Come on, K, don't hold out on me."

"You really want to hear this?"

He walked over to join her on the couch, then picked up her legs and draped them across his lap. Just like old times. "Yes, I really want to hear this."

Karen shrugged. "Okay, you asked for it. Well, first off, there's the lawsuit I'm expecting from one of the most powerful families in New York State—"

"The Van Schriks."

"Uh-huh. So we might need to pay for a lawyer; I'll see how that plays out tomorrow. Then the property taxes and the water bill went up again this year, Pan's tuition is going up next semester, Jerry Barron's playing coy again about handing out raises . . . and Pan wants her own car."

He chuckled. "Learner's permit burning a hole in her pocket?"

Karen smiled. "That's what *I* said."

He took both of her hands in his. "Okay, so here's what we'll do. Tomorrow I'll deposit the check; when it clears I'll send you the extra money. It's probably nowhere near what you need, but it's something."

She shook her head. "No, you're right, the money should go into Pan's college fund. I'll figure something out." She eyed him suspiciously. "Why are you being so generous? Is the museum doing *that* well?"

"Only in my head," Dave said with a smile. "Actually, the place is doing okay. Could be better, but things should improve now that school's out for the summer. You remember how business tends to pick up on the weekends. But, you know . . ." His eyes took on a wistful gaze as an idea began to form. "The Spear of Longinus, right in my basement . . ."

Karen frowned. She knew that look in his eyes; it always meant trouble. "Dave . . ."

He laughed. "Don't get upset, K, I'm not going to do anything crazy. It's just . . ." He shook his head forlornly. "*Man.* Why couldn't this thing have dropped in my lap in time for Easter? I would've made a killing!"

"And gone straight to hell for it."

" 'I'm on the hiiiighway to hell,' " he warbled off-key, then laughed at Karen's stern expression. "Enough with the stink-eye, already. Annie and I already made the deal, and Pan'll get the extra cash. I can live on ramen noodles and canned sardines for a little longer."

"Oh, God, you're still eating that crap?" Karen stuck out her tongue. "Ukk."

"I am." He glanced down and his eyes widened in surprise. "And you, I just realized, are still wearing your wedding ring." He held up her left hand and pointed to the single gold band that stood out against the steel rings on her other fingers.

Karen blushed. "Force of habit."

Dave smiled slyly. "Really."

"Yes, really. And so what?" She held up his hand. "I don't see *you* wearing *yours.*"

Now it was his turn to blush, as he reached under his shirt to pull out the ring dangling from its chain.

A tiny gasp slipped past Karen's lips.

"What can I say?" Dave took her hands again. "I still love you, K."

"I . . ."

An ill-timed—and unwanted—banging at the museum's front door spoiled the moment.

Surprised by the interruption, Karen pulled her hands away and glanced toward the entrance. "That was a quick trip." She swung her feet onto the floor and sat up straight on the couch, like a teenager whose parents had caught her making out with her boyfriend.

"I don't think it's the girls," Dave said. The banging became louder, more insistent. "Oh, no, wait. That Millar guy—"

"The one who sold you that thing in the cellar?"

"Yeah. He e-mailed me this morning that he was in town and wanted to discuss it. I told him to stop by." Dave glanced at the clock. "Sure took his time getting here. Oh, well." He patted Karen on the knee. "Back in a minute." He rose from the couch and headed for the door.

"Tell him you already sold it," Karen said. "Unless he's got a better offer."

"Yes, ma'am," he replied.

"And Dave?"

He stopped in the doorway.

She gestured toward her wedding band. "We'll talk about this later—okay?"

He smiled warmly. "You bet." Then he hurried to put an end to the pounding before the front door was knocked off its hinges.

It wasn't Morrison Millar, though. When Dave opened the door he found a pair of young female Goths standing on the other side. They were Asian and appeared to be in their early twenties—although with the right makeup and hairstyle a teenager could easily pass for an adult, as he knew from observing Pan and her friends—

and were dressed in what looked like Tim Burton-inspired *Alice in Wonderland* costumes, one midnight black, the other bright pink, and both frilled in white. The style was called Gothic Lolita; he remembered that because Pan's friend Tory Kwon dressed this way.

The girls stood beneath a large black umbrella—designed as a catlike head complete with stubby vinyl ears on top—held by the one in pink, who smiled brightly at Dave. Her black-clad counterpart, however, glared at him through narrowed eyes, her mood as dark as storm clouds.

"Oh, hey, girls," he said. "I'm sorry, but the museum's not open today. But if—"

"You are David Zweeback?" Black Alice asked, in an accent he couldn't place. Was it Japanese? Chinese? Korean, maybe? Queens was such a mishmash of cultures it could be any of them, and he'd always been terrible with accents.

"*Zwie*back. Yes."

"I am Lady Kiyoshi Sasaki of House Otoyo." She gestured toward her pink counterpart. "This is my sister, Miyuki."

Japanese, then. He nodded amiably. "Okay. What can I do for you?"

"You purchased item one-seven-nine from Morrison Millar," Kiyoshi said. "It was delivered to this address two days ago. You will tell us where it is."

"Slow down a minute," Dave said. "Are you the people Annie called to pick it up?" He looked the girls up and down. They didn't seem strong enough to lift an empty cardboard box, let alone a wooden crate. "I was expecting somebody a little . . . burlier."

"The item is here?" Kiyoshi asked.

"Yeah, I've got it down—"

Her right hand shot out blindingly fast, the heel of the palm slamming into the center of his chest like a battering ram to send him flying across the museum. He crashed through a glass case containing vintage Halloween masks, bounced his head off a wooden shelf on which horror action figures were displayed, and dropped to the floor in a heap.

Dave gasped for breath, but every inhalation felt as though a red-hot spike was being shoved through his rib cage. Something wet and warm was running down his collar and he reached up to touch the back of his head; his fingers came away bloodstained.

Behind him, Karen cried, "Dave!"

Pink Alice—Lady Miyuki—swept past him so quickly her legs were a blur. Karen screamed.

"Leave her alone!" Dave struggled to his feet, but a swift kick to the jaw from one of Kiyoshi's thick-soled Mary Janes laid him flat.

Karen fell beside him, savagely pushed by Miyuki, and scrambled to place herself between the intruders and her ex. *"Dave?"* she asked, nudging him. *"David! Answer me!"*

"Fine . . . I'm . . ." he mumbled before lapsing into unconsciousness.

A veritable army of male and female Asian Goths poured through the door, every one of them dressed in faux Victorian garb like Kiyoshi and her sister. Some, however, carried very non-Victorian automatic rifles and began setting up defensive positions behind the door and front display window.

"Who are you people?" Karen demanded. "What do you want?"

Kiyoshi stepped forward to tower over her.

"You will take us to the Prize," she ordered. "Now."

"So, what's your friend's problem?" Javi asked Pan quietly as they strolled back to Annie's car.

"Who—Sheena?" Pan glanced over her shoulder. About ten feet behind them, Sheen and Annie were engaged in some kind of conversation. Sheen appeared to be in a good mood, using a lot of hand gestures to emphasize her point, but no matter how animated the discussion became, it didn't prevent her from stealing occasional glances Javi's way to burn him with her death stare.

Pan grinned at Javi. "You mean other than her overwhelming hatred for the Yankees, and the fact I'm actually *talking* to one of the Bleacher Bums instead of punching him in the face? Not a thing."

"Oh, okay," he said. "That explains why your dad looked like he wanted to kill me, too. I saw that Mr. Met bobblehead on his desk."

"No," she said with a laugh, "he wants to kill you 'cause you're a guy and I'm his daughter. Mom, too. She's not a baseball fan, but she'd probably be happy to jump in and hold your arms while Dad worked you over."

"Nice family you come from." He eyed her closely. "And where do *you* stand on the whole baseball thing?"

"Let's! Go! Mets! Let's! Go! Mets!" she said, pumping her fists upward with each word.

"Now *hit* him!" Sheen called out from behind.

Javi rolled his eyes. "Oh, great."

Pan laughed. "She doesn't mean it."

"No, I meant me dating a Mets fan. My dad'll kill me."

Pan's heart stopped, just for a second. "Is . . . is that what we're doing?" she asked haltingly. "Dating?"

"You mean what we're doing right now?" Javi said. "Not so much." He leaned in close with a wolfish smile. "Too many prying eyes."

"I see you, Jeter!" Sheen yelled. "Watch it!"

Javi laughed. "Like I was saying. But I was thinking we could maybe go on a real date sometime, if that's cool with you."

Pan swallowed nervously. "I'd like that." She paused. "So I haven't . . . weirded you out yet?"

He seemed surprised by the question. "Where'd you ever get that idea?"

"Well, I mean, I wouldn't think you run into a lot of girls who can do . . . you know . . ."

"I haven't," Javi said. "So? Okay, so you're different. You got magic healing powers and you can stare into the hearts of monsters and stuff like that; you're probably even bulletproof, for all I know. But I mean, what's so bad about that? It makes you . . . I don't know, like a superheroine or something."

Pan snorted. "Hardly."

"Now, me, on the other hand . . . I got a shape-shifter who hunts monsters for a godmother—right? My grandma—okay?—used to be her running buddy back in the day, helping her fight monsters all over the world, and that is the God's honest truth. I've seen the pictures!

"Oh!" he added with a grin. "And check this out: Yesterday I met this girl bad enough to get in a monkey's face and make him back down just when he was getting ready to crack my skull open. And she did it without even going all medieval on his ass or nothing! How cool is *that?*"

Pan was so totally embarrassed by the compliment she turned her head away, using her hair to cover her face.

"So with all of that," Javi continued, "you think you got a *chance* of 'weirding me out'? Ain't no way, no how, Cookie." He brushed aside her hair so he could look her in the eye. "But y'know what?" he added softly. "I'm willing to give it some time. Who knows? Maybe you'll surprise me."

The chill of excitement that raced up her spine and out through her limbs was so powerful she almost tripped over her own feet. Javi slipped an arm around her waist to steady her.

"I got you." He put her back on her feet, but didn't remove his arm.

"Okay, you lured him in!" Sheen yelled. "Now *HIT* him, already!"

Pan laughed.

Unfortunately, that good feeling didn't last.

Annie suddenly halted. "Do you feel that?" She began looking around.

"What's wrong?" Sheen asked.

Annie turned around to face the way they'd come. They'd walked a block west from the museum, but had a clear view of the three stretch limousines that now pulled up at the corner of Thirty-seventh Street—and the Elegant Gothic Lolitas that swarmed out of them. Led by two Japanese girls—one in black, the other in pink—the sizable group headed in the direction of the House of Horrors.

Pan and Javi walked back to join Annie and Sheen.

"What's going on?" Pan asked. She looked past them to spy the Japanese arrivals. "What's with the Goth Lolis?"

"I don't know," Sheen replied. "Tourists?"

"They're not tourists, they're—" Annie gasped. "Oh, my God, they're here for Zaqiel!" She stamped her foot. "Damn it, I *knew* that vampire hit squad wasn't going to be the end of this."

"Wait—what?" Pan asked.

"Come on!" Annie turned on her heel and began jogging in the opposite direction. With the three teens racing to keep up with her, she dug into her backpack and came out with her cell. By the time Pan caught up to her the call had already gone through.

"Alexander? It's Mom. I'm still in Queens. Listen, I've got a situation. You remember the skeleton your people are supposed to pick up? Well, they're going to need armed backup. I think House Otoyo just showed up . . . Yes, quick as you can." She rolled her eyes. "Of *course* I'll stay out of trouble until you get here. Okay, see you soon. Love you." She hung up.

"Alexander's your son?" Pan asked.

"Yes. He's such a worrier." Annie smiled warmly. "But I love him anyway." She came to a sudden stop. "Here we are."

They were standing in front of a long black vehicle that looked like an old station wagon that had been pimped out for one of those *The Fast and the Furious* movies, only sleeker and more badass. Pan could definitely see Vin Diesel behind the wheel of this ride.

"Is this your car?" she asked.

"Before you say anything, it's not a hearse, it's a nineteen sixty-nine Ford Murena GT," Annie said proudly as she pulled a purple-haired Troll key ring from her backpack. "It's got a V-8 engine with four hundred and twenty-nine horsepower, and has the absolute most butter-soft leather seating. There are only twelve like it in the entire world."

"So it's a souped-up, limited-edition hearse." Pan smiled. "I love it."

Javi and Sheen joined them.

"Nice hearse," Sheen remarked.

Annie shook her head in despair and walked around to the rear hatch. She opened it, then pushed aside a black tarpaulin that concealed a pair of steel footlockers. After fumbling through a multitude of keys on the ring she found the one she wanted, then quickly unlocked the cases and threw them open.

"Whoa," Javi whispered in awe.

Pan had never seen that many weapons in her life outside of a Jason Statham action movie. Handguns, knives, rifles, machine guns—it was like a National Rifle Association sample sale.

"Oh my God!" Sheen howled. "Who're you—Rambo?"

"Sylvester Stallone *wishes* he had these kinds of toys. Unfortunately, I need to travel light for this." Annie picked up a couple of huge sheathed knives and clipped them to her belt. "Now, I want you kids to stay here—but the minute you hear shooting, get out as fast as you can." She closed the hatch, tossed the keys to Javi, and stepped onto the sidewalk. "Don't scratch my car," she warned.

"I thought you promised your son you were gonna stay out of trouble," Pan said.

"He knows better. Besides, if House Otoyo is here, your parents are going to need my help. I can't wait for the cavalry to arrive."

"Why not?"

Annie hesitated before answering. "Because once they've collected Zaqiel, their leader, Lady Sasaki, won't have any further use for Karen and David . . . except maybe for their blood."

"What?"

"They're vampires, Pan." Annie held up a hand before the girl could respond. "Yes, vampires exist, just like the monsters you've been seeing most of your life. And I'll be happy to tell you all about them, and their clan houses—but later. Right now I have to get your parents out of there. You three get going."

"I'm not going anywhere," Pan said. "You go do whatever you've gotta do, but I'm gonna help Mom and Dad."

Annie gently placed her hands on the girl's shoulders. "Pandora, I know you want to be brave, but be realistic. As clichéd as it sounds, if you try to help you'll only get in the way."

"Okay, but I—"

"My best chance of reaching Karen and David is to strike fast and keep moving; distract the vampires so much that they forget about your parents and focus on me. I can't be worrying about you, too."

"But I—"

Annie turned to Javi. "Javier, talk to her. I need to scout the area so I can plan my attack." And with that she shape-shifted into the form of a large hawk and took to the air.

"That is *so* damn cool," Sheen remarked.

"But I know a way in!" Pan yelled at the high-soaring bird, then snarled. *"Damn it!"*

Javi watched Annie pinwheel through the bright summer sky and scratched his head. "I thought vampires could only come out at night."

Pan waited until Annie had flown far enough away before starting back in the direction of the museum herself.

Sheen placed a hand on her arm. "Wait a minute. Where're you goin'?"

"I'm getting my parents," Pan replied sternly. "You got a problem with that?"

A warm smile slowly lit her Sheen's features. " 'Course not, Zee. I just didn't want you doin' anything that crazy-stupid without me." She looked at Javi. "What about you, A-Rod? You in?"

"Well," he said with a smile, "*somebody's* gotta protect you girls from all the scary vampires, right? Might as well be me."

"My hero," Sheen said drolly, and turned back to her friend. "So what's the plan?"

Pan flashed a sly smile. "You guys like Greek food?"

There was dried blood in Dave's mouth, but for the life of him he couldn't imagine how it got there. And for some reason he had trouble opening his eyes. From the rough texture of whatever was pressing against his cheek, however, he could tell he was lying facedown on a hard, cold surface—it felt like concrete. How had he gotten there?

Then the excruciating pain that had been lying in wait behind his confusion leaped from the darkness to smash him back to consciousness, and he remembered everything.

The Elegant Gothic Lolitas, Kiyoshi and Miyuki, dressed like Victorian Era vampires. Getting blasted across the museum with a single punch, then kicked in the head when he tried to help—

Karen.

Dave forced his eyes open, to find himself on the museum's unfinished basement floor—hence the feeling of concrete under his cheek—a few feet from the skeleton's unfolded left wing. Right now feet was *all* he saw from his position: eight pairs of highly polished boots and shoes, all clustered around the skeleton's torso. More members of the Goth gang, obviously. One pair in particular caught his attention: black, thick-soled Mary Janes. Kiyoshi's. He'd know those ass-kickers anywhere; his throbbing jaw confirmed it.

He rolled his eyes upward to see what was going on, and was surprised by the look on Kiyoshi's face. Was that reverence she was showing for the angel-thing—or fear? Whichever it was, she didn't seem to be in any hurry to touch either it or the Spear of Longinus; neither did any of the other members of the Humbert Humbert Undead Society.

Except for Pink Alice, that is. Standing next to her black-clad counterpart, Miyuki leaned forward and reached out for the spear's broken handle.

Kiyoshi grabbed her sister by the shoulder and yanked her back. A great deal of angry gesturing and apparently harsh Japanese words from the dark Goth followed, resulting in Miyuki lowering her gaze in subservience as she muttered some kind of apology. A hint of a smile peeped out of the corners of Kiyoshi's dark-lipsticked mouth, and she drew the other girl into a brief, comforting hug.

But where was Karen?

Moving cautiously so as not to draw the gang's attention, Dave turned and raised his head. Karen was beside him, sitting on the cellar steps and nervously fiddling with a Creature From the Black Lagoon bobblehead doll, using her thumbs to pry and twist the spring underneath the oversize plastic cranium until the Creature's head was turned completely around.

"You break it, you bought it," Dave whispered.

Karen jumped a tiny bit, but managed to tighten her grip on the toy before it fell from her hands. She put the doll down and lowered herself to the floor, then threw her arms around Dave's neck. He did the same, grateful to find her unharmed.

When they finally pulled away, Dave turned his head to discover they were being watched by their captors. Eight pairs of lips drew back in horrific smiles too wide for any human mouth; eight pairs of sharklike teeth gleamed brightly under the basement's fluorescent lighting.

"Oh, God," Karen whispered hoarsely.

Dave slid forward to move Karen behind him. "What . . . What the hell *are* you?" he asked the creatures.

Lady Kiyoshi suddenly appeared beside him; she'd moved across the basement in the time it took him to blink. Delicate fingers reached out to dig black-lacquered nails into his shoulder and yank him to his feet.

"No!" Karen jumped up to help him and was shoved hard against the stairs by Kiyoshi's free hand. She gasped and rubbed her sore back.

"Leave her alone!" Dave snapped at the girl.

"You will remove the Spear of Longinus from the skeleton," she commanded.

"What's stopping *you*?" he growled. "Afraid of breaking a nail?"

That little act of defiance was rewarded by having his head bounced off the brick wall behind him. Painful as that was, it *did* serve to remind him of the precariousness of his situation. These people were violent and dangerous—and, apparently, not human—so maybe pissing them off by talking back wasn't exactly the smartest move he could be making . . .

"We cannot touch the spear," Kiyoshi said.

"You mean you're afraid of it."

Kiyoshi snarled. "You will remove it from the skeleton." She turned and began dragging him toward it.

Dave dug in his heels, attempting to slow her progress, but it was like trying to halt a moving bus by hanging onto its rear bumper. "Wait wait wait!" he said. "How do you know this . . . How do you know it won't kill *me*?"

"I do not," she replied. "But among us you have the greatest chance of surviving"—her eyes suddenly turned as black as a doll's—"because you are still human." Kiyoshi's talons sunk deep into the back of Dave's neck. "Now do as I say, or I will have your wife torn apart before your eyes."

A flash of pink-hued movement, and Miyuki was beside Karen. Talons yanked her head back, exposing Karen's throat to those nightmarish teeth.

"No—don't!" Dave cried, and tried to pull away from Kiyoshi. Instead, she applied pressure, forcing him to bend forward until his nose was almost touching the ancient wooden handle.

"*Remove. the. spear,*" Kiyoshi growled. "Or she dies."

Dave's shoulders slumped in defeat. "Okay," he said softly.

Karen's eyes were brimming with tears. "Dave . . ." she croaked. "Don't . . ."

"It'll . . . it'll be okay, hon," Dave said, trying to sound braver than he felt. He smiled weakly. "Love you, K."

And reached for the spear.

Thirty vampires. Ten on the street, twenty inside the museum, and all armed. The limousine drivers didn't count—they were human, and could be dealt with easily enough. But there was only one of her, and backup was who knew how far away.

This was a problem.

From her perch atop a lamppost on the corner of Thirty-seventh Street, Annie watched through hawk's eyes as the members of House Otoyo took up defensive positions inside Renfield's House of Horrors and on the sidewalk in front of it. Those outside were trying their best to appear inconspicuous so as to not arouse the suspicions of passersby, but not even a perception-filter spell could disguise the unusual sight of grown men and women dressed in frills, satin, and velvet. Thankfully, no one stopped to ask questions, or—worse—make caustic remarks about the male vampires' somewhat effeminate wardrobe choices.

There was nothing effeminate about the guns they were brandishing, however. These vampires had come prepared for a street war, which meant they were expecting to have to fight for ownership of Zaqiel's bones and the Spear of Longinus. House Karnstein's hit squad last night, now House Otoyo . . . just how many clans were searching for Zaqiel?

And why the sudden interest in him?

She looked up and down the street for the tenth time. Still no sign of Alexander and his Knights. Either they were tied up in traffic, or he was having a devil of a time assembling his forces, given that most of the brotherhood was at their Denver convention.

Screw it, she thought. *I can't wait any longer—not with David and Karen trapped in there.*

She took to the air, looking for some type of back door that would allow her access to the museum without alerting the vampires to her presence. They'd know she was around soon enough—when she started killing them.

Pan already knew about a back-door entrance to the museum. It wasn't at ground level, though, but in a dank, smelly tunnel that ran below the streets. And that's where she'd led Sheen and Javi after a mad dash into the Greek diner that was a block west of the House of Horrors. The owners, George and Calisto Lambiris, had long ago grown accustomed to the strange girl with the strange name popping into their establishment, so they'd said little beyond the obligatory "How are you? How's your father?" as Pan led her friends into the kitchen and then down the stairs in the back to the tunnel. She'd had to fight the urge to steal some food to nosh on during the underground journey—the spanakopita here was *so* good, and the mouth-watering scents of Calisto's cooking made her stomach rumble—but she hadn't left the kitchen *entirely* empty-handed . . .

"So, how'd you know about this place?" Sheen asked as they trudged along the dimly lit passage. Bare lightbulbs hung every dozen feet or so from wires along the route, providing much-needed illumination.

"Don't you remember last night, when I touched the skeleton's wings and they came shooting out of the coffin and we all went running for cover? You wanted to run out the front door, but Dad said he'd locked it?"

"I remember you doin' really somethin' stupid last night," Sheen replied, "and me almost soilin' an awesome new dress 'cause of it—a new dress you woulda been payin' the dry-cleaner bill for. Is *that* what you're talkin' about?"

Pan rolled her eyes. Her friend could be *such* a drama queen. "Anyway, Dad told you there were two other ways out of the basement: the cellar doors in the front that go up to the street, and a door in the back—"

"That leads to some tunnel," Sheen interjected. "Okay, I remember that." She looked around. The tunnel and its branches were made of brick, the curved ceiling about ten feet above their heads and the sides wide enough for two people to walk abreast. "So, this is it, huh?" She shrugged. "Looks okay. How many times you been down here?"

"Like eight or nine. When the weather was really crappy sometimes, I'd go this way to pick up the takeout me and Dad ordered. Just watch your step—it's . . . pretty gross down here."

That was an understatement. The concrete floor was speckled with dirt and dead bugs, rotting food scraps and odorous fecal mounds—apparently there were some pretty big rats down here—and the air was heavy with a salty, mildewed tang.

Javi sniffed disdainfully. "*Damn*—what crawled in here and died?"

"The stink's coming all the way over from the East River," Pan explained. "These used to be bootleggers' tunnels during Prohibition; they run all the way to the river. Boats would pull up to a dock and unload shipments of illegal booze, and the tunnels gave mobsters access to the beer gardens and speakeasies that used to be around here." She caught sight of her friends' curious expressions and added, "I looked it up on Wikipedia."

"Oh, so then it's *gotta* be true," Sheen replied sarcastically.

They turned a rounded corner and started down another passageway.

"So, Ms. Urban Explorer, what do we do when we get there?" Sheen asked.

"Well, the door goes into the building's furnace room behind Dad's storage area," Pan replied. "I figure we sneak in there and see how many Goth Lolis there are—scout the area, like Annie's doing outside. And then we can plan our next move."

"Still don't see why we couldn't have grabbed some guns from Annie's car," Javi said.

She frowned. "Because I'm not a killer, that's why."

"Okay, so *you* wouldn't have to carry one, but I could've taken one. For protection, y'know. I mean, I've got her keys and they were *right there.*"

"I *said* no guns—all right?" she snapped. "Besides, Sheen and I don't know how to use them—do you?"

"Well . . . paintball guns, I do," Javi slowly admitted. "But I play a lot of first-person shooters, too. And they got these old *House of the Dead* arcade games at the Concourse Plaza Multiplex up in my neighborhood—I kick all *kinds'a* ass on those."

"Yeah, well, I think we're *way* beyond video games here," she replied dryly.

"So, then I guess the question is," Sheen chimed in, "if these guys that busted into your dad's place are really vampires, how *are* we supposed to fight them?"

"Well, I grabbed these when we ran through Mrs. Lambiris's kitchen," Pan said, and pulled a handful of garlic bulbs from one of her jacket pockets. "I figured we could mash them up and . . . I don't know, smear the juice on our necks so the vampires couldn't bite us."

Sheen grimaced. "Eww. That's just *gross*, Zee."

"Or we could throw them," Javi suggested. "My coach says I got a cannon for an arm. Getting hit with one'a those things oughtta hurt like hell."

"But aren't these Japanese vampires?" Sheen asked. "What's *garlic* gonna to them? Shouldn't you be usin', like, packets of wasabi or somethin'?"

"Hey, what do you want from me?" Pan replied. "I'm making this up on the fly." Then she came to a halt and her mood immediately became somber. "We're here."

They'd come to a small set of rickety wooden steps that ended at a metal door.

Pan stared at the portal. There was a sudden tingling in her body; every muscle was on fire, and her heart was racing wildly. She was scared of something terrible happening to her parents; of putting her friends at risk; of dying at the hands of the monsters she'd spent so many years fearing.

Yet even though she was terrified, even though she knew what dangers awaited her, she also knew she'd keep going, because on the other side of that door were her mother and father, and they needed her help.

But what if she was too late? What if, as she'd feared, the vampires had already fed on her parents? Drained them of blood and tossed their lifeless corpses in a corner?

As if sensing her distress, Sheen stepped up from behind and placed her hands on Pan's shoulders. "I'm right here, Zee," she whispered, and gave an encouraging squeeze. "You can do this, okay? Let's just go get your folks."

Pan reached up to place her hands over Sheen's, and squeezed back. Then she took a deep, steadying breath and drew herself up to her full height. "Okay." She turned to face her friends and pulled out the garlic bulbs.

"I am *not* smearing that crap on me," Sheen insisted. "Not even to keep Count freakin' Dracula at bay."

"Then we'll try it Javi's way." Pan placed the garlic on the steps, then dug out her key ring from her other jacket pocket. She selected the one for her school locker—she didn't care about that one—and scored the bulbs, then mashed them against the steps until juice began running from the cuts. The tunnel quickly filled with eye-stinging, garlicky fumes. Blinking back tears, Pan held out two each to her friends, keeping two for herself.

"Hey! What did I say about getting this crap on me?" Sheen said. "*This* is getting crap on me." Pan just frowned at her. Sheen sighed and took her share, holding the bulbs by their stems. "*So gross . . .*"

"When you throw them, don't throw like a girl, like you usually do," Pan instructed her, then smiled. "Throw them like Ammi was right in front of you."

Sheen's mood instantly improved. "Really? Oh, then a couple'a bloodsuckers are *definitely* gonna be losin' eyes today."

"Who's Ammi?" Javi asked.

"Long story," Pan said dismissively. "You guys ready?"

Sheen nodded quietly. Javi said, "Let's do this."

They slowly climbed the stairs, and with each step her fears began to reassert themselves. Pan nervously scraped her bottom teeth against her left thumbnail, peeling away the polish. She was scared, sure, but more than anything she needed to be strong, needed to be confident. Mom and Dad *would* be alive; she *would* save them.

She reached the top step and grabbed the doorknob.

"Please, *please* be alive," she whispered.

And opened the door.

31

"Nothing happened."

Dave stood with the Spear of Longinus clutched in his sweaty right hand, and stared at the broken weapon he'd pulled from the skeleton's chest. The metal point glowed softly in the harsh fluorescent lighting, with an energy that prickled his skin and momentarily took his breath away, but hadn't killed him.

"How about that?" He chuckled nervously and turned to Karen. "I felt for sure God was gonna—"

To his surprise, she was alone on the steps. The pink-garbed Miyuki had disappeared.

The scrape of shoes against the concrete floor behind him shifted his attention away from his ex. He looked around to find that their captors had moved to the far corners of the cellar. Apparently, they too had been of the opinion that holy retribution was sure to be unleashed when the spear was removed, and had taken steps to avoid being caught in the blast radius.

Dave stared at the remnant of the ancient weapon, then cast a brief sidelong glance toward the pair of metal cellar doors that led to the street. One tug on the release handle and the gas struts on both sides of the entrance would automatically open it; all he and Karen had to do was make it across the twelve-foot gap that lay between them and freedom.

Is that all? he thought sarcastically.

He slowly moved toward Karen and held out his free hand. "K . . . come over here." She glanced at the vampires, who remained where they were, and hurried to join him.

"What do you think you are you doing?" Kiyoshi asked.

Dave began nudging Karen toward the cellar doors. "We're leaving. I took out the spear like you wanted; now we're gonna go. You can pack up that lousy skeleton and get it the hell out of here. The keys are in my office—be sure to lock up the place when you're done."

Kiyoshi was the first to step forward—though cautiously, and not too close. "Throw the spear away," she commanded.

"What—the thing that's keeping you and the goon squad at a distance?" Dave barked a short laugh. "Not a chance." The Cheshire grin surfaced. "But if you want it, how about you come over here and take it?" He thrust it toward her.

The vampire girl drew back. Dave might not have burst into flame or been turned into a pillar of salt from touching the spear, but clearly she wasn't inclined to see if the same held true for the children of the night.

Karen nudged him in the ribs. "Dave, what're you *doing*?" she hissed in a stage whisper. "Don't antagonize them—you'll only make things worse."

Dave ignored the comment, but kept moving toward the doors. "What's the deal, anyway?" he asked Kiyoshi. "Isn't the spear what you came here for?" He nodded toward Zaqiel's remains. "Or was it Mr. Bones over there?"

"I am . . . uncertain," her ladyship admitted in a halting voice. Dave was surprised to discover that even the living dead could blush with embarrassment. "I have heard the story of Longinus and the spear, and there have long been rumors about its part in the death of the fallen angel Zaqiel . . ." She stared at the bones for a few moments, and then an idea seemed to take shape. "Perhaps the Prize is information he possesses!"

"But he's dead," Karen said. "I mean, deader than you. He's a *skeleton*, for heaven's sake—he can't tell you anything!"

"You are mistaken," Kiyoshi said sharply. "Zaqiel is more than a skeleton, he is our ancestor—one of the Ancients; one of the First Reborn. Therefore, we can revive him."

"Wait a second. A fallen angel that's also . . . a vampire?" Karen sighed wearily. "This whole day is just screwing with my head . . ."

Kiyoshi looked to her sister. "The regeneration must be started immediately. Blood is required for the process."

Miyuki merely stared back at her dark sister; apparently English was not a language she understood. The clan leader immediately realized her error and undoubtedly barked the same order in Japanese because, as one, the vampires all turned toward Dave and Karen.

"Yeah . . ." Dave muttered. "Like I didn't see *this* coming."

Then he pushed Karen toward the cellar doors and threw the spear at Kiyoshi.

The clan leader shrieked as her sister leaped to intercept the relic, but Dave didn't hang around to see what happened next. He spun on his heels . . . and took all of two steps before the spear punctured his left shoulder and he fell into Karen's arms.

A pink dress entered his black-spotted field of vision. Miyuki reached out to grab hold of the spear's broken shaft—and savagely yanked it from his shoulder.

Dave gritted his teeth and tried hard to not scream. He looked into Karen's frightened eyes and forced a lopsided smile.

"I'm good, I'm fine," he muttered.

"Liar. You're bleeding," she said, smiling as she blinked back tears.

"I'll walk it off," he replied, trying to sound humorous and failing. Then he thought: Wait. Where was the explosion? The wrath of God unleashed on the unholy? There was a bloodsucking corpse holding something allegedly used to stab the big man's only son—why, then, was this vampire not bursting into flame?

Maybe because it's only a story, *numbskull,* he thought with some measure of disappointment.

He turned to watch her. Miyuki apparently enjoyed the way his blood ran along the point, grinning as it slid across the softly glowing metal. Dave noticed, however, that she avoided *touching* the metal; her hands never strayed above the wooden handle. That was probably how she'd grabbed it when he threw it at her sister—as long as she didn't make contact with the pointy end it was safe for even a vampire to hold.

All right, so maybe it's not *just a story* . . . It was something hopeful to wish for, anyway.

Kiyoshi said something in Japanese, and her more colorful sibling shrugged and dropped the spear—directly onto the skeleton. Which led, in turn, to the Goth vampire leader yelling at her sister. Dave couldn't understand the words, but, having a teenaged daughter, he could tell by the exaggerated eye rolling Miyuki did that "What-*ev*-er" was apparently a universal response to all authority figures. Even among the living dead.

"What's going on?" Karen asked.

"A sisterly spat, it looks like. Don't really know, don't really care," he replied, ignoring his throbbing shoulder. "But I *do* know a distraction when I see one." He reached past her and yanked the handle. The doors sprung open and he pushed her up the steps. "Run, K!"

Karen scrambled up the steps and out onto the sidewalk, praying that Dave was right behind her.

She made it all of fifteen feet or so before a hand grabbed a fistful of her hair and slammed her down on the concrete.

Dazed, Karen opened her eyes to find Miyuki leaning over her, a horrifying shark-tooth smile stretched across pink-glossed lips. Behind her stood three bodyguards, who laughed at Karen's plight—until the heads of two of them suddenly went spiraling into the air amid twin geysers of blood.

Karen screamed—not as loudly as the vampires, though—and tilted her own head back to look at her would-be savior.

Annie was a blur, leaping past the decapitated bodies and driving two of the biggest serrated knives Karen had ever seen into the chest of the third bodyguard as he fumbled to raise his handgun. The weight of the huntress slammed him to the ground, and a quick slash of her knives added his head to the small collection that was rolling around on the pavement.

Then Annie turned toward Miyuki, a predator's smile baring her teeth. The vampire shrieked and dove into the basement.

Karen jumped to her feet and pointed toward the cellar doors.

"Annie, Dave is still—"

Annie, however, wasn't looking at her—she was looking *past* her. "Never mind that! Get out of here!" she barked, charging forward. "Go now!"

Karen turned in the direction Annie was heading. There was another group of vampires, ten or so, rushing to meet the huntress—and they were all pointing guns.

"Oh, crap," Karen muttered, and dove for cover behind a red-and-black Smart Car parked at the curb as the first shots were fired.

Annie went into a baseball slide that took her underneath the barrage, and within striking range of her enemies. Karen, meanwhile, huddled behind the car as the bullets Annie had avoided ricocheted off other vehicles and the sidewalk. Then, strangely enough, the sounds of gunfire and triggered car alarms were drowned out by high-pitched screams.

Karen cautiously peeked out from cover to see what was happening, and gasped in shock.

Annie was in the middle of the pack, spinning and twisting, blades flashing, dodging bullets as she decimated the gun-wielding vampires with just a pair of knives. Her moves were fluid and graceful, almost balletic, as she weaved a path of destruction through the ranks. In less than a minute, there were ten more heads bouncing into the gutter.

She straightened up and whipped her hair back, then looked over her vampire-blood-spattered shoulder at Karen—and winked. "Who says you can't bring a knife to a gunfight?" she quipped.

Karen pointed past her. "Look out!"

Annie turned. More of House Otoyo's clan members were pouring out of the museum. Some of them had big knives, too. The huntress stood her ground and waited for them to come to her.

Just then, a black SUV and a quartet of dark blue vans screeched to a halt on the far side of Thirty-fifth Avenue. The Gothic Lolitas spun around, ignoring the huntress to face the new arrivals.

"*Now* what?" Annie said with a snarl.

Two men stepped from the SUV: one white, one black, both built like weight lifters and wearing tailored suits. They were engaged in an argument they'd obviously started in the car.

". . . No, you slack-jawed Neanderthal," the black man was saying in a British accent, "the problem is that you don't know how to read directions from a bloody Google map! We'd have been here hours ago if you hadn't led us all the way out to bloody Flushing!"

"Is not my fault!" his companion replied. He sounded Russian. "Thirty-five Avenue here, Thirty-five Avenue in this Flooshing . . . It makes no sense. Only a madman would lay out streets in such a way!"

As the argument raged on, they were too engrossed in making their respective points to notice the altercation just across the street. But as another man—tall, thin, wearing a dark blue suit—walked around from the passenger side of the SUV, he spotted Annie and the Gothic Lolitas right away.

"Why, it's House Otoyo and La Bella Tenebrosa!" he called out pleasantly. "How nice to see you all again!"

That brought his friends' argument to a halt.

"House Orlock," Annie muttered with a sneer. "Terrific."

The doors of the vans flew open, and a veritable army of the undead—well dressed and *very* well armed—leaped out to take positions.

The shooting began almost immediately.

Down in the basement, Dave, held fast in the grip of two of Kiyoshi's minions, had been positioned above the skeleton and was on the verge of becoming a blood offering to a fallen angel when all hell broke loose upstairs.

Miyuki dropped into the basement and landed in a heap by her sister's feet. She began speaking quickly in Japanese, but Dave didn't need a translator—the gunfire that erupted out on the street told him all he needed to know.

"*Karen!*" he cried, and struggled to pull away from his captors, even though there was no chance of success.

There was more gunfire, followed by the sounds of glass shattering, bullets pinging off brick and cars and the metal cellar doors, and the screams of men, women, and children caught in what sounded like a full-scale war.

Kiyoshi barked orders at the vampires holding Dave. They tossed him aside, pulled out their guns, and rushed up the cellar steps—only to be cut down in a hail of bullets.

Bullets, Dave suddenly realized, that were capable of killing dead people—who should be immune to such things. How could *that* be?

The vampires tumbled down the stairs, and Kiyoshi directed her remaining henchman to drape the bodies over the skeleton. He moved swiftly to obey. Lady Sasaki's goons might be dead—permanently, this time—but clearly they still had their uses. She'd needed blood in order to resurrect the angel; now she had it.

As precious life-fluid spilled across the ancient bones, thick smoke billowed from the remains. Dave gagged from the stench of rotted meat that singed his nostrils, and watched in astonishment as veins and arteries, muscles and intestines were regenerated—slowly at first, then with increasing rapidity. Patches of dark skin formed around the limbs, then spread upward to cover the torso, the wings, and finally the head.

And then for the first time in nearly two centuries, the fallen angel Zaqiel took a deep breath, opened his eyes . . . and roared in anger:

"SEBASTIENNE!"

32

"What the hell was that?" Sheen whispered fearfully.

Pan froze in the doorway, her body halfway into the furnace room, her hand still on the knob. "I . . . don't know. It didn't sound like Dad." Thankfully.

"Whoever that guy is," Javi said, "he sounds *really* pissed off. And did you hear? He was yelling for Annie."

Pan nodded. She'd gotten so used to calling Sebastienne by her nickname, she'd forgotten what "Annie" was short for. What disturbed her, though, was that if the guy was bellowing for Annie it meant she wasn't down here kicking vampire ass; that she hadn't already come to Mom and Dad's rescue in the time it took Pan and her friends to sneak in the back way.

What was Annie *waiting* for?

"Maybe we oughtta rethink this . . ." Sheen murmured.

"No," Pan said firmly, and stepped all the way inside. "I'm doing this. Look, Sheen, you and Javi can go back and call for help, but I'm not leaving Mom and Dad."

"Even if that means they might kill you?" Javi asked.

She hesitated, then forced herself to look him square in the eye. "Yes."

"Okay." Javi then handed her his garlic cloves. "Then I'm gonna need something better than a couple'a smelly vegetables to hit them with." He looked around the furnace room, his gaze settling on a two-foot-long metal pipe that was propped in a corner. "Here we go." He retrieved the makeshift weapon and made a few practice swings.

"What's your batting average?" Pan asked.

"Three twenty-two last season. Why?"

She nodded toward the pipe. "Just wanted to make sure you know how to use that thing."

"Better believe it, Cookie," Javi said with a grin. "My coach says I'm a five-tool player."

"Well, he got the *tool* part right . . ." Sheen muttered.

"Quit it," Pan said with an I-mean-it glare. Sheen shrugged. "Now, c'mon. Let's go see what they're doing." Pan crept over to the inner door, fighting the urge to just run out and start throwing garlic bulbs like fastballs.

What she saw when she opened it, though, stopped her cold and took her breath away.

From the reaction that Zaqiel received from Japan's Undead Marching Society you would have thought God Himself had made an appearance in the museum's basement, instead of one of His castoffs. All three vampires had dropped to their knees and bowed their heads in respect.

Dave watched as the fallen angel scanned his surroundings with a mix of curiosity and anger. It was clear from his expression that he had no idea where he was, what year he'd awakened in, or who these black-clad supplicants genuflecting before him were, but it was also evident that he was looking for someone in particular—and pissed off by their absence.

His gaze settled on Dave. "Where is she?" he asked in perfect English. "Where is the one who betrayed me—the one who *murdered* me?" His lips pulled back in a snarl. *"Answer* me, monkey. *Where is Sebastienne?"*

Dave knew whom Zaqiel was inquiring about—but he also knew that admitting he was friends with the angel's killer would be a really big mistake. The wisest thing to do, he decided, was play dumb. "Uh . . . I don't—"

"My lord," Kiyoshi began hesitantly, her gaze still directed at the floor. "Forgive this one for interrupting, but the dark one has been spotted outside this very establishment. She attempted to kill my sister."

Dave started. Annie had come back—and was fighting with the vampires? Then maybe she'd been able to help Karen get away—that would certainly explain Miyuki's panicked dive into the basement after she and her thugs had gone after K . . . and why the vampire girl had come back alone. Dave started to breathe a sigh of relief, but then another question entered his mind:

If Annie's here . . . where are the kids?

Zaqiel at last focused on the group kneeling around him. The anger that Dave had seen in his expression softened just a touch; in fact, Zaqiel appeared amused by the gathering. "And who would *you* be, child?"

Kiysohi raised her head to answer, but one glimpse of her black, soulless eyes and gruesome teeth identified her immediately.

"You are children of the Reborn?" Zaqiel said, surprised.

"Hai," the girl said with a quick nod.

Zaqiel smiled. "Excellent. Then rise, my children of darkness," he said with surprising warmth, "and let me gaze upon your beautiful faces."

The vampires did as requested, beaming with pride as they looked up at their ancestor. The angel reached out with hands still slick with their clansmen's blood and gently placed his fingertips under the jaws of Lady Sasaki and her sister.

"Exquisite," he said approvingly as he gave their chins a playful pinch—which left behind tiny blood spots on their porcelain skin. "Japan was always one of my favorite countries."

Miyuki giggled, but her darker sibling snapped at her in Japanese. The message was pretty clear: *Stop acting silly and show some respect.*

"Now tell me," Zaqiel said to Kiyoshi. "Where might I find my beloved murderess?"

"Annie, please!" Karen said. "You've got to help Dave!"

The two women were huddled behind a delivery van across the street as the war continued raging around them. At some point the police had arrived, and now it was a three-way confrontation with casualties on all sides—not to mention the innocent bystanders who'd been hit by stray bullets.

Annie was massaging her temples, trying to quell the psychic overload that had driven her to her knees moments before. During the battle, she'd been able to ignore the warning sensation that she always experienced in the presence of supernatural creatures—and which had become a constant, nagging buzz in her head with so many vampires nearby—but the unexpected jolt that had surged through her mind had been the equivalent of licking an exposed live wire . . . while wearing metal braces on her teeth.

But what could have caused it? Something powerful, certainly; no doubt something vastly evil as well. Annie winced as her sinuses throbbed. If she could just clear her head for a moment, she could sort it all out . . .

"Annie!" Karen shouted, concerned. "What's wrong?"

"Could you *please* stop yelling? It *really* doesn't help." Annie pinched the bridge of her nose between thumb and forefinger to alleviate the pressure in her skull. "Just give me a second. I haven't felt anything this intense since . . ." She suddenly stiffened. "Oh, no . . ." she whispered. "No, no, no . . ."

"What is it?"

The huntress looked over her shoulder, toward the museum. "It's Zaqiel . . . I can feel him," she croaked, then her eyes widened in horror. "Oh, God, I can *feel* him! He's alive!"

Karen started. "What—the angel? That's impossible!"

"Of course it isn't! It's—" Annie's eyes widened as she looked past Karen. "Oh, damn . . ." She grabbed Karen by the hand—"Run!"—and bolted down the block.

Stumbling to keep up, Karen turned her head to see what had spurred Annie to run away from the battle—in time to see one of the silk-suited vampires fire a shoulder-mounted missile launcher at his Japanese counterparts. The poorly aimed rocket soared past House Otoyo's defenders . . . and straight toward the fleeing women.

The museum shook from a loud explosion outside; it was followed by what sounded like a glass mountain collapsing—actually the shattering of every window on the block—and the ear-piercing screech of a parking lot's worth of car alarms.

Dave gasped. "Karen . . ."

Zaqiel tilted his head toward the ceiling. "What is that infernal racket?"

"A rival house has arrived in pursuit of the same prize that we did, my lord, and now seek to forcibly take it from us." Kiyoshi winced. "We . . . did not know that *you* were the Prize, of course . . ."

"A rival house of *vampires*?" the angel asked, and Kiyoshi nodded. She almost seemed embarrassed by the admittance. Zaqiel shook his head. "Unacceptable. My children should not be fighting amongst themselves—they should be ruling this world as my brothers and I had intended to do. And you shall, with my guidance. But first this imbecilic warring must end—immediately."

Before Kiyoshi could protest, Zaqiel spun on his heels and strode to the open cellar doors. He leaped upward, using his powerful wings to lift him above the battlefield, where he bellowed:

"*ENOUGH!*"

The shooting stopped, just like that.

"*Damn* . . ." Dave whispered.

No doubt as equally impressed with Zaqiel's leadership skills as Dave was, Kiyoshi, Miyuki, and their bodyguard began climbing the steps to observe their ancestor, now that he had everyone's attention.

It took a couple of seconds before Dave realized that, in their excitement to go topside, the vampires had forgotten all about him.

"Thank you, Jesus," he muttered, looking toward the ceiling. Then he winced as his gaze fell on the discarded Spear of Longinus. He glanced up again. "Oops. Sorry."

Apology made, the next step was getting out of the museum, so he could go looking for Karen. With any luck, Annie had gotten her safely away before the shooting started.

And if not . . . ?

Dave shook his head. This wasn't the time or place for negative thoughts. Annie seemed to know what she was doing; given the current situation, he doubted there was anyone better qualified to protect K.

Yeah, he thought wryly, *but who's gonna protect you from K when she focuses on the fact that you brought all this trouble down on everyone's heads when you bought that stupid skeleton?*

A tiny smile quirked the corners of his mouth. If Karen was unharmed, if he had the chance to see her again, she could scream at him all she liked. He'd almost look forward to it.

Keeping watch on the undead Goths, Dave began inching toward the rear of the basement, and the tunnel that he knew was just past the furnace room. He looked over his shoulder to gauge the distance he needed to cover—

And found his daughter staring back at him from the doorway.

Miyuki Sasaki stood beside her sister and watched as the angel Zaqiel—hard-bodied and blood-dappled—hovered above the war zone on ebon wings.

"So beautiful . . ." she whispered in awe.

He drifted down the street, his gently flapping wings dispersing the thick, acrid smoke of numerous car fires that blazed all around. Above, the air thrummed with the reverberations of media and law enforcement helicopters that swarmed the area like mosquitoes thirsting for blood; below, bodies—both human and undead— littered the asphalt. House Orlock might have possessed superior numbers when the siege began, but from the casualties that Miyu could see, it was House Otoyo that was winning the battle. She smiled, beaming with clannish pride.

"My children—hear me!" Zaqiel commanded. Surprisingly, the combatants on both sides lowered their weapons, though neither clan leader had given the order. Could it be, Miyu wondered, that they recognized him as their ancestor, as one of the progenitors of the vampiric race? "I, Zaqiel of the First Reborn, say unto you this day: Lay down your weapons, for the warring among your houses ends—*now*!

"You have come seeking a great prize, and I tell you that the prize has always been within your grasp. Unity among all clans; the subjugation of the human race— *that* is the true prize!"

Miyu clapped with delight at his stirring declaration, ignoring Kiyoshi's frown of disapproval. Always the serious one, was dear Yoshi . . .

"But the prize shall never be yours," Zaqiel continued, "until you put aside this pointless infighting, combine your forces, and bring the humans to heel! And if I must be the one to lead you on the journey, then I . . . I . . ."

His voice faltered, and the strength seemed to drain from his body. Wings beating irregularly, he floated toward the ground—and into the welcoming arms of his children.

Miyu gasped. "Yoshi, what is wrong with him? He's not going to die, is he? You just revived him!"

Kiyoshi smiled warmly and patted her sister's arm. "Do not worry. The fallen one has simply overtaxed himself. Once he has fed and rested properly he will be fine . . . and then he and I shall have a very long talk about the future of the Reborn." A sly grin pulled at the corners of her mouth. "Clan unity and world domination . . ." she said. "What an excellent idea—under my leadership, of course . . ."

Miyu gave a vague nod, not paying attention to Yoshi's plotting—really, when *wasn't* she plotting something?—and glanced back toward the cellar entrance.

Miyu grinned. If the angel required sustenance, she knew exactly where to find a supply of fresh blood. . . .

33

"Dad!" Pan ran forward to hug him. The impact almost knocked him off his feet, but he managed to remain upright. "I knew you were okay . . . I knew it."

Dad, however, didn't seem quite as happy to see *her*.

"Pan, what're you *doing* here?" he asked.

She stepped back to look up at him. "You forgot to take me to Stone Cold Creamery, so we came back to drag you and Mom out."

"We?" He looked past her to see Sheen and Javi standing in the furnace room. "Damn it, you kids shouldn't be here!"

Pan peered around him. "Where's Mom?"

He gestured toward the open cellar doors. "I think she managed to get away. I heard that Annie's raising all kinds of hell."

"*Mom's* out there?" Pan asked, her voice spiking in panic. "With that angel loose and all the vampires shooting at each other? We've gotta go get her!" She tried to step around him, but he moved to block her.

"We *can't* go out that way. They're all clustered around the top of the stairs." Dad stole a glance back over his shoulder, then turned back to her, his expression a mixture of concern and fear. "Pan, we have to get out through the tunnel—now. Those things might come back any minute."

Even sooner than that.

A dark-haired, black-eyed Japanese girl seemingly materialized behind his left shoulder, a malevolent ghost from an Asian horror film like *Ringu* or *Ju-on: The Grudge*—only this one was dressed all in pink and glammed up. She was too cute to be a vengeful spirit, though, and her brightly colored outfit and nails totally killed any scary vibe she might have been trying to give off.

Then she grinned, revealing a mouthful of dagger-sharp teeth, and became the scariest monster Pan had ever seen.

OH, MY GOD, IT'S A REAL VAMPIRE! she thought, although what came bursting past her lips was more of a shriek than an actual sentence, matched in volume by both Sheen *and* Javi. It was a regular three-part harmony of terror.

The Goth Loli giggled, then dug her pink-polished nails into Dave's neck and yanked him back. He spun around and lashed out with his fist, catching her across the left cheek with a blow that would have staggered most people.

Miyuki smiled—and threw him across the basement. Dave smashed through a crate of knickknacks, finally coming to rest at the base of the steps leading to his office.

He didn't get up.

"DAD!" Pan screamed.

Giggling softly, Miyuki went to retrieve her prey, ignoring his would-be rescuers . . . or perhaps just saving them for the next course.

"NO!" Pan cried. She leaped forward and landed on the vampire's back, wrapping her arms around the creature's neck. "You leave him alone!" she ordered, and smeared the garlic bulbs she was holding against the girl's face.

The Goth Loli shrieked as the juice ran into her black orbs. Pan tossed away the bulbs and clamped her hands over Miyuki's mouth as the girl stumbled wildly, trying to locate the streetside exit but blinded by the garlic.

Pan looked over to Sheen and Javi. "Help me, you guys! We can't let her get a—"

Miyuki leaped into the air and slammed Pan's head against the ceiling, then tossed her aside. Pan crashed through a card table piled with magazines and struck the floor; old copies of *Fangoria, Famous Monsters of Filmland,* and *Vampirella* rained down on her. Dazed, she struggled to get up, but her brain felt disconnected from her limbs. All she could do was watch helplessly as the undead girl lightly touched down in front of her.

Miyuki wiped teary eyes with a frilly sleeve. Then delicate lips rolled back to expose a horrifying grin, and she moved in for the kill.

Karen groaned, slowly opened her eyes, and thought, *Why am I lying on my back?*

It was certainly a beautiful day on which to laze away a Sunday afternoon, the sky so magnificently blue and cloudless and . . . filled with police and news helicopters hovering overhead?

Karen frowned. That didn't seem right. And as her ringing ears cleared, neither did the constant blaring of car alarms along the block, nor the sirens in the distance that were getting closer, nor the moans and screams of . . . whoever was moaning and screaming. What was going on?

And why did her face feel so sticky? She reached up to wipe off whatever it was, then inspected her fingers.

Blood.

Startled, she sat up to find Annie sprawled lifelessly across her lap. The back of the huntress's T-shirt was tattered, the skin beneath looking like raw hamburger meat and riddled with shrapnel.

It was *Annie's* blood that was all over her, Karen realized.

Now it all came rushing back: the vampire gun battle; the missile; running down the street with Annie to escape it. Then, just before the projectile struck the asphalt and detonated, Annie had pulled Karen close, placing herself in harm's way and taking the brunt of the explosion. The shock wave had lifted the two women into the air and over a parked car, and then . . . darkness.

Annie had saved her life.

Karen gently prodded the huntress's shoulder. "Ms. Mazarin?" No response. "Annie?" She reached out with her index and middle fingers and pressed them against Annie's neck to check for a pulse. Thankfully, it was there—and surprisingly strong, given her injuries.

Then Karen remembered something else—or rather some*one* else.

Dave!

She slowly pulled herself out from under Annie, careful to avoid flipping the unconscious woman onto her back and worsening her condition. Then she stood up on wobbly legs, leaning against a nearby SUV for support until she felt strong enough to walk.

The shooting's stopped, she suddenly realized. She looked up the block, toward where the fighting had been fiercest, but from her position behind the huge vehicle it was difficult to see if any of the creatures were still around. Maybe they'd left while she was unconscious?

God, I hope so. All I want to do is find out that Dave is okay, and then hopefully we can put this nightmare behind us . . .

"I'll . . . I'll be right back," she said to Annie, knowing full well the woman couldn't hear her. "I've got to check on . . ." Karen paused. She'd been about to say *my husband.* ". . . on Dave . . ." It was probably force of habit, she told herself.

Like wearing her wedding ring, nine months after the divorce?

"I still love you, K," he'd said.

It was true that she still had feelings for him, but . . . *love* him? She wasn't sure.

A tiny smile quirked the corners of her mouth. If Dave was unharmed, if she had the chance to see him again, she could figure it all out later. *That is, after I'm done kicking his ass for buying that stupid skeleton and dragging us into this mess.*

Still a tad shaky on her feet, Karen staggered out from behind the SUV—and walked straight back into the nightmare.

The vampires were still here, only instead of fighting they were gathered in the middle of the street, around a tall, handsome black man who had . . . wings?

"It's Zaqiel . . . I can feel him," Annie had said. *"Oh, God, I can feel him! He's alive!"*

Karen gasped. A fallen angel. Alive. Allied with a horde of bloodsucking killers.

And gazing at her with an extremely hungry look.

As one, the vampires turned to see what had caught their master's eye.

"Mrs. Zweeback—what perfect timing," Kiyoshi said. Her black eyes sparkled. "Our father is literally *dying* for a drink . . ."

Javi came racing to Pan's aid and swung away with the metal pipe, catching Miyuki across the back of her skull. The Goth Loli's head snapped forward, then to the side as Javi managed to get in a second strike. On his third swing, however, she grabbed the pipe with one hand and wrenched it from his grip—then rapped him on the temple with it. The boy went down in a heap.

Miyuki tossed aside the weapon and knelt beside Javi. Her hands whipped forward, the right grabbing his jaw as the left gripped his hair and turned his head to expose his neck. Her teeth hovered above his jugular vein.

And then Miyuki cried out as something razor-sharp sliced across her back amid a tiny crackle of lightning that raced up and down her spine. Gritting her teeth against the pain she dropped Javi and spun around—to find Sheen holding the Spear of Longinus inches from her face.

"Hands off my friend's property, you grabby bitch," Sheen said, and thrust the spear at her.

Miyuki yelped. In a flash of pink and white, she evaded the attack and hared up the steps to the sidewalk. Apparently one taste of the spear's power was enough for her.

Sheen took a moment to make certain the vampire wasn't going to turn around and launch another assault; when that didn't happen she released a slow, tremulous breath.

At her feet, Javi groaned and tried to get up.

Sheen slid a hand around his back and helped him to his feet. "You all right?"

"Been better," he replied weakly. "Hey, thanks for the assist."

"Me helpin' out a Yankees fan," Sheen said in mock distress. "I think that's one'a the signs of the Apocalypse." She smiled. "Don't tell anybody, okay? I'll never live it down."

"*Dad!*" Pan sat bolt upright, ignoring the pain of her aching back and head. She staggered to her feet and ran across the basement while her friends followed, then dropped to her knees beside him. He looked so lifeless . . . "Dad?"

He slowly opened one eye. "H . . . hey, p-pun'kin," he croaked.

She blinked away tears of relief. "Don't move! Okay? Just stay right there!"

"Wasn't . . . planning on . . . going anywhere . . ." His voice faded as he lapsed into unconsciousness.

"Is . . . is your dad . . . ?" Sheen croaked.

"He's gonna be okay," Pan said. *I hope.*

"He won't be if we keep hanging around here," Javi remarked as he glanced at the open cellar doors. "*None* of us will be."

"So what do we do now?" Sheen asked.

Pan turned to answer—and that's when she noticed the Spear of Longinus in Sheen's hands. Waves of golden energy crackled around its tip, visible only to her eyes; a faint, powerful hum reverberated in her mind.

For a moment she was surprised to find it still here. The very weapon used to kill Zaqiel, and the notion of hiding it or destroying it so it couldn't be used against him a second time apparently hadn't occurred to anyone.

"I think we should pick your dad up and go back through the tunnel," Javi replied, "before those vampires come back in here."

"*What?*" Pan snapped. "With Mom in the middle of all that fighting? No way!"

"*Yes* way. For all you know, Annie's already found your mom and got her squirreled away somewhere until this thing blows over. We can't just go running into the middle of whatever's going on up there—that'd be crazy."

"Oh, I get it," she growled. "You're afraid."

Sheen started. "Zee!"

"Afraid ain't got *nothing* to do with it. It's about being *smart*, and knowing when's a good time to fight. The three of us and a lead pipe, against a street full of vampires with guns? *That* ain't a good time to fight."

"But we've got the spear!"

Javi crouched down beside her. "Look, Cookie," he said gently, "we are totally outta our depth here. We ain't monster hunters and we ain't soldiers. But this is what Annie does, all the time. She can handle this; we can't. And the longer we hang around here arguing about it, the bigger the chance Shark Girl is gonna come back with reinforcements. And once they start chewing on our necks, there'll be *nobody* left down here to help your dad. You don't want that happening, do you?"

"No," Pan said quietly, yet the thought of running away, of leaving her mother among the monsters, made her want to throw up.

Sheen kneeled down to join them. She placed a hand on her best friend's arm. "I think lover boy here has a point, Zee. You gotta think of your dad first. Then we can figure out how to find your mom."

A loud cheer from the street reached their ears. The sound of an army gathering around its leader in celebration, Pan wondered—or an undead horde eager to slake its thirst?

It was followed by a shriek of pure terror.

"MOM!" Pan pulled away from her friends, grabbed the spear from Sheen's hand, and bolted up the stairs. "You guys get Dad outta here!"

She hit the street and saw the vampires—a mixture of Goth Lolis and silk-suited thugs—gathered down by Thirty-fifth Avenue. And amid the fine suits and polished leather and dainty frills . . . a glimpse of a Harley-Davidson T-shirt.

"Mom!" she gasped, and ran forward.

"Pan—don't!" Sheen cried.

Pan glanced over her shoulder and caught sight of Javi and Sheen standing on the sidewalk, their features frozen in horror. They both appeared ready to join her, but she waved them back. The look of utter despair on Sheen's face broke her heart.

"Look, I'm sorry if I pissed you off before," Pan had said to her best friend what now felt like a hundred years ago. *"I know you're only looking out for me, and I do—I really do—appreciate what you did when all that stuff was going on between me and Ammi. I don't ever want you thinking I don't. 'Cause I do. Really. So . . . are we good? You and me?"*

"Sure, Vampira, we're good. BFF and all that—right?"

"Yeah."

"Love ya, Zee."

Love you, too, jungle queen, she thought.

And then she was among the dead.

"Get away from her!" she shrieked, drawing their attention. *"You leave my mother alone, you sons of bitches!"*

She swung the spear from side to side in wild two-handed arcs that threatened to pull her off-balance. The vampires—some obviously fearful of the relic, the majority amused by her antics—gave her a wide berth, then closed ranks behind her. There'd be no retreat from this fight, no chance for escape. She didn't care; all that mattered was her mother.

The crowd opened up enough for her to see Karen lying on the ground, eyes closed.

"Mom!" Pan ran to her side, ignoring the creatures gathered around her, and cradled her head in her lap. Karen's neck was riddled with punctures; tiny crimson beads pooled around the wounds.

"Mo . . . Mom?" Pan croaked through the tears that burned her eyes. She stroked Karen's face. The skin was ice cold. "Mommy, no . . ." she wailed.

Pan threw back her head and howled in misery—and the vampires laughed.

No, not vampires.

Monsters.

She'd lived with monsters for almost her entire life—watching them, avoiding them, fearing them. Allowing them to crush her spirit and screw with her head. To rob her of a normal childhood. With Annie's help she'd thought she had come to terms with their existence, to understand that they were just another part of the world around her, but now they'd taken away one of the two most important people in her life—and reveled at her despair.

Her lips drew back in a feral snarl.

Monsters.

How she hated them. How she wished every one of them dead.

"Comes the monkey-child to the rescue," a voice rumbled, deep as thunder, "only to discover she is far, far too late."

She wiped away her tears and looked over her shoulder. Zaqiel stood a few yards away, majestic ebon wings spread wide, his mouth stained a bright red. From her mother's blood.

Pan gripped the Spear of Longinus in shaky hands and rose to her feet. It was a powerful weapon—she could tell by the way her skin crackled with preternatural energy. It flowed into her, strengthening her limbs, bolstering her faded spirit, calming her frazzled nerves. She had never felt so at peace with herself, so in control.

The vampires stopped laughing.

She turned to face the angel.

"Put it down, child," Zaqiel commanded with a nod toward the spear, his eyes betraying his fear of it. "Otherwise I promise your death shall be an agonizing one."

She didn't bother with threats or snarky comebacks; she just charged at him. With a cry of rage, she jumped as high as she could, aiming the spear at the devil's heart.

She never came close.

Zaqiel sidestepped her attack, one hand reaching out to grasp Pan's left arm as the other swept down to break her right wrist—and its grip on the relic. The spear dropped into his hand, the soft thud of wooden handle against flesh drowned out by her high-pitched screech—which in turn was cut short as he whipped her around by the arm to slam her through the windshield of a nearby SUV. The glass exploded around her as she tumbled over the dashboard and into the passenger seat, coming to rest with her right leg tangled in the steering wheel and her head on the rubber floor mat.

Pan sobbed. Her leather jacket had protected her from the brunt of the impact, but there was glass in her hair, her scalp and face were bleeding, her right knee felt loose, and the throbbing of her broken wrist threatened to rob her of what little consciousness she'd been able to hang on to before she'd gone through the windshield.

And what did she have to show for all this pain? Nothing. Her mother was dead. She couldn't help her; couldn't save her. She hadn't even been able to scratch Zaqiel with the damn spear.

Failure, she thought despondently. *I'm such a failure . . .*

The passenger-side door was wrenched off its hinges, and Pan yelped as Zaqiel appeared in the gap. He glared at her as though she were a bug in need of extermination.

Spear clutched in one hand, the fallen angel reached in with the other and yanked Pan from the vehicle, then threw her to the ground. A bomb seemed to detonate inside her brain as her head bounced off the asphalt.

He grabbed a fistful of her T-shirt and hauled the barely conscious girl to her feet. She opened her eyes to find what seemed to be the devil himself inches from her face.

"Hey," she said brightly, as though greeting an old friend. She knew that she was slipping into shock from her injuries. It was making her giddy. "Y-ya know what? I'ma . . . I'ma kill you so bad y'gonna wish you'd s-stayed dead."

"Insolent little monkey," he growled.

And then he shoved the spear through her chest.

34

Pan gasped as the spear tip smashed through her rib cage, rupturing her heart before exiting through her back to rip into the lining of her leather jacket. Trembled spasmodically as a surge of electricity coursed through her from head to toe, stronger than anything she'd experienced during her encounter with the megamall security guard. Heard the rattle of her breath as her left lung collapsed and blood gushed from her mouth. Realized that this must be what it felt like when a vampire got staked.

And thought it odd that she hadn't died already.

Zaqiel drew her close, his fetid breath warm on her face, and lightly pressed his lips over hers. At first she thought he was kissing her but then his tongue darted over and into her mouth, and she realized he was lapping up her blood. After a few deep swallows he pulled away and licked his lips.

"Exquisite," he murmured. "Such a—"

Whatever he'd meant to say was interrupted by a sizable explosion. One of the vans parked on Thirty-fifth Avenue erupted in a ball of flame. Pan looked past Zaqiel to see someone in a dark business suit standing on the roof of a green Kia, a big, gray-metal box balanced on their left shoulder. As she watched, a missile came flying out from one of the box's tubes, and two seconds later another van blew apart.

The intruder lowered the rocket launcher to reveal a rugged-looking man in his sixties, with shoulder-length silver hair and craggy features. "Now that I have your attention . . ." he bellowed to the undead, then turned to look over his shoulder. "Take 'em out!"

A loud war cry filled the air as a dozen men and women in combat gear ran onto the block, carrying some serious weaponry.

Annie's cavalry had arrived.

They unleashed a heavy barrage of gunfire that tore into the vampire ranks, blowing off heads and ripping apart torsos. Whatever their ammunition was made of, it caused the re-deadified corpses to burst into flame.

The vampires scattered—some for cover, some to take up defensive positions, but most of them to escape. The ones who weren't fast enough joined their overcooked brethren as piles of ashes.

A Goth Loli girl dressed in black—almost a twin to the one in pink from the basement attack—ran over to Zaqiel and gently tugged at his arm. "My lord, we must away. The huntress's reinforcements have arrived and the losses for both houses during our skirmish severely weakened our position. We cannot match their strength. Escape is our only option."

The angel snarled. Apparently God's outcast didn't like taking orders.

And then a voice rang out across the battlefield:

"ZAQIEL!"

All heads turned toward the dark-haired, blood-spattered huntress. She was stumbling up the street, obviously weak from her injuries yet still capable of slashing away with a pair of serrated knives to cut down any vampire that foolishly ventured within striking distance. And she was getting closer to her angelic prey with every step.

Zaqiel snarled. "Sebastienne."

The Goth Loli gave another light tug on his arm. "Please, my lord. If you are to lead us to a new age we cannot lose you now in a meaningless battle. You can always kill the dark one another time."

Zaqiel gnashed his teeth, weighing his decision, then nodded sharply. "Very well." He released his hold on Pan's shirt and hurried away, following the Goth Lolis to a black limousine parked close by.

Pan fell, the descent seeming to take a lifetime. Her knees crunched against the asphalt and she tipped over, crashing onto her left side; she felt the vibration travel up and down the length of the relic. It tickled.

Now. Now I'm gonna die, she thought, and closed her eyes. It was okay, though.

She'd never really been big on religion, but from everything she'd heard Heaven was supposed to be a really cool place . . . at least according to Hollywood movies. Whatever. If it meant she'd be able to see Mom again, then God's crib couldn't be all that bad. *Hope I'm still not carrying around this friggin' spear in my chest when I get there . . .*

Multicolored lights flashed and spun and crackled in the darkness behind her lids, a private fireworks display. She smiled. "So pretty . . ."

Outside her eyes, there were more explosions and gunfire, more screams and shouting. And then:

"Pan!" a familiar voice cried from what seemed to be a great distance. *"Oh, God, no!"* She tried to open her eyes and see who it was, but it was easier to just lay here in darkness and allow the world to slip away. It didn't hurt so much, this way, didn't scare her. Still, she knew that voice . . .

"PAN!" it called again—and this time she recognized the speaker.

"Mom . . . ?" she croaked.

"Let me go!" Karen yelled. "Let me—" Her cry was cut short by the meaty thud of bone striking flesh, followed by the sounds of multiple car doors slamming and vehicles peeling out. Then silence.

Feet pounded up to her, and she heard Sheena scream, *"PAN! PAN! Help her! Please, somebody help my friend!"*

A strong hand clutched her shoulder. "Pan?" Javi called. "Just hang on, okay? We got help coming." His breath hitched as he added, "Hey, look, we . . . we ain't even been out on our first date or nothing, so d-don't you go dying on me, Cook . . . Cookie. All right? Y-you're gonna be o-okay."

Warm tears spattered her face; gentle fingers brushed aside hair that had fallen over her eyes.

"Gonna . . . gonna be okay . . ." Javi whispered.

Mom's not dead, she thought dimly. *She's not dead! She's alive!* Then there was still a chance she could be rescued.

Hang . . . hang on, Mom . . . I'm coming to . . . coming to get you . . .

A tiny smile bowed her lips.

It remained even as she drew her last breath.

TO BE CONTINUED IN

THE SAGA OF PANDORA ZWIEBACK · BOOK 2

BLOOD REIGN

STEVEN A. ROMAN
BESTSELLING AUTHOR OF THE CHAOS ENGINE TRILOGY

ABOUT THE AUTHOR

STEVEN A. ROMAN is the bestselling author of the novels *X-Men: The Chaos Engine Trilogy* and *Final Destination: Dead Man's Hand*. His writing has garnered praise from such authors as World Fantasy Award–winner Charles de Lint, Bram Stoker Award–winner Elizabeth Massie, and fantasist and crime fiction novelist Neal Barrett Jr.

His short fiction has appeared in the anthologies *The Best New Zombie Tales 2, The Dead Walk Again!, Doctor Who: Short Trips: Farewells, If I Were an Evil Overlord, Tales of the Shadowmen 4: Lords of Terror, The Ultimate Hulk,* and *Untold Tales of Spider-Man.* He also wrote the graphic novels *Lorelei: Building the Perfect Beast, Stan Lee's Alexa,* and *Sunn,* and co-wrote the direct-to-DVD animated short *X-Men: Darktide.*

In addition to writing Steve worked as a fiction editor, then later as Editor-in-Chief, for ibooks, inc., a New York–based publishing company. Among the many titles he edited during his tenure were: original licensed novels based on *Terminator 2, The Transformers, Witchblade,* Spider-Man, and *Ghostbusters;* the fantasies *Dragonkin, Moebius' Arzach,* and *The Orc's Treasure;* the science fiction series *Isaac Asimov's Robot Mysteries;* and the Young Adult SF spoof *Britney Spears is a Three-Headed Alien!*

Steve's current writing projects include the novels *Blood Reign: The Saga of Pandora Zwieback, Book 2* and *Doctor Omega and the Megiddo Factor,* and the Mature Readers graphic novel *Lorelei: Sects and the City.*